≽A MODERN GRAPHIC RETELLING OF *ANNE OF GREEN GABLES*≼

Anne
of West
Philly

A MODERN GRAPHIC RETELLING OF *ANNE OF GREEN GABLES*

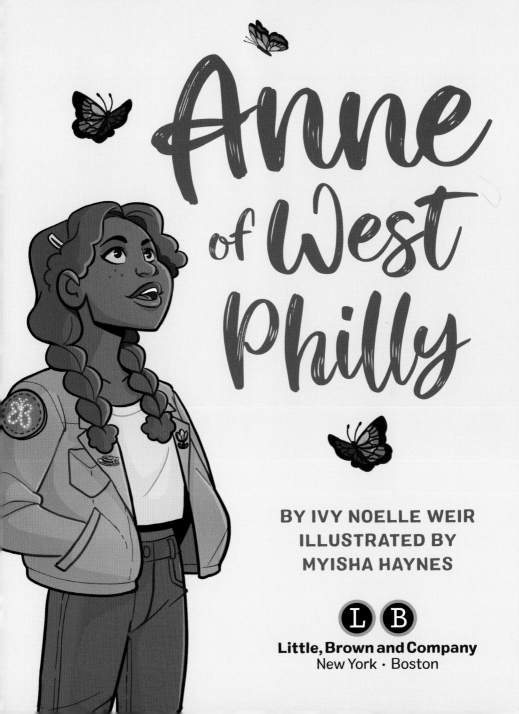

Anne of West Philly

BY IVY NOELLE WEIR
ILLUSTRATED BY
MYISHA HAYNES

LB
Little, Brown and Company
New York • Boston

About This Book

This book was edited by Rachel Poloski and designed by Ching N. Chan. The production was supervised by Bernadette Flinn, and the production editor was Lindsay Walter-Greaney. The text was set in Colby, and the display type is Westhouse.

Story by Ivy Noelle Weir; art by Myisha Haynes; colors by Edwin Surya W., Delanda Gracesya R., Angela Olivia, Dwi Febri Novita, Tannia Venansjah, and Trio Vilten of Caravan Studio
Sensitivity read by Steenz

Little, Brown and Company
Hachette Book Group
1290 Avenue of the Americas, New York, NY 10104
Visit us at LBYR.com

First Edition: March 2022

Little, Brown and Company is a division of Hachette Book Group, Inc.
The Little, Brown name and logo are trademarks of Hachette Book Group, Inc.

The publisher is not responsible for websites (or their content) that are not owned by the publisher.

Library of Congress Cataloging-in-Publication Data is available.

ISBNs: 978-0-316-45978-5 (hardcover), 978-0-316-45977-8 (paperback), 978-0-316-45974-7 (ebook), 978-0-316-45972-3 (ebook), 978-0-316-45975-4 (ebook)

PRINTED IN CHINA

1010

Hardcover: 10 9 8 7 6 5 4 3 2 1

Paperback: 10 9 8 7 6 5 4 3 2 1

For Hattie and Casper —INW

*To my loving family: Mom,
Dad, and Darion—the
Matthew to my Marilla—MH*

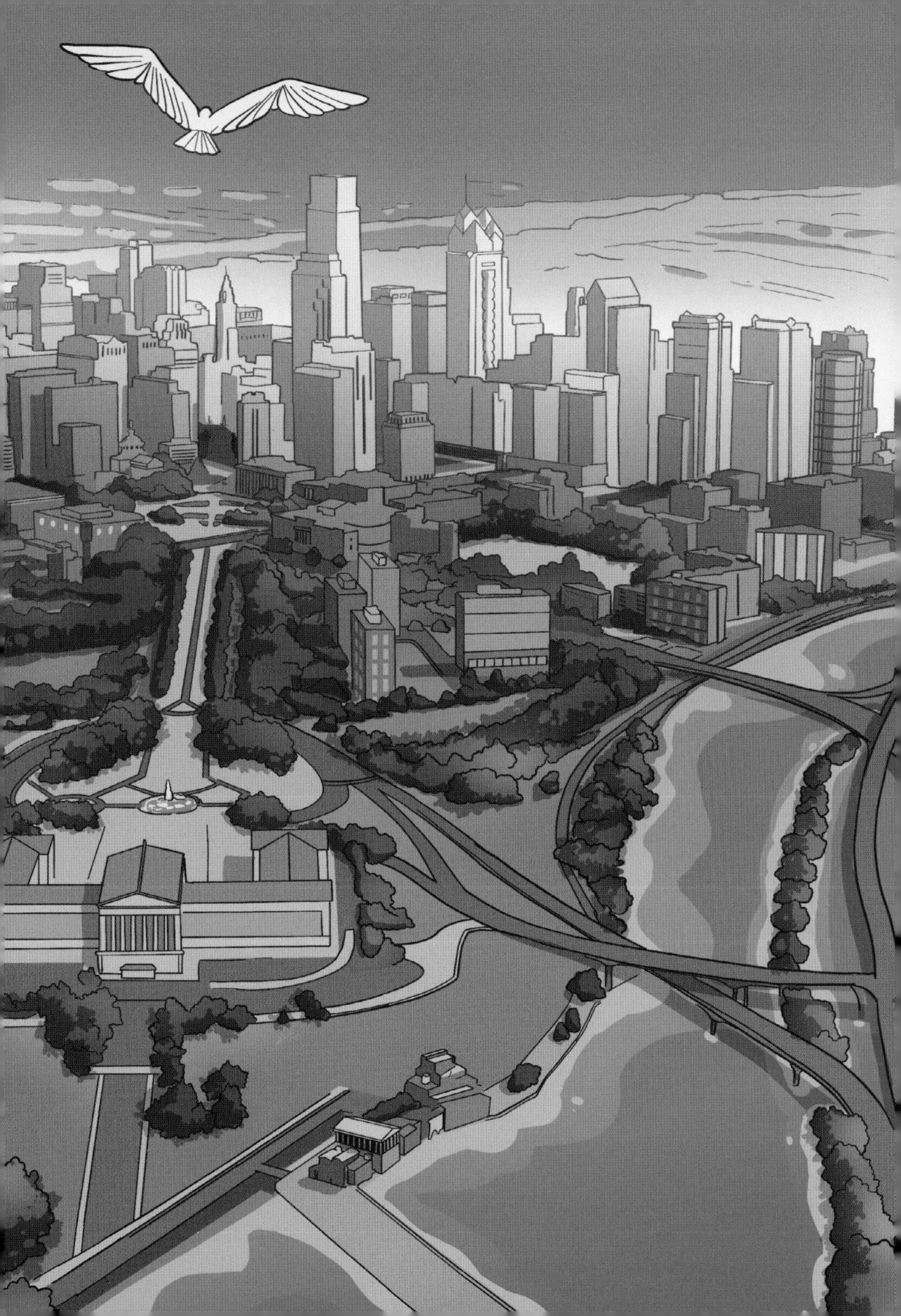

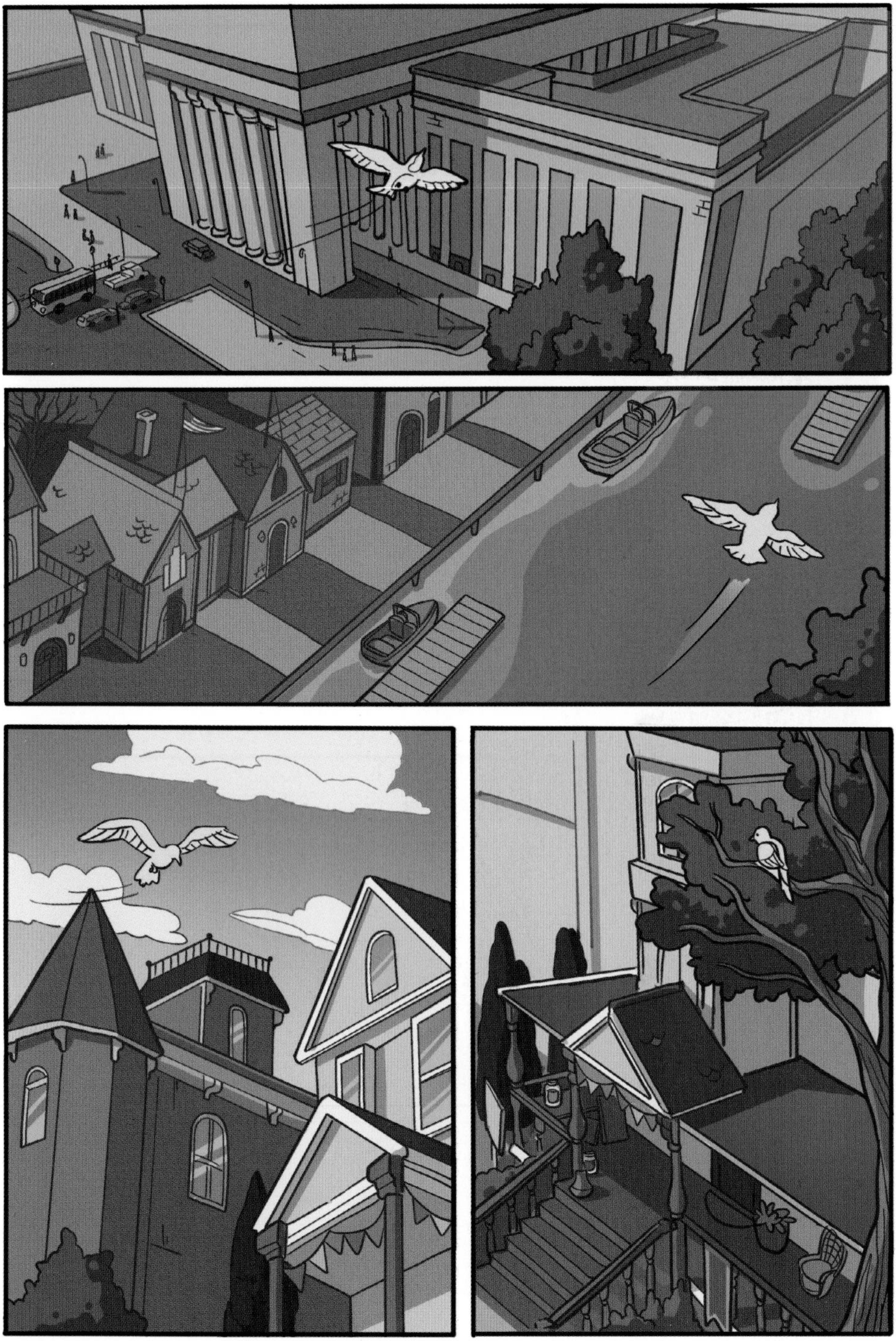

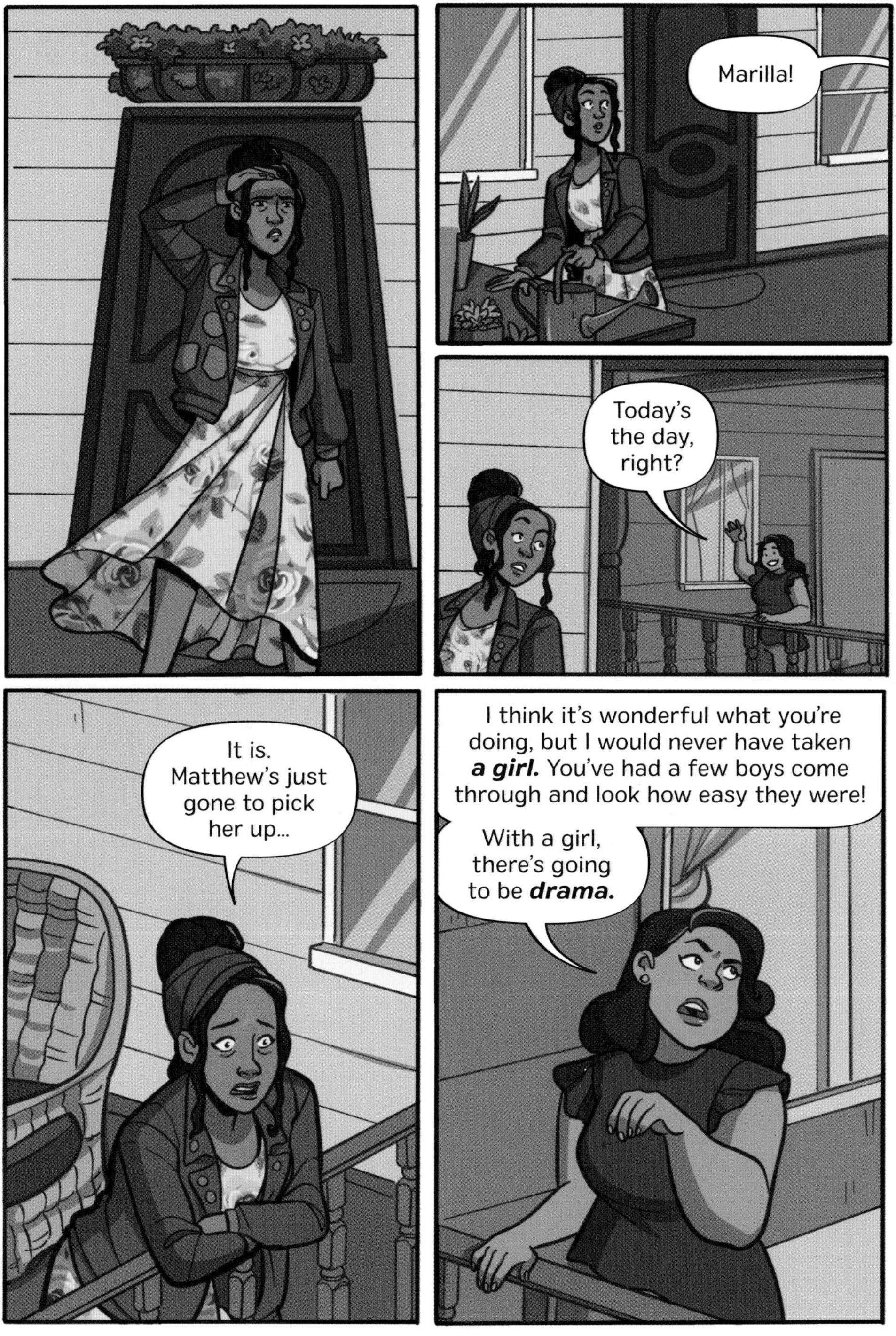
Marilla!
Today's the day, right?
It is. Matthew's just gone to pick her up...
I think it's wonderful what you're doing, but I would never have taken ***a girl.*** You've had a few boys come through and look how easy they were!
With a girl, there's going to be ***drama.***

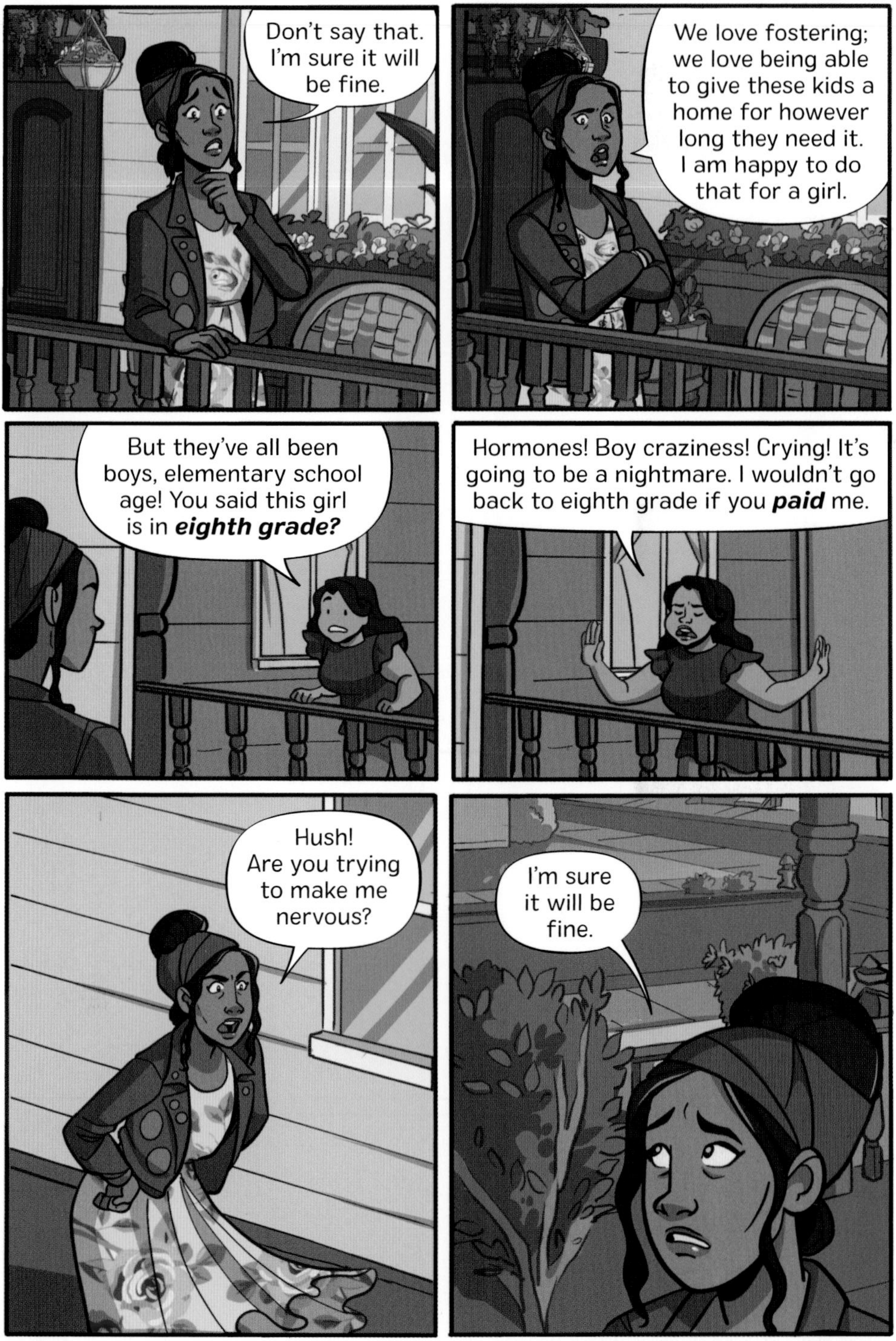
Don't say that. I'm sure it will be fine.
We love fostering; we love being able to give these kids a home for however long they need it. I am happy to do that for a girl.
But they've all been boys, elementary school age! You said this girl is in ***eighth grade?***
Hormones! Boy craziness! Crying! It's going to be a nightmare. I wouldn't go back to eighth grade if you ***paid*** me.
Hush! Are you trying to make me nervous?
I'm sure it will be fine.

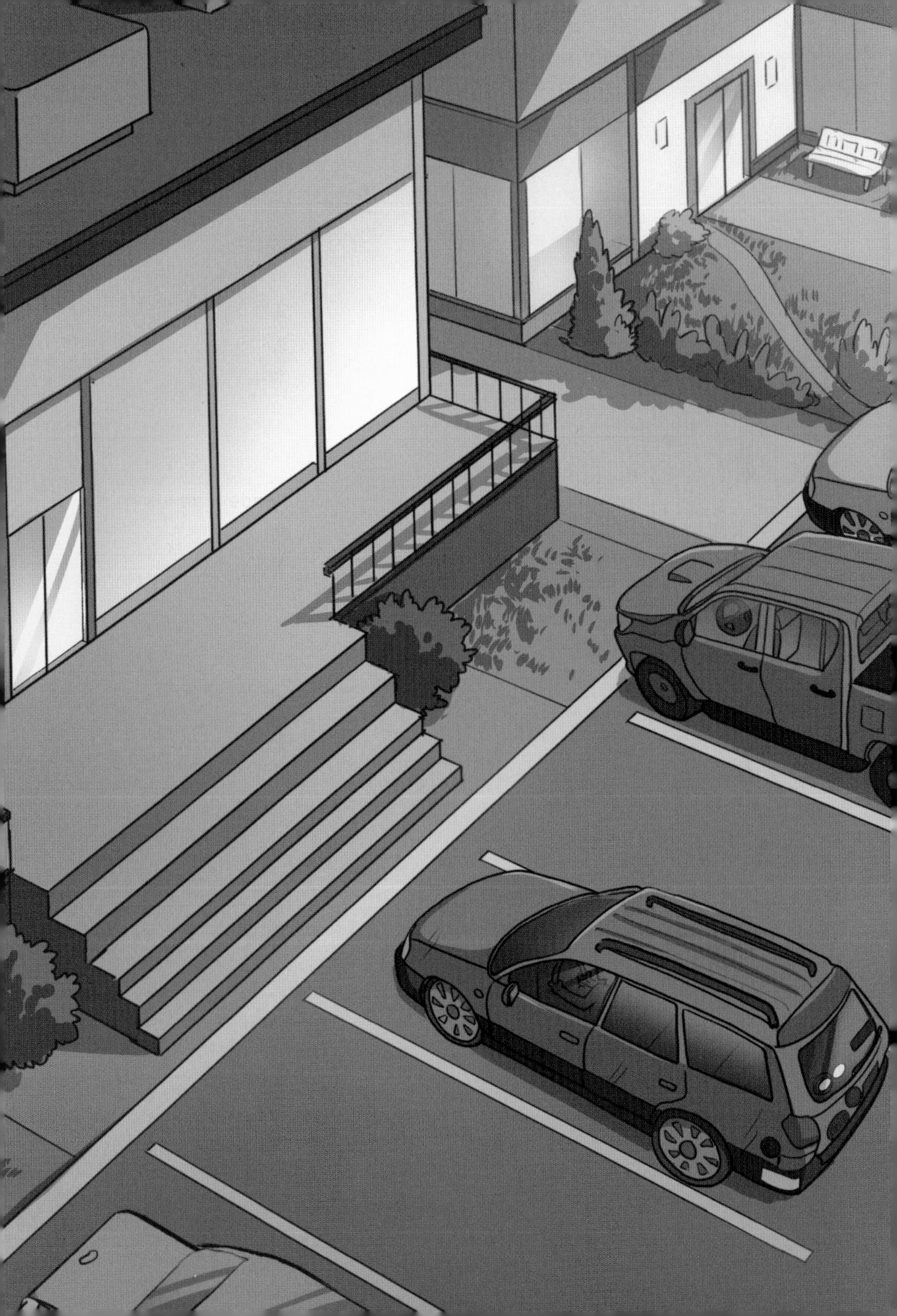

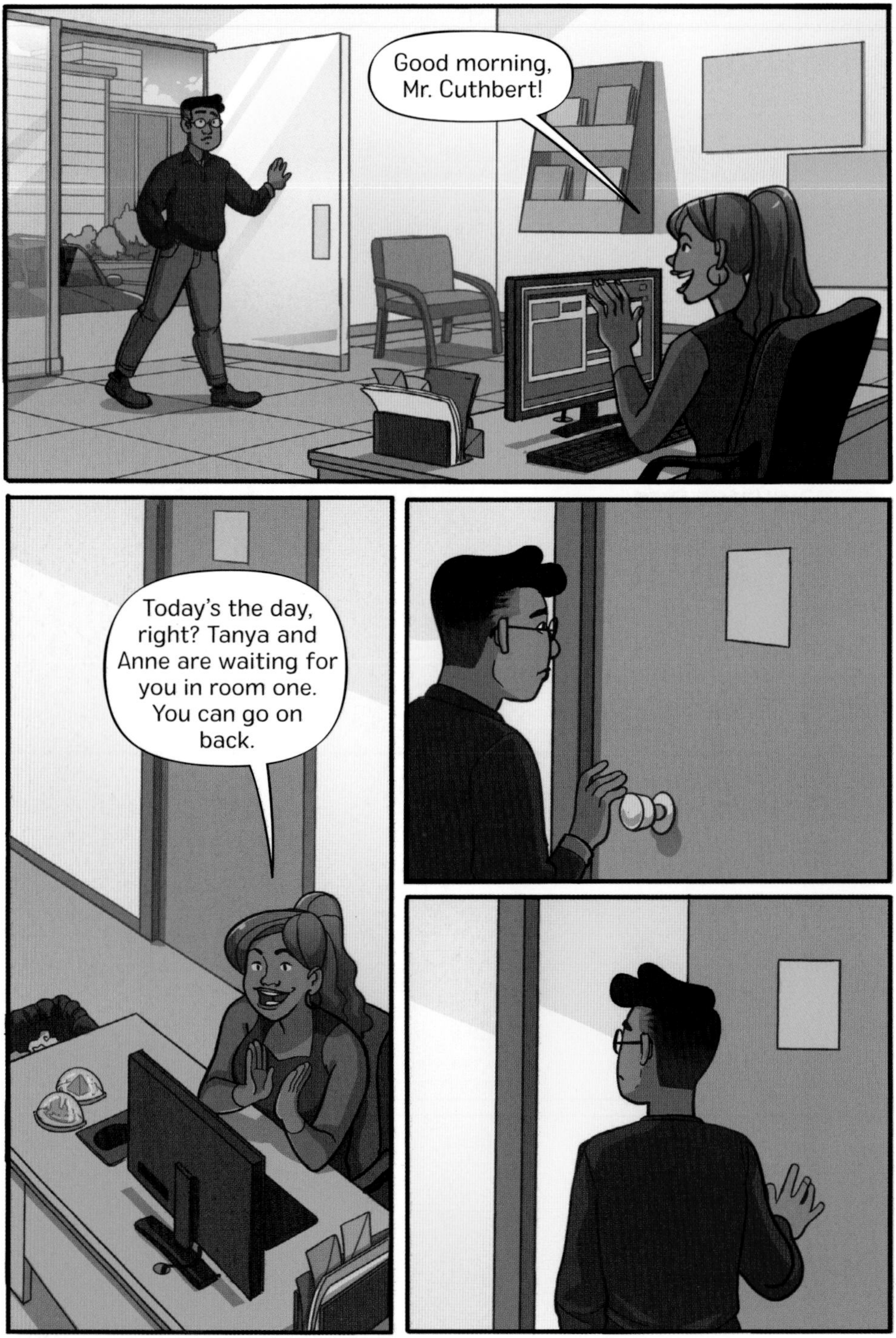
Good morning, Mr. Cuthbert!
Today's the day, right? Tanya and Anne are waiting for you in room one. You can go on back.

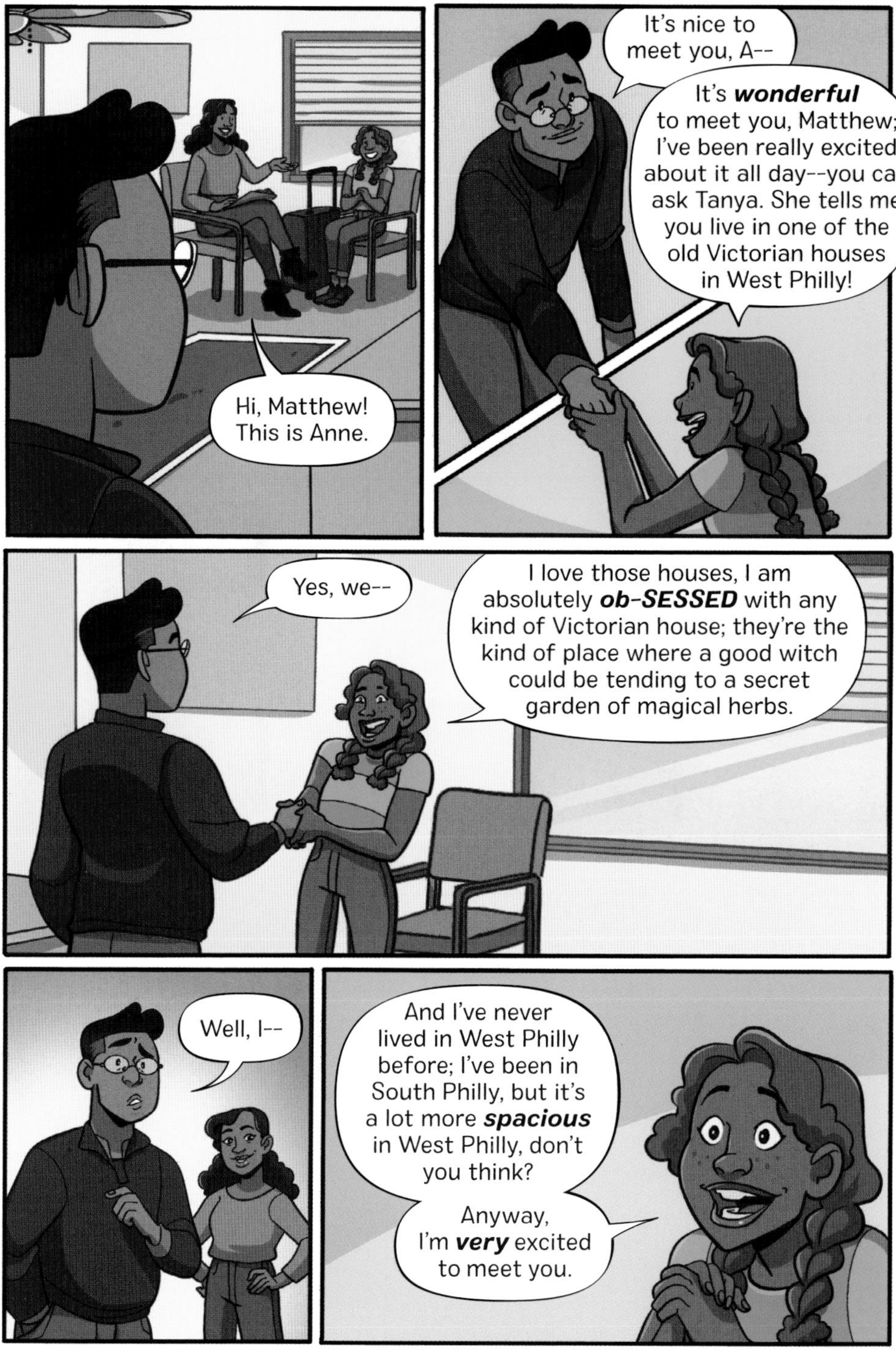
Hi, Matthew!
This is Anne.
It's nice to meet you, A--
It's ***wonderful*** to meet you, Matthew; I've been really excited about it all day--you can ask Tanya. She tells me you live in one of the old Victorian houses in West Philly!
Yes, we--
I love those houses, I am absolutely ***ob-SESSED*** with any kind of Victorian house; they're the kind of place where a good witch could be tending to a secret garden of magical herbs.
Well, I--
And I've never lived in West Philly before; I've been in South Philly, but it's a lot more ***spacious*** in West Philly, don't you think?
Anyway, I'm ***very*** excited to meet you.

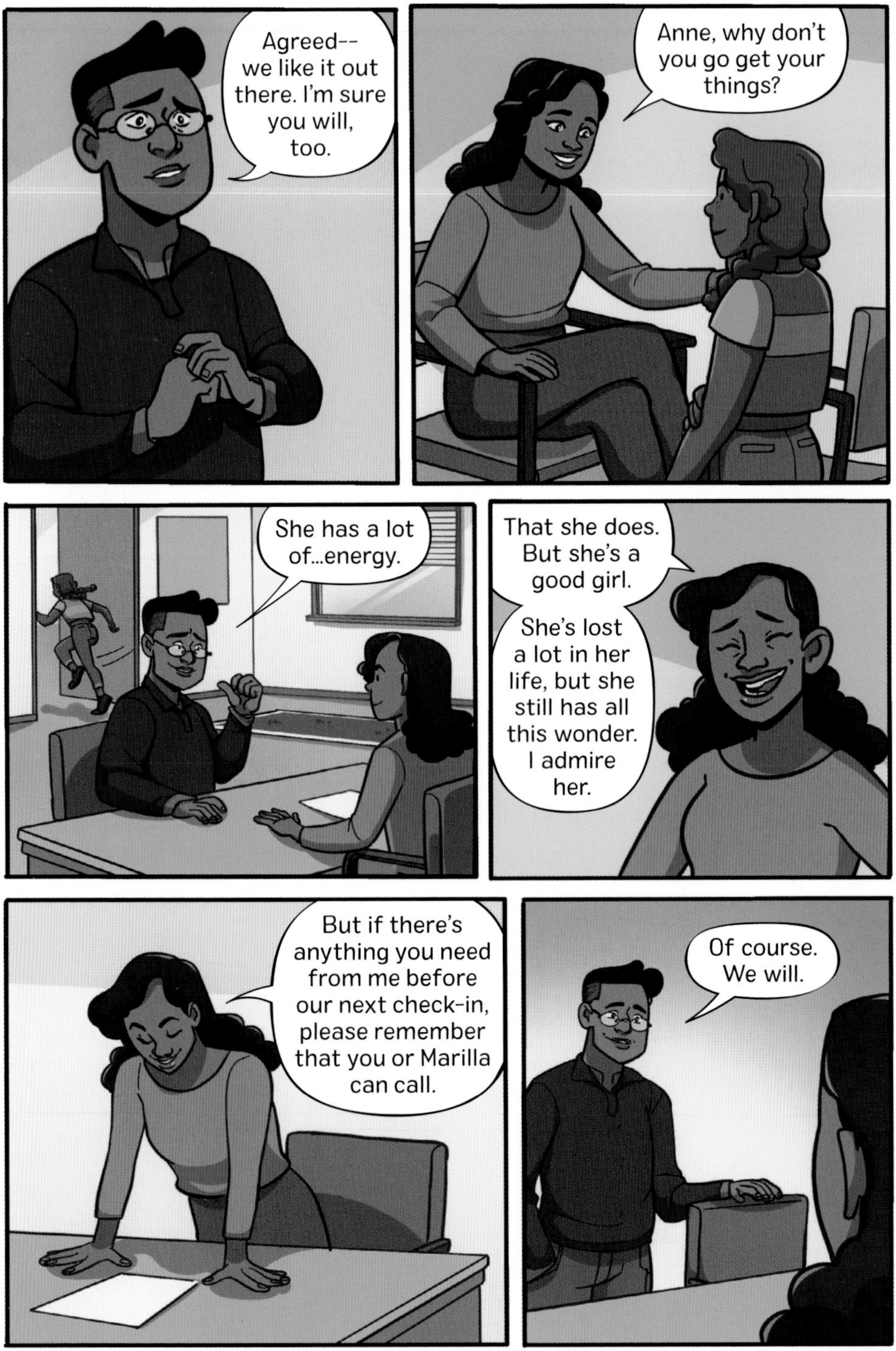
Agreed-- we like it out there. I'm sure you will, too.
Anne, why don't you go get your things?
She has a lot of...energy.
That she does. But she's a good girl.
She's lost a lot in her life, but she still has all this wonder. I admire her.
But if there's anything you need from me before our next check-in, please remember that you or Marilla can call.
Of course. We will.

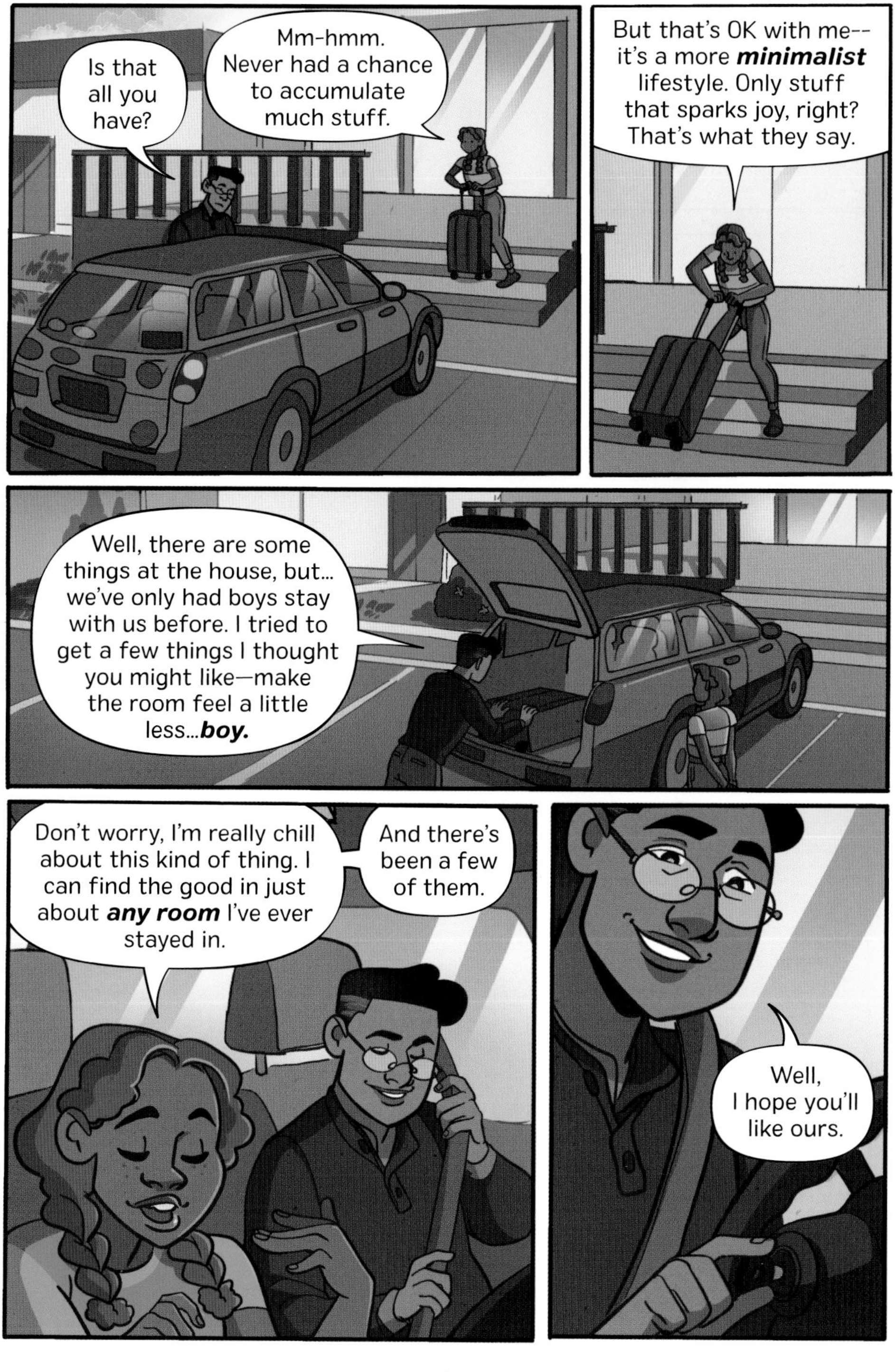
Is that all you have?
Mm-hmm. Never had a chance to accumulate much stuff.
But that's OK with me-- it's a more **minimalist** lifestyle. Only stuff that sparks joy, right? That's what they say.
Well, there are some things at the house, but... we've only had boys stay with us before. I tried to get a few things I thought you might like—make the room feel a little less...**boy.**
Don't worry, I'm really chill about this kind of thing. I can find the good in just about **any room** I've ever stayed in.
And there's been a few of them.
Well, I hope you'll like ours.

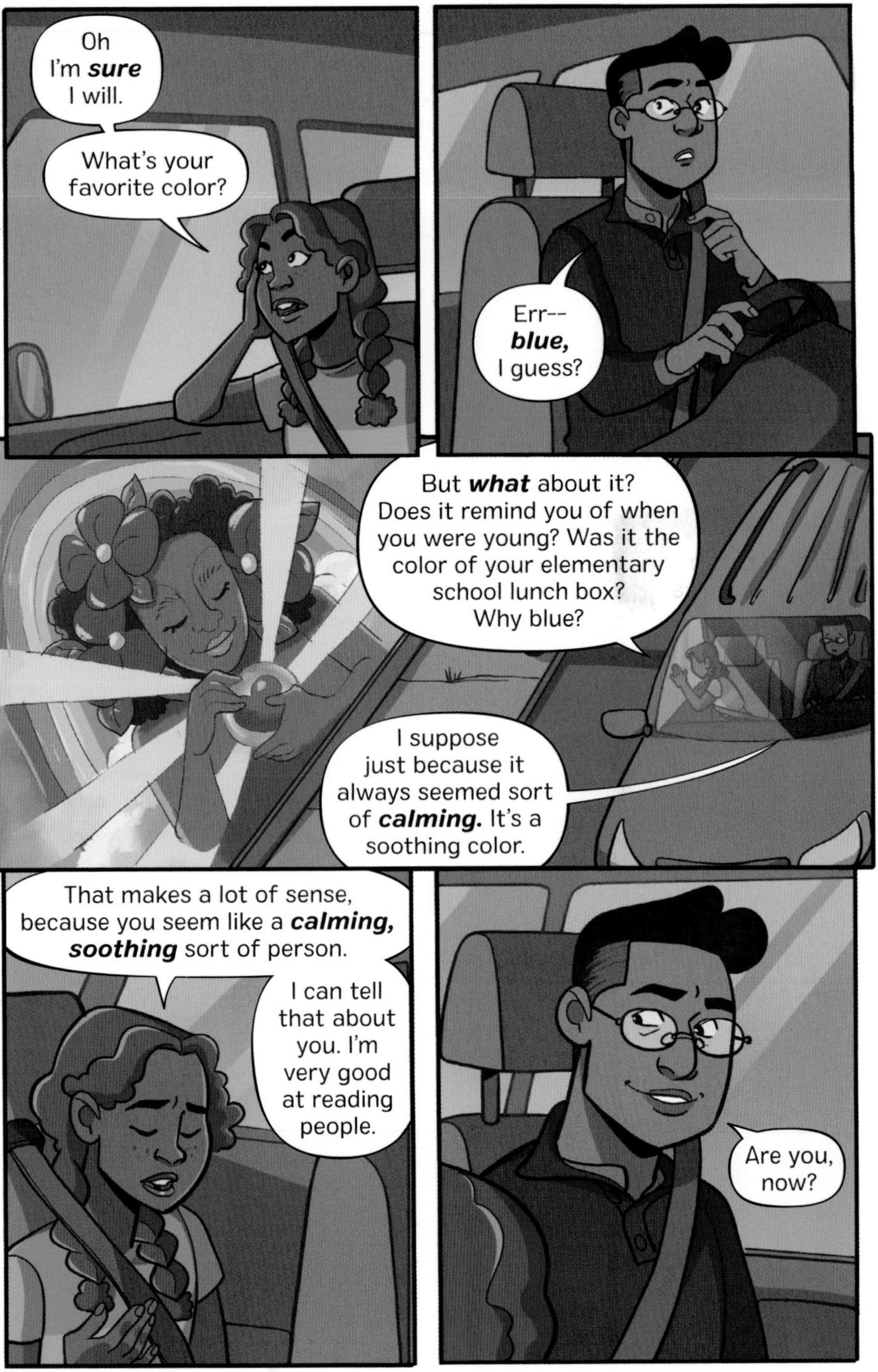
Oh I'm ***sure*** I will.
What's your favorite color?
Err-- ***blue,*** I guess?
But ***what*** about it? Does it remind you of when you were young? Was it the color of your elementary school lunch box? Why blue?
I suppose just because it always seemed sort of ***calming.*** It's a soothing color.
That makes a lot of sense, because you seem like a ***calming, soothing*** sort of person.
I can tell that about you. I'm very good at reading people.
Are you, now?

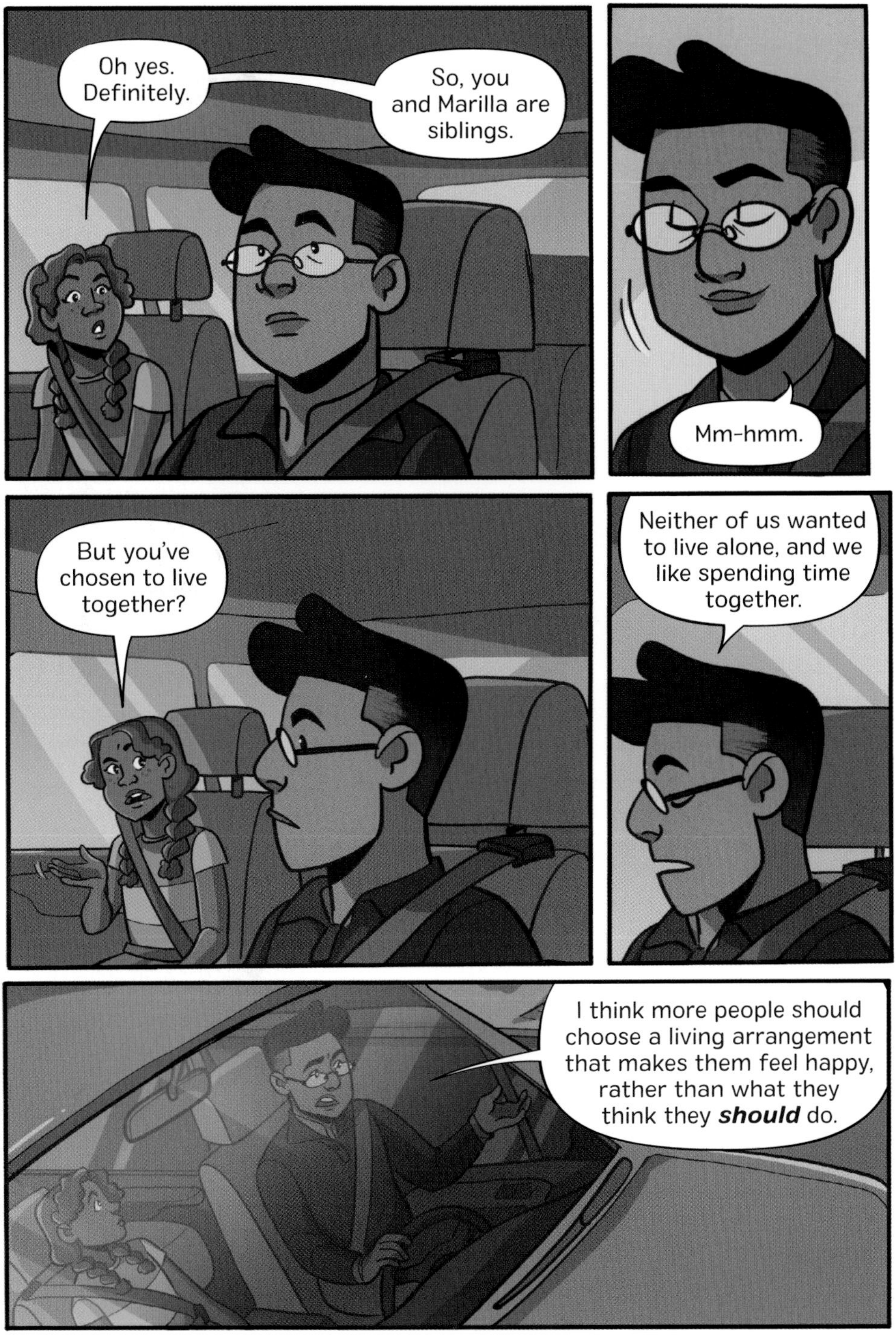
So, you and Marilla are siblings.
Oh yes. Definitely.
Mm-hmm.
But you've chosen to live together?
Neither of us wanted to live alone, and we like spending time together.
I think more people should choose a living arrangement that makes them feel happy, rather than what they think they ***should*** do.

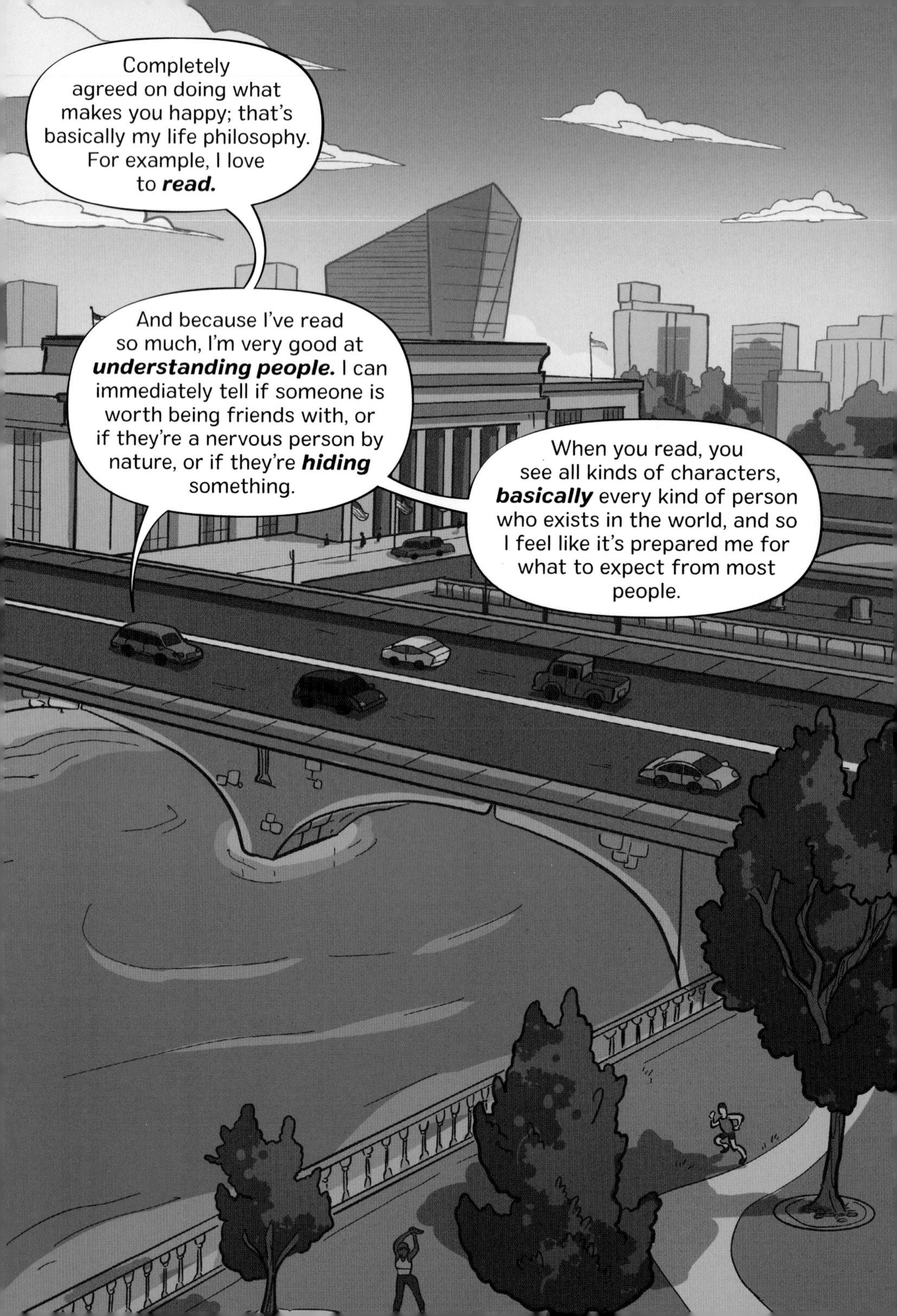
Completely agreed on doing what makes you happy; that's basically my life philosophy. For example, I love to ***read.***
And because I've read so much, I'm very good at ***understanding people.*** I can immediately tell if someone is worth being friends with, or if they're a nervous person by nature, or if they're ***hiding*** something.
When you read, you see all kinds of characters, ***basically*** every kind of person who exists in the world, and so I feel like it's prepared me for what to expect from most people.

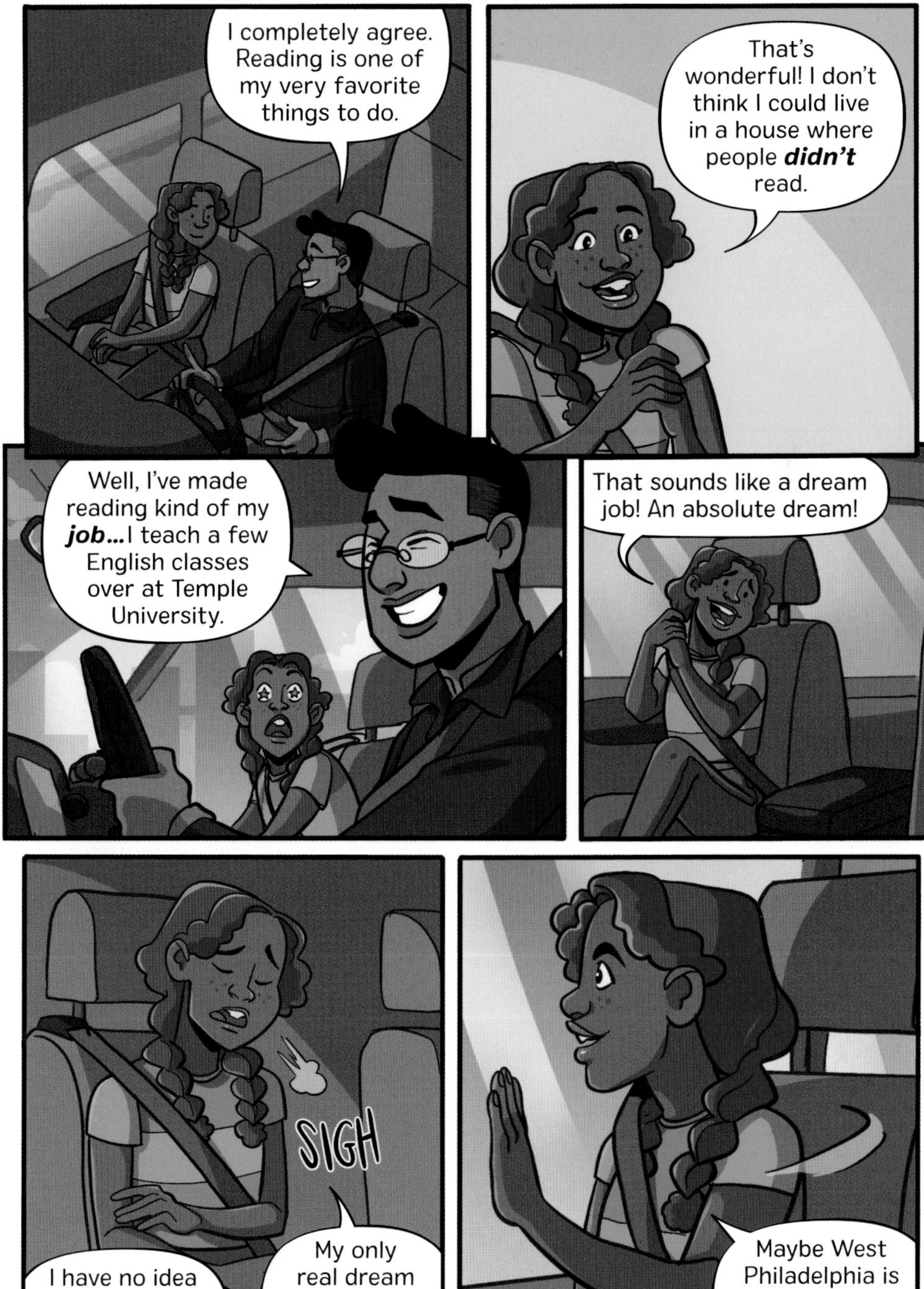
I completely agree. Reading is one of my very favorite things to do.
That's wonderful! I don't think I could live in a house where people ***didn't*** read.
Well, I've made reading kind of my ***job…*** I teach a few English classes over at Temple University.
That sounds like a dream job! An absolute dream!
SIGH
I have no idea what my dream is, job-wise.
My only real dream is to have an ***exciting*** life.
Maybe West Philadelphia is where I find my exciting life.

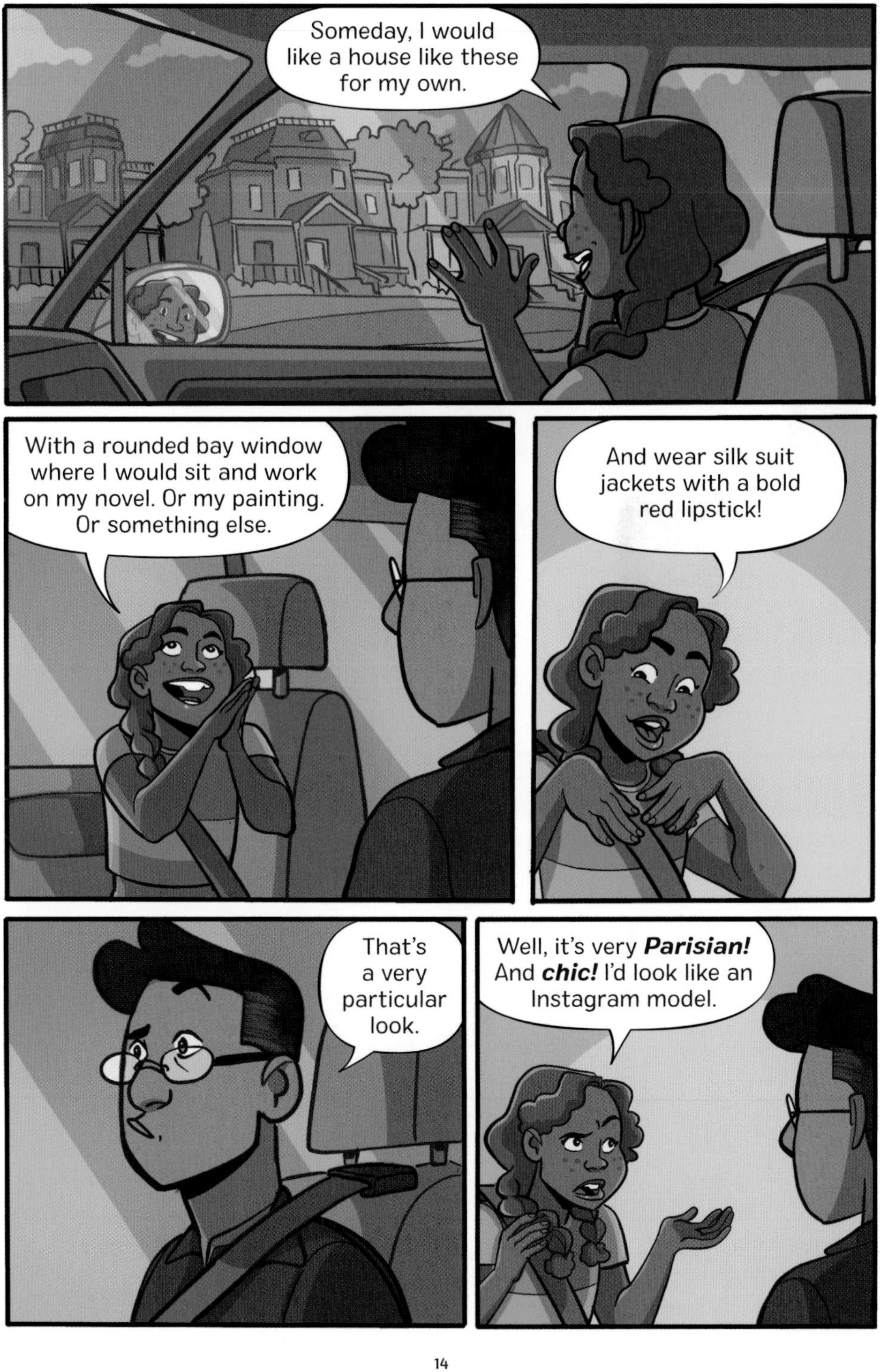
Someday, I would like a house like these for my own.
With a rounded bay window where I would sit and work on my novel. Or my painting. Or something else.
And wear silk suit jackets with a bold red lipstick!
That's a very particular look.
Well, it's very ***Parisian!*** And ***chic!*** I'd look like an Instagram model.

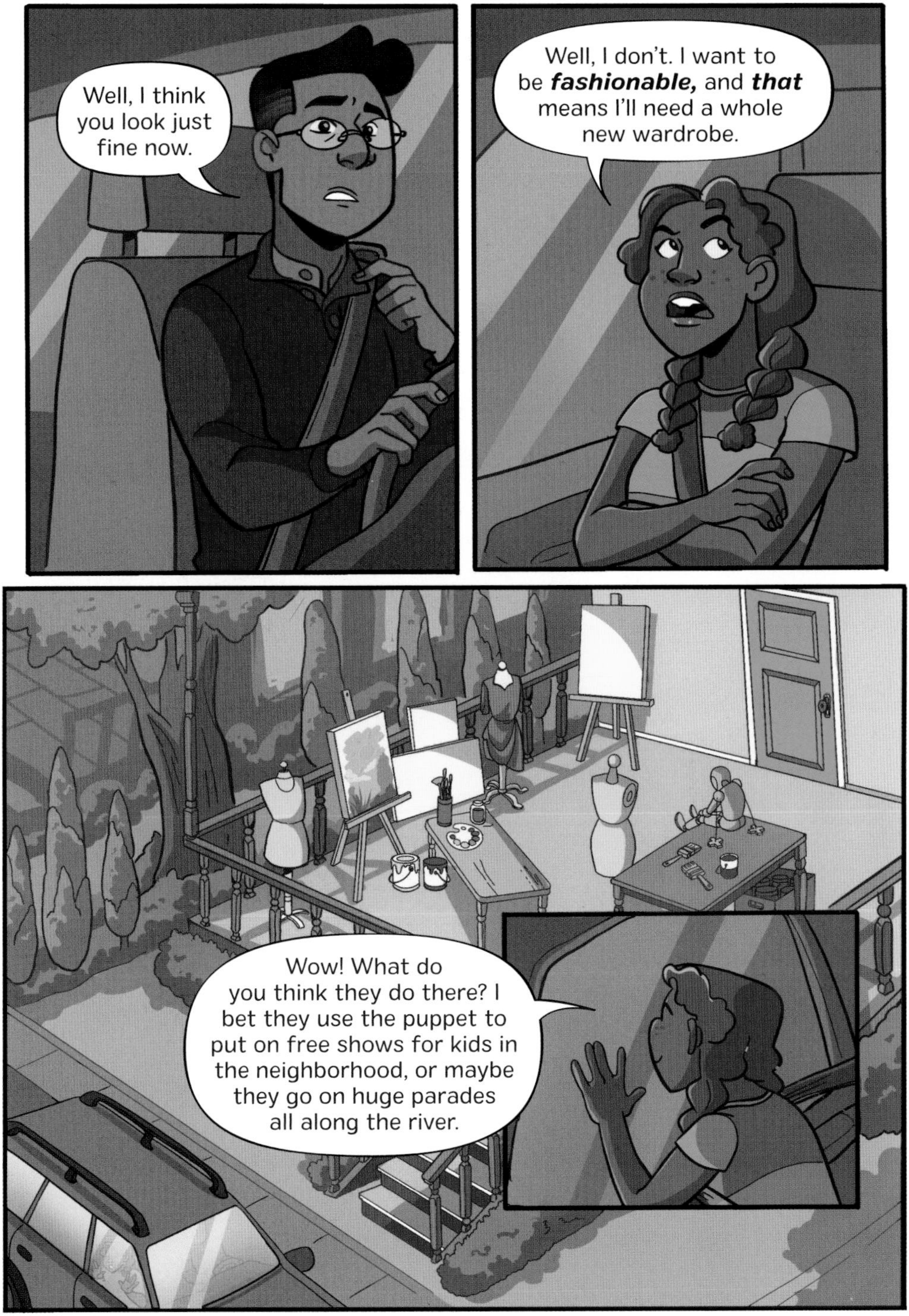
Well, I think you look just fine now.
Well, I don't. I want to be ***fashionable,*** and ***that*** means I'll need a whole new wardrobe.
Wow! What do you think they do there? I bet they use the puppet to put on free shows for kids in the neighborhood, or maybe they go on huge parades all along the river.

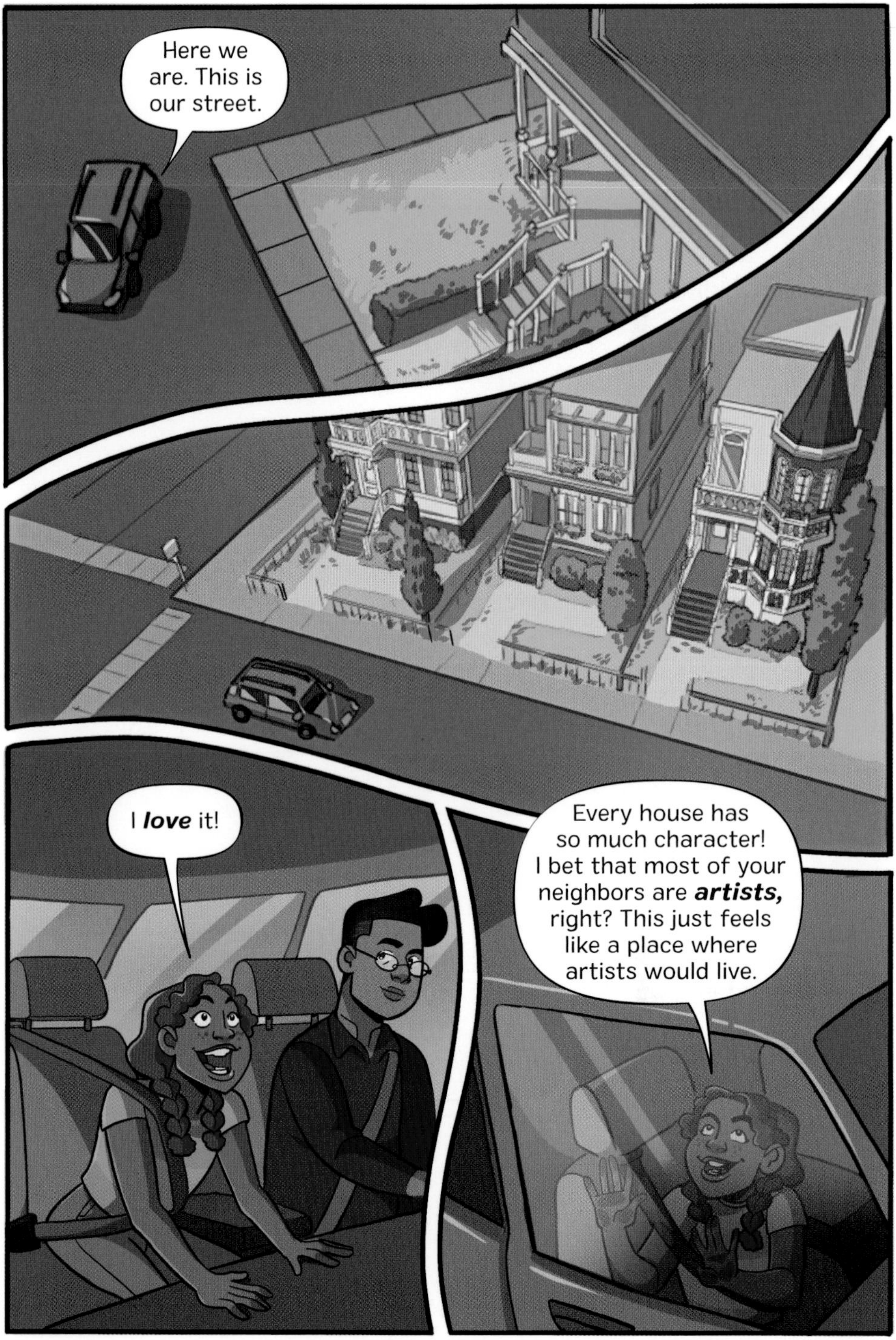
Here we are. This is our street.
I *love* it!
Every house has so much character! I bet that most of your neighbors are ***artists,*** right? This just feels like a place where artists would live.

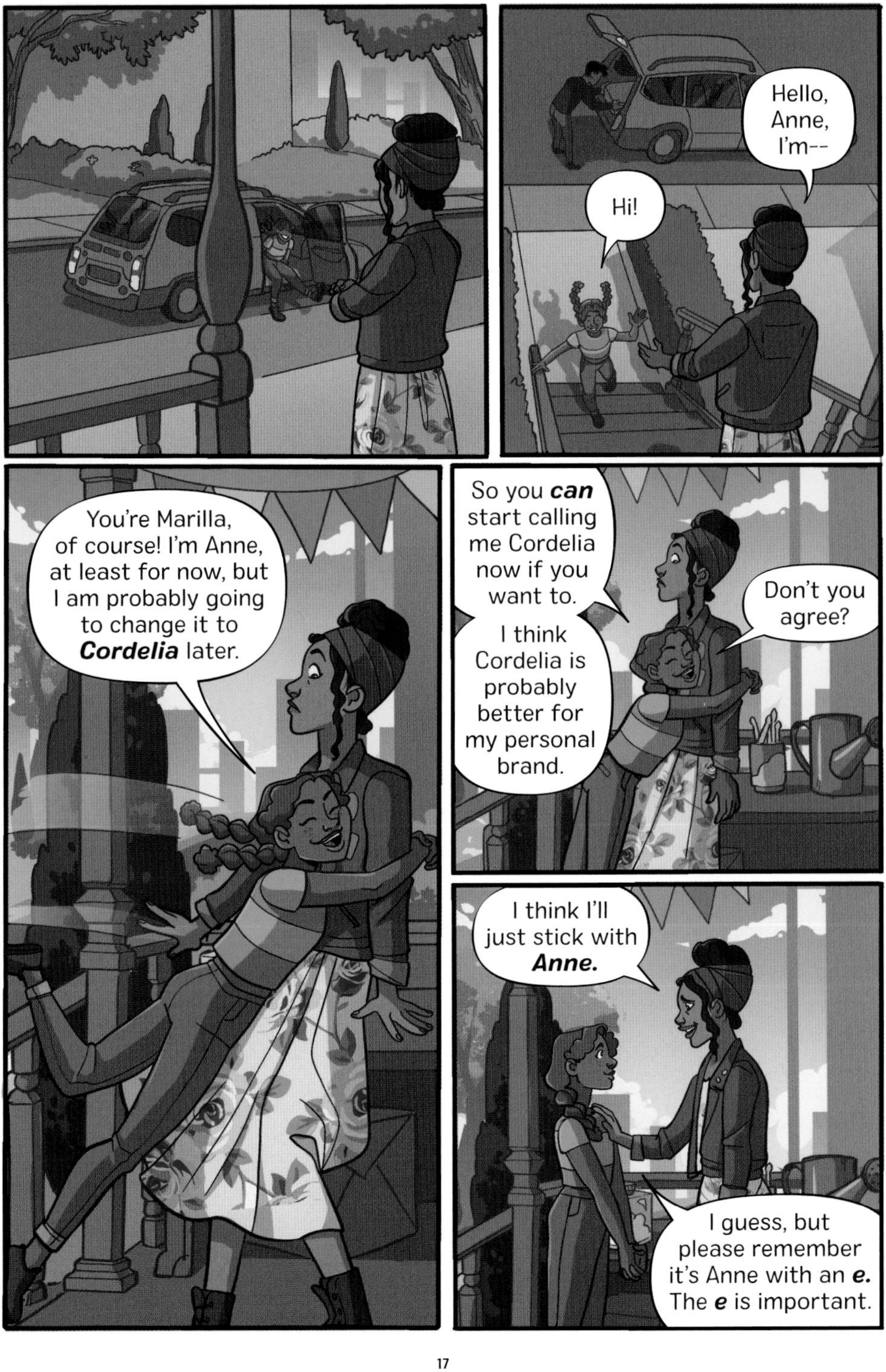
Hello, Anne, I'm--
Hi!
You're Marilla, of course! I'm Anne, at least for now, but I am probably going to change it to *Cordelia* later.
So you *can* start calling me Cordelia now if you want to.
I think Cordelia is probably better for my personal brand.
Don't you agree?
I think I'll just stick with *Anne.*
I guess, but please remember it's Anne with an *e.* The *e* is important.

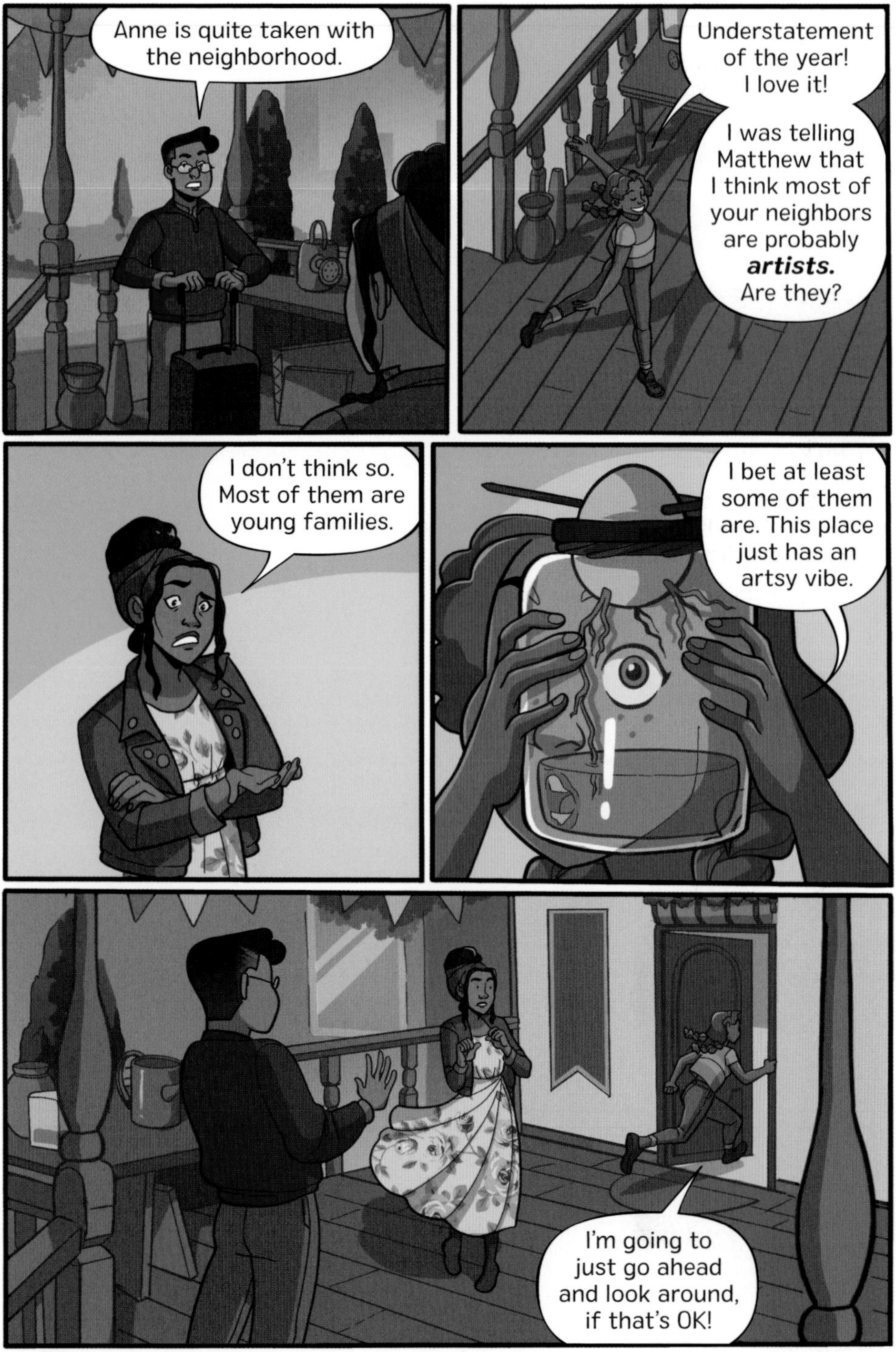
Anne is quite taken with the neighborhood.
Understatement of the year! I love it!
I was telling Matthew that I think most of your neighbors are probably ***artists.*** Are they?
I don't think so. Most of them are young families.
I bet at least some of them are. This place just has an artsy vibe.
I'm going to just go ahead and look around, if that's OK!

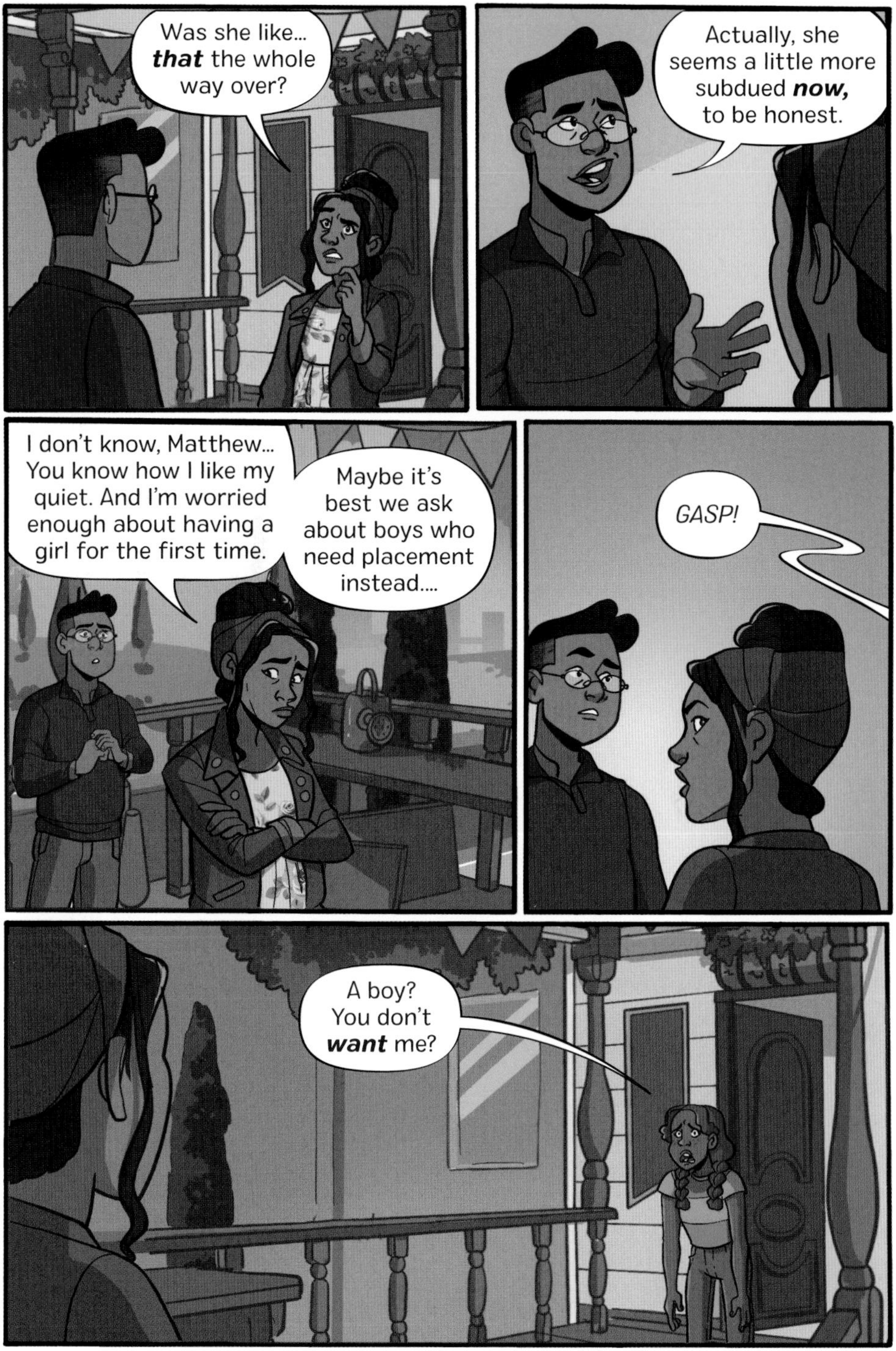
Was she like... **that** the whole way over?
Actually, she seems a little more subdued **now,** to be honest.
I don't know, Matthew... You know how I like my quiet. And I'm worried enough about having a girl for the first time.
Maybe it's best we ask about boys who need placement instead....
GASP!
A boy? You don't **want** me?

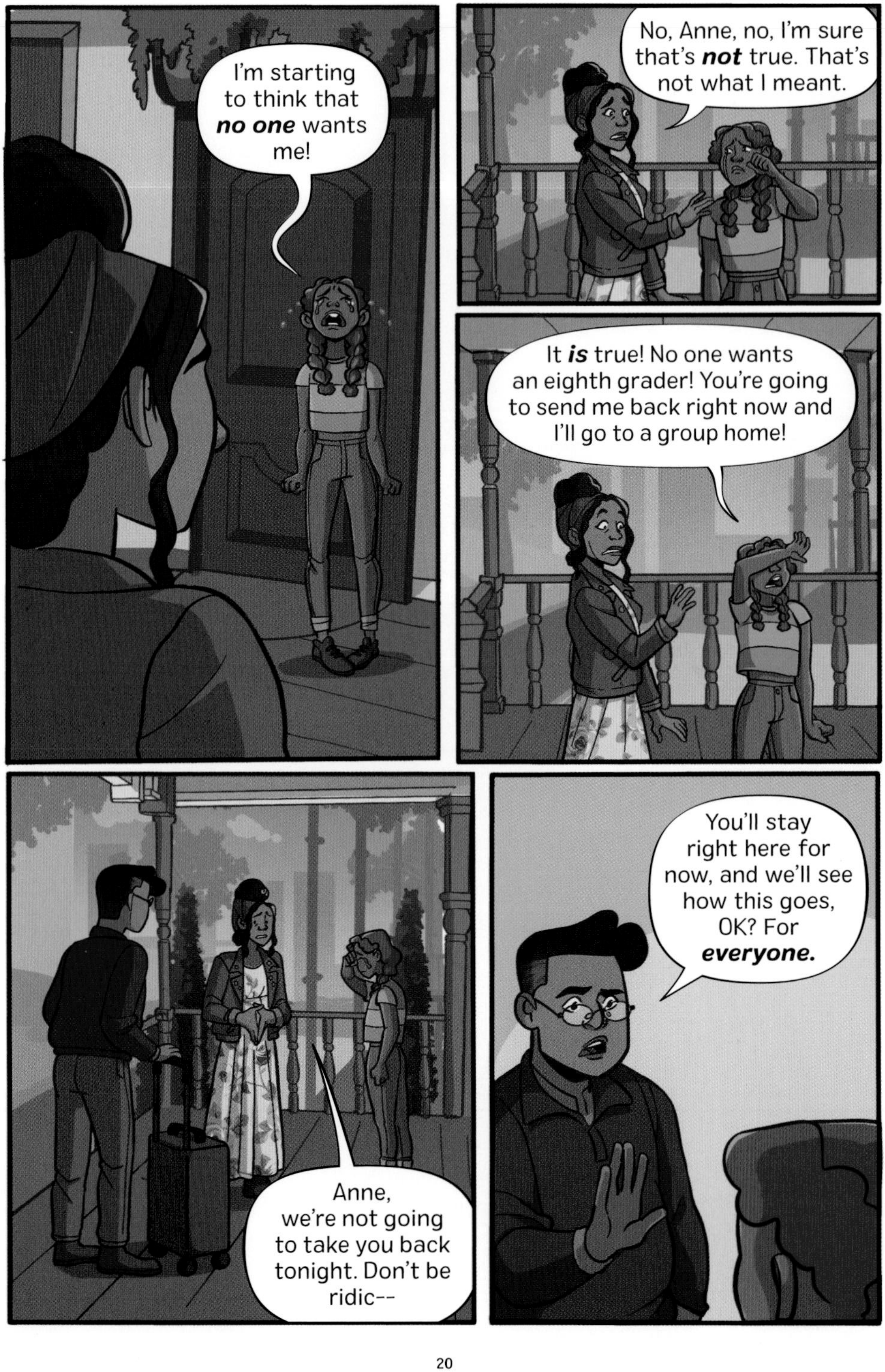

I'm starting to think that ***no one*** wants me!
No, Anne, no, I'm sure that's ***not*** true. That's not what I meant.
It ***is*** true! No one wants an eighth grader! You're going to send me back right now and I'll go to a group home!
Anne, we're not going to take you back tonight. Don't be ridic--
You'll stay right here for now, and we'll see how this goes, OK? For ***everyone.***

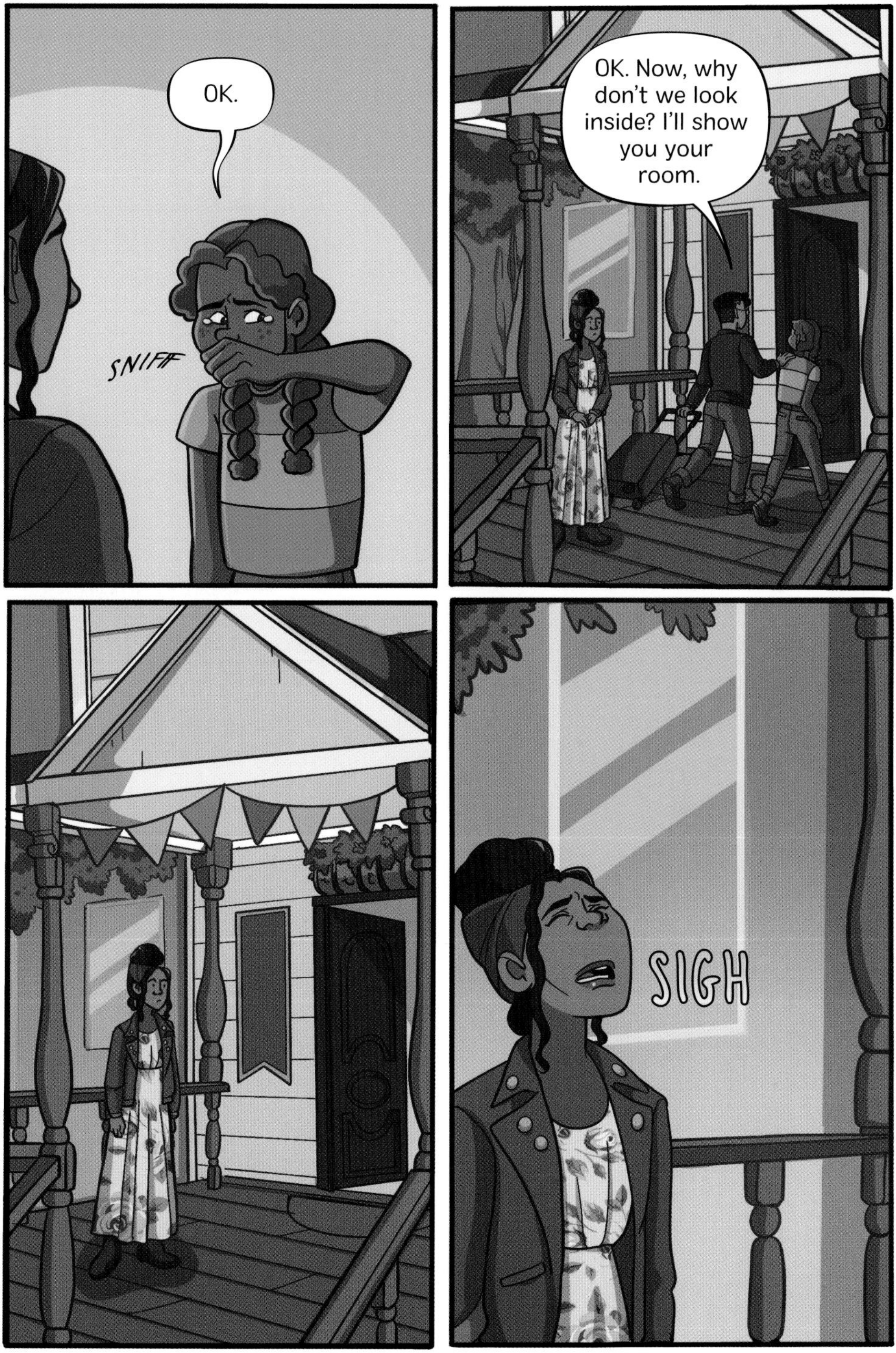

OK.
SNIFF
OK. Now, why don't we look inside? I'll show you your room.
SIGH

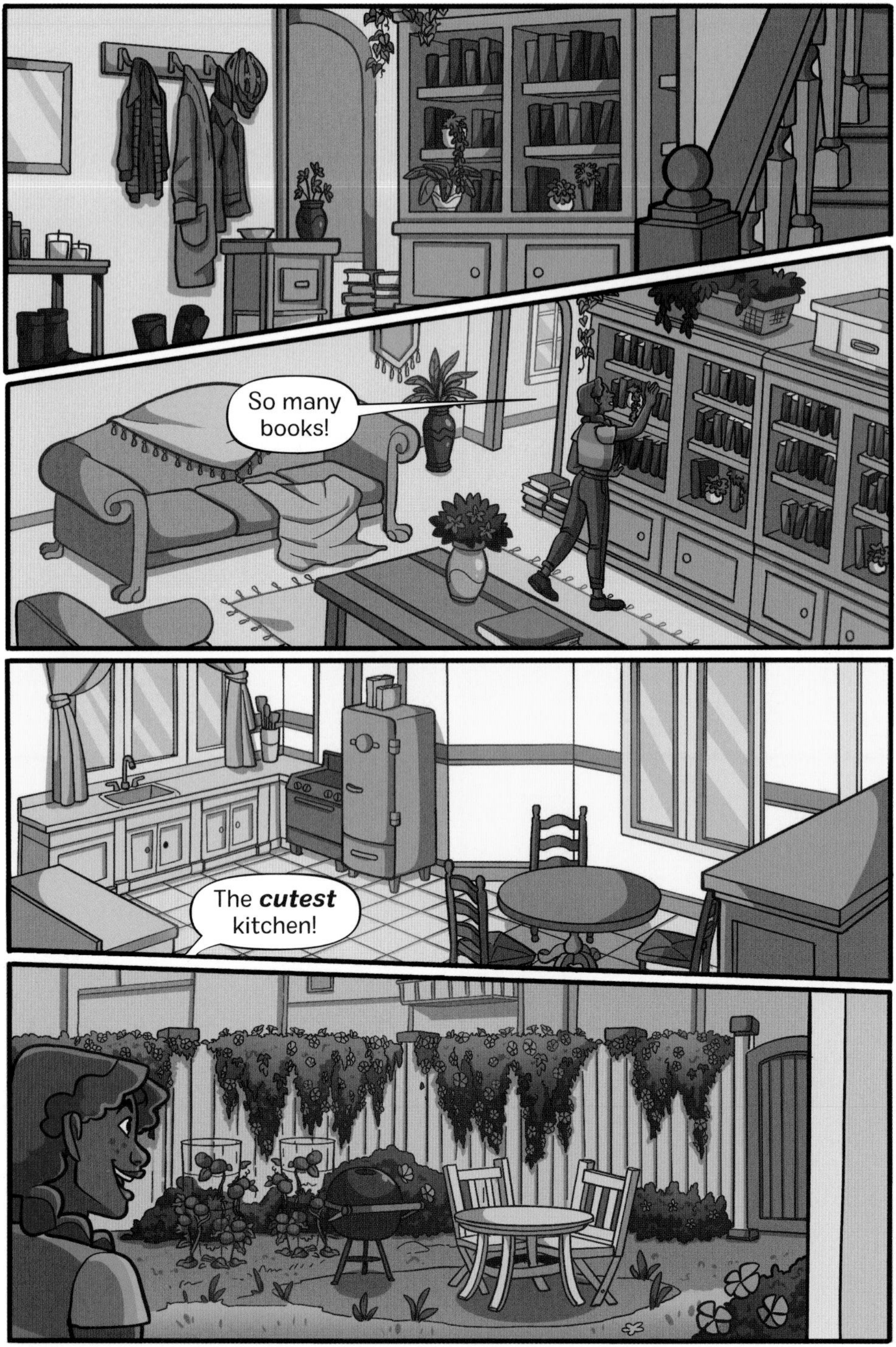
So many books!
The *cutest* kitchen!

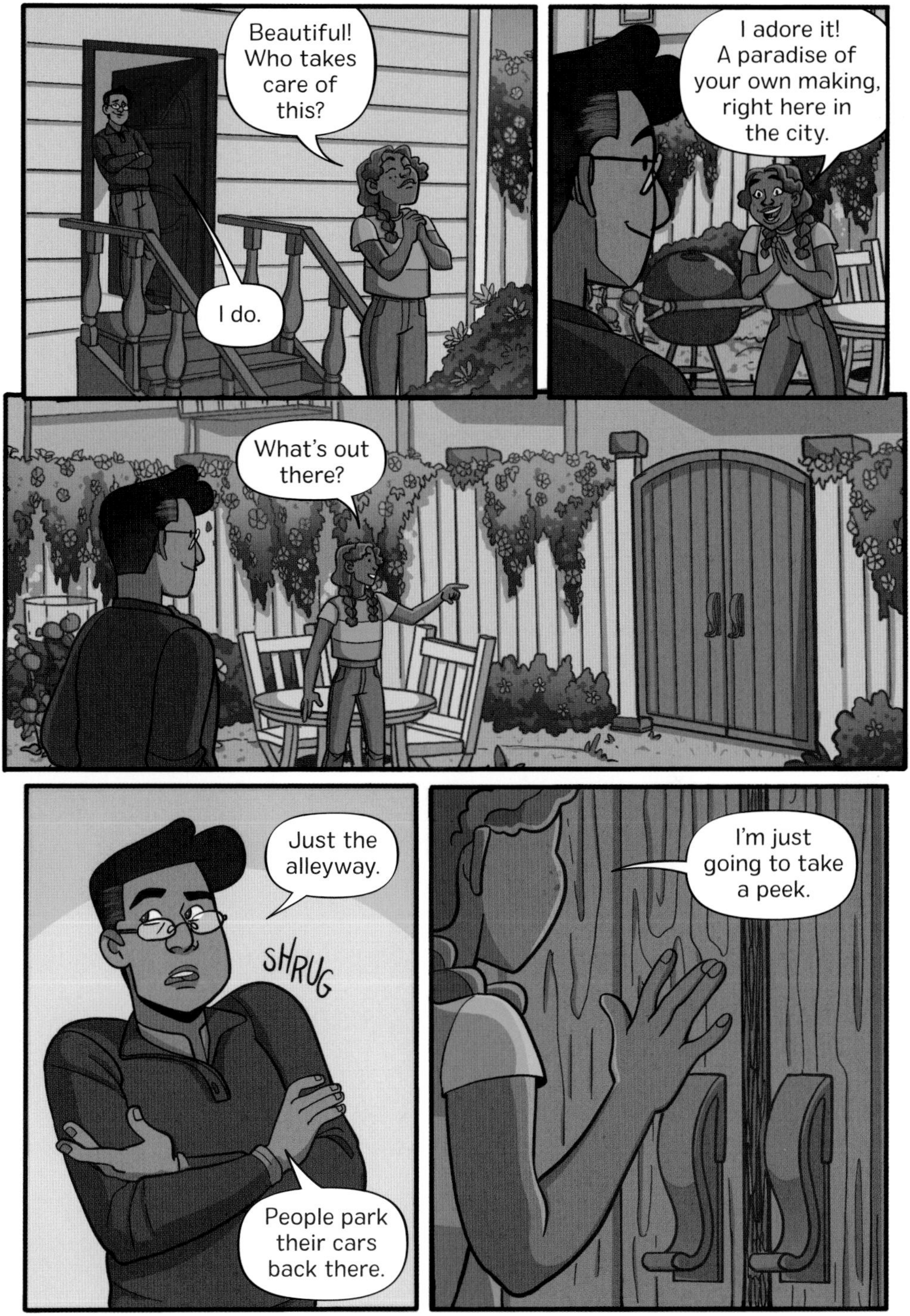
Beautiful! Who takes care of this?
I do.
I adore it! A paradise of your own making, right here in the city.
What's out there?
Just the alleyway.
SHRUG
People park their cars back there.
I'm just going to take a peek.

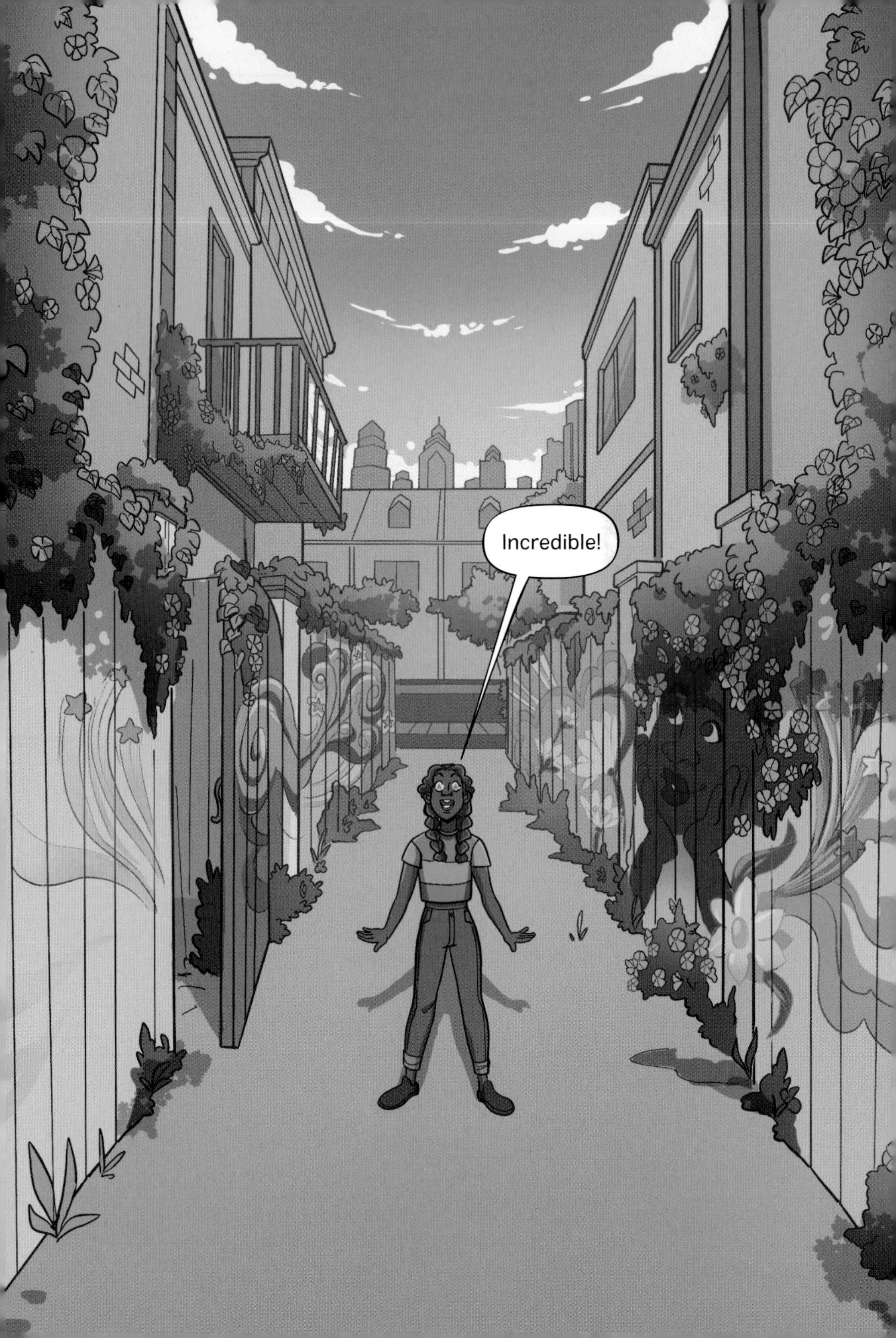
Incredible!

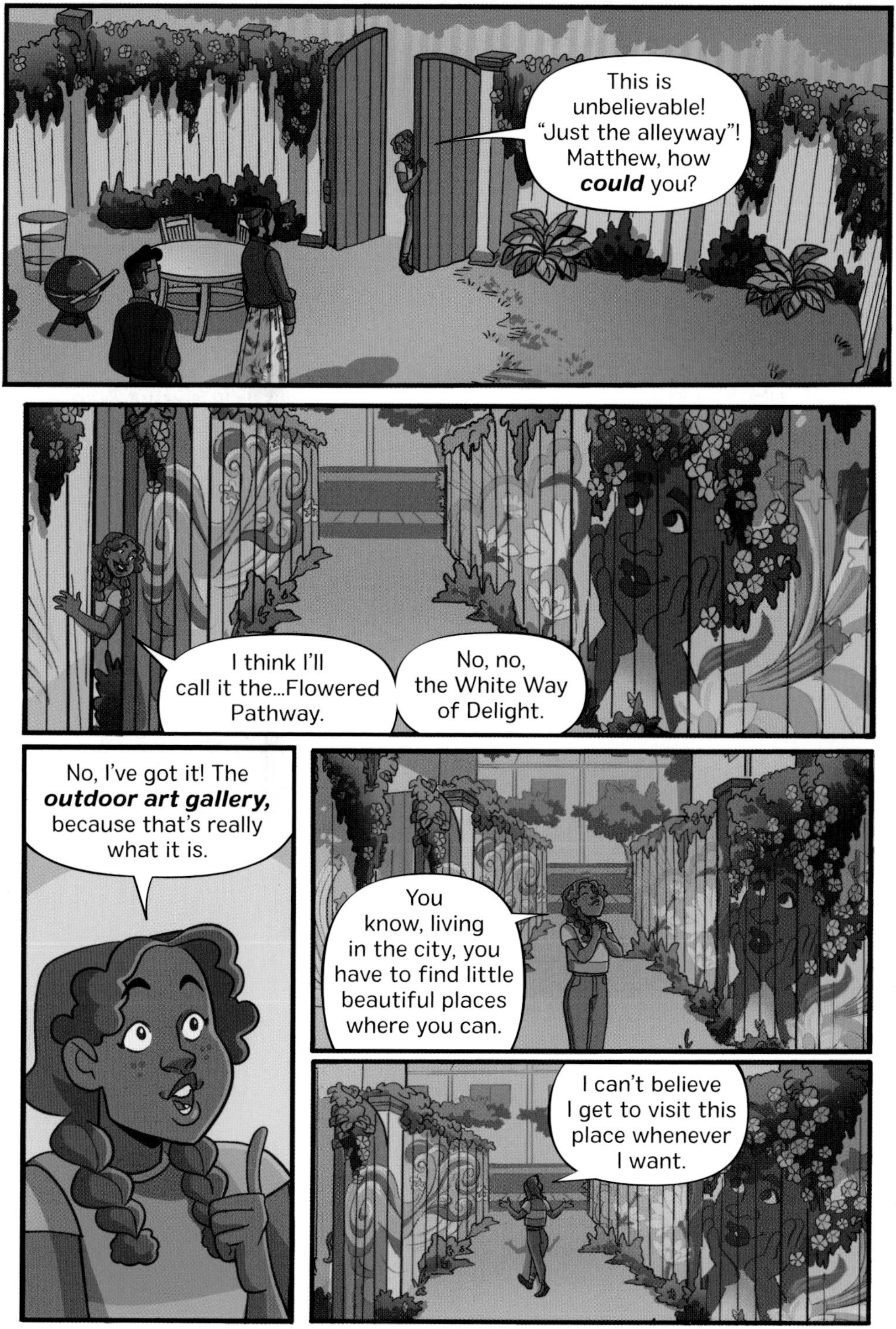
This is unbelievable! "Just the alleyway"! Matthew, how **could** you?
I think I'll call it the...Flowered Pathway.
No, no, the White Way of Delight.
No, I've got it! The ***outdoor art gallery,*** because that's really what it is.
You know, living in the city, you have to find little beautiful places where you can.
I can't believe I get to visit this place whenever I want.

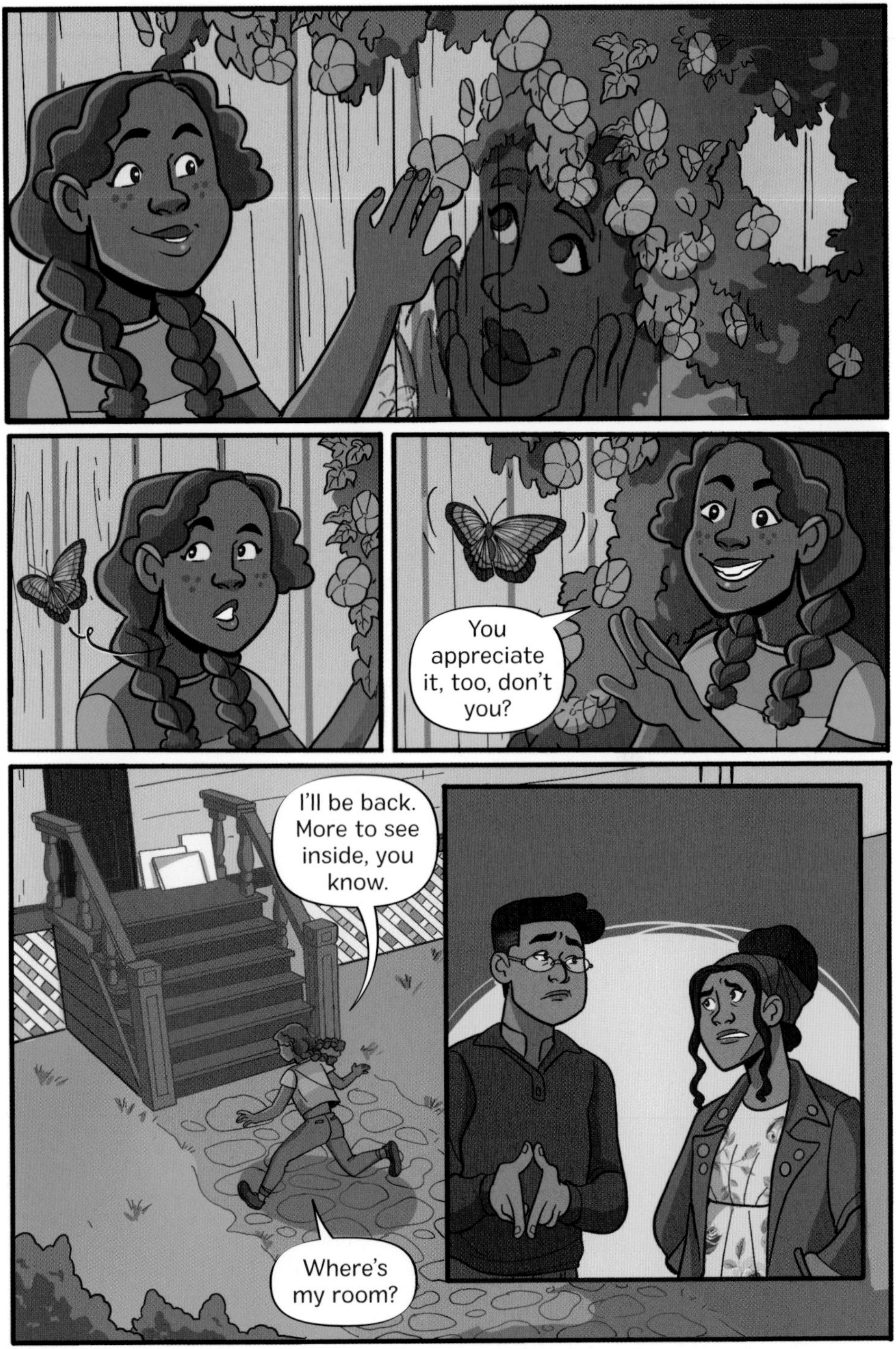
You appreciate it, too, don't you?
I'll be back. More to see inside, you know.
Where's my room?

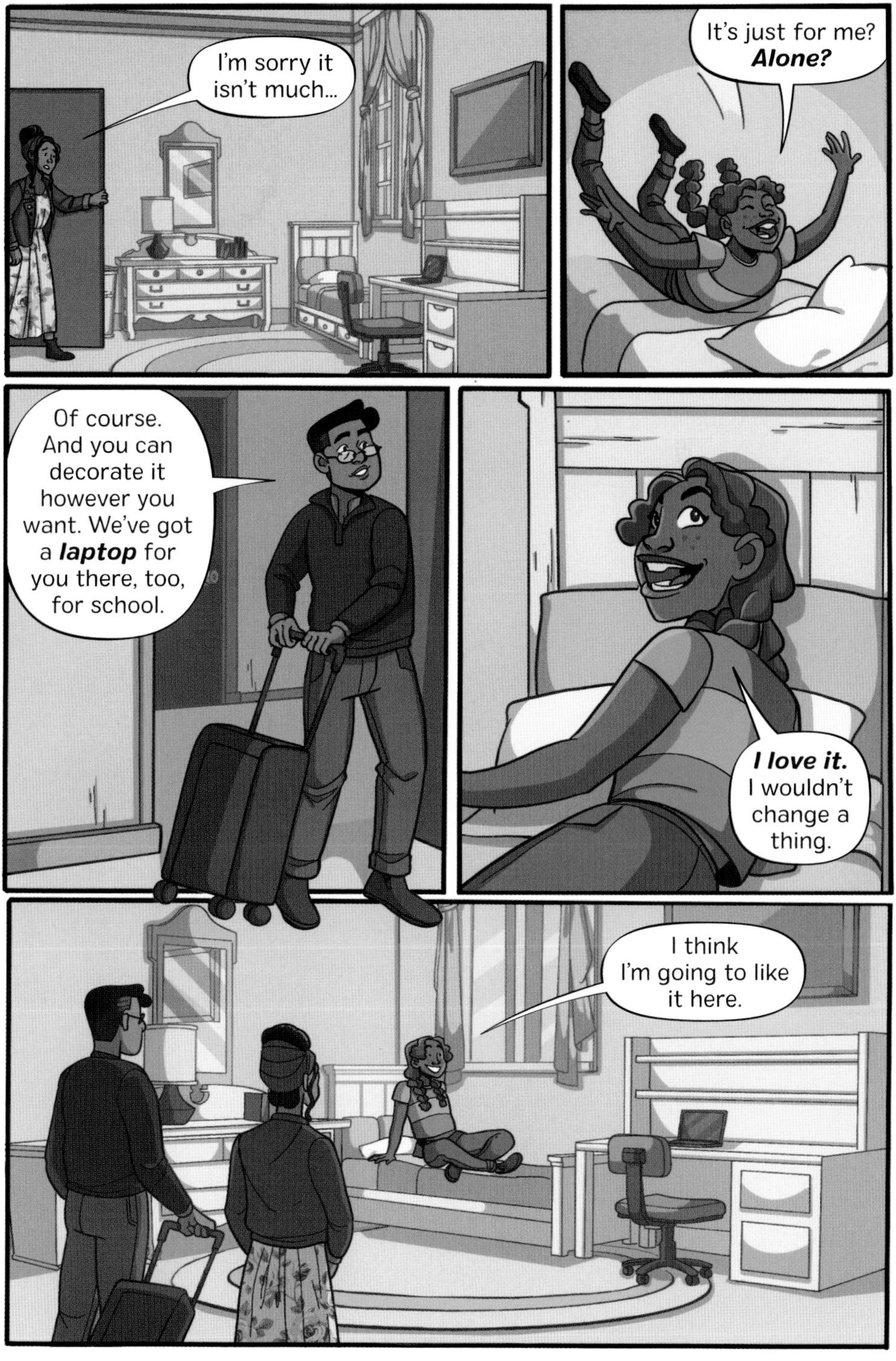
I'm sorry it isn't much...
It's just for me? ***Alone?***
Of course. And you can decorate it however you want. We've got a ***laptop*** for you there, too, for school.
I love it. I wouldn't change a thing.
I think I'm going to like it here.

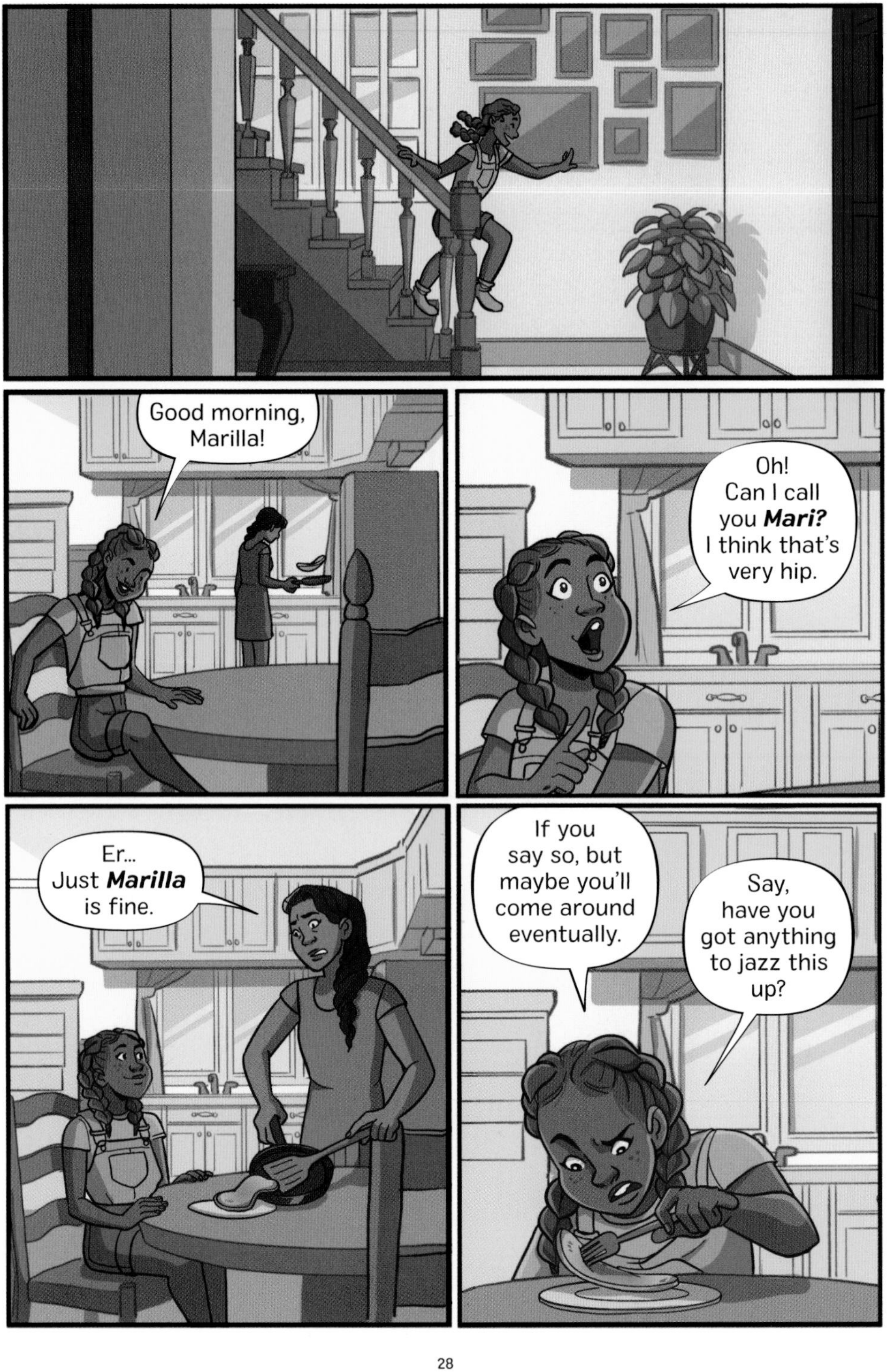
Good morning, Marilla!
Oh! Can I call you ***Mari?*** I think that's very hip.
Er... Just ***Marilla*** is fine.
If you say so, but maybe you'll come around eventually.
Say, have you got anything to jazz this up?

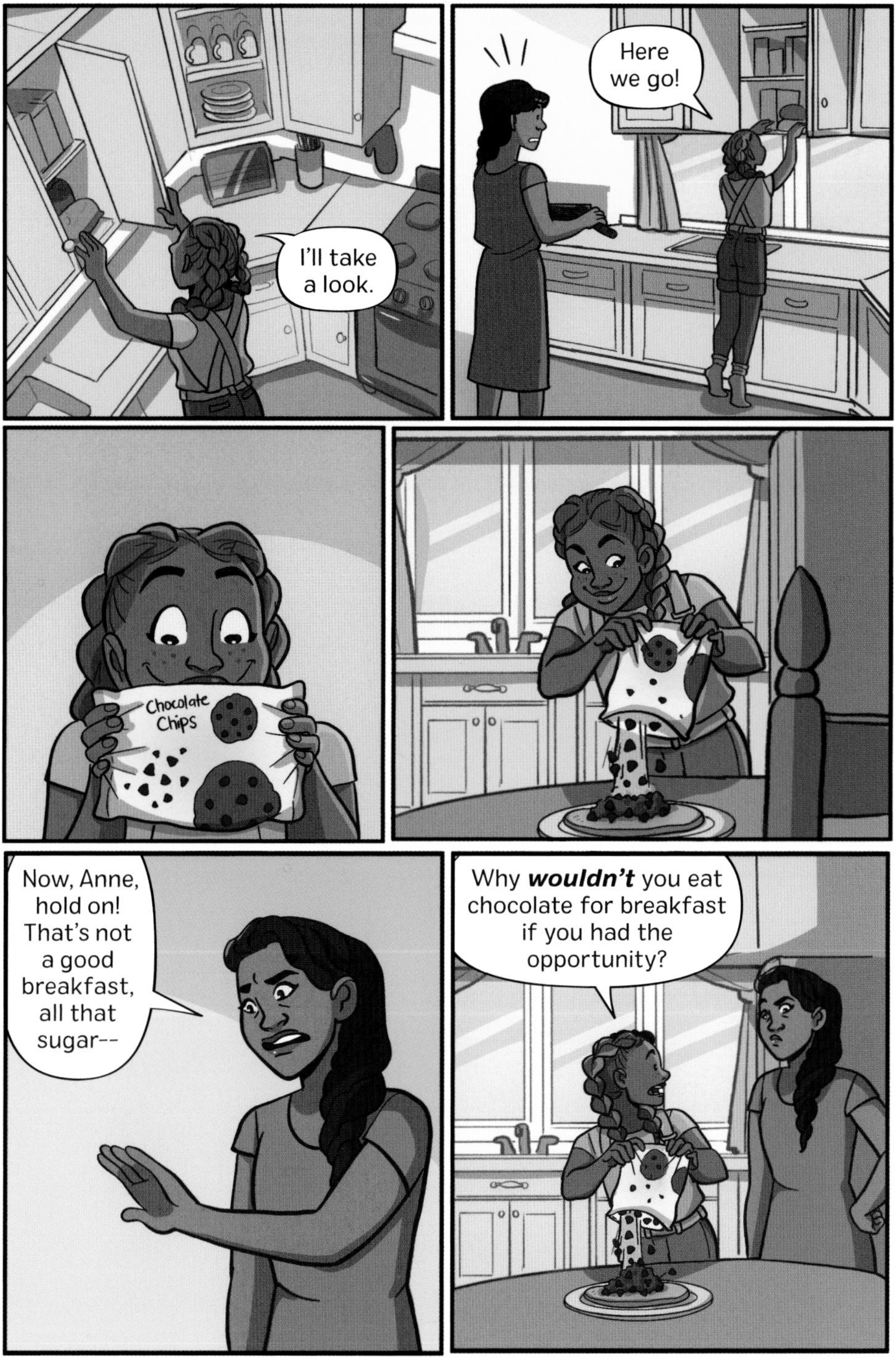
I'll take a look.
Here we go!
Chocolate Chips
Now, Anne, hold on! That's not a good breakfast, all that sugar--
Why ***wouldn't*** you eat chocolate for breakfast if you had the opportunity?

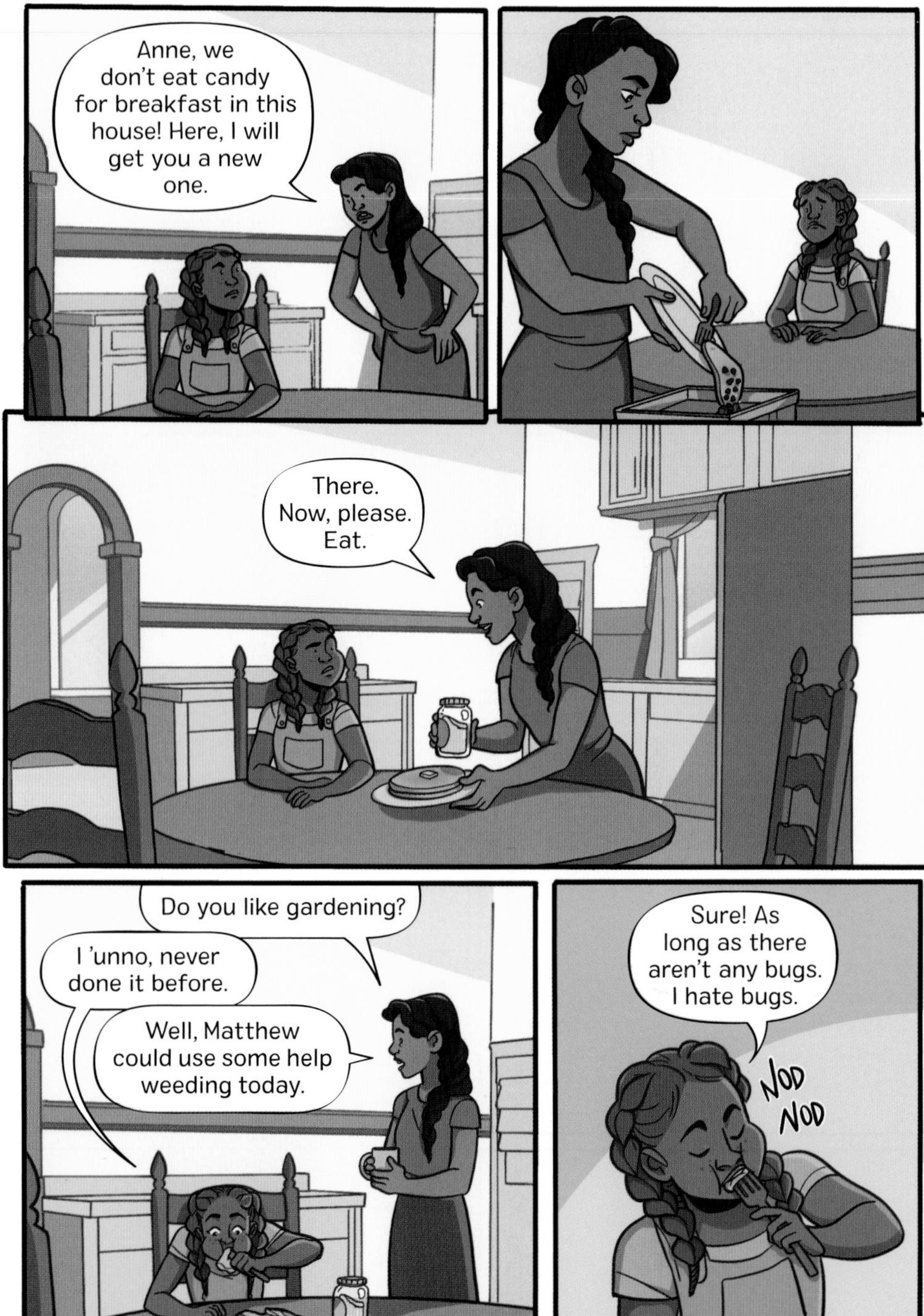
Anne, we don't eat candy for breakfast in this house! Here, I will get you a new one.
There. Now, please. Eat.
Do you like gardening?
I 'unno, never done it before.
Well, Matthew could use some help weeding today.
Sure! As long as there aren't any bugs. I hate bugs.
NOD NOD

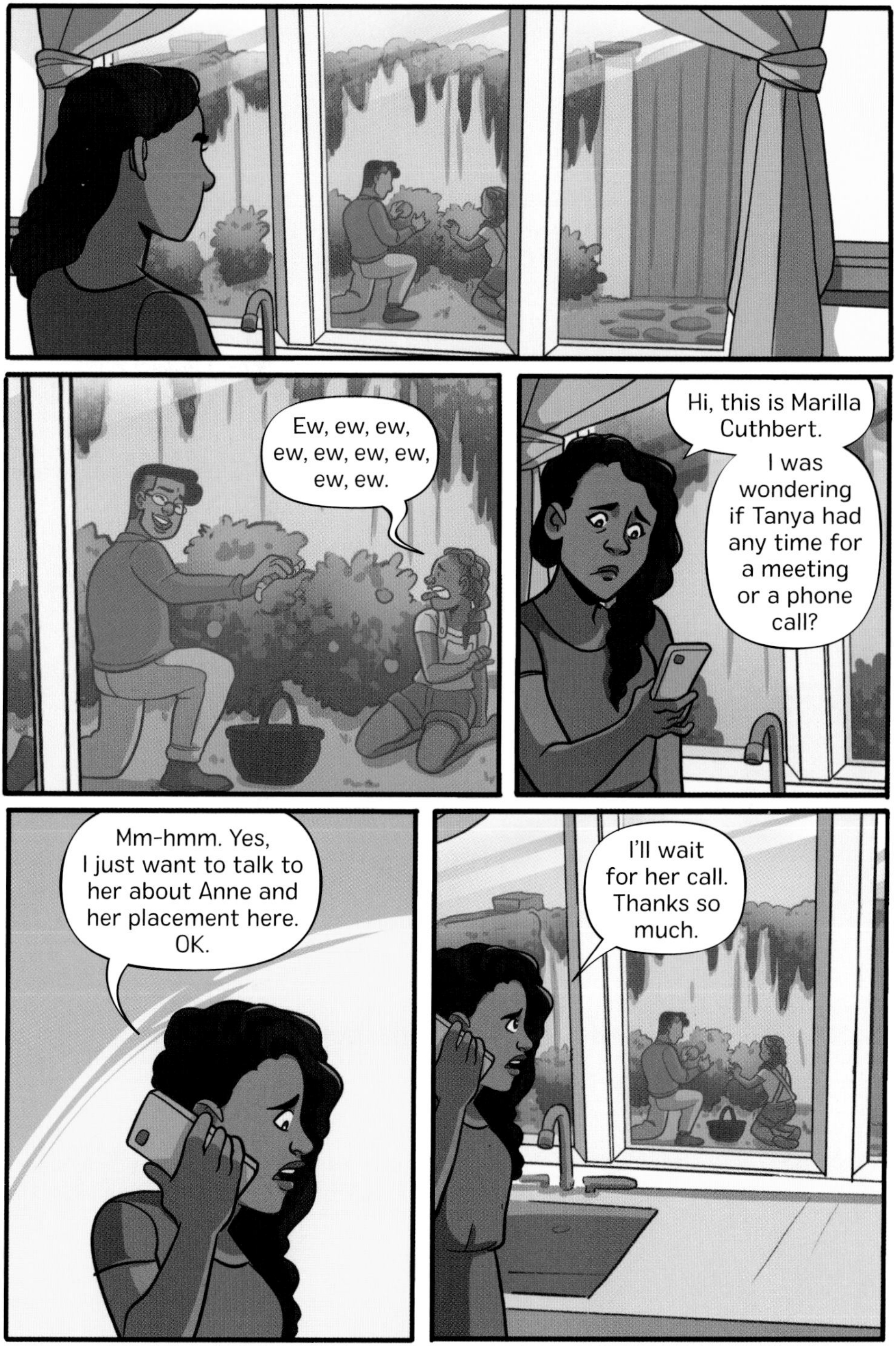
Ew, ew, ew,
ew, ew, ew, ew,
ew, ew.
Hi, this is Marilla Cuthbert.
I was wondering if Tanya had any time for a meeting or a phone call?
Mm-hmm. Yes, I just want to talk to her about Anne and her placement here. OK.
I'll wait for her call. Thanks so much.

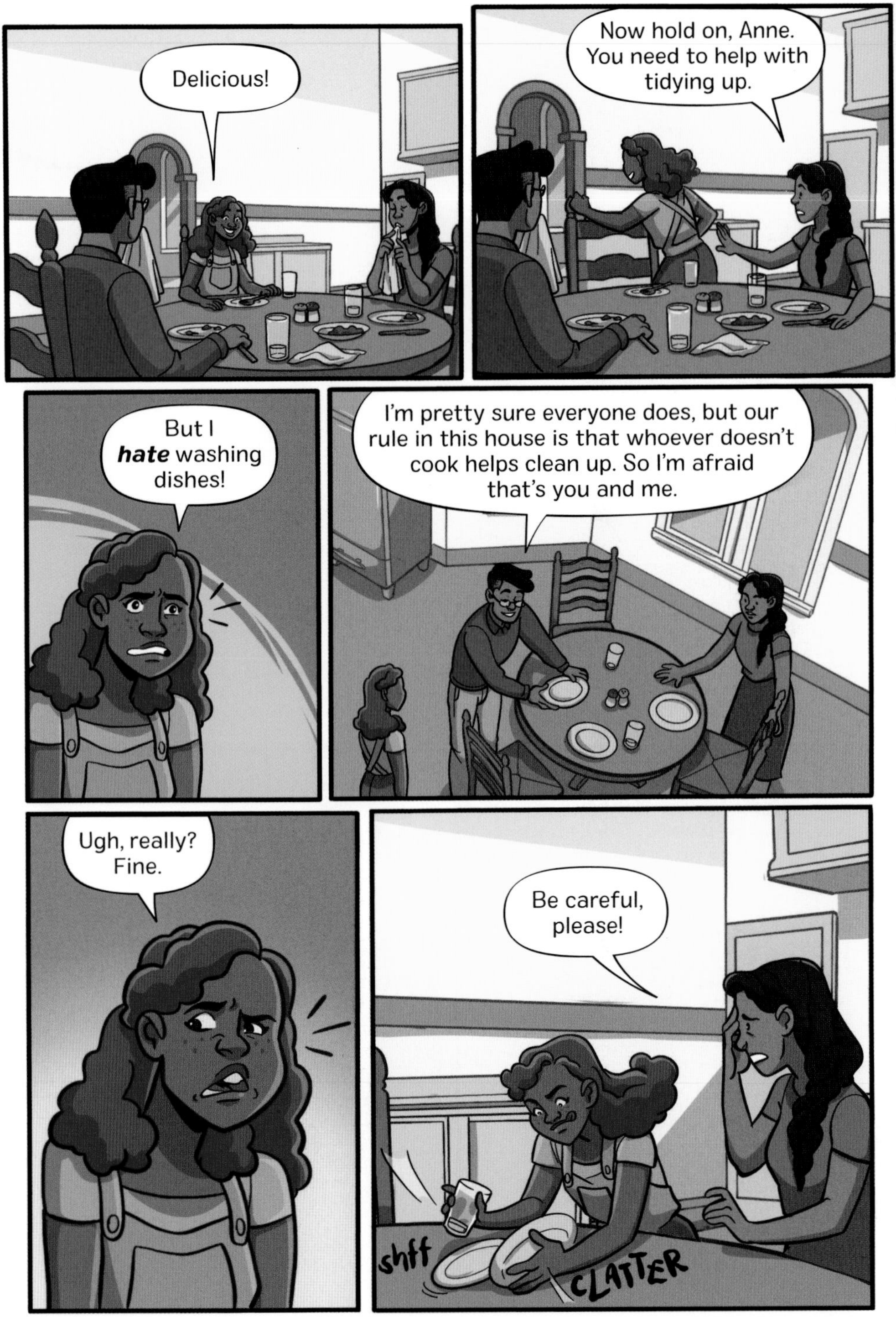

Delicious!
Now hold on, Anne. You need to help with tidying up.
But I *hate* washing dishes!
I'm pretty sure everyone does, but our rule in this house is that whoever doesn't cook helps clean up. So I'm afraid that's you and me.
Ugh, really? Fine.
Be careful, please!
shff
CLATTER

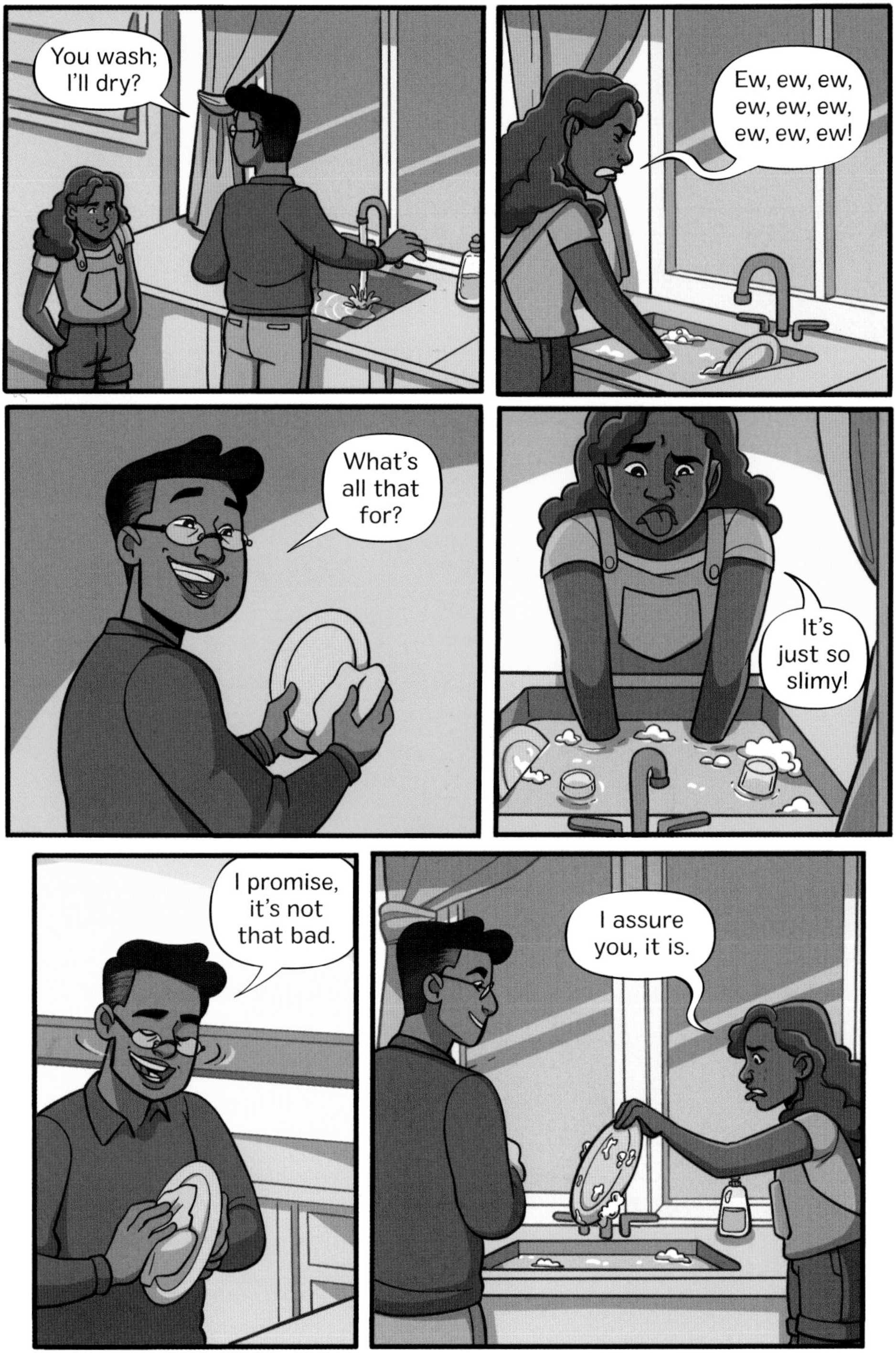
You wash; I'll dry?
Ew, ew, ew, ew, ew, ew, ew, ew, ew!
What's all that for?
It's just so slimy!
I promise, it's not that bad.
I assure you, it is.

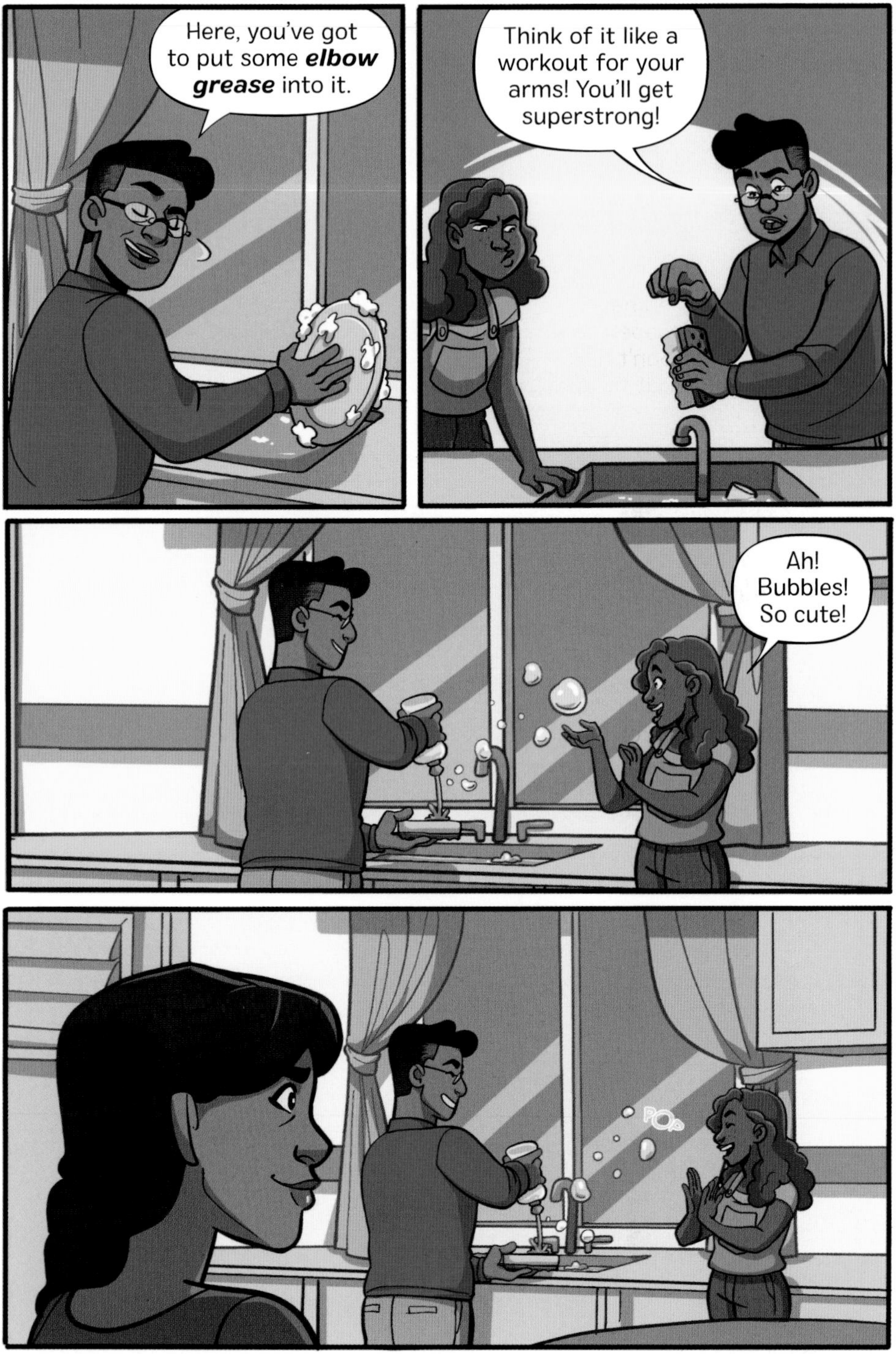

Here, you've got to put some ***elbow grease*** into it.
Think of it like a workout for your arms! You'll get superstrong!
Ah! Bubbles! So cute!
POP

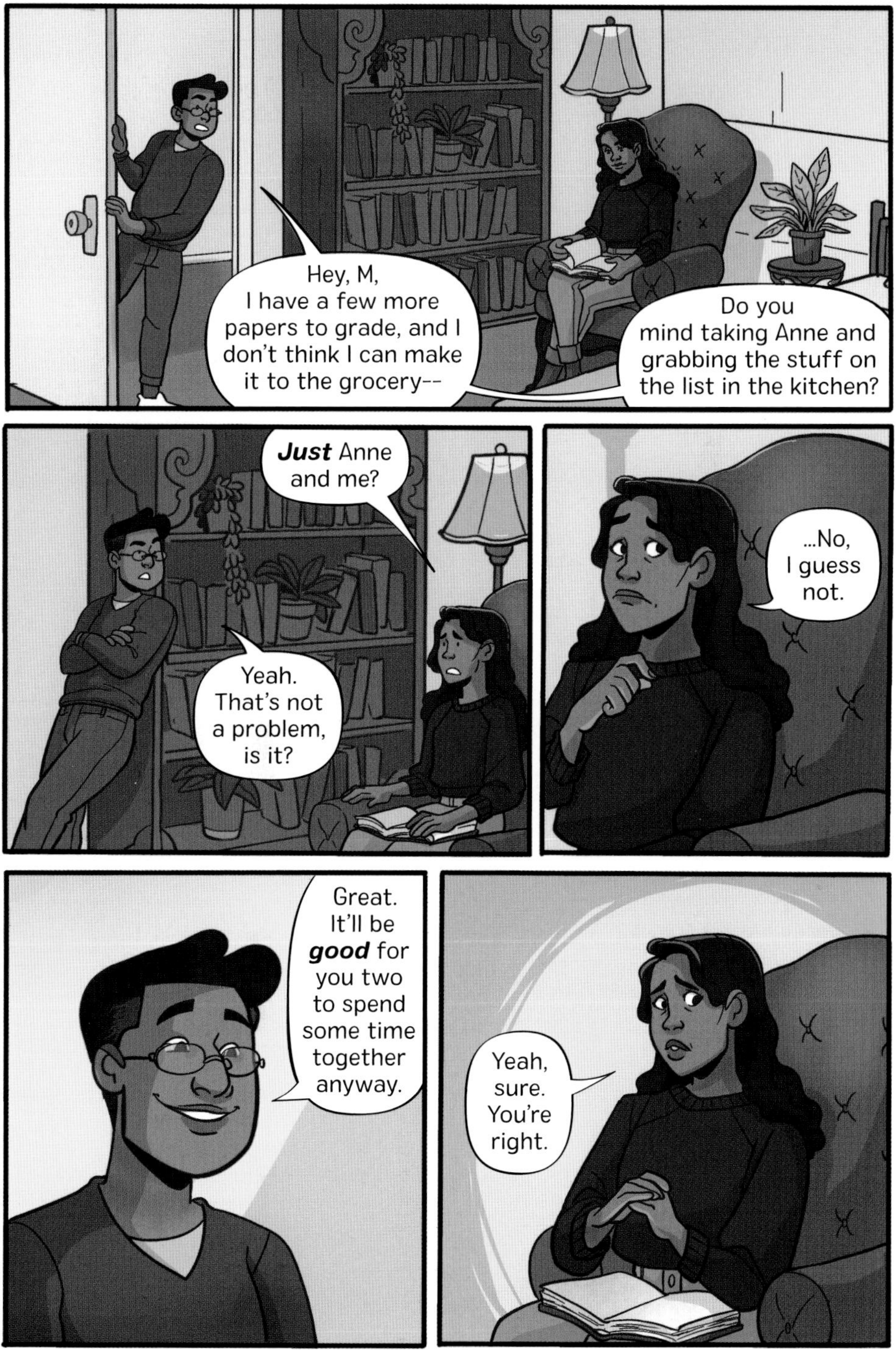
Hey, M, I have a few more papers to grade, and I don't think I can make it to the grocery--
Do you mind taking Anne and grabbing the stuff on the list in the kitchen?
Just Anne and me?
Yeah. That's not a problem, is it?
...No, I guess not.
Great. It'll be *good* for you two to spend some time together anyway.
Yeah, sure. You're right.

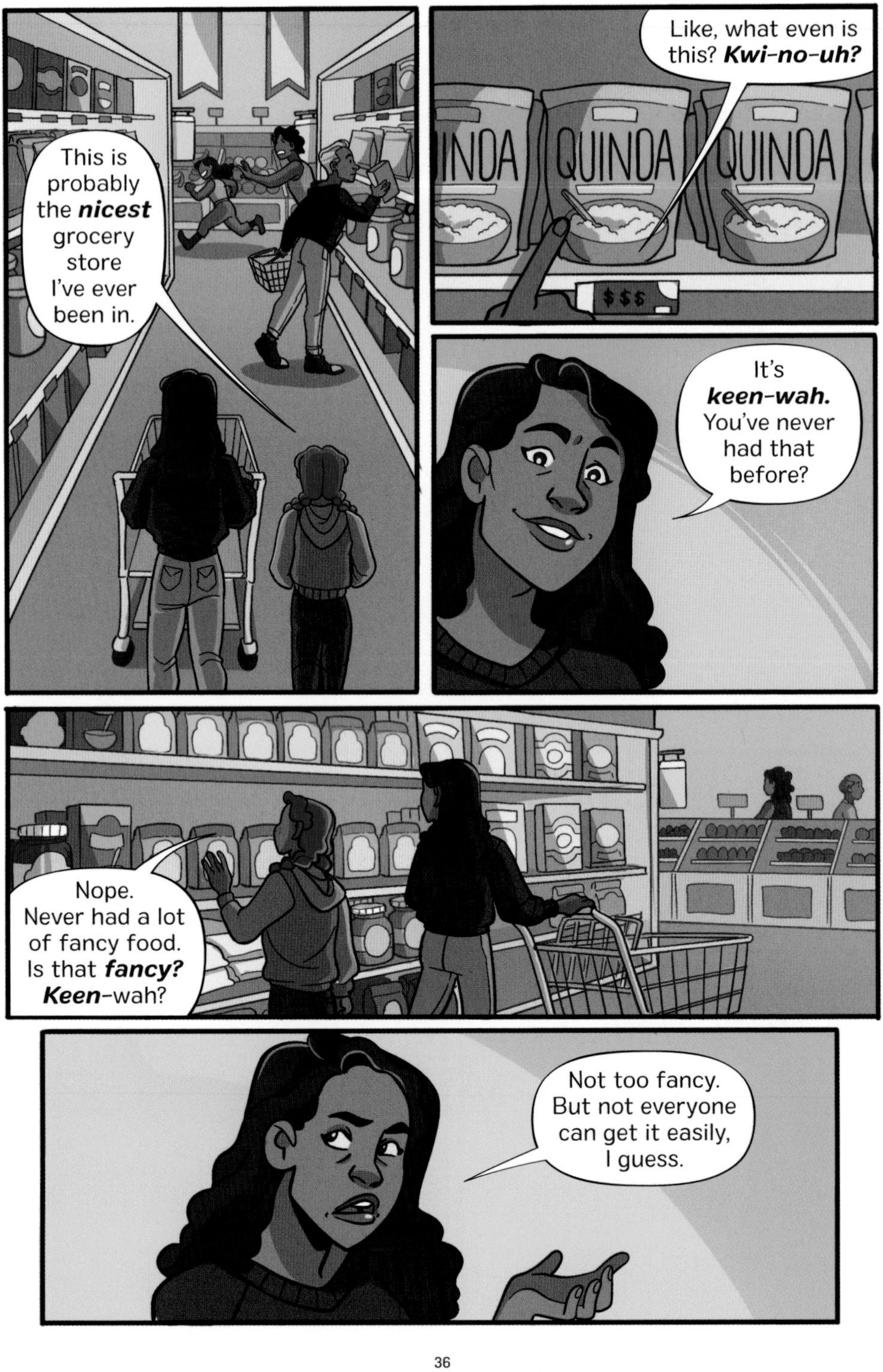
This is probably the *nicest* grocery store I've ever been in.
Like, what even is this? ***Kwi-no-uh?***
QUINOA
$$$
It's ***keen-wah.*** You've never had that before?
Nope. Never had a lot of fancy food. Is that ***fancy? Keen***-wah?
Not too fancy. But not everyone can get it easily, I guess.

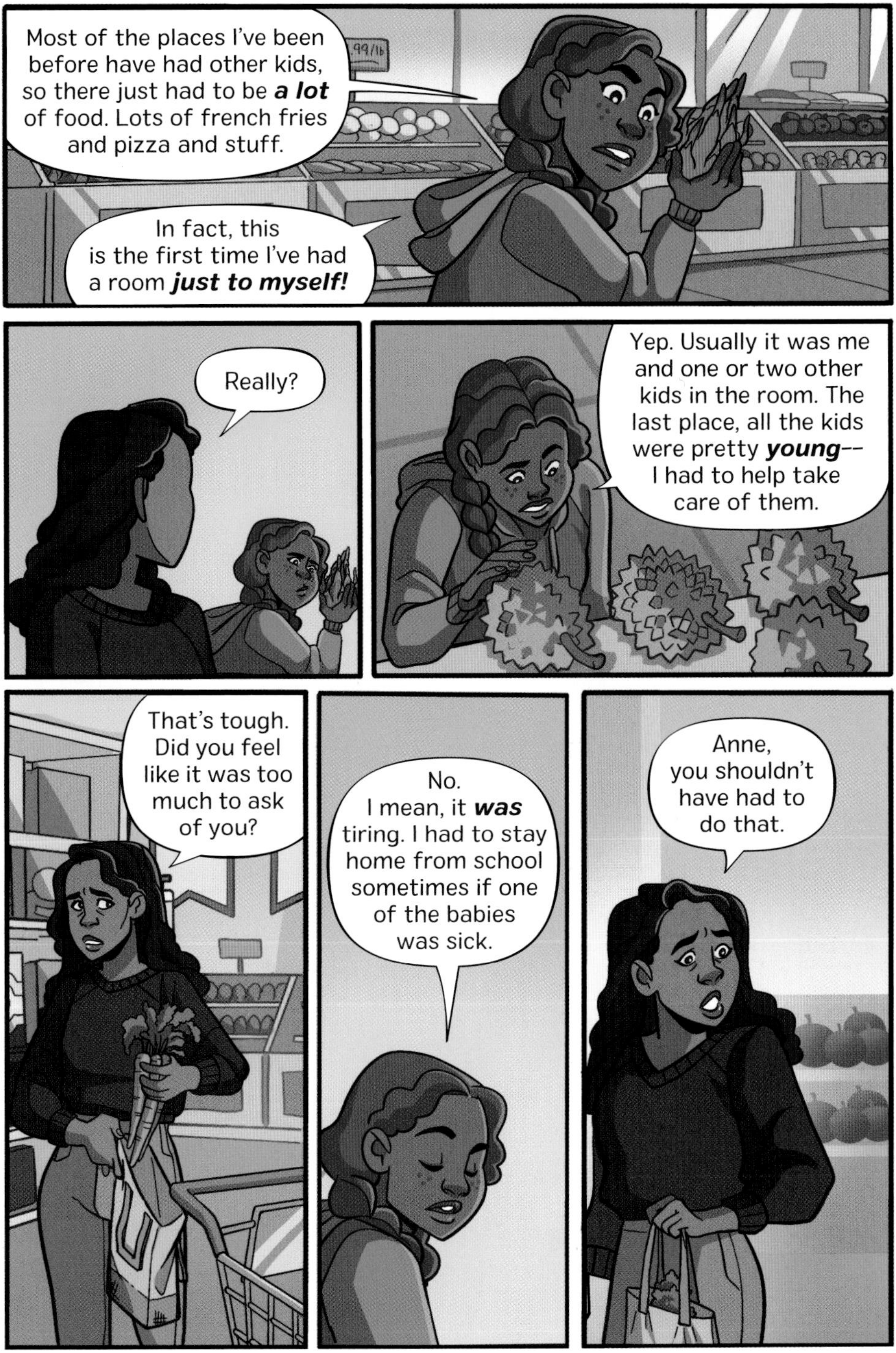
Most of the places I've been before have had other kids, so there just had to be ***a lot*** of food. Lots of french fries and pizza and stuff.
In fact, this is the first time I've had a room ***just to myself!***
Really?
Yep. Usually it was me and one or two other kids in the room. The last place, all the kids were pretty ***young***-- I had to help take care of them.
That's tough. Did you feel like it was too much to ask of you?
No. I mean, it ***was*** tiring. I had to stay home from school sometimes if one of the babies was sick.
Anne, you shouldn't have had to do that.

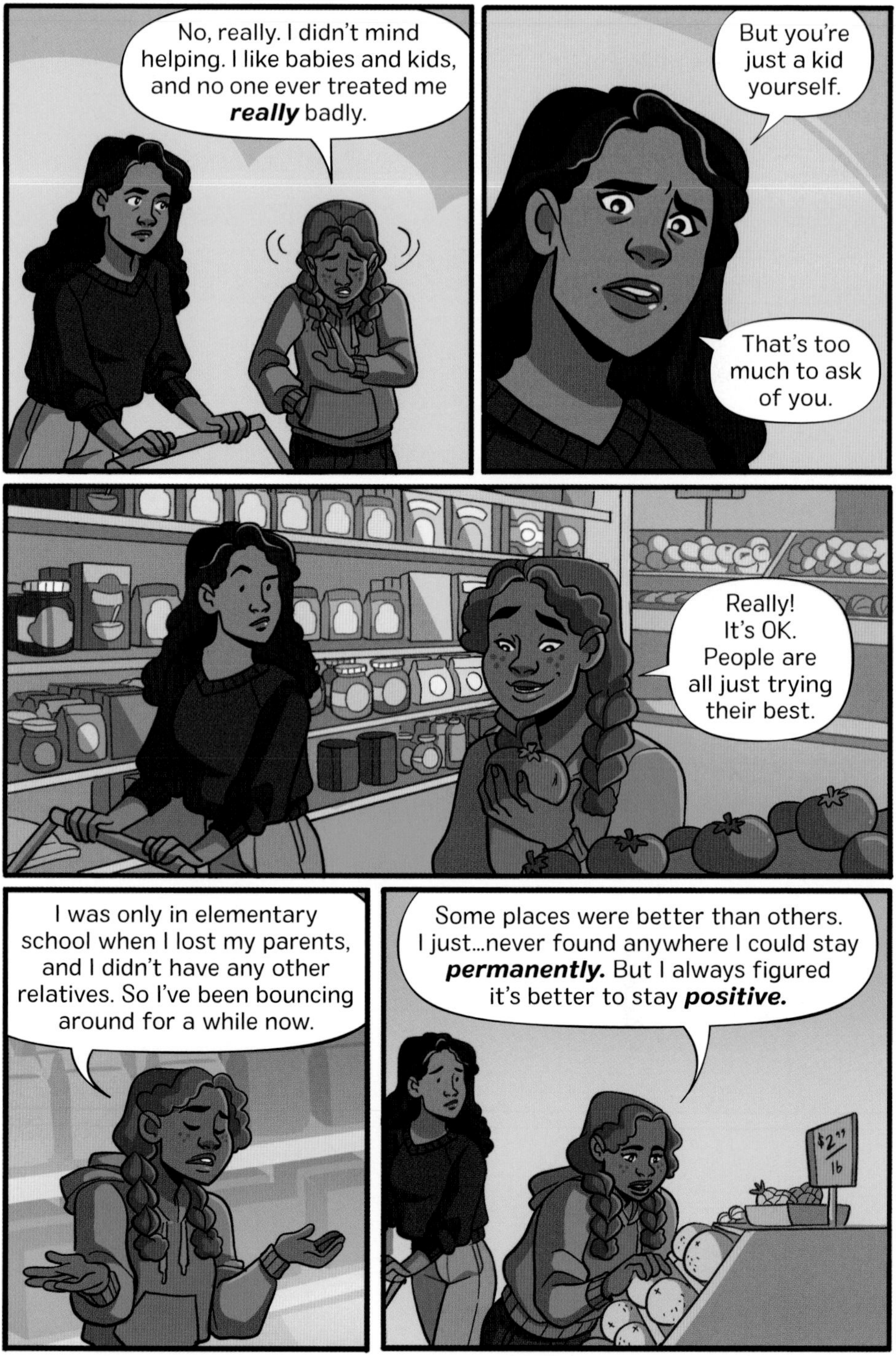
No, really. I didn't mind helping. I like babies and kids, and no one ever treated me ***really*** badly.
But you're just a kid yourself.
That's too much to ask of you.
Really! It's OK. People are all just trying their best.
I was only in elementary school when I lost my parents, and I didn't have any other relatives. So I've been bouncing around for a while now.
Some places were better than others. I just...never found anywhere I could stay ***permanently.*** But I always figured it's better to stay ***positive.***
$2.99 /lb

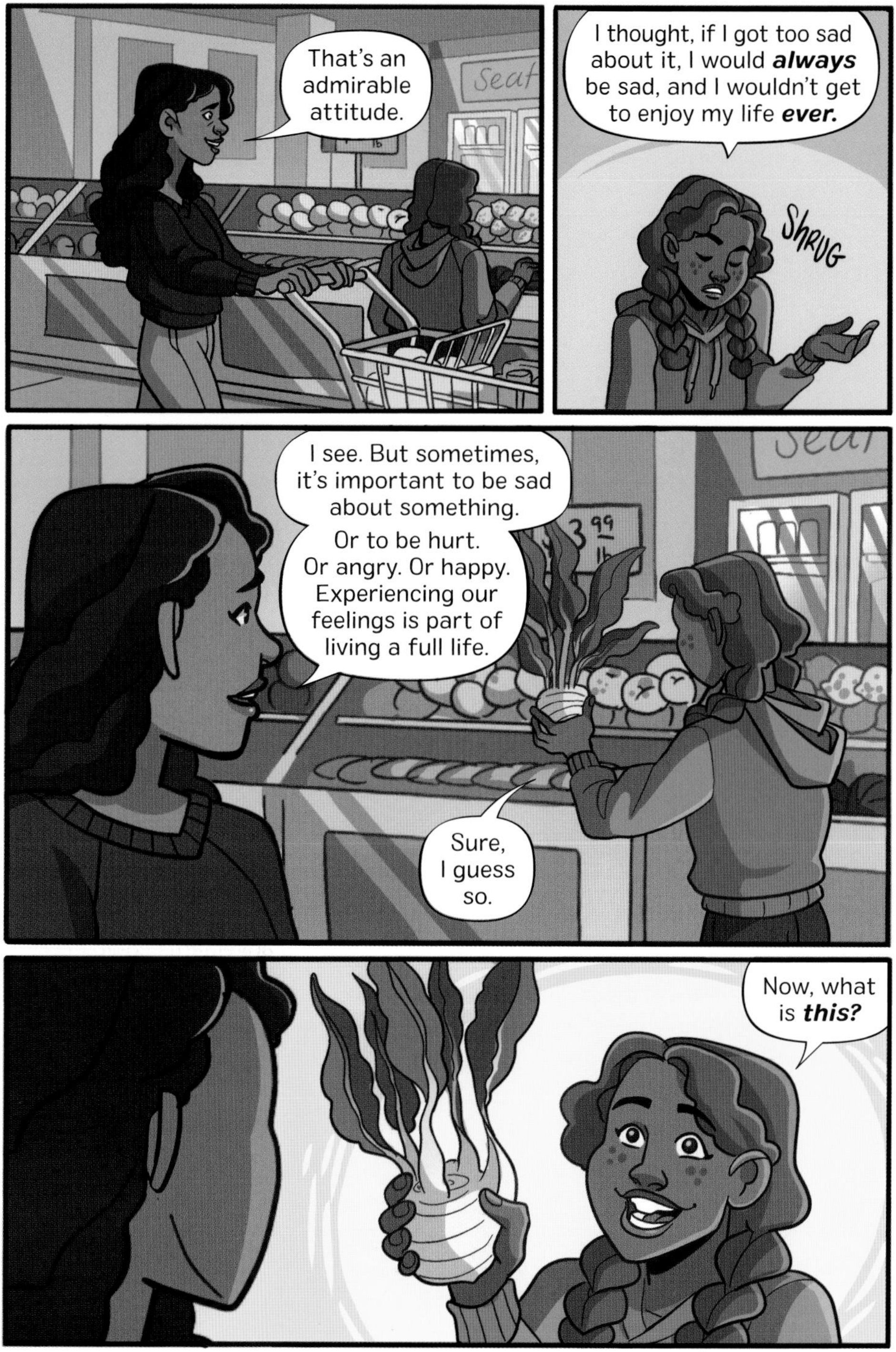
That's an admirable attitude.
I thought, if I got too sad about it, I would **always** be sad, and I wouldn't get to enjoy my life **ever.**
SHRUG
I see. But sometimes, it's important to be sad about something.
Or to be hurt. Or angry. Or happy. Experiencing our feelings is part of living a full life.
Sure, I guess so.
Now, what is **this?**

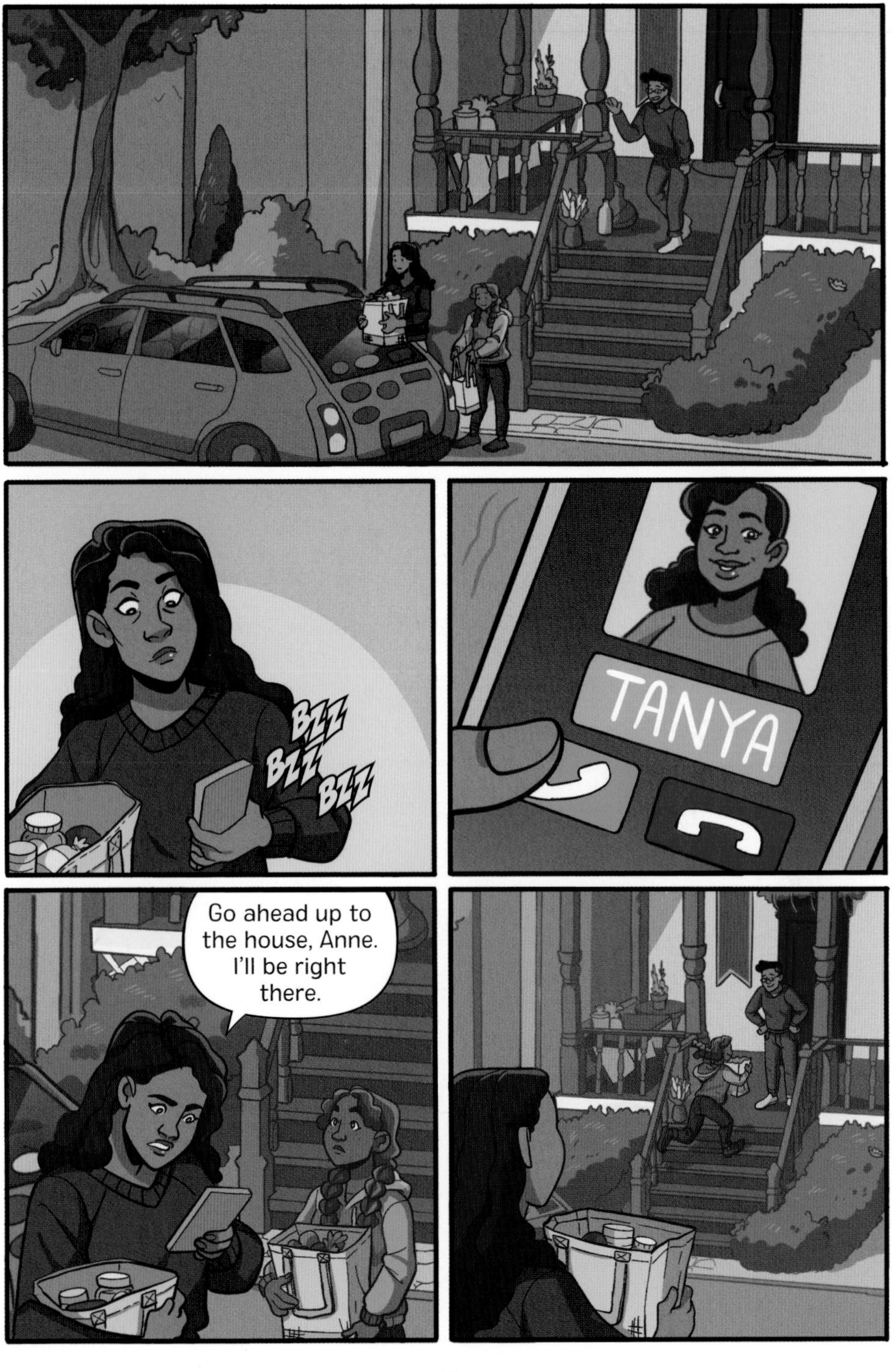
BZZ
BZZ
BZZ
TANYA
Go ahead up to the house, Anne. I'll be right there.

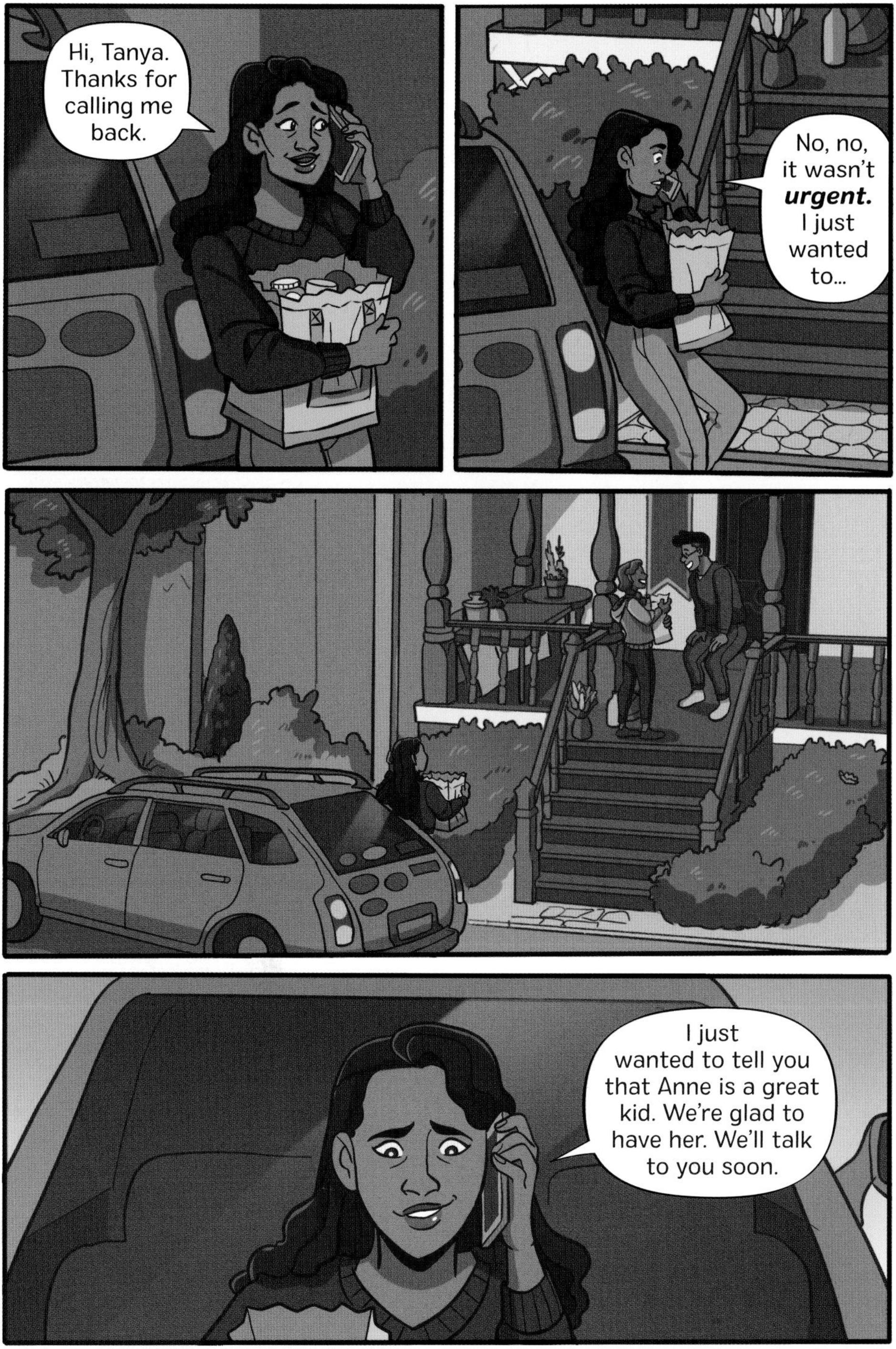
Hi, Tanya. Thanks for calling me back.
No, no, it wasn't ***urgent.*** I just wanted to...
I just wanted to tell you that Anne is a great kid. We're glad to have her. We'll talk to you soon.

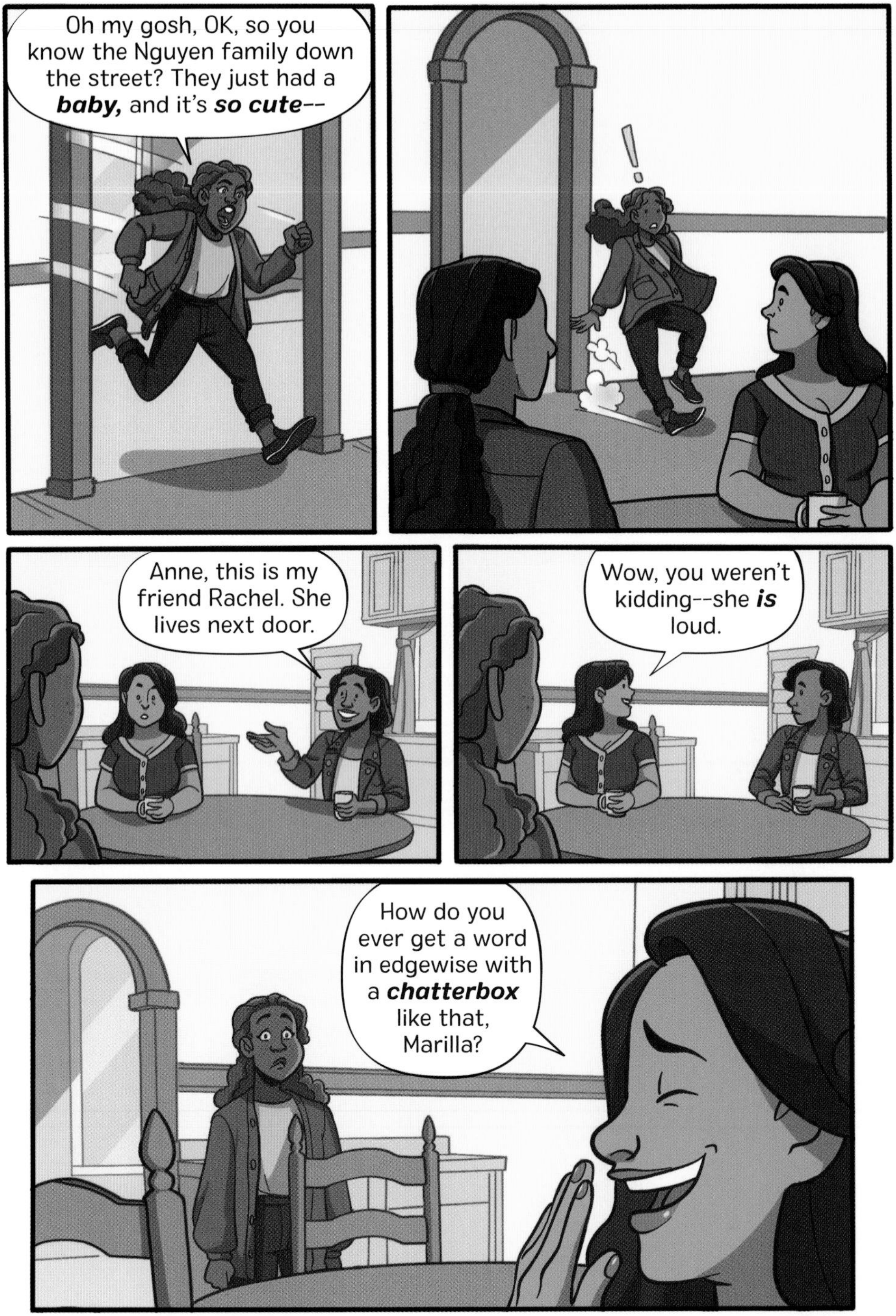
Oh my gosh, OK, so you know the Nguyen family down the street? They just had a ***baby,*** and it's ***so cute***--
!
Anne, this is my friend Rachel. She lives next door.
Wow, you weren't kidding--she ***is*** loud.
How do you ever get a word in edgewise with a ***chatterbox*** like that, Marilla?

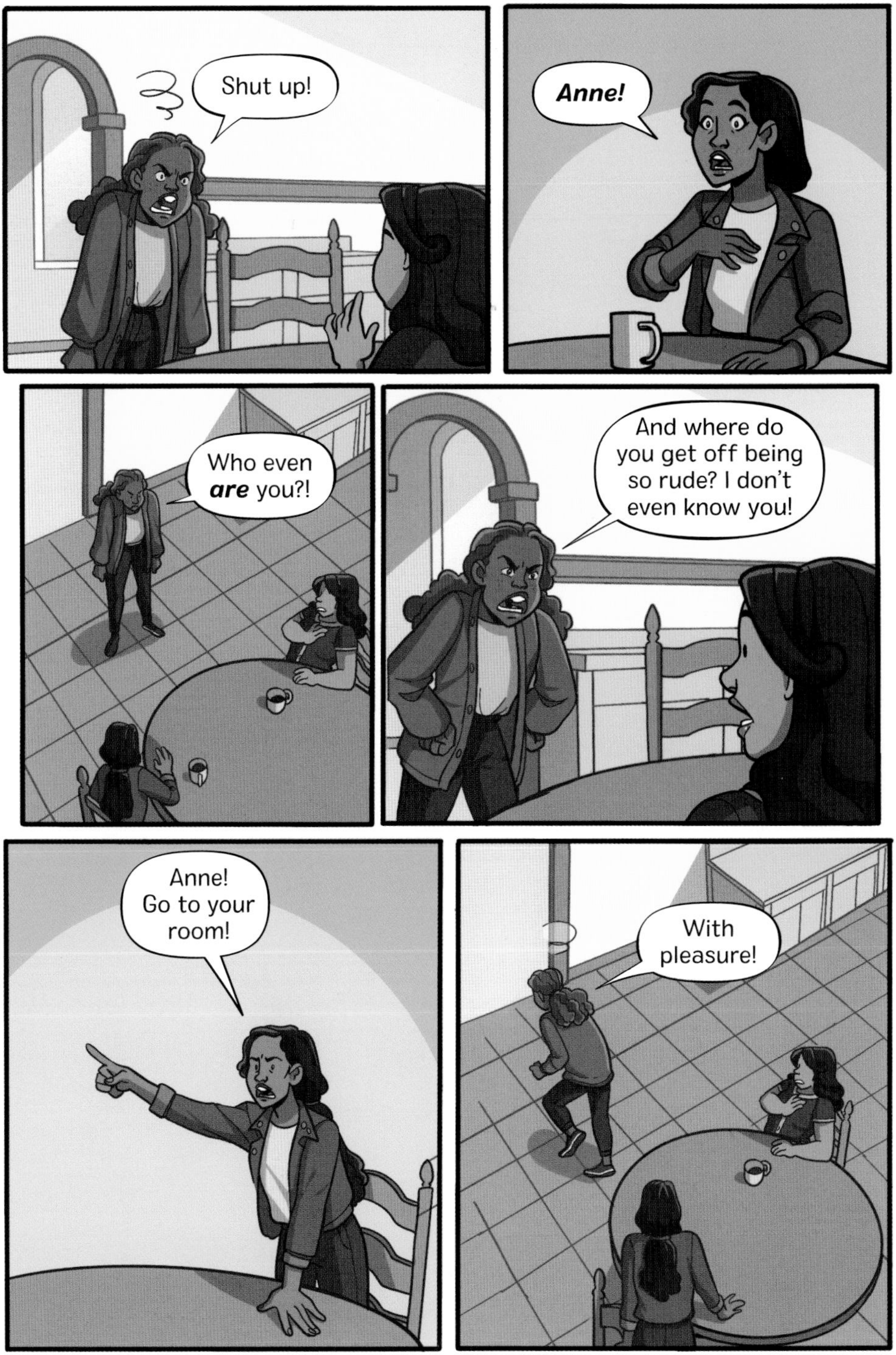
Shut up!
Anne!
Who even ***are*** you?!
And where do you get off being so rude? I don't even know you!
Anne! Go to your room!
With pleasure!

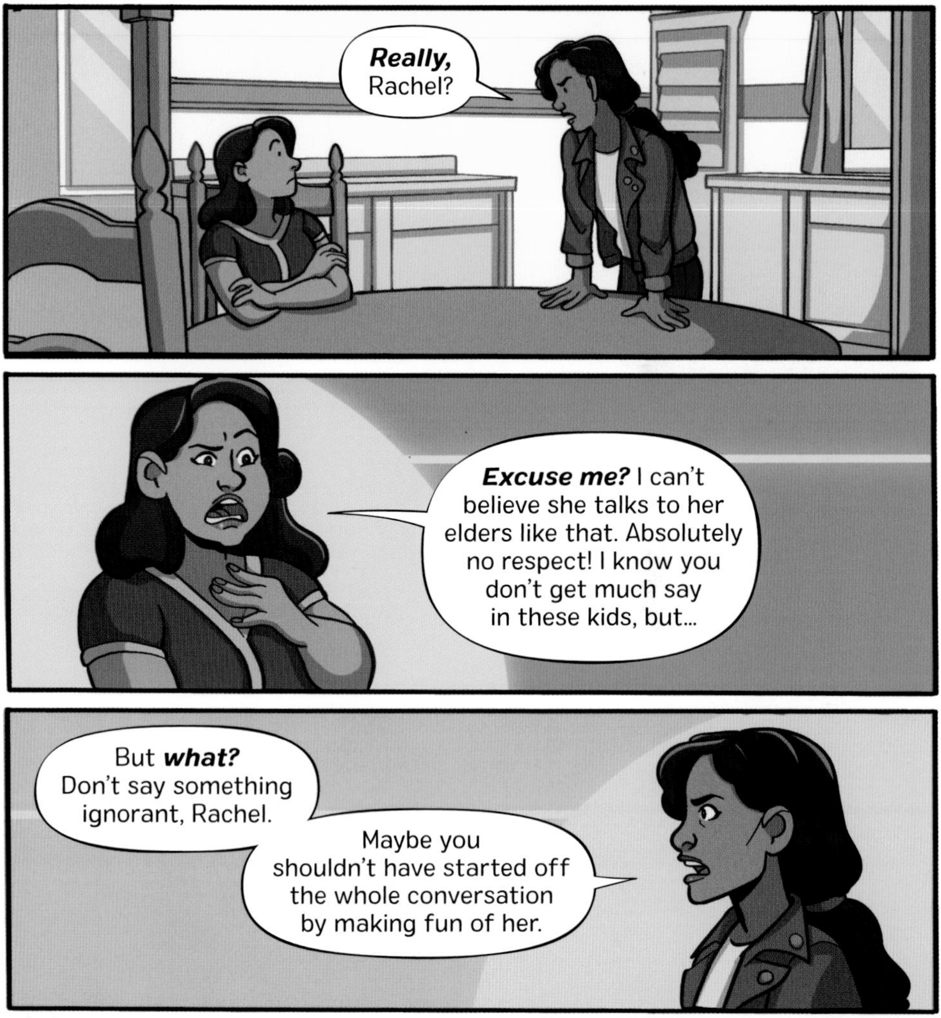
Really, Rachel?
Excuse me? I can't believe she talks to her elders like that. Absolutely no respect! I know you don't get much say in these kids, but...
But **what?** Don't say something ignorant, Rachel.
Maybe you shouldn't have started off the whole conversation by making fun of her.
Well, don't think I was out of line.
Do you think it's going to be any **easier** for her at school?

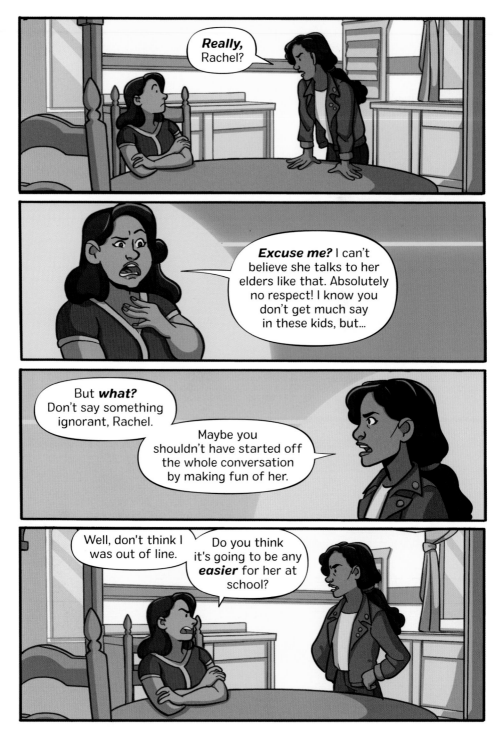

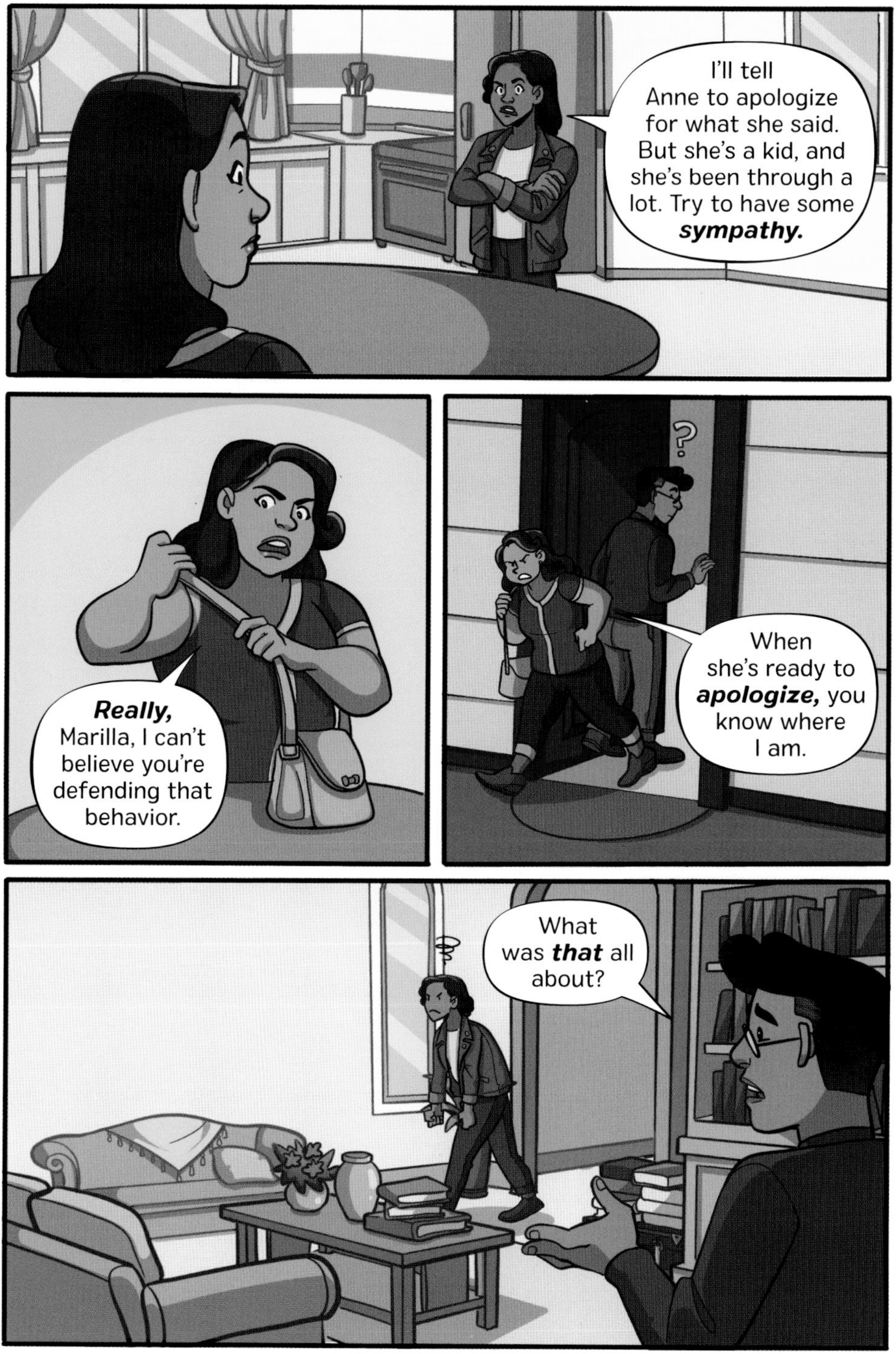
I'll tell Anne to apologize for what she said. But she's a kid, and she's been through a lot. Try to have some ***sympathy.***
Really, Marilla, I can't believe you're defending that behavior.
?
When she's ready to ***apologize,*** you know where I am.
What was ***that*** all about?

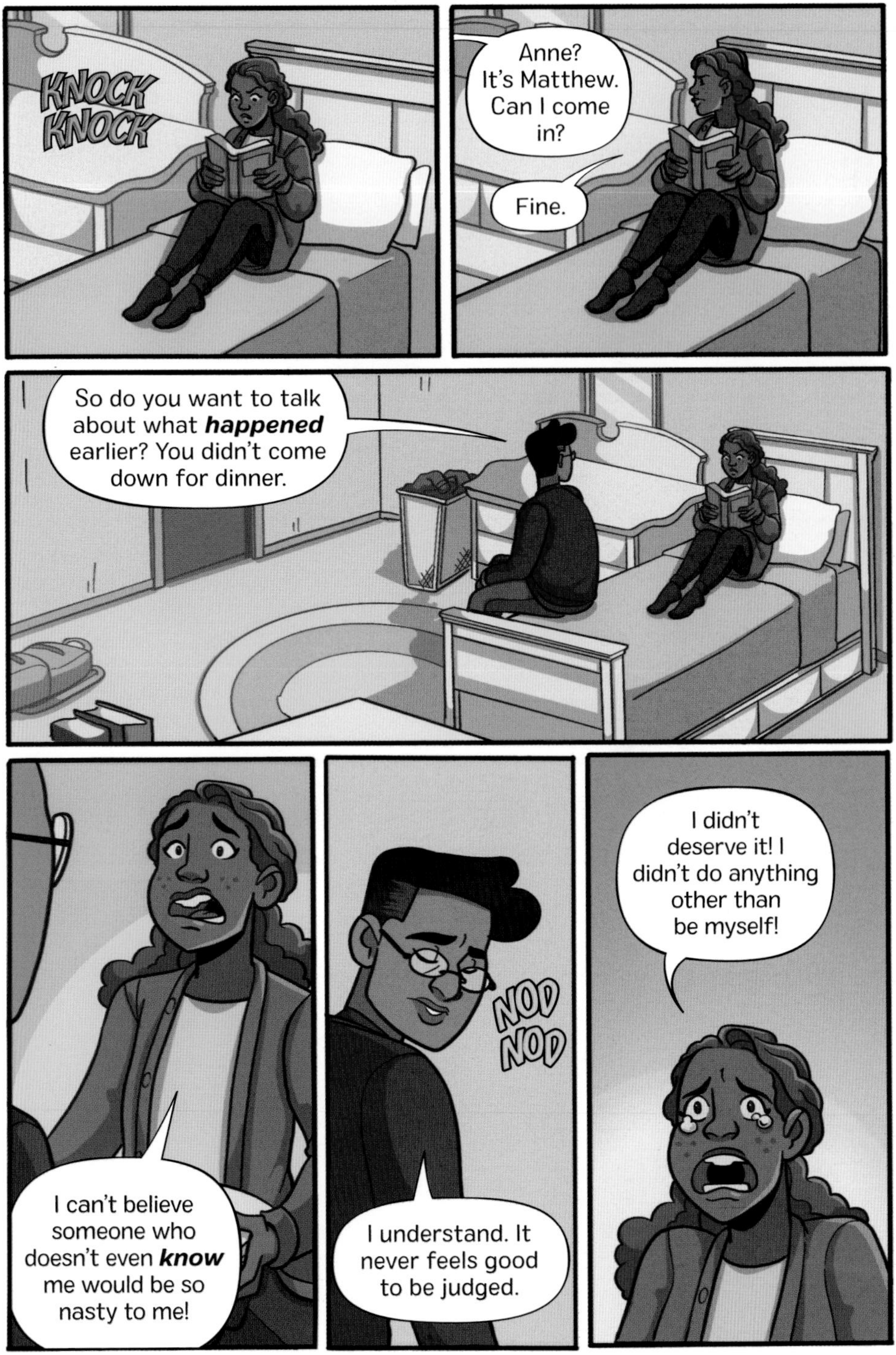
KNOCK KNOCK
Anne? It's Matthew. Can I come in?
Fine.
So do you want to talk about what ***happened*** earlier? You didn't come down for dinner.
I can't believe someone who doesn't even ***know*** me would be so nasty to me!
NOD NOD
I understand. It never feels good to be judged.
I didn't deserve it! I didn't do anything other than be myself!

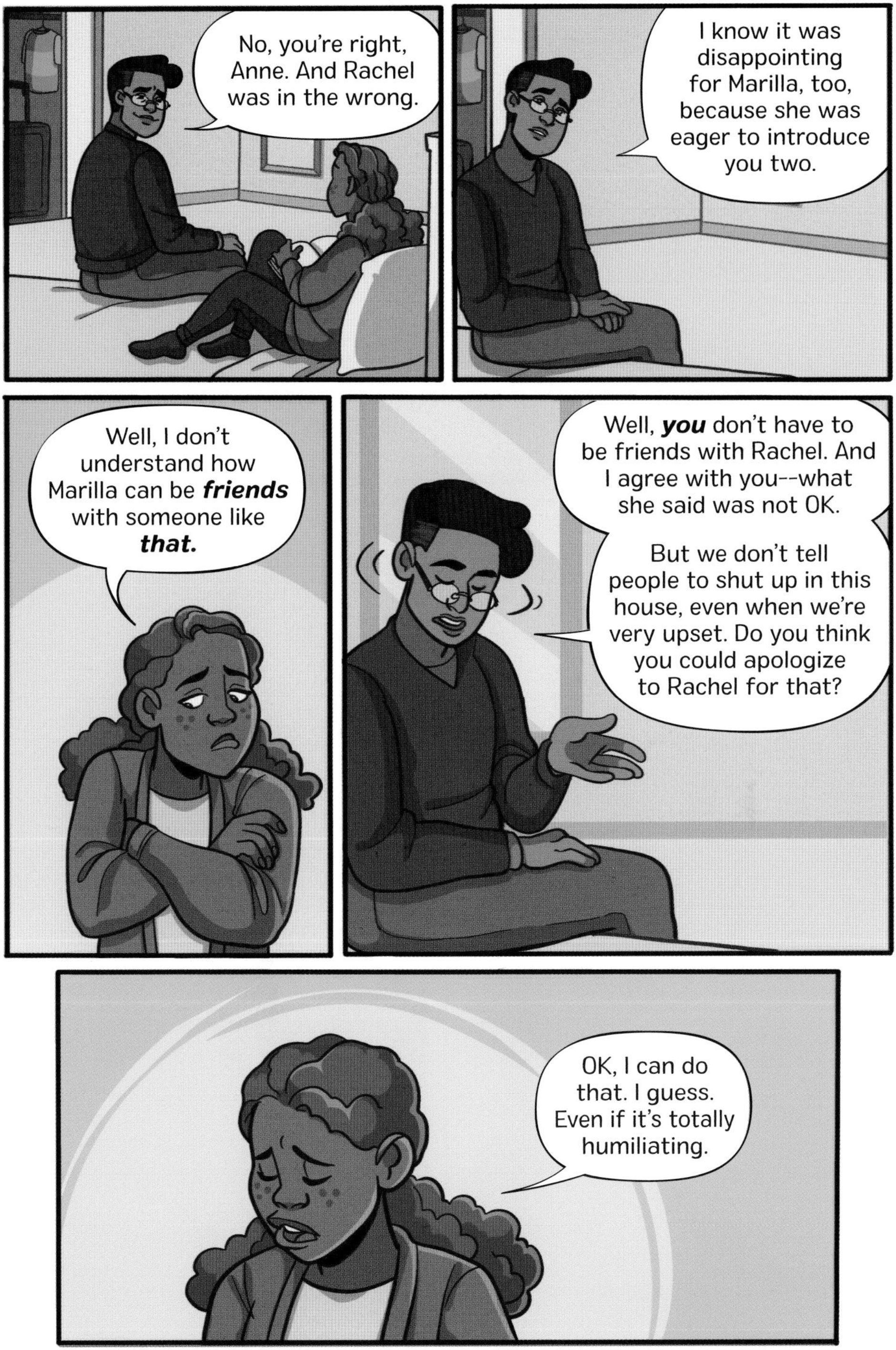
No, you're right, Anne. And Rachel was in the wrong.
I know it was disappointing for Marilla, too, because she was eager to introduce you two.
Well, I don't understand how Marilla can be ***friends*** with someone like ***that.***
Well, ***you*** don't have to be friends with Rachel. And I agree with you--what she said was not OK.
But we don't tell people to shut up in this house, even when we're very upset. Do you think you could apologize to Rachel for that?
OK, I can do that. I guess. Even if it's totally humiliating.

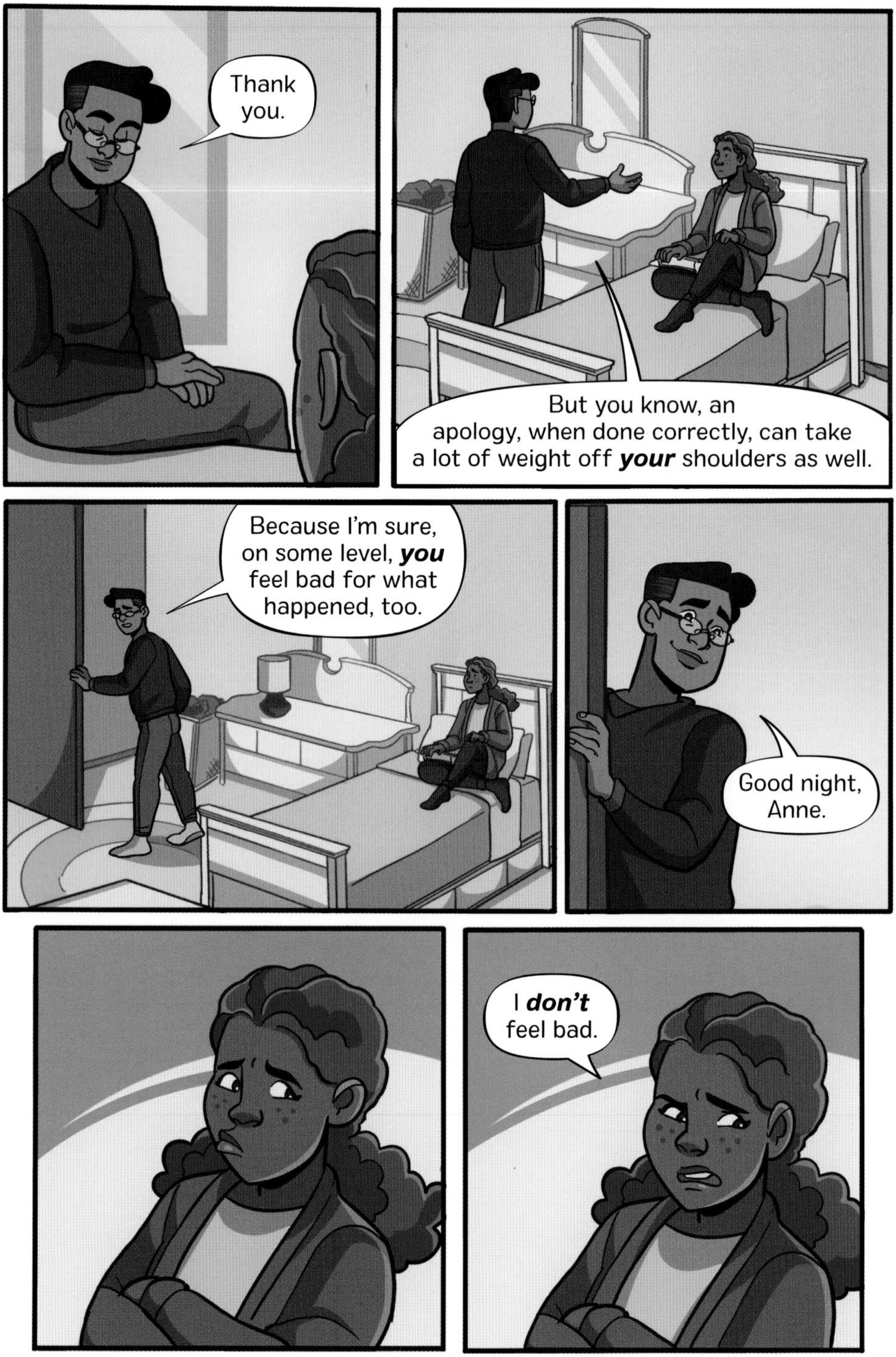
Thank you.
But you know, an apology, when done correctly, can take a lot of weight off ***your*** shoulders as well.
Because I'm sure, on some level, ***you*** feel bad for what happened, too.
Good night, Anne.
I ***don't*** feel bad.

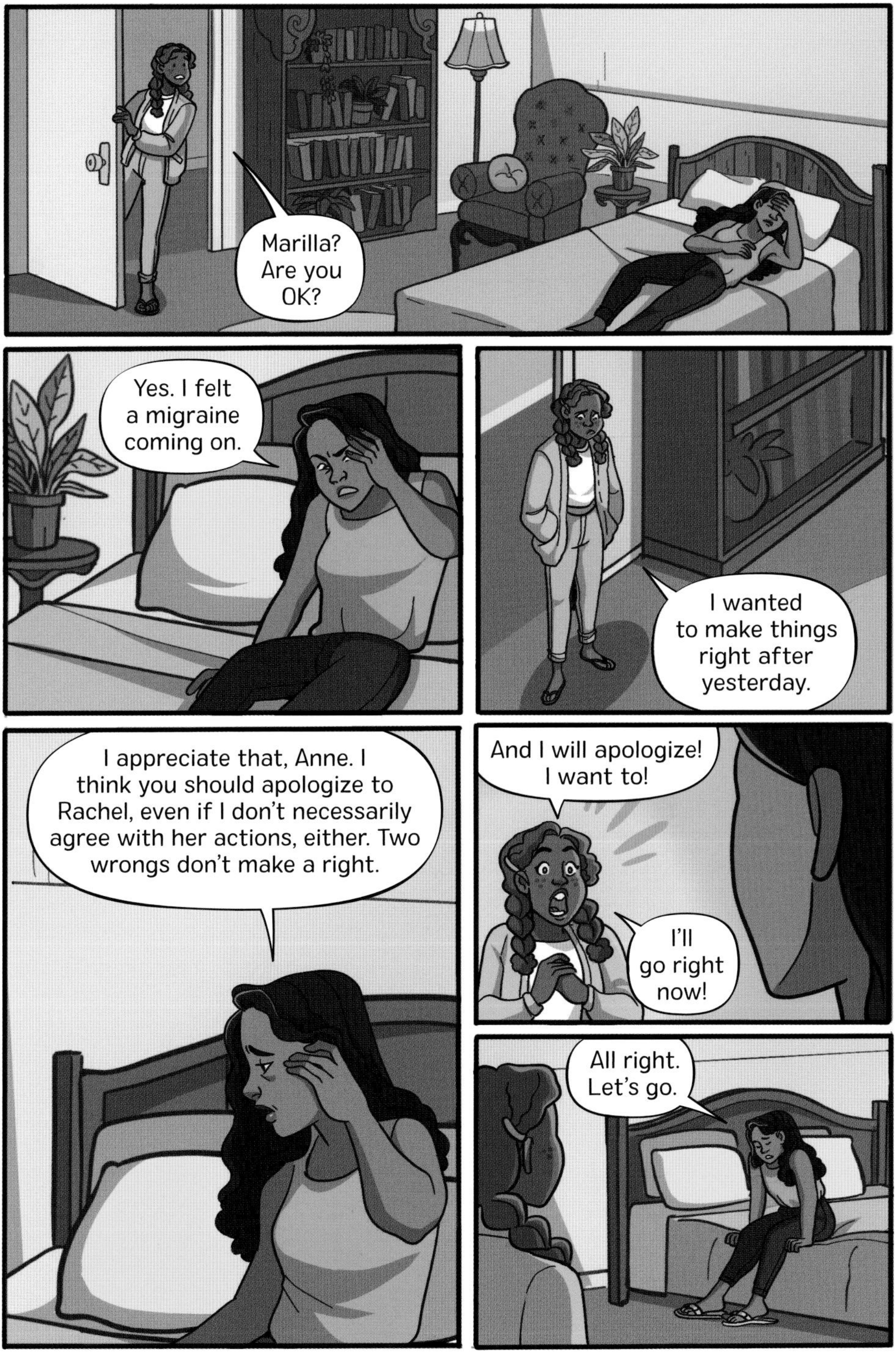
Marilla? Are you OK?
Yes. I felt a migraine coming on.
I wanted to make things right after yesterday.
I appreciate that, Anne. I think you should apologize to Rachel, even if I don't necessarily agree with her actions, either. Two wrongs don't make a right.
And I will apologize! I want to!
I'll go right now!
All right. Let's go.

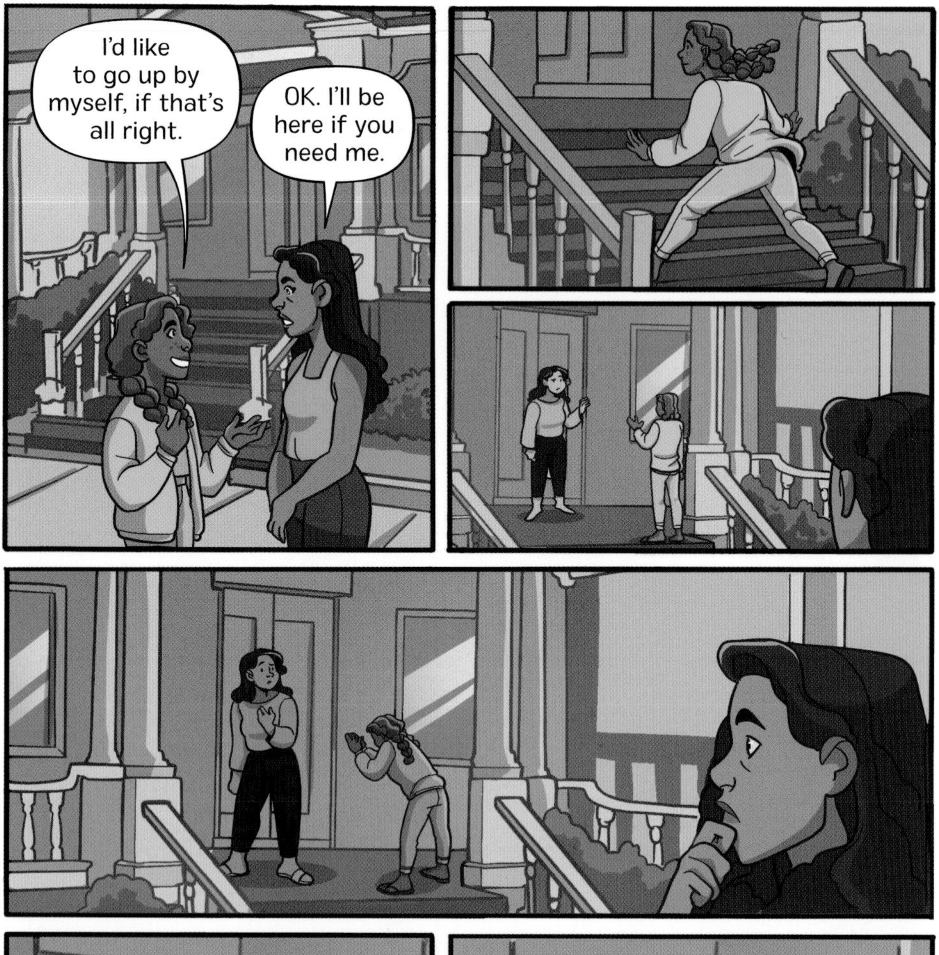
I'd like to go up by myself, if that's all right.
OK. I'll be here if you need me.
NOD NOD

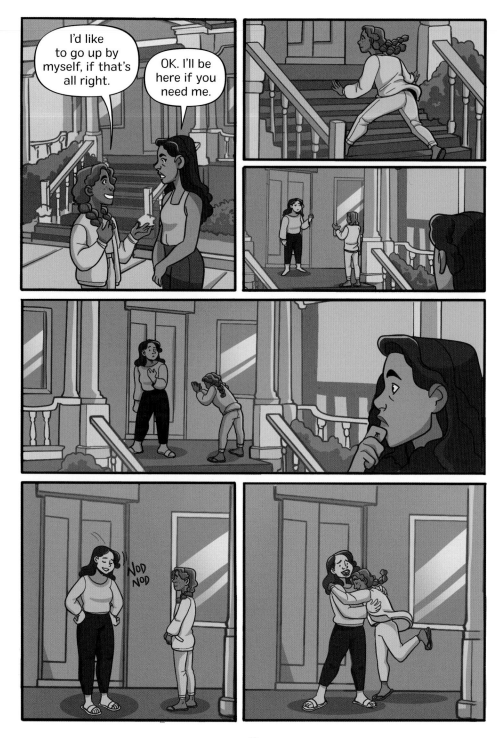

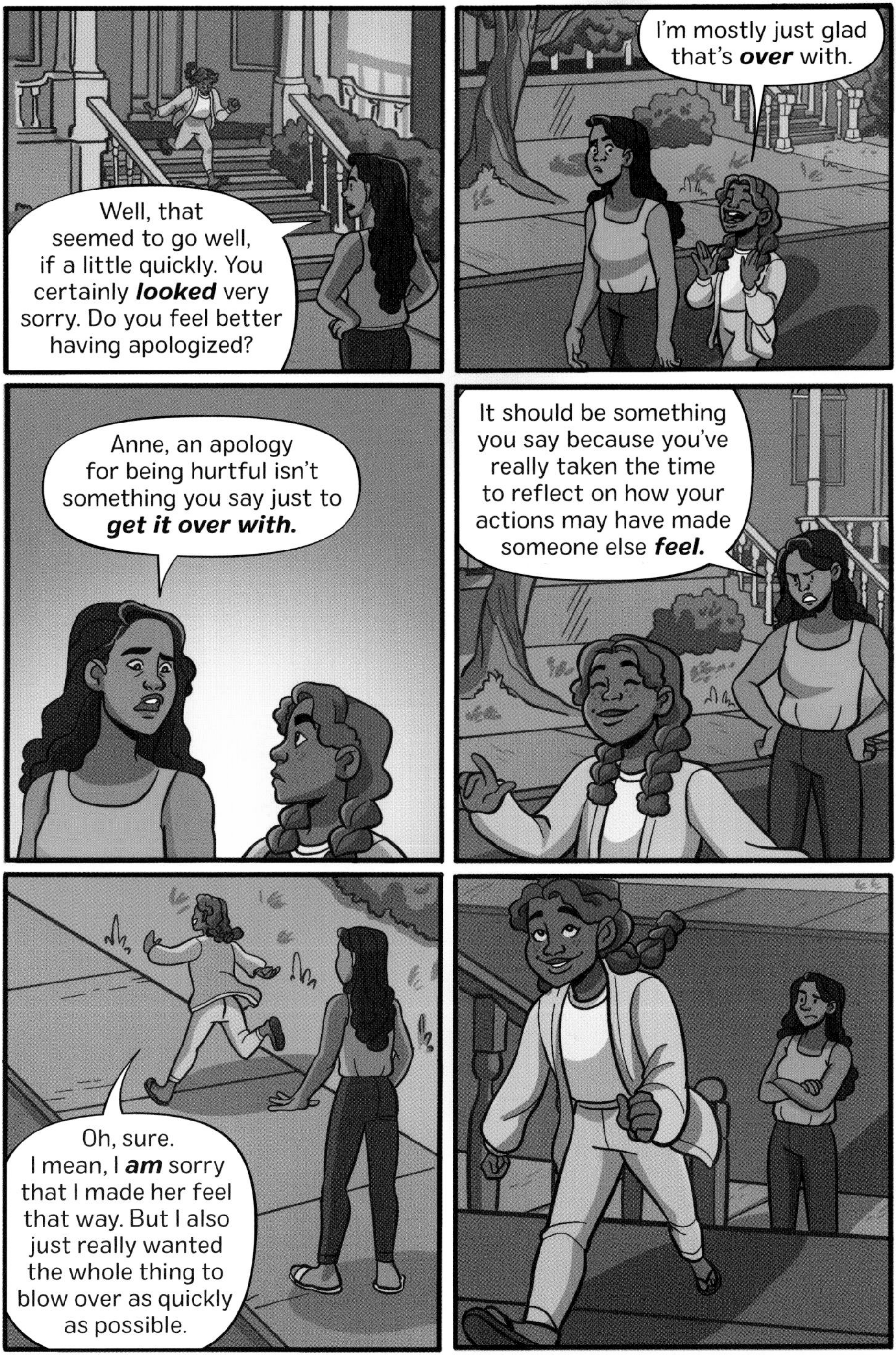
Well, that seemed to go well, if a little quickly. You certainly **looked** very sorry. Do you feel better having apologized?
I'm mostly just glad that's **over** with.
Anne, an apology for being hurtful isn't something you say just to **get it over with.**
It should be something you say because you've really taken the time to reflect on how your actions may have made someone else **feel.**
Oh, sure. I mean, I **am** sorry that I made her feel that way. But I also just really wanted the whole thing to blow over as quickly as possible.

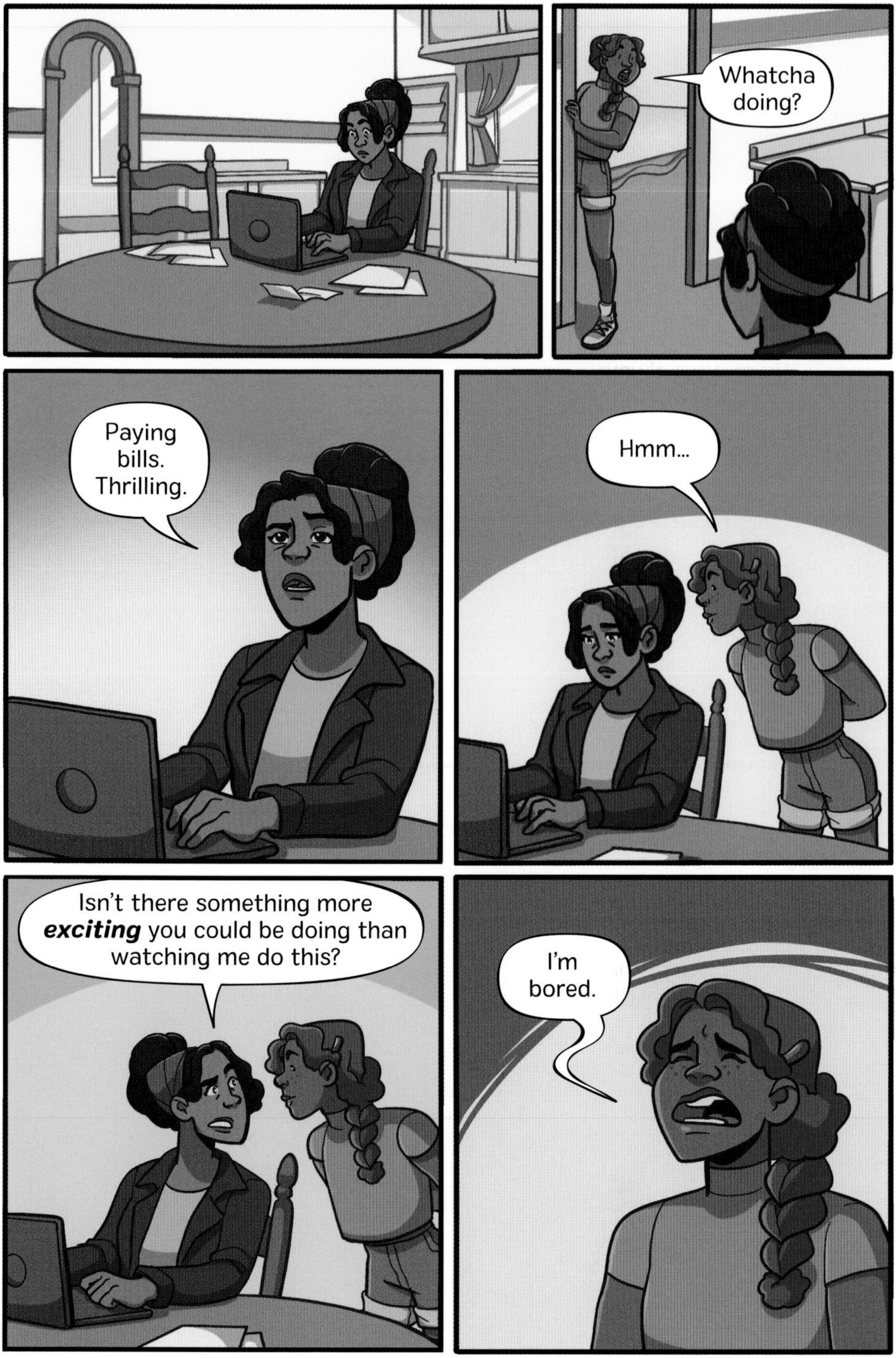
Whatcha doing?
Paying bills. Thrilling.
Hmm...
Isn't there something more ***exciting*** you could be doing than watching me do this?
I'm bored.

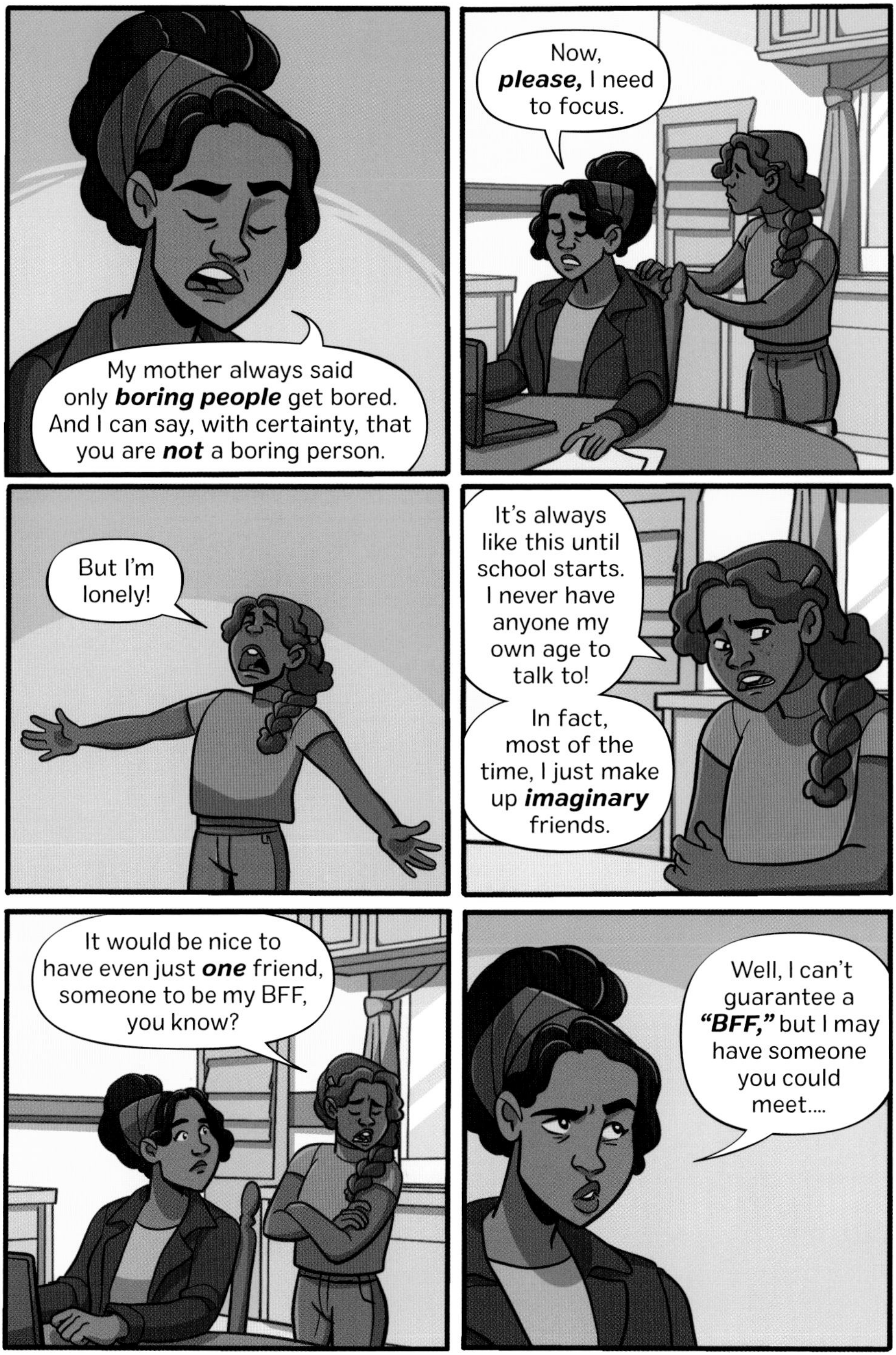
My mother always said only ***boring people*** get bored. And I can say, with certainty, that you are ***not*** a boring person.
Now, ***please,*** I need to focus.
But I'm lonely!
It's always like this until school starts. I never have anyone my own age to talk to!
In fact, most of the time, I just make up ***imaginary*** friends.
It would be nice to have even just ***one*** friend, someone to be my BFF, you know?
Well, I can't guarantee a ***"BFF,"*** but I may have someone you could meet....

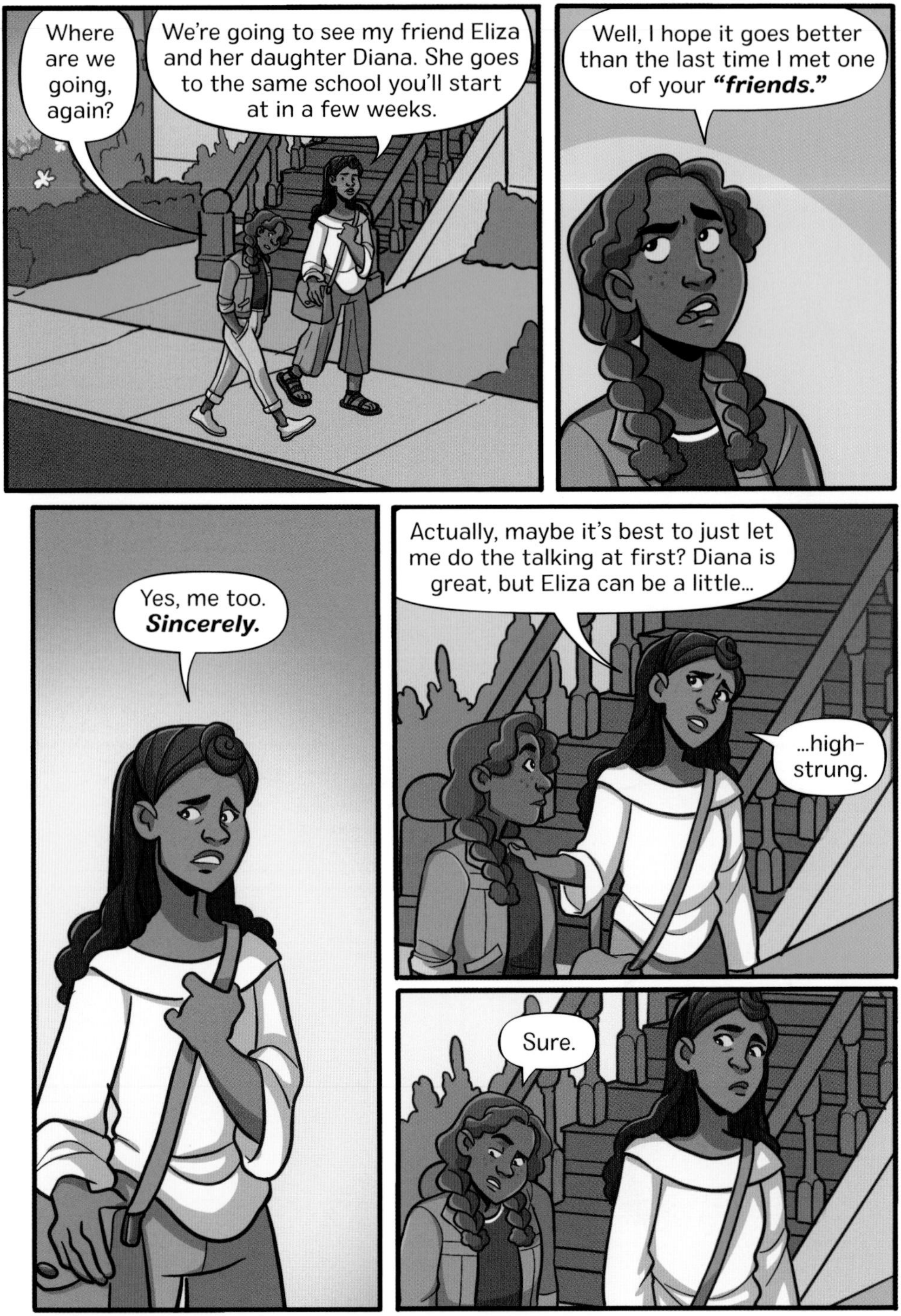
Where are we going, again?
We're going to see my friend Eliza and her daughter Diana. She goes to the same school you'll start at in a few weeks.
Well, I hope it goes better than the last time I met one of your ***"friends."***
Yes, me too. ***Sincerely.***
Actually, maybe it's best to just let me do the talking at first? Diana is great, but Eliza can be a little...
...high-strung.
Sure.

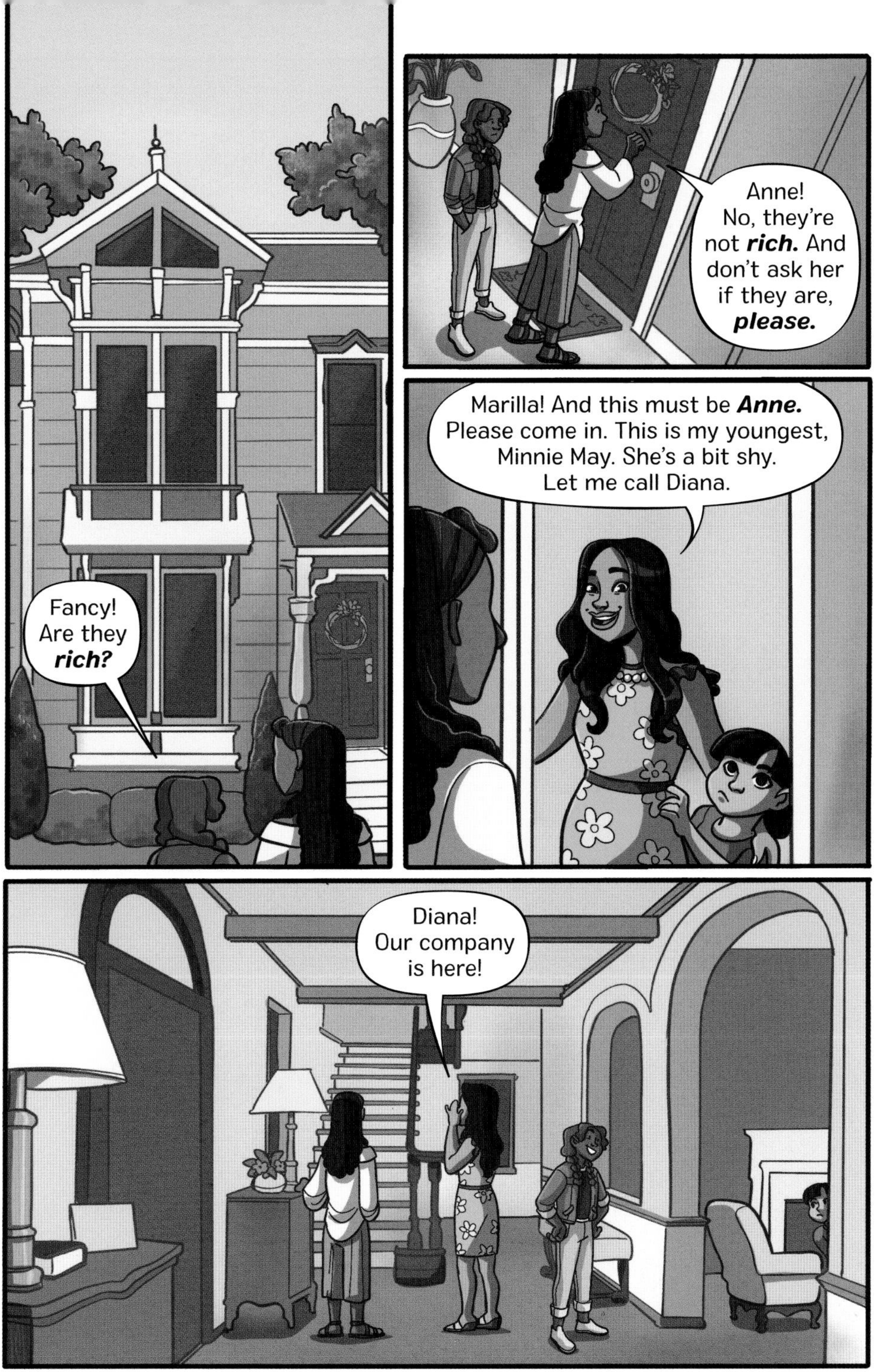
Fancy!
Are they
rich?
Anne!
No, they're
not ***rich.*** And
don't ask her
if they are,
please.
Marilla! And this must be ***Anne.***
Please come in. This is my youngest,
Minnie May. She's a bit shy.
Let me call Diana.
Diana!
Our company
is here!

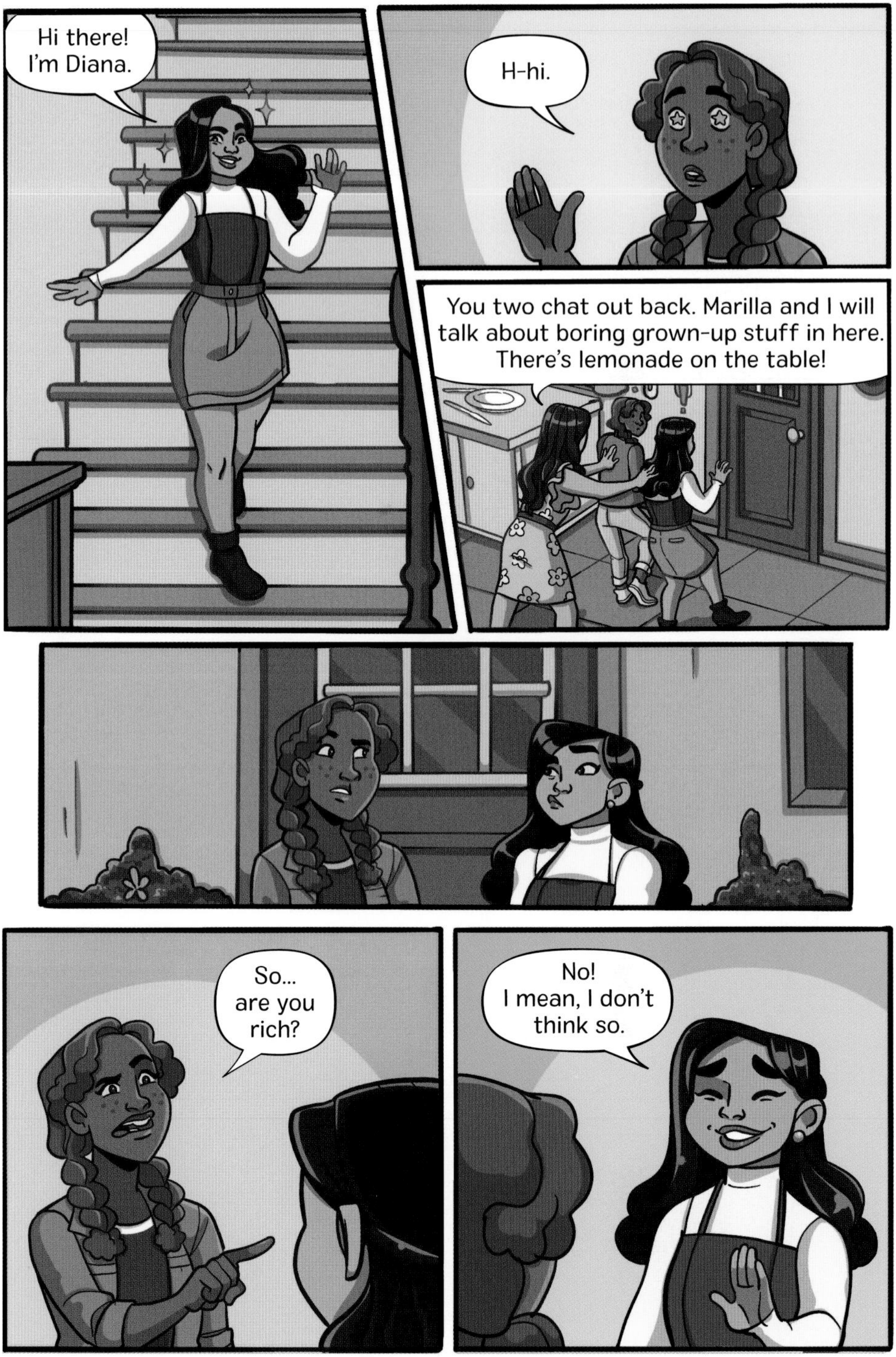

Hi there! I'm Diana.
H-hi.
You two chat out back. Marilla and I will talk about boring grown-up stuff in here. There's lemonade on the table!
So... are you rich?
No! I mean, I don't think so.

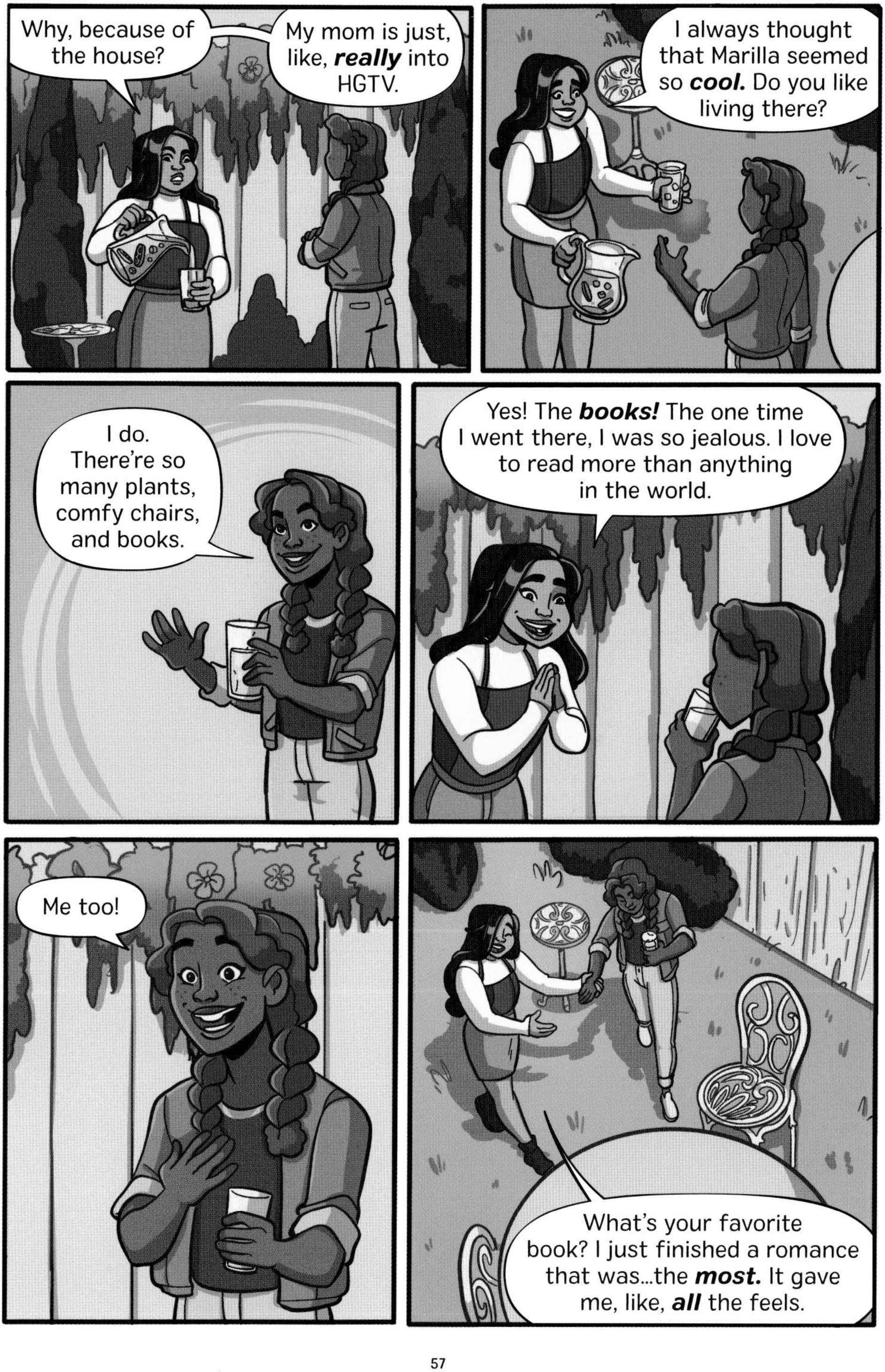
Why, because of the house?
My mom is just, like, ***really*** into HGTV.
I always thought that Marilla seemed so ***cool.*** Do you like living there?
I do. There're so many plants, comfy chairs, and books.
Yes! The ***books!*** The one time I went there, I was so jealous. I love to read more than anything in the world.
Me too!
What's your favorite book? I just finished a romance that was...the ***most.*** It gave me, like, ***all*** the feels.

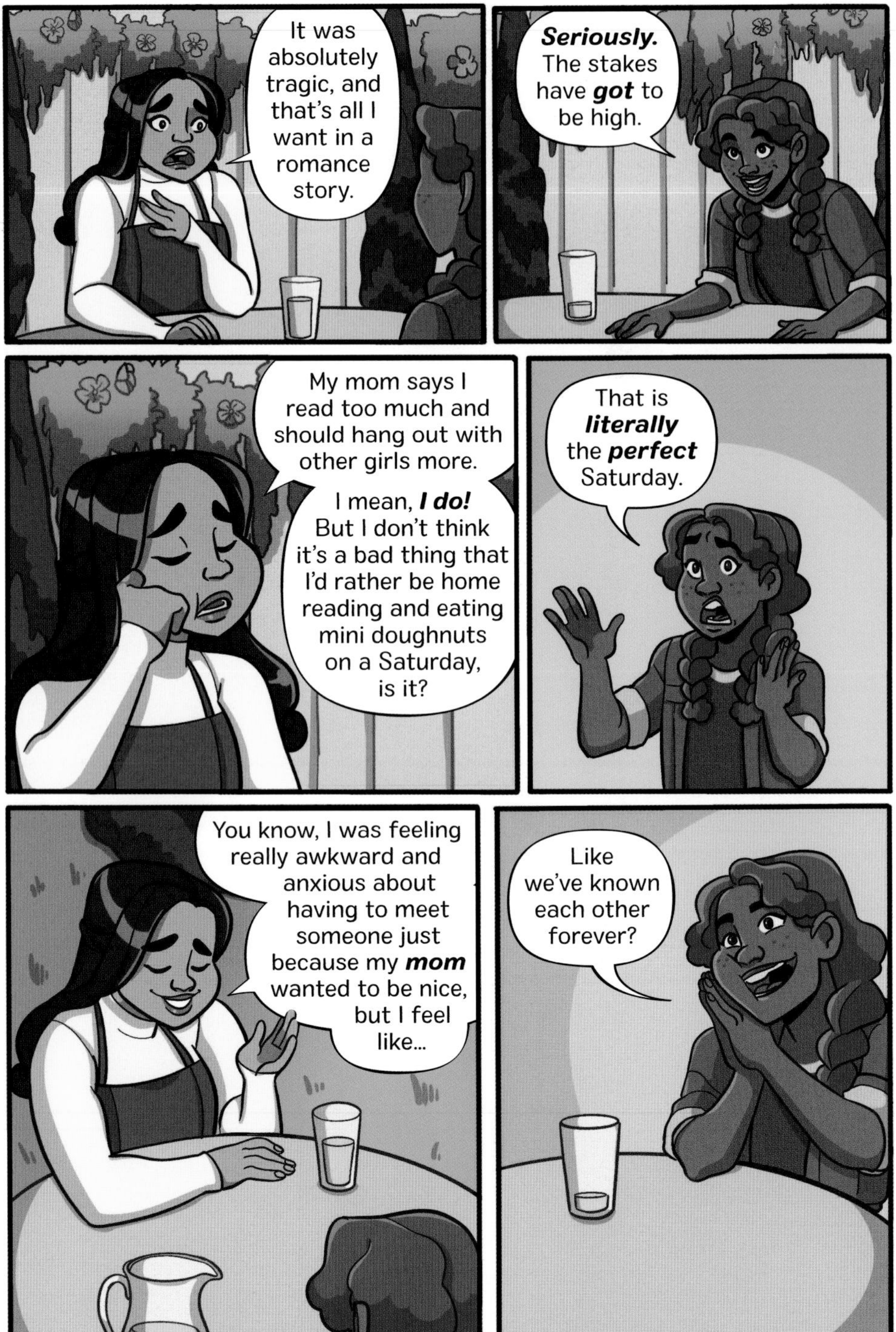

It was absolutely tragic, and that's all I want in a romance story.
Seriously. The stakes have ***got*** to be high.
My mom says I read too much and should hang out with other girls more.
I mean, ***I do!*** But I don't think it's a bad thing that I'd rather be home reading and eating mini doughnuts on a Saturday, is it?
That is ***literally*** the ***perfect*** Saturday.
You know, I was feeling really awkward and anxious about having to meet someone just because my ***mom*** wanted to be nice, but I feel like...
Like we've known each other forever?

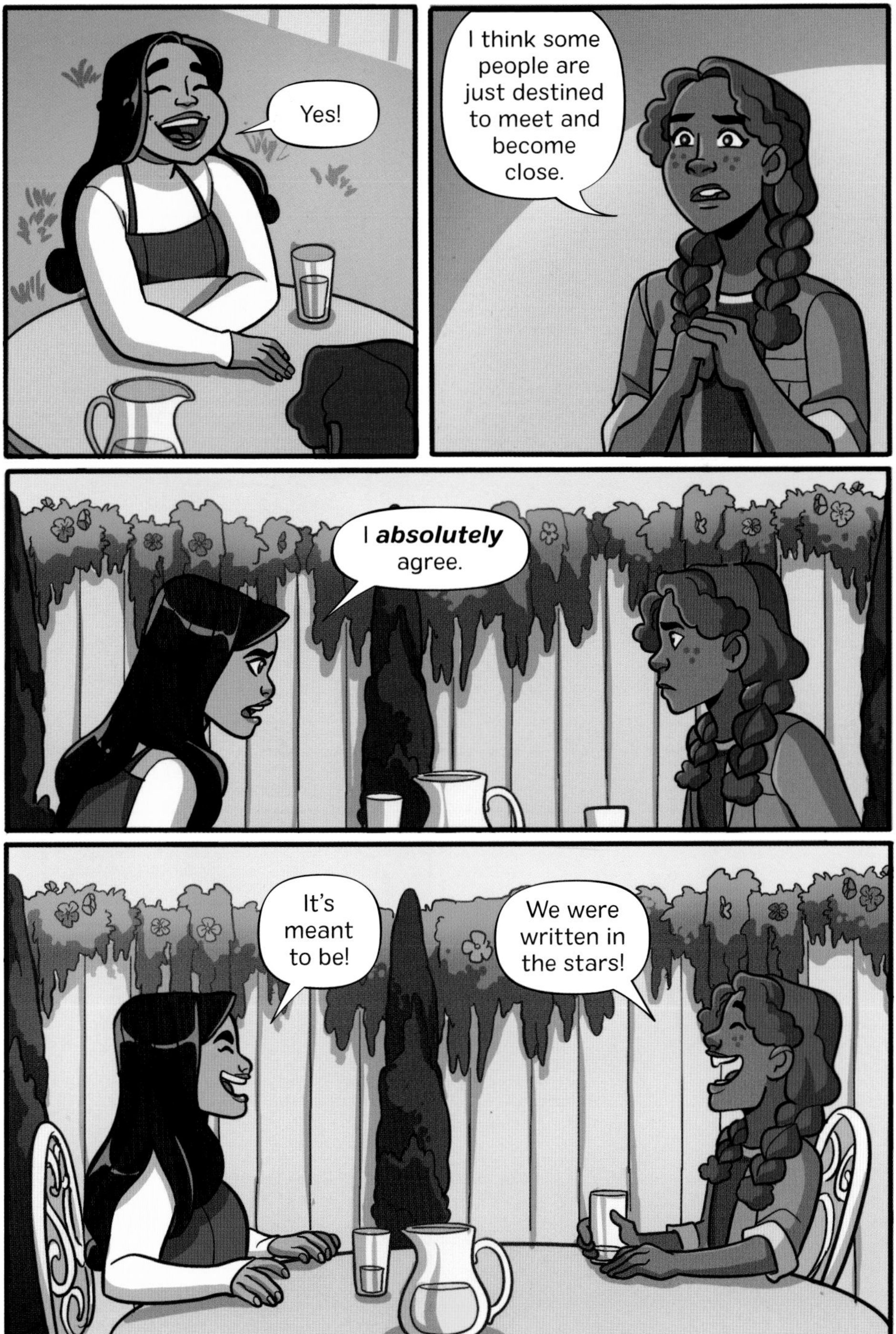

Yes!
I think some people are just destined to meet and become close.
I **absolutely** agree.
It's meant to be!
We were written in the stars!

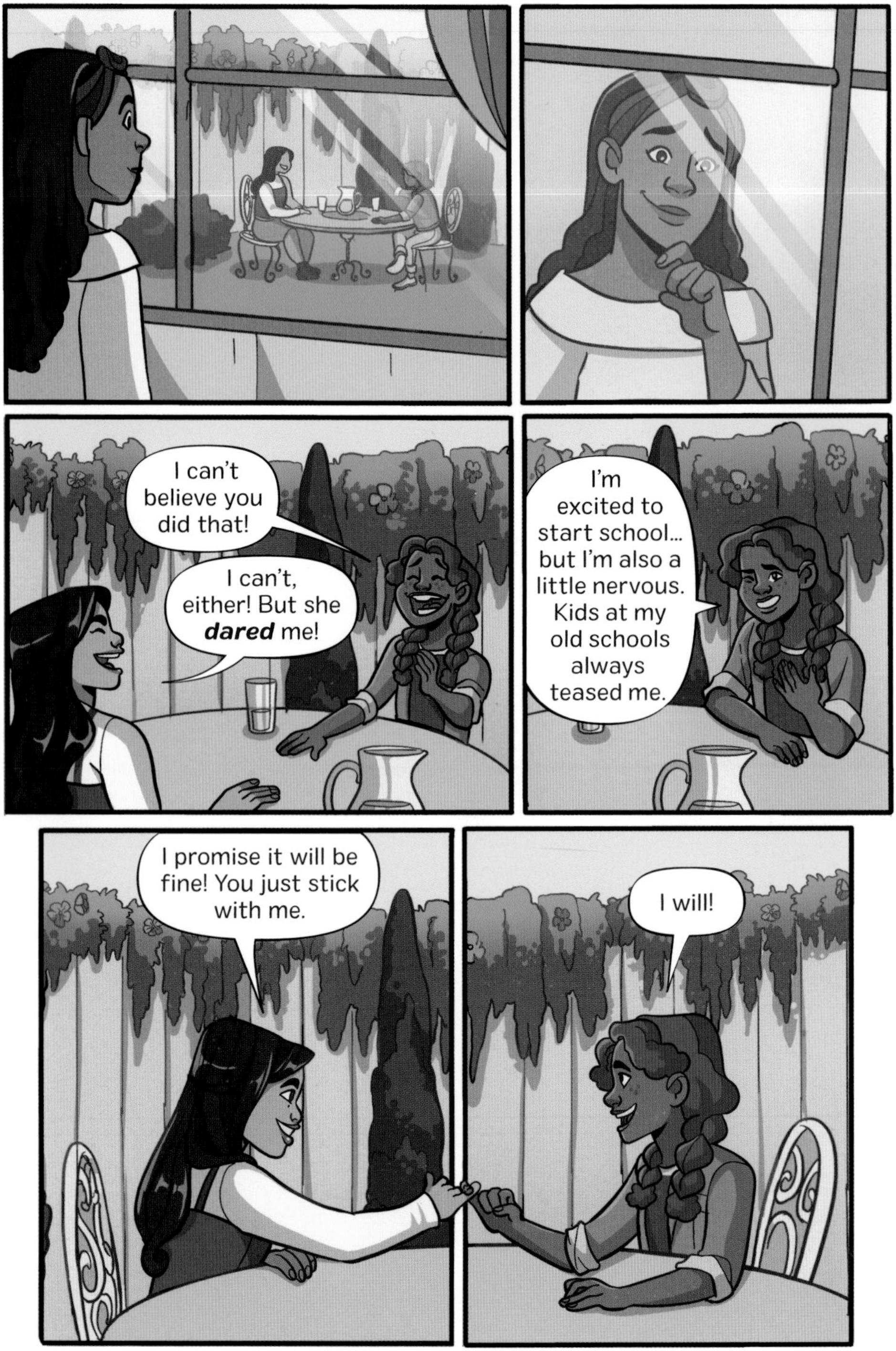
I can't believe you did that!
I can't, either! But she ***dared*** me!
I'm excited to start school... but I'm also a little nervous. Kids at my old schools always teased me.
I promise it will be fine! You just stick with me.
I will!

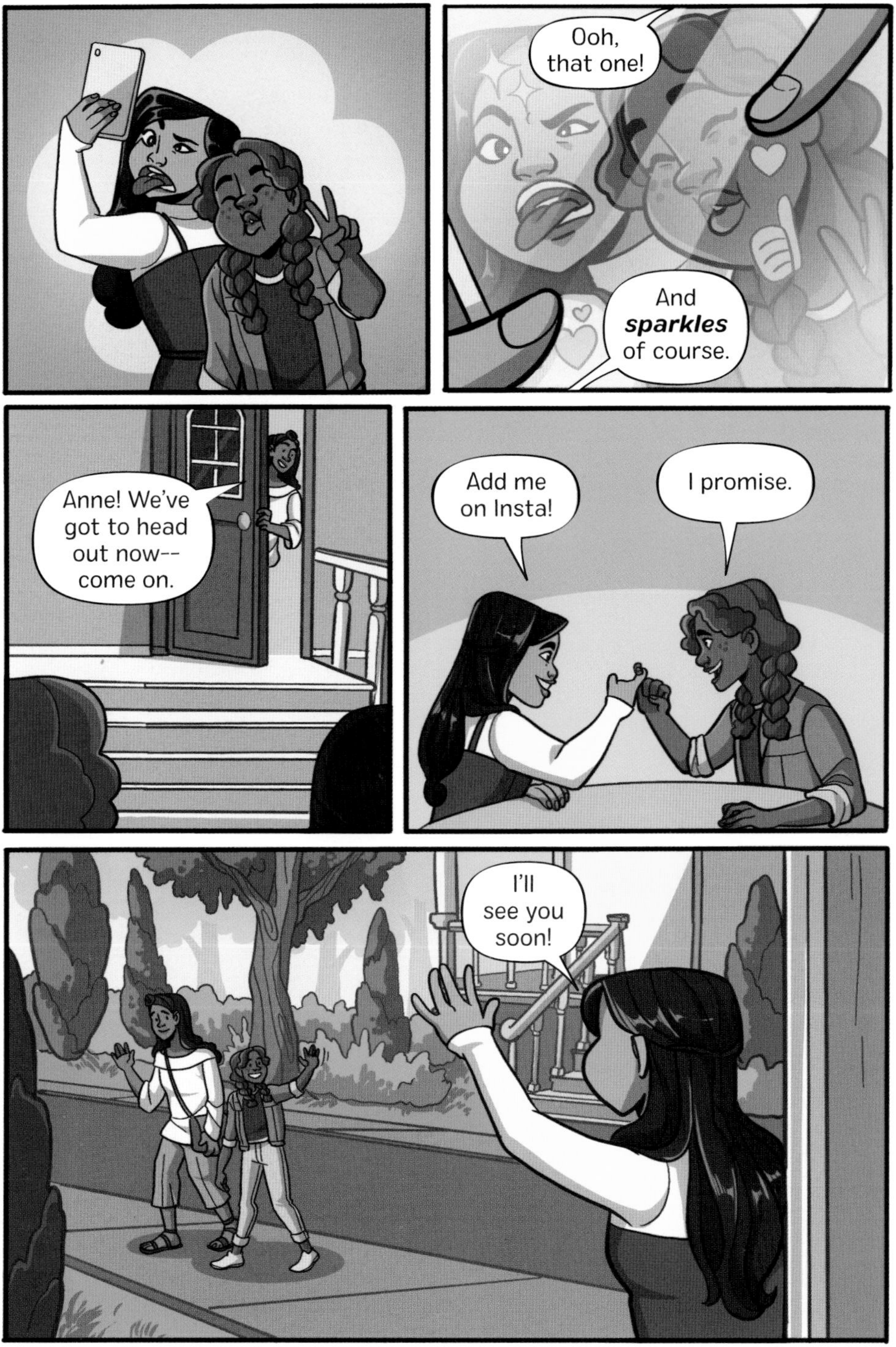
Ooh, that one!
And *sparkles* of course.
Anne! We've got to head out now--come on.
Add me on Insta!
I promise.
I'll see you soon!

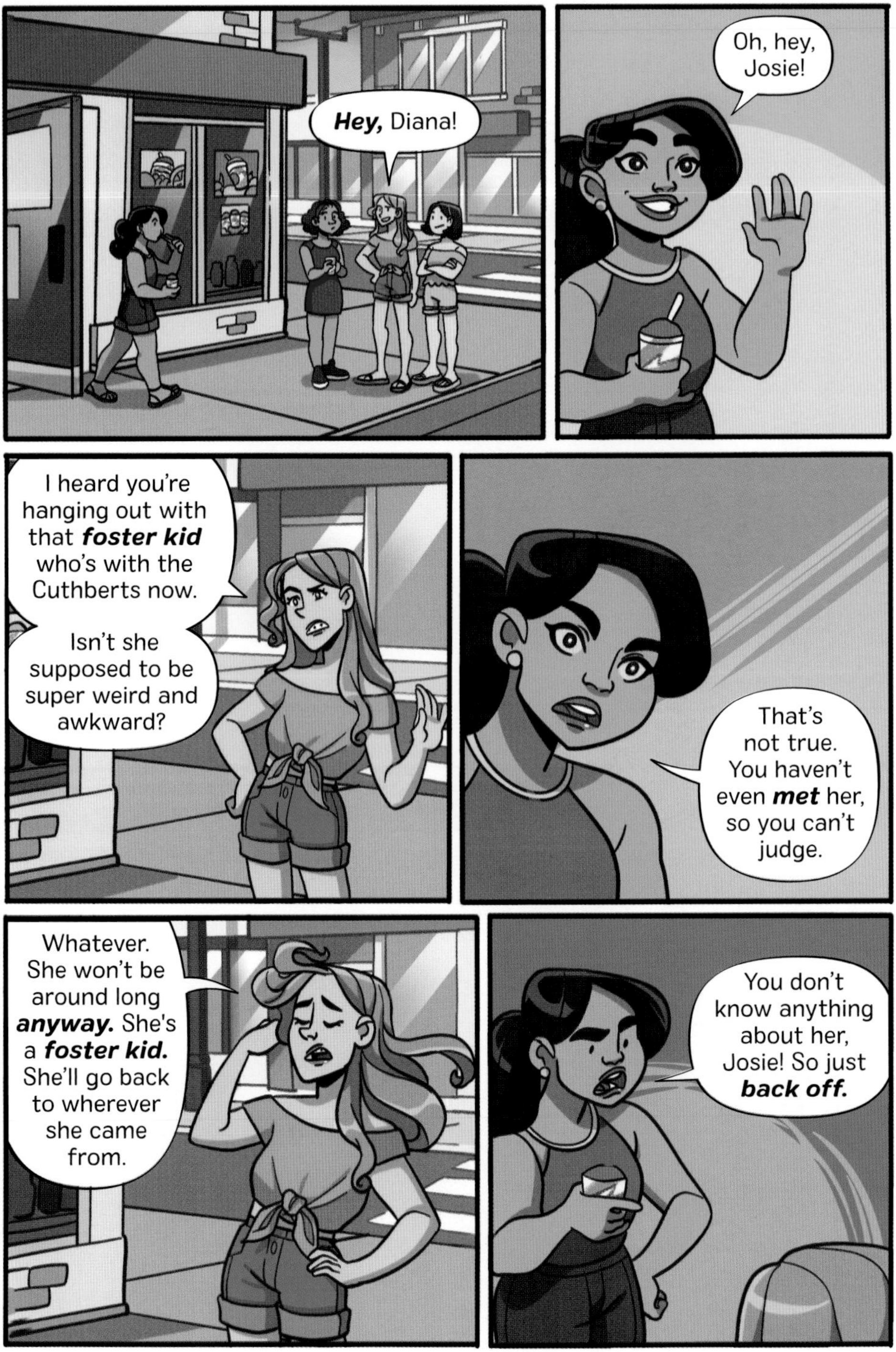
Hey, Diana!
Oh, hey, Josie!
I heard you're hanging out with that foster kid who's with the Cuthberts now.
Isn't she supposed to be super weird and awkward?
That's not true. You haven't even met her, so you can't judge.
Whatever. She won't be around long anyway. She's a foster kid. She'll go back to wherever she came from.
You don't know anything about her, Josie! So just back off.

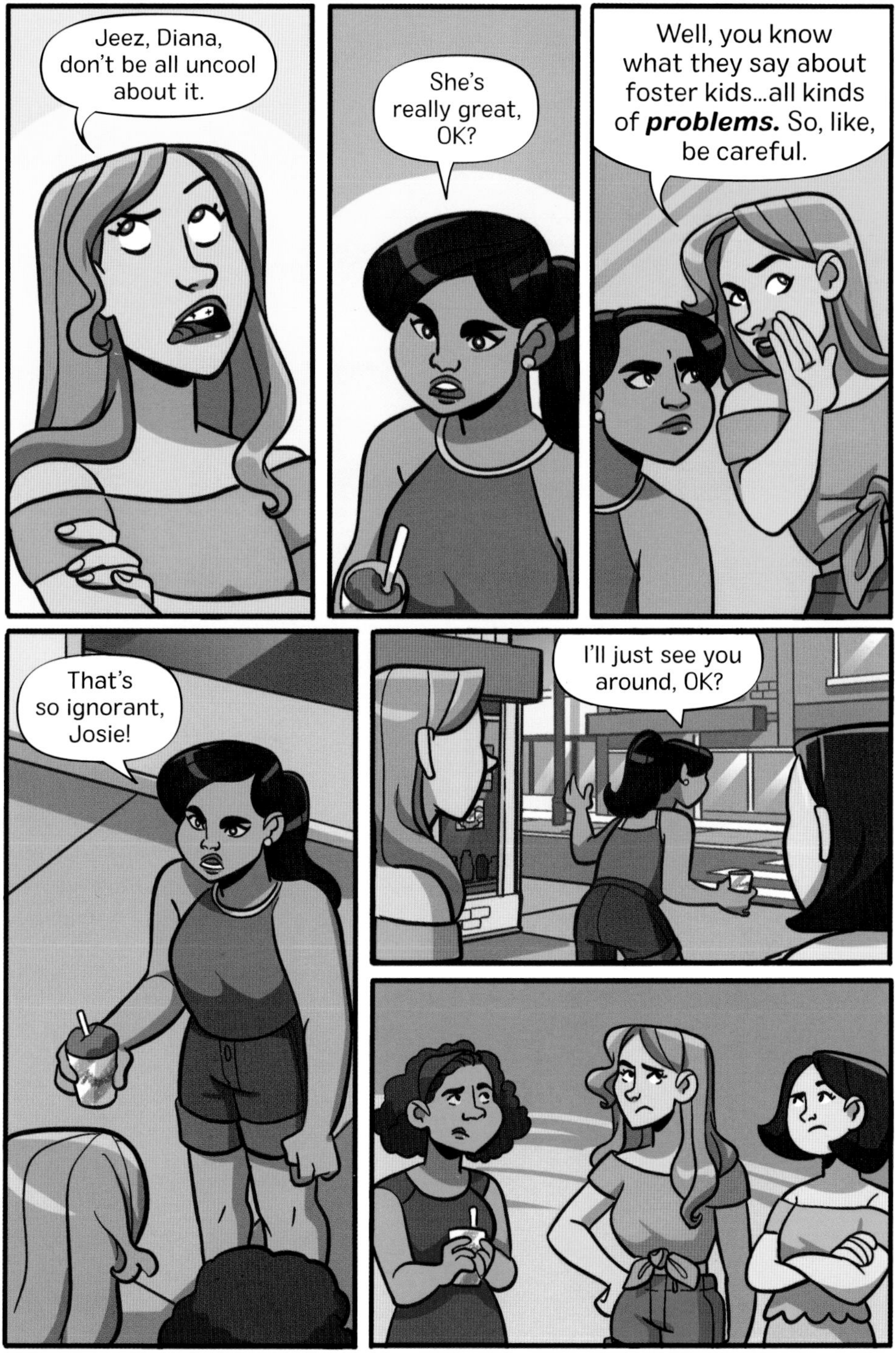
Jeez, Diana, don't be all uncool about it.
She's really great, OK?
Well, you know what they say about foster kids...all kinds of ***problems.*** So, like, be careful.
That's so ignorant, Josie!
I'll just see you around, OK?

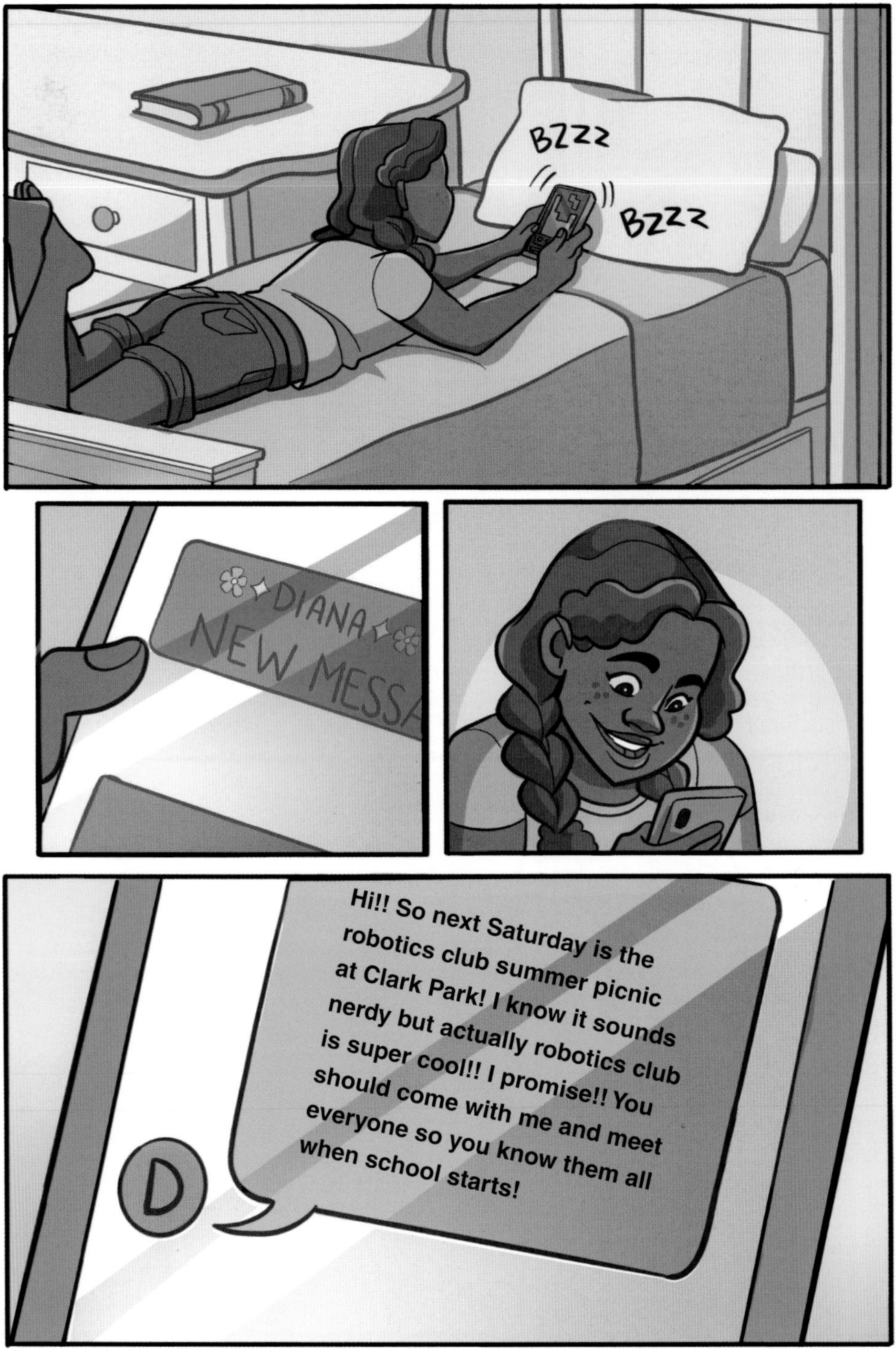
BZZZ
BZZZ
DIANA
NEW MESSA
Hi!! So next Saturday is the robotics club summer picnic at Clark Park! I know it sounds nerdy but actually robotics club is super cool!! I promise!! You should come with me and meet everyone so you know them all when school starts!
D

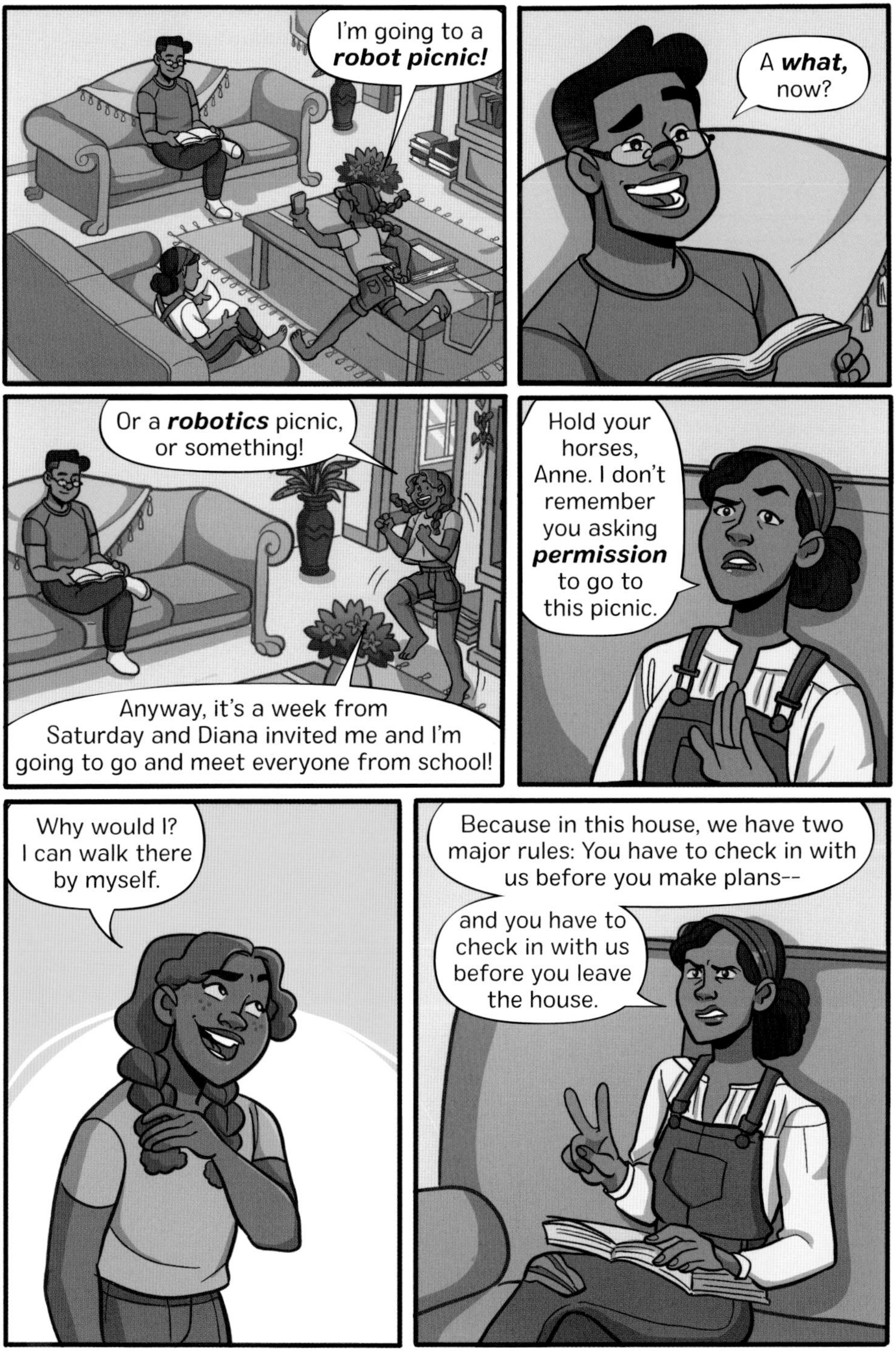

I'm going to a **robot picnic!**
A **what,** now?
Or a **robotics** picnic, or something!
Anyway, it's a week from Saturday and Diana invited me and I'm going to go and meet everyone from school!
Hold your horses, Anne. I don't remember you asking **permission** to go to this picnic.
Why would I? I can walk there by myself.
Because in this house, we have two major rules: You have to check in with us before you make plans--
and you have to check in with us before you leave the house.

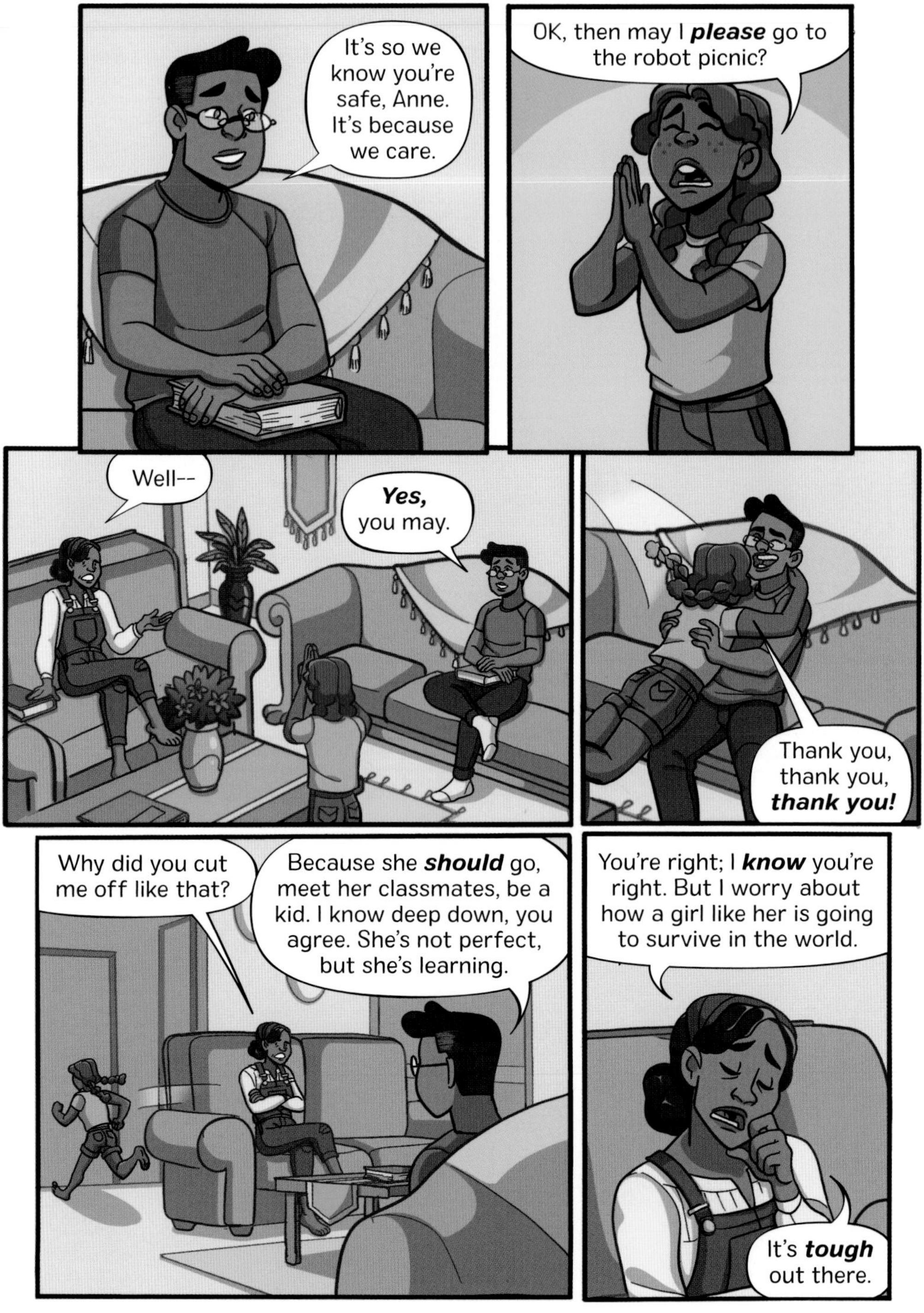
It's so we know you're safe, Anne. It's because we care.
OK, then may I ***please*** go to the robot picnic?
Well--
Yes, you may.
Thank you, thank you, ***thank you!***
Why did you cut me off like that?
Because she ***should*** go, meet her classmates, be a kid. I know deep down, you agree. She's not perfect, but she's learning.
You're right; I ***know*** you're right. But I worry about how a girl like her is going to survive in the world.
It's ***tough*** out there.

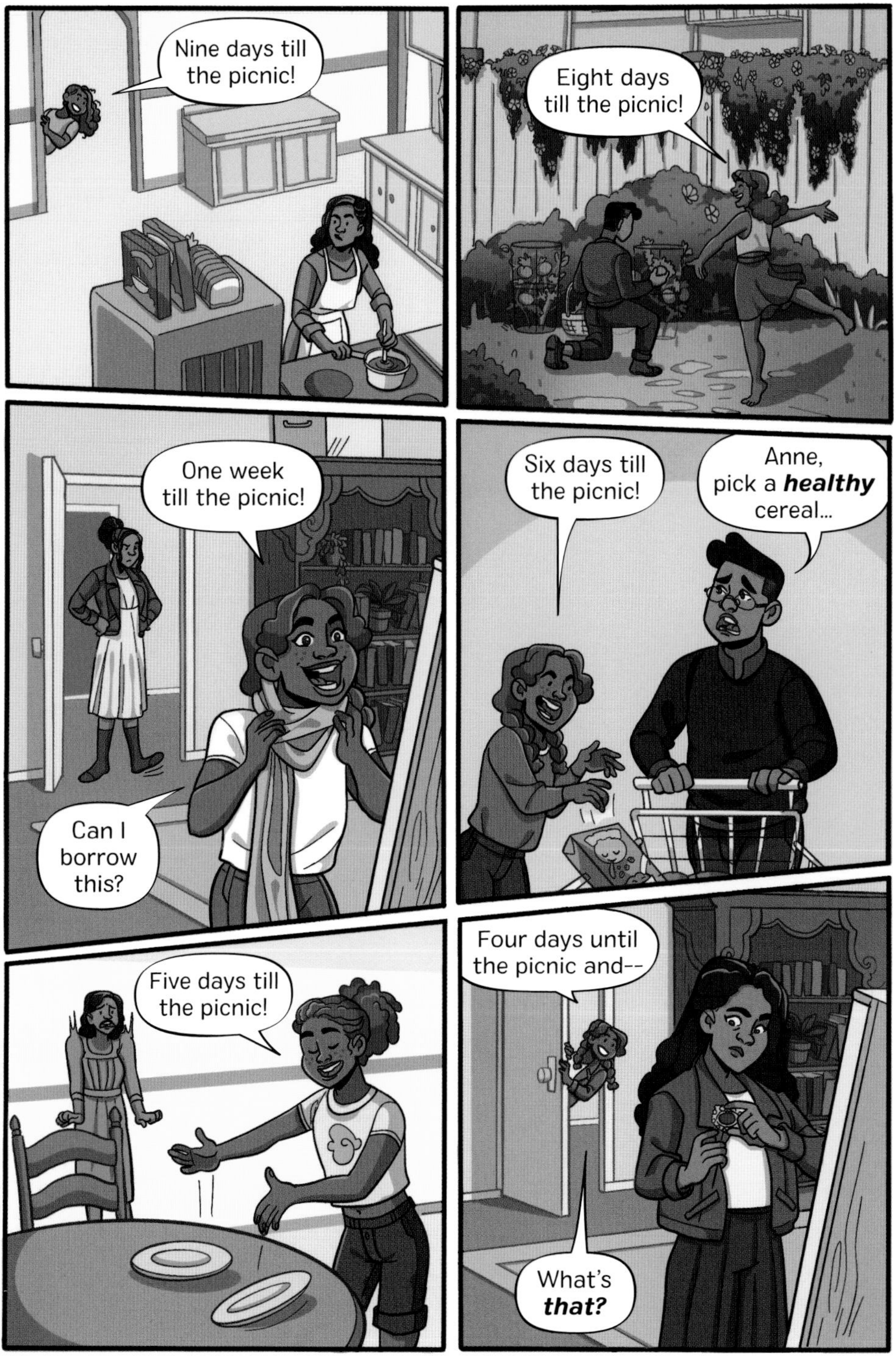
Nine days till the picnic!
Eight days till the picnic!
One week till the picnic!
Can I borrow this?
Six days till the picnic!
Anne, pick a ***healthy*** cereal...
Five days till the picnic!
Four days until the picnic and--
What's ***that?***

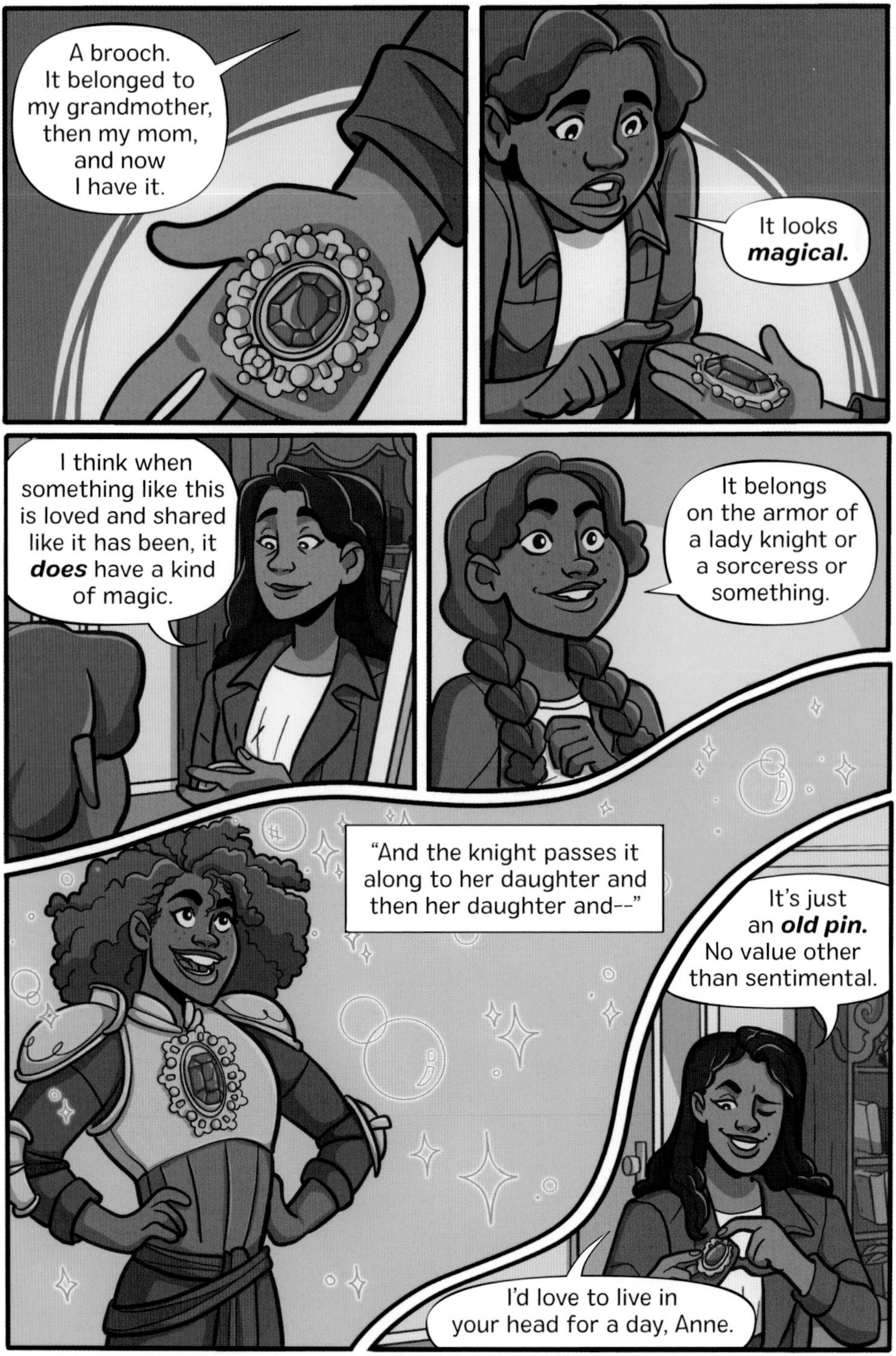
A brooch. It belonged to my grandmother, then my mom, and now I have it.
It looks ***magical.***
I think when something like this is loved and shared like it has been, it ***does*** have a kind of magic.
It belongs on the armor of a lady knight or a sorceress or something.
"And the knight passes it along to her daughter and then her daughter and--"
It's just an ***old pin.*** No value other than sentimental.
I'd love to live in your head for a day, Anne.

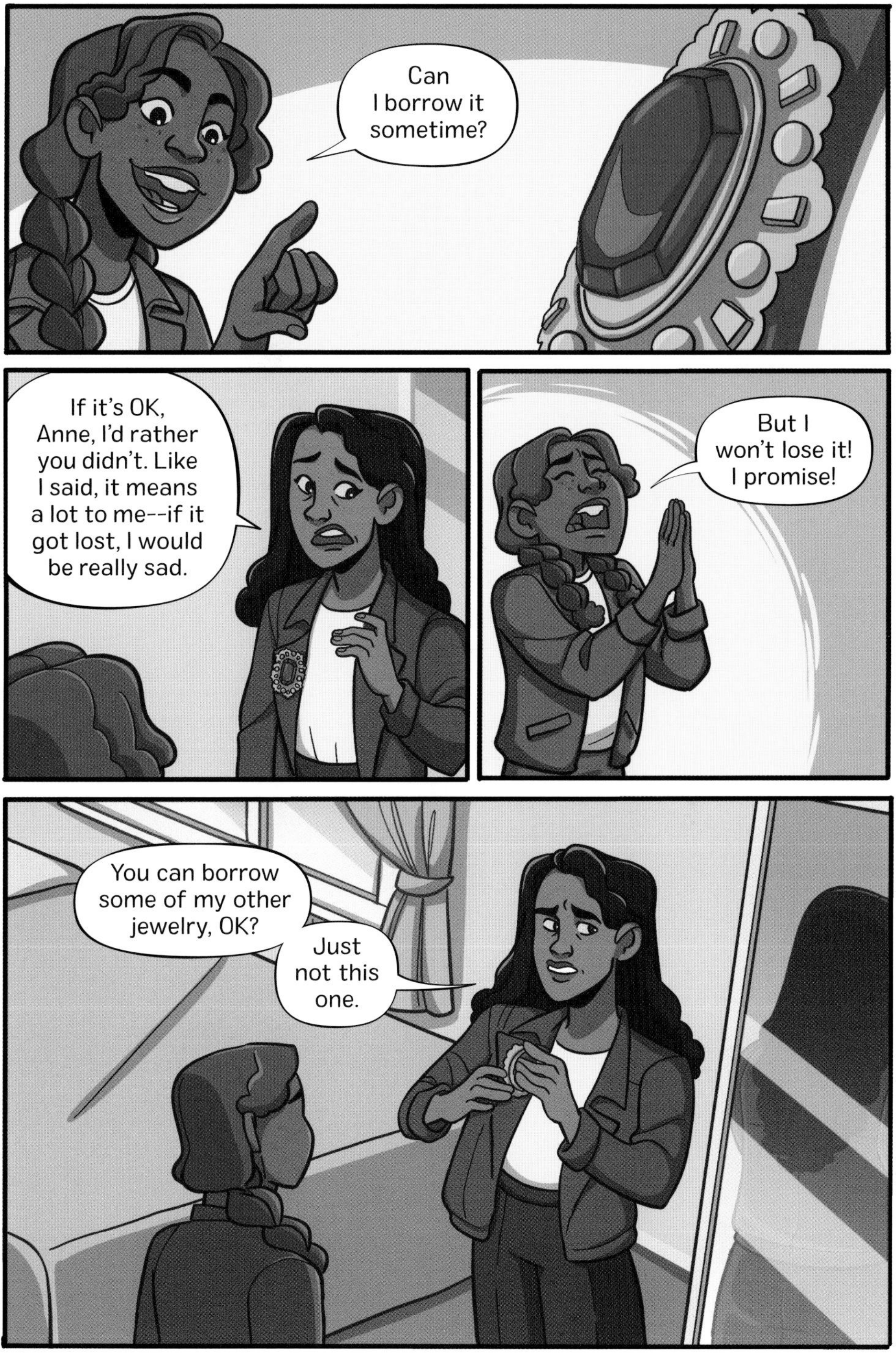

Can I borrow it sometime?
If it's OK, Anne, I'd rather you didn't. Like I said, it means a lot to me--if it got lost, I would be really sad.
But I won't lose it! I promise!
You can borrow some of my other jewelry, OK?
Just not this one.

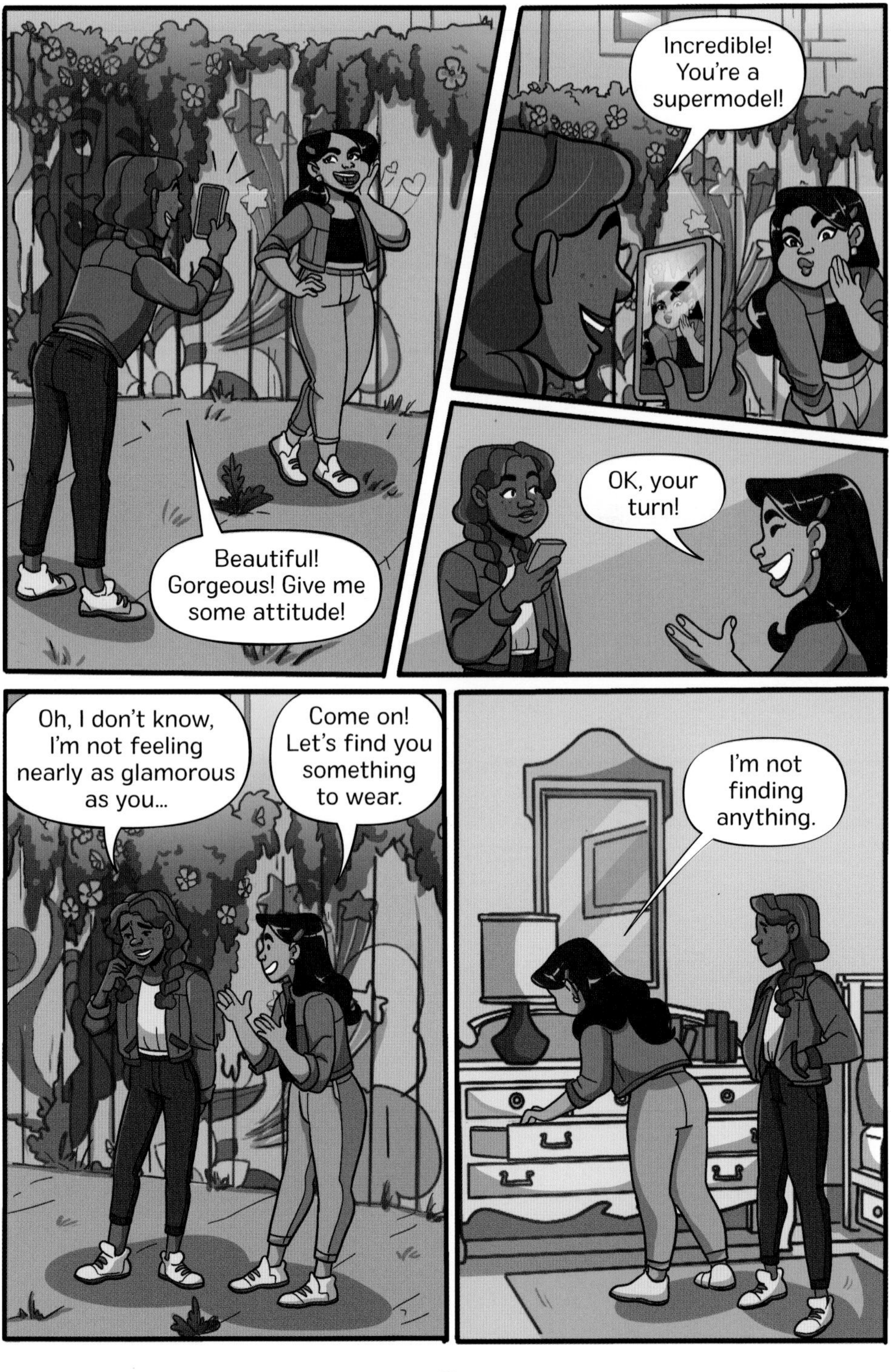
Beautiful! Gorgeous! Give me some attitude!
Incredible! You're a supermodel!
OK, your turn!
Oh, I don't know, I'm not feeling nearly as glamorous as you...
Come on! Let's find you something to wear.
I'm not finding anything.

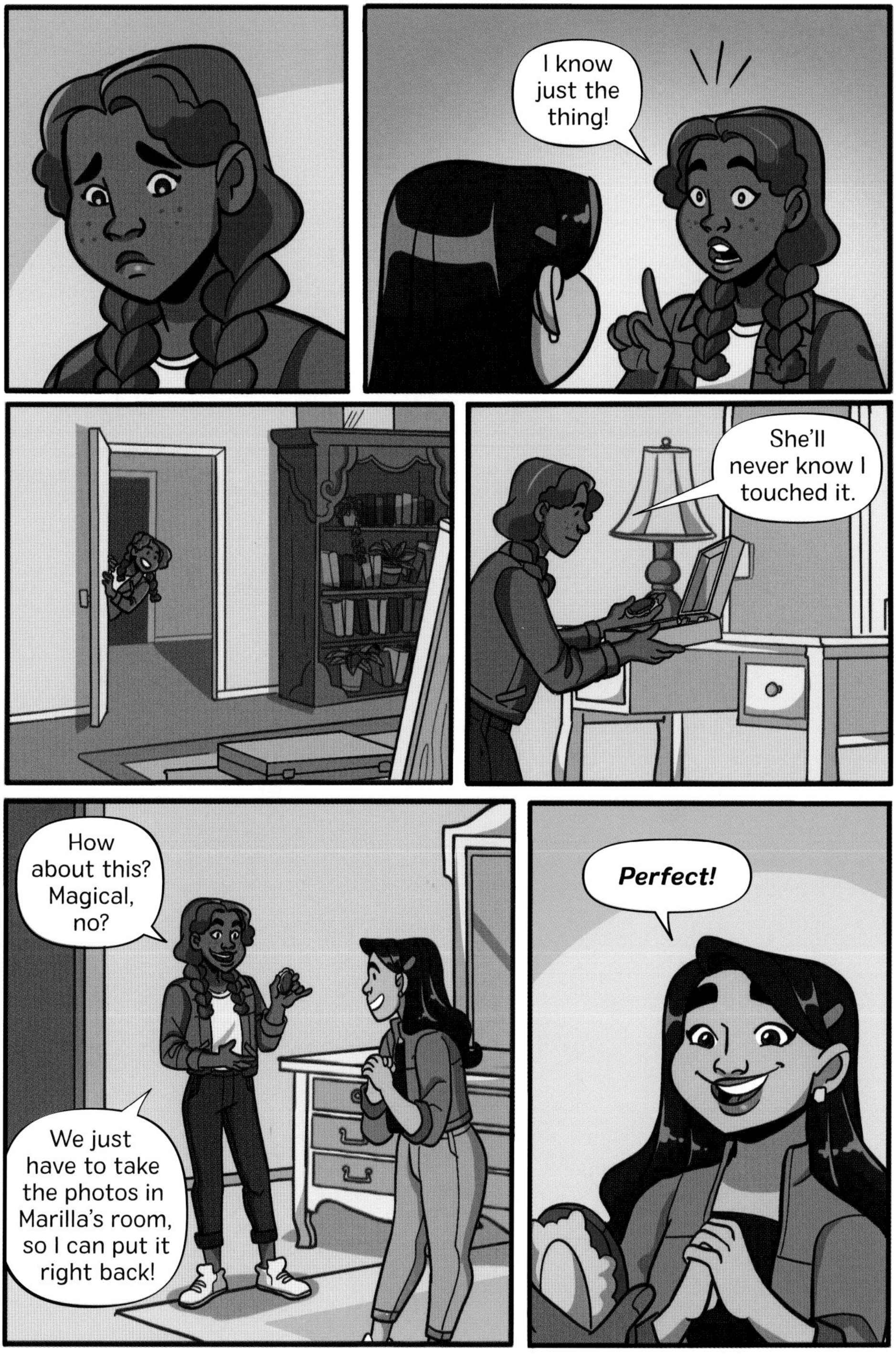
I know just the thing!
She'll never know I touched it.
How about this? Magical, no?
We just have to take the photos in Marilla's room, so I can put it right back!
Perfect!

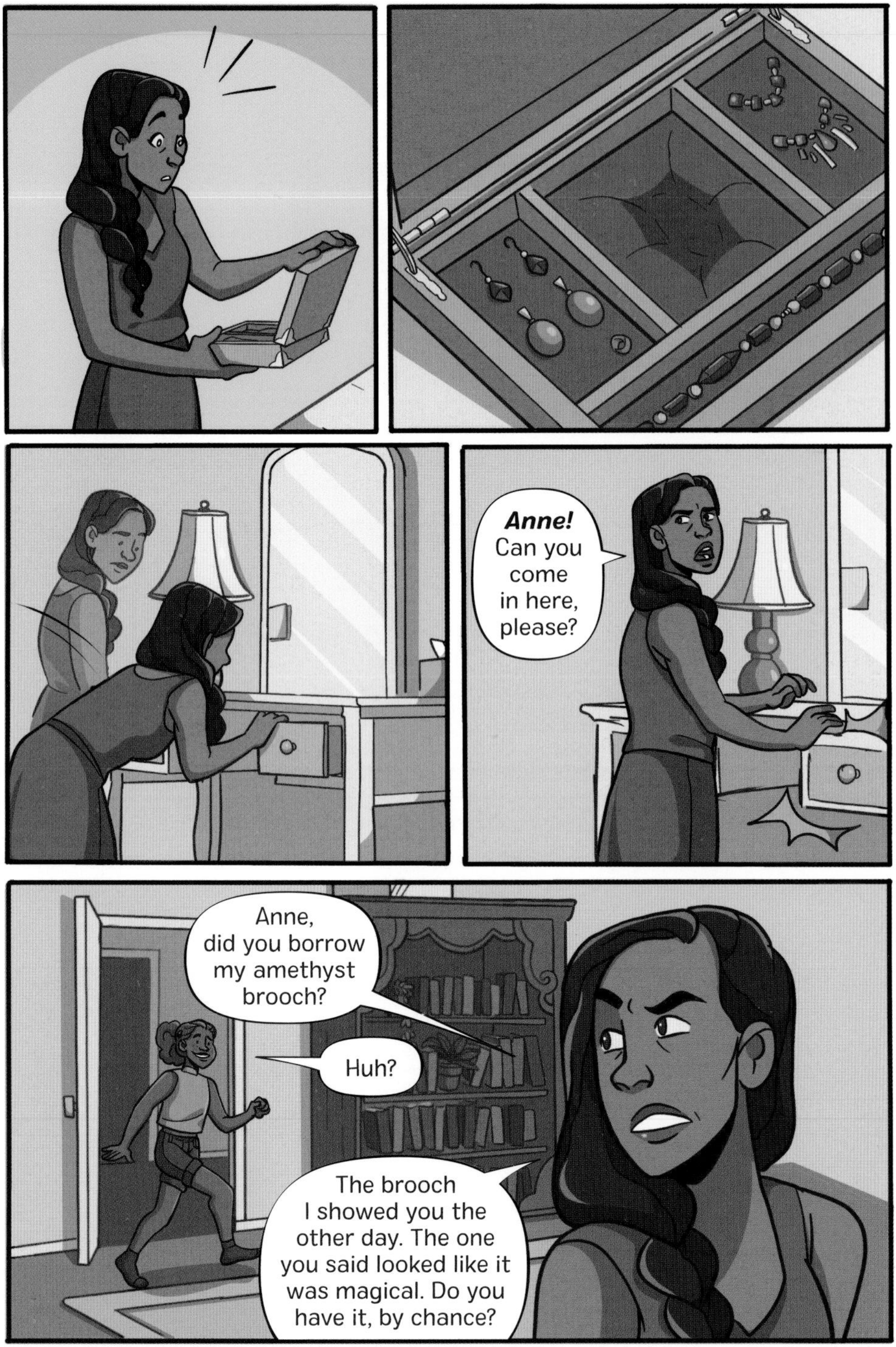

Anne! Can you come in here, please?
Anne, did you borrow my amethyst brooch?
Huh?
The brooch I showed you the other day. The one you said looked like it was magical. Do you have it, by chance?

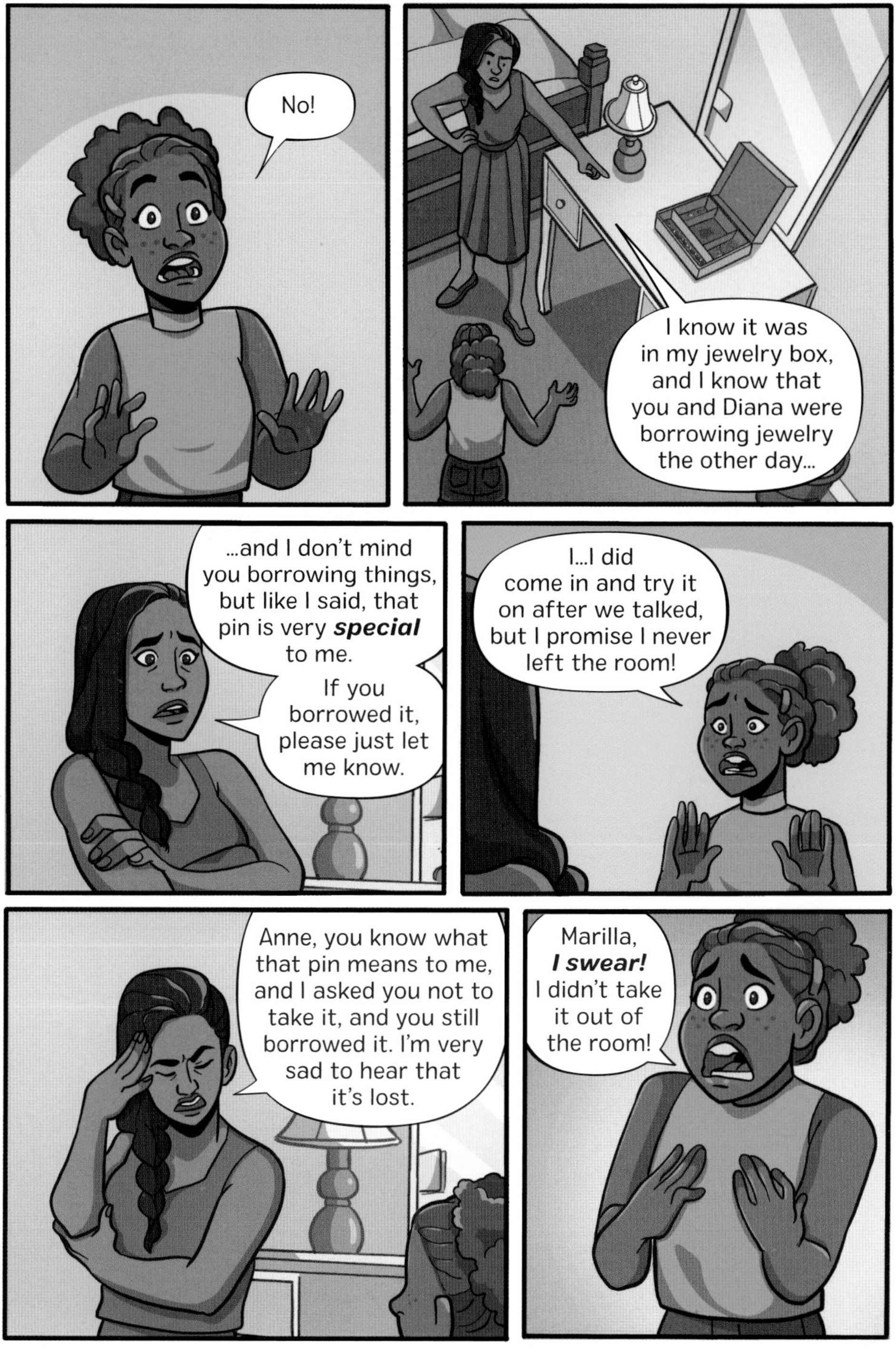

No!
I know it was in my jewelry box, and I know that you and Diana were borrowing jewelry the other day...
...and I don't mind you borrowing things, but like I said, that pin is very ***special*** to me.
If you borrowed it, please just let me know.
I...I did come in and try it on after we talked, but I promise I never left the room!
Anne, you know what that pin means to me, and I asked you not to take it, and you still borrowed it. I'm very sad to hear that it's lost.
Marilla, ***I swear!*** I didn't take it out of the room!

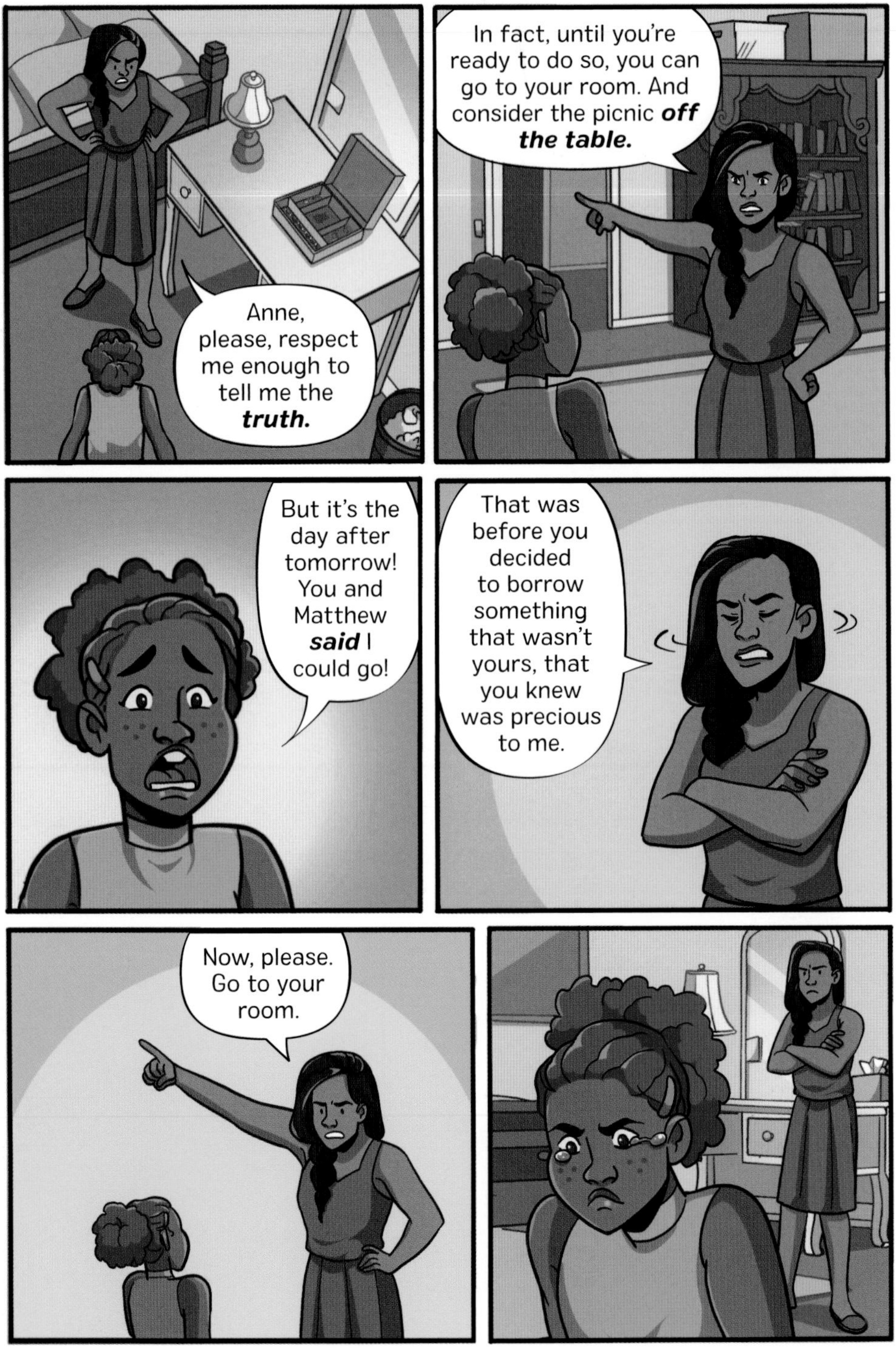
Anne, please, respect me enough to tell me the *truth.*
In fact, until you're ready to do so, you can go to your room. And consider the picnic *off the table.*
But it's the day after tomorrow! You and Matthew *said* I could go!
That was before you decided to borrow something that wasn't yours, that you knew was precious to me.
Now, please. Go to your room.

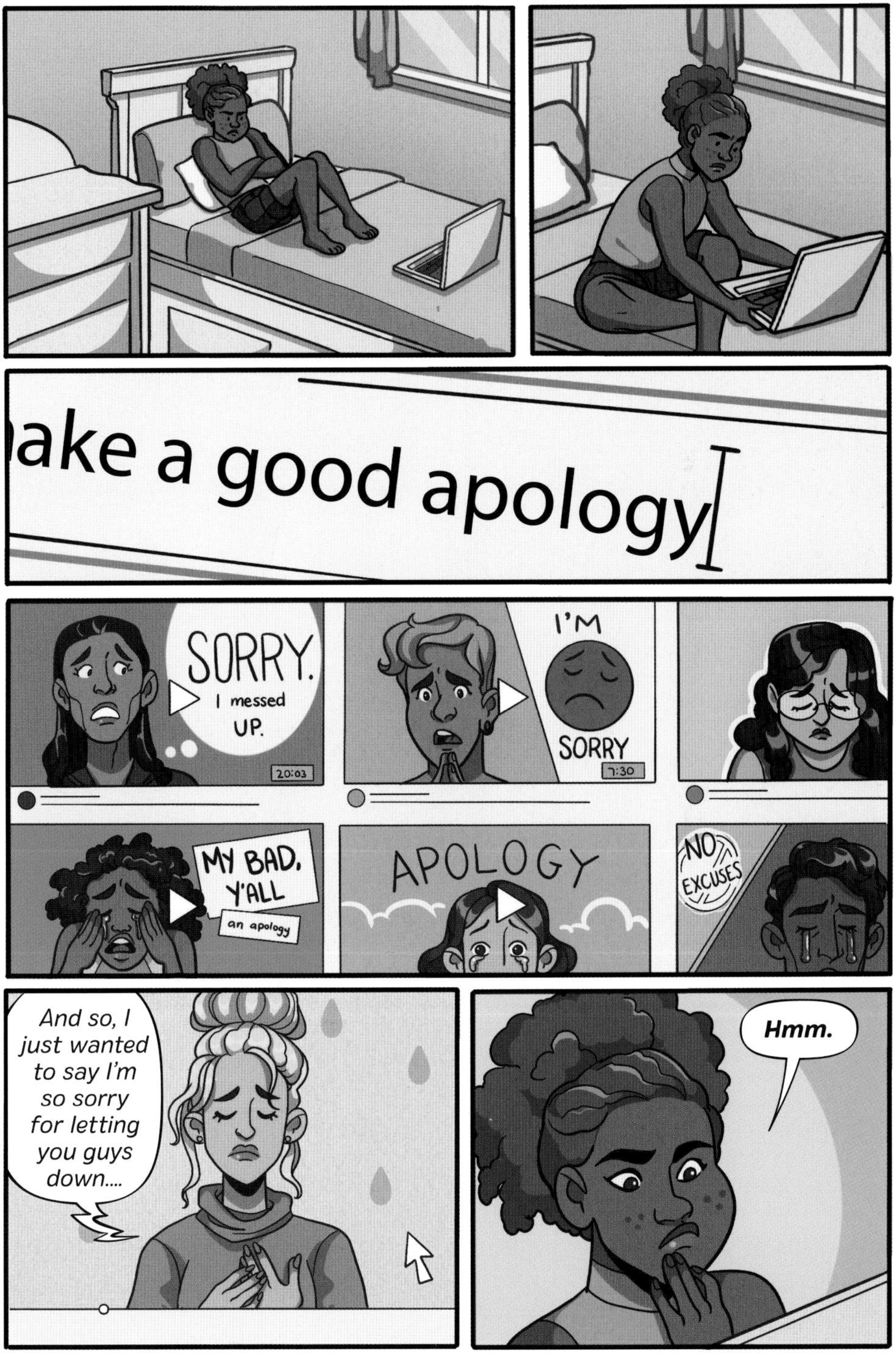
ake a good apology
SORRY.
I messed UP.
20:03
I'M
SORRY
7:30
MY BAD, Y'ALL
an apology
APOLOGY
NO EXCUSES
And so, I just wanted to say I'm so sorry for letting you guys down....
Hmm.

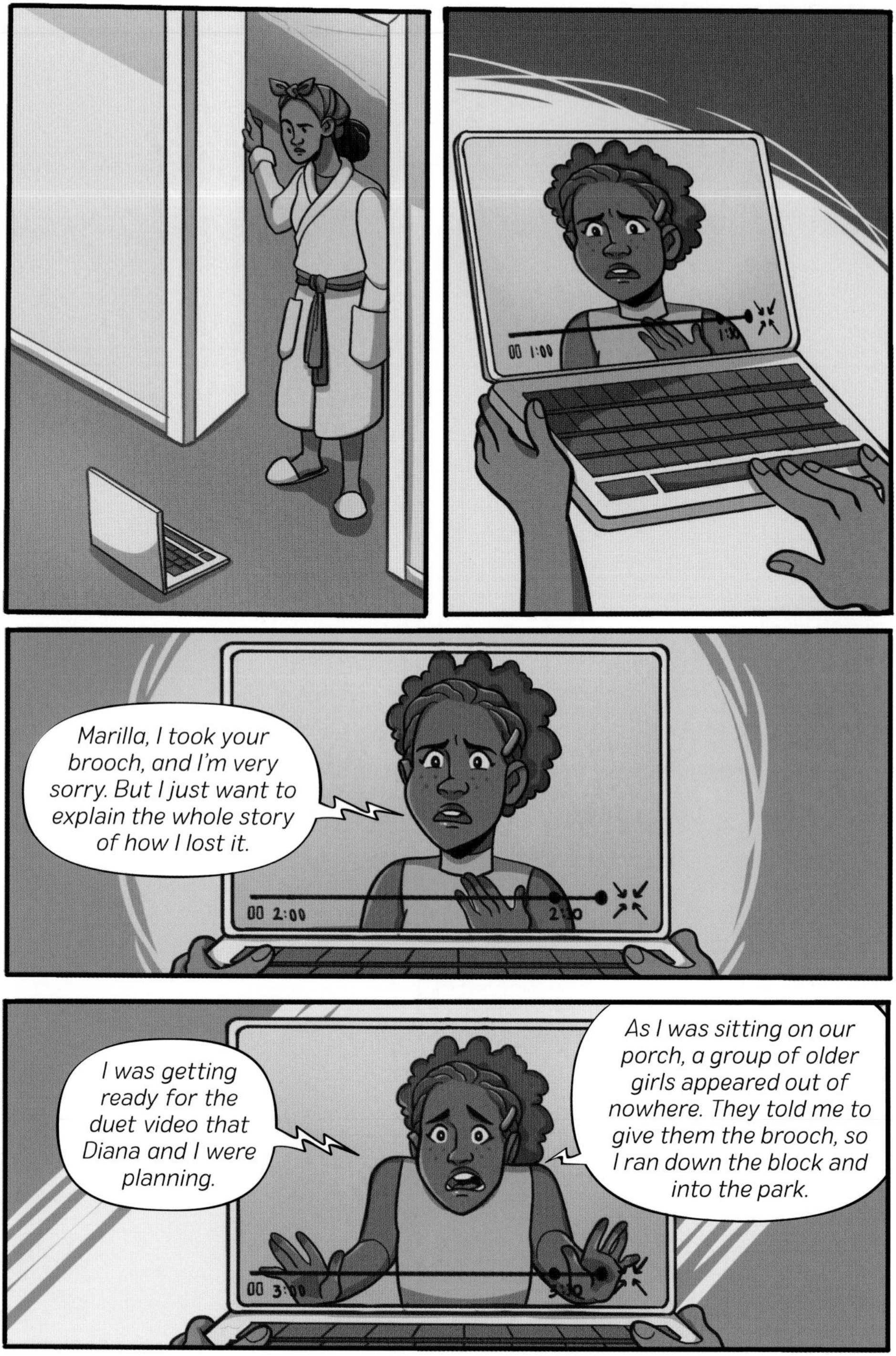

00 1:00
Marilla, I took your brooch, and I'm very sorry. But I just want to explain the whole story of how I lost it.
00 2:00
I was getting ready for the duet video that Diana and I were planning.
As I was sitting on our porch, a group of older girls appeared out of nowhere. They told me to give them the brooch, so I ran down the block and into the park.

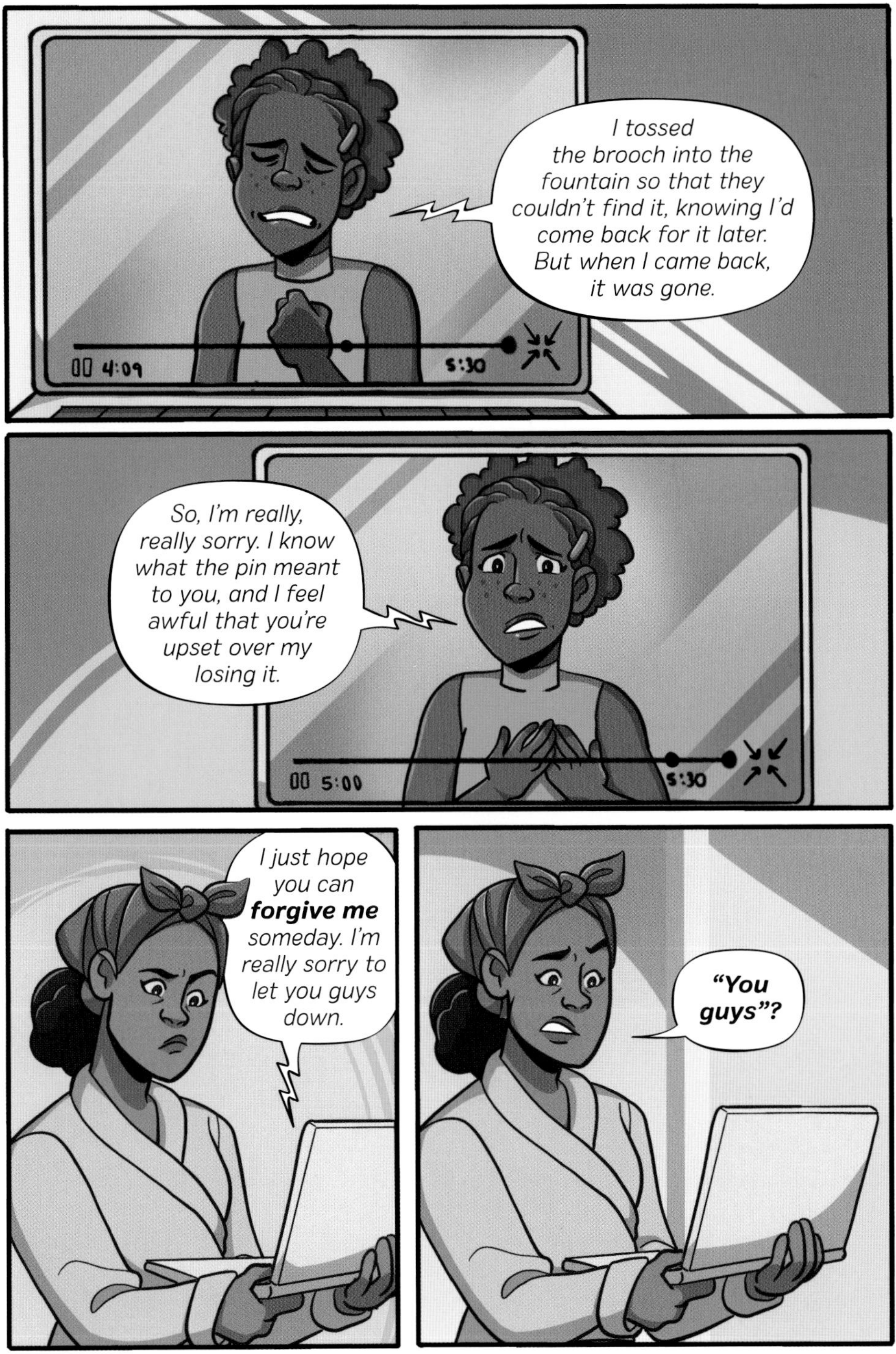
I tossed the brooch into the fountain so that they couldn't find it, knowing I'd come back for it later. But when I came back, it was gone.
4:09
5:30
So, I'm really, really sorry. I know what the pin meant to you, and I feel awful that you're upset over my losing it.
5:00
5:30
I just hope you can **forgive me** someday. I'm really sorry to let you guys down.
"You guys"?

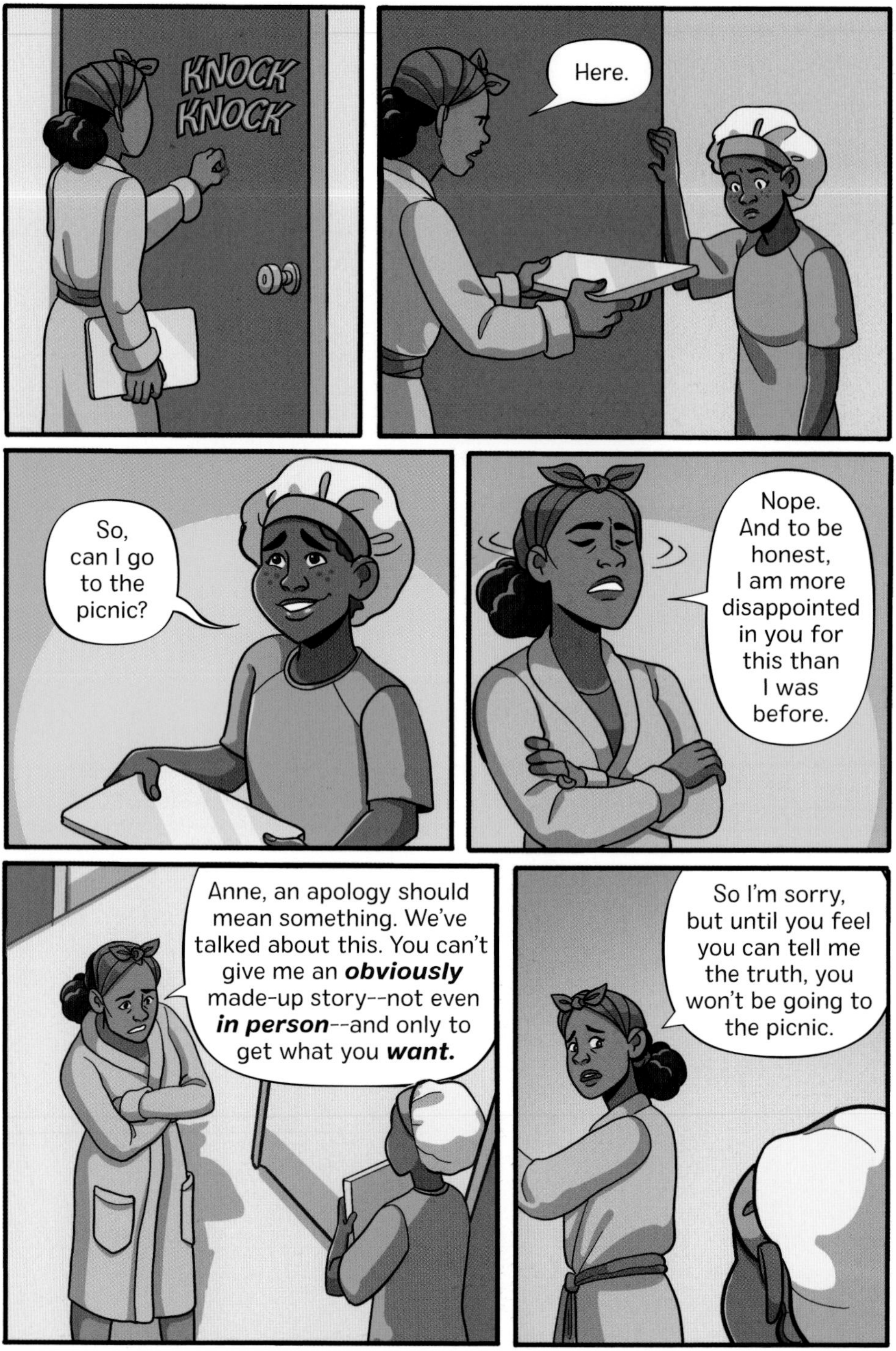

KNOCK KNOCK
Here.
So, can I go to the picnic?
Nope. And to be honest, I am more disappointed in you for this than I was before.
Anne, an apology should mean something. We've talked about this. You can't give me an ***obviously*** made-up story--not even ***in person***--and only to get what you ***want.***
So I'm sorry, but until you feel you can tell me the truth, you won't be going to the picnic.

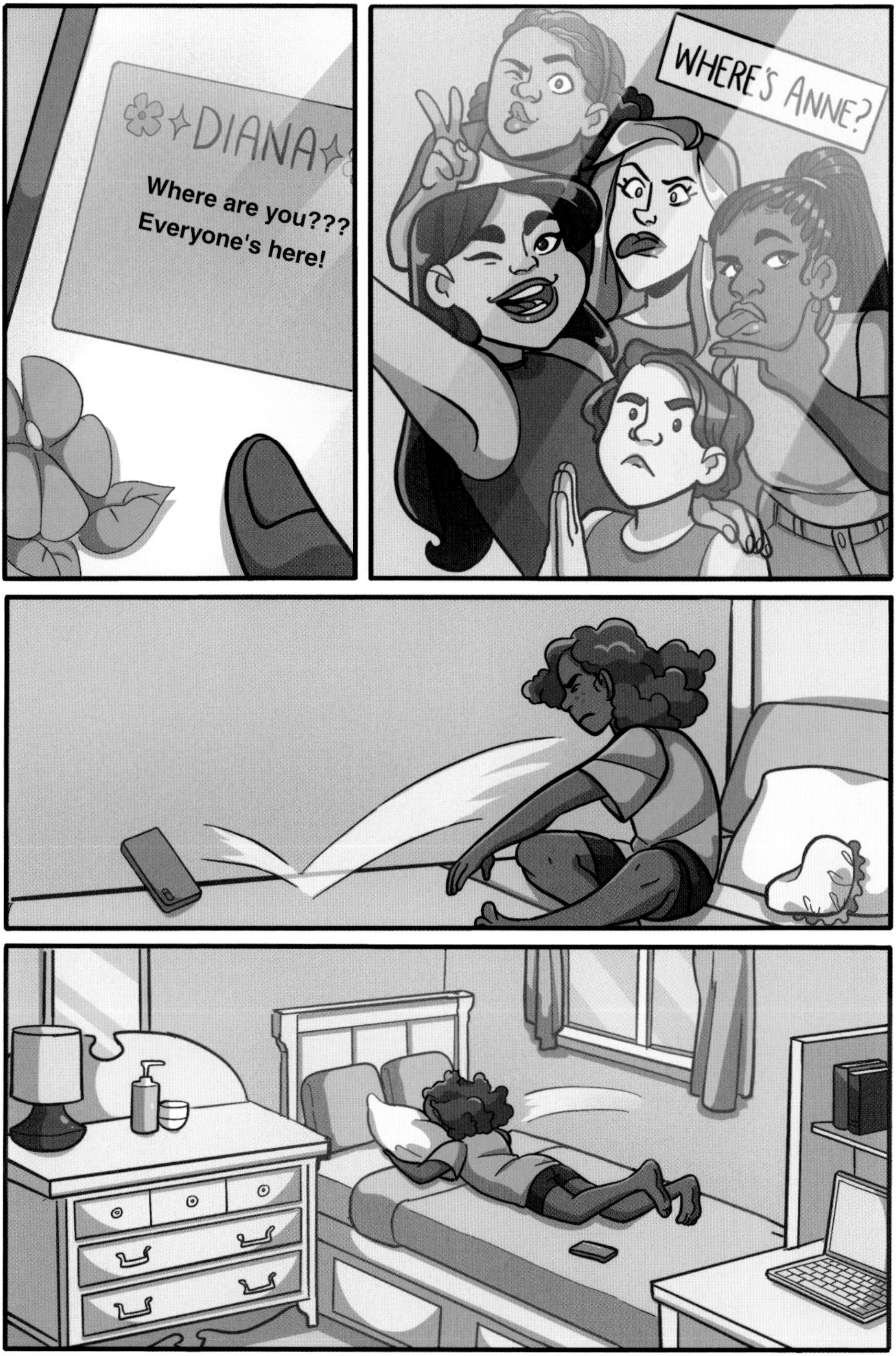
DIANA
Where are you???
Everyone's here!
WHERE'S ANNE?

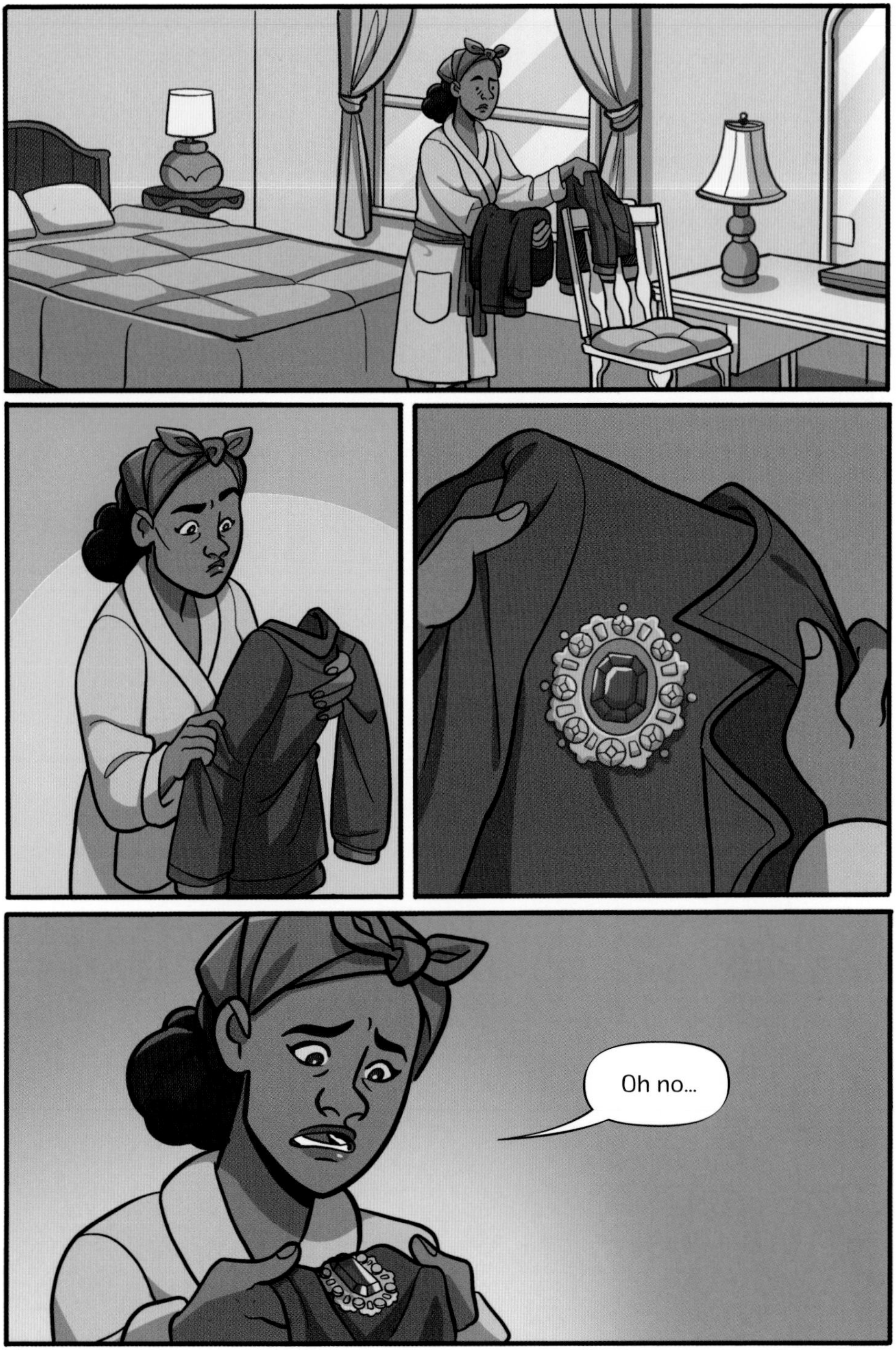
Oh no...

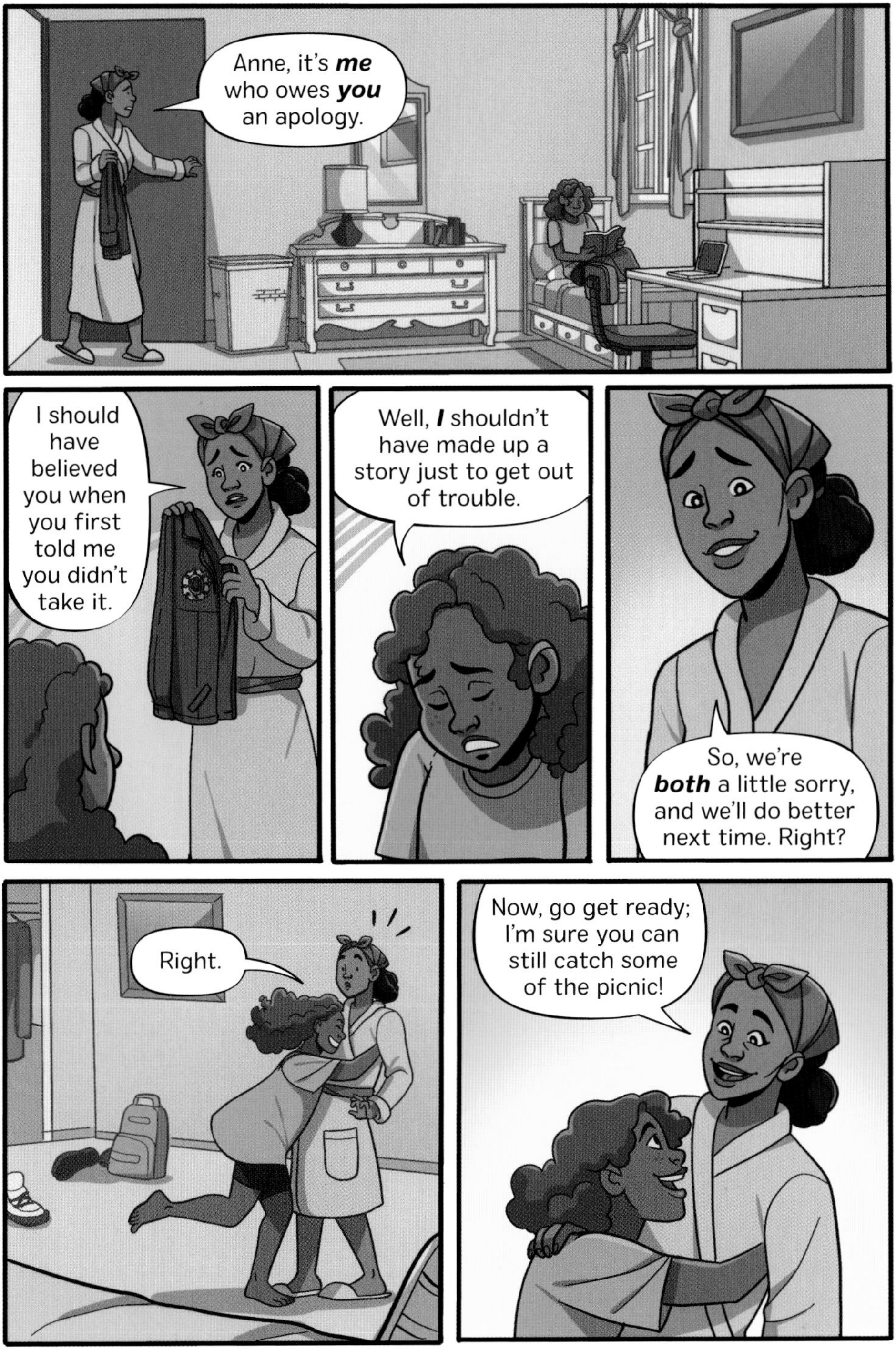
Anne, it's ***me*** who owes ***you*** an apology.
I should have believed you when you first told me you didn't take it.
Well, ***I*** shouldn't have made up a story just to get out of trouble.
So, we're ***both*** a little sorry, and we'll do better next time. Right?
Right.
Now, go get ready; I'm sure you can still catch some of the picnic!

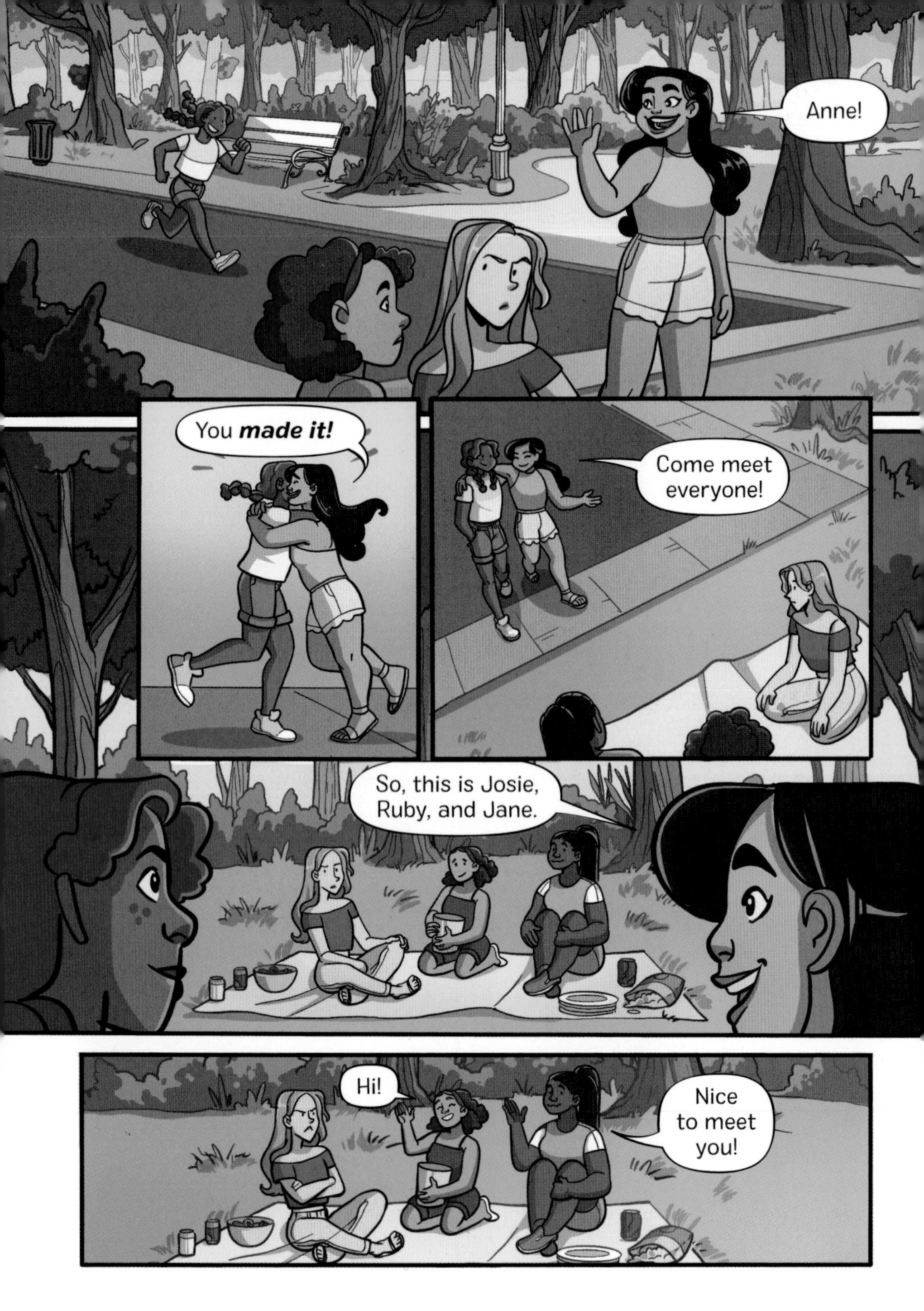
Anne!
You **made it!**
Come meet everyone!
So, this is Josie, Ruby, and Jane.
Hi!
Nice to meet you!

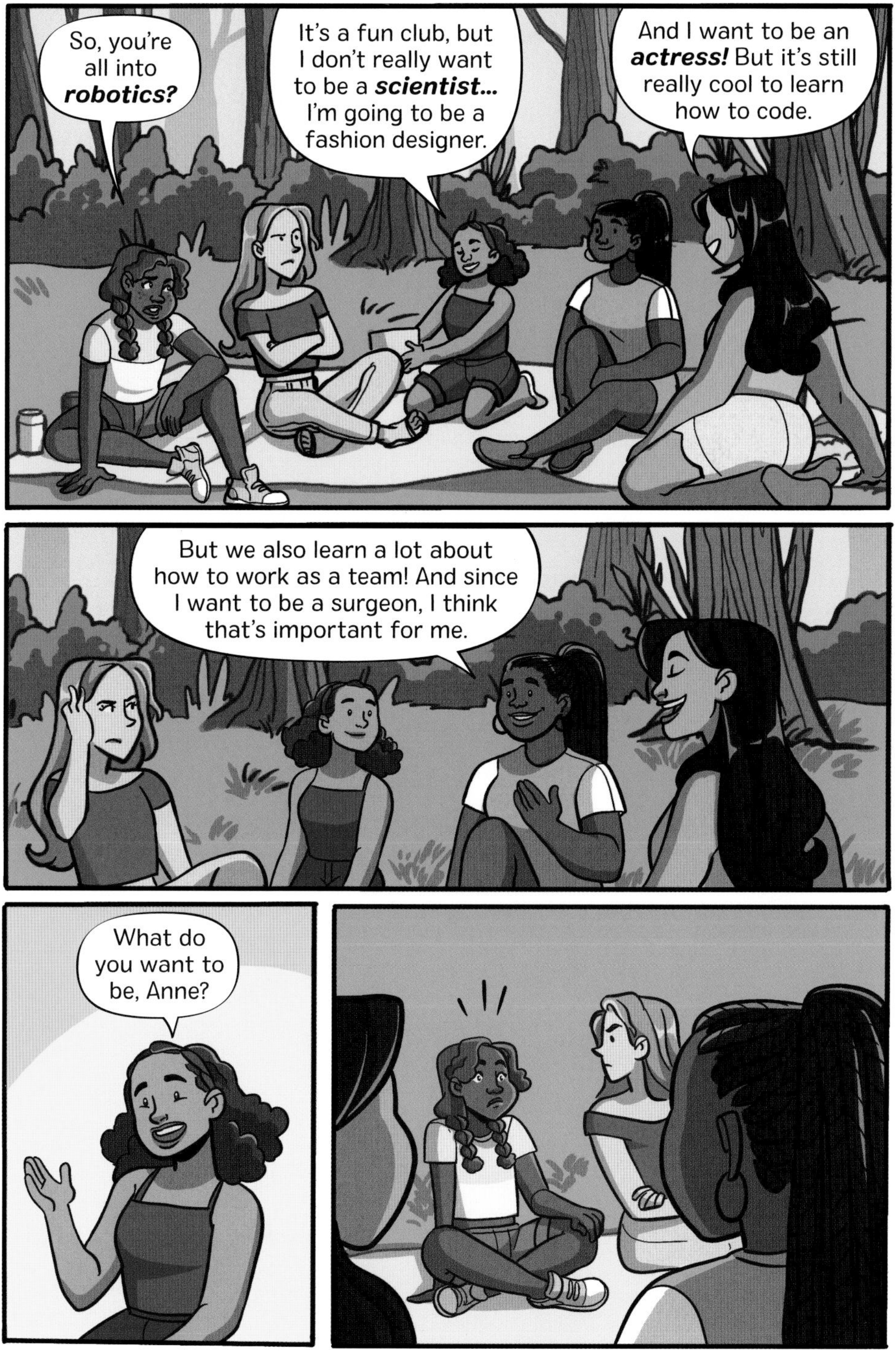
So, you're all into ***robotics?***
It's a fun club, but I don't really want to be a ***scientist...*** I'm going to be a fashion designer.
And I want to be an ***actress!*** But it's still really cool to learn how to code.
But we also learn a lot about how to work as a team! And since I want to be a surgeon, I think that's important for me.
What do you want to be, Anne?

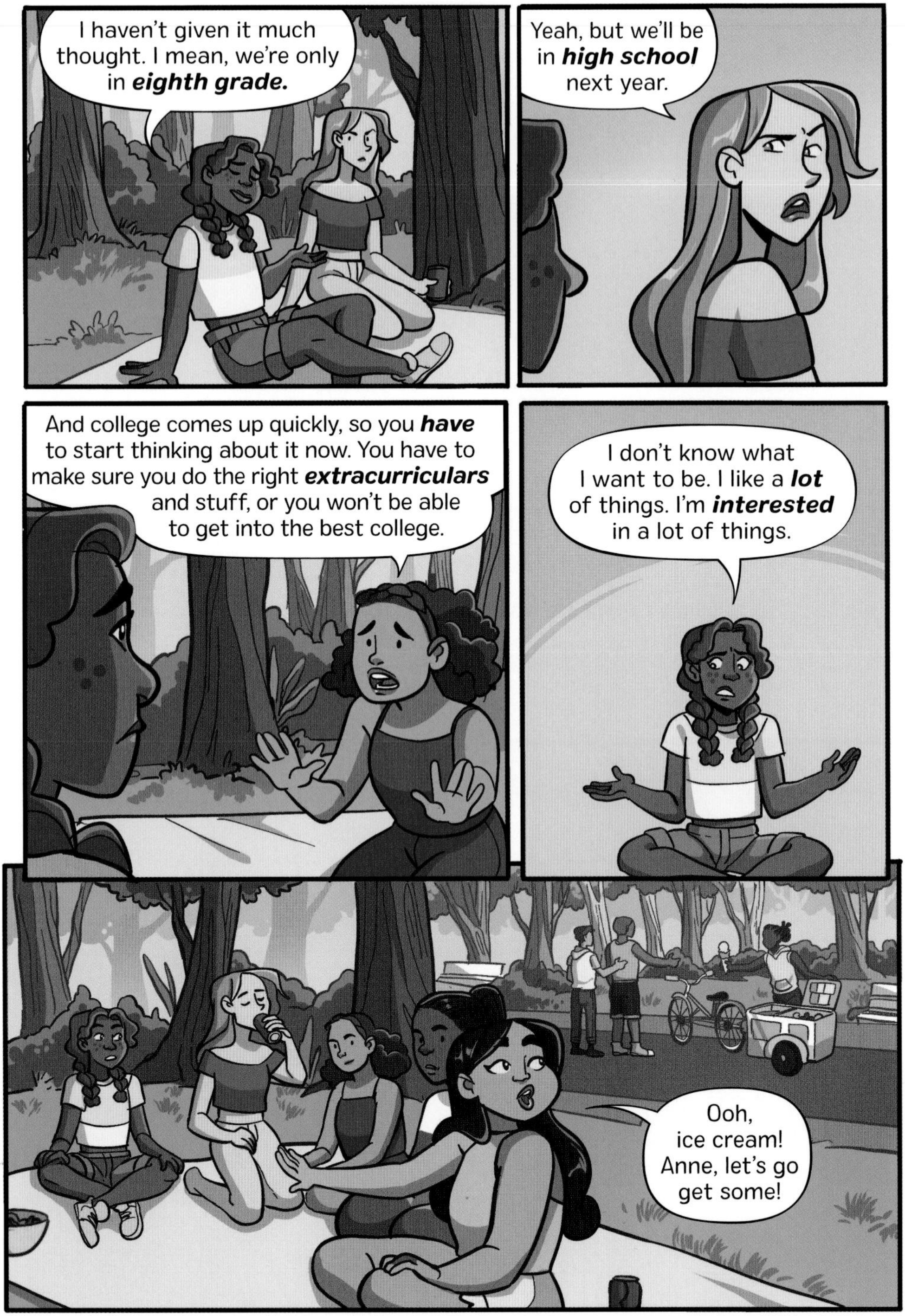
I haven't given it much thought. I mean, we're only in ***eighth grade.***
Yeah, but we'll be in ***high school*** next year.
And college comes up quickly, so you ***have*** to start thinking about it now. You have to make sure you do the right ***extracurriculars*** and stuff, or you won't be able to get into the best college.
I don't know what I want to be. I like a ***lot*** of things. I'm ***interested*** in a lot of things.
Ooh, ice cream! Anne, let's go get some!

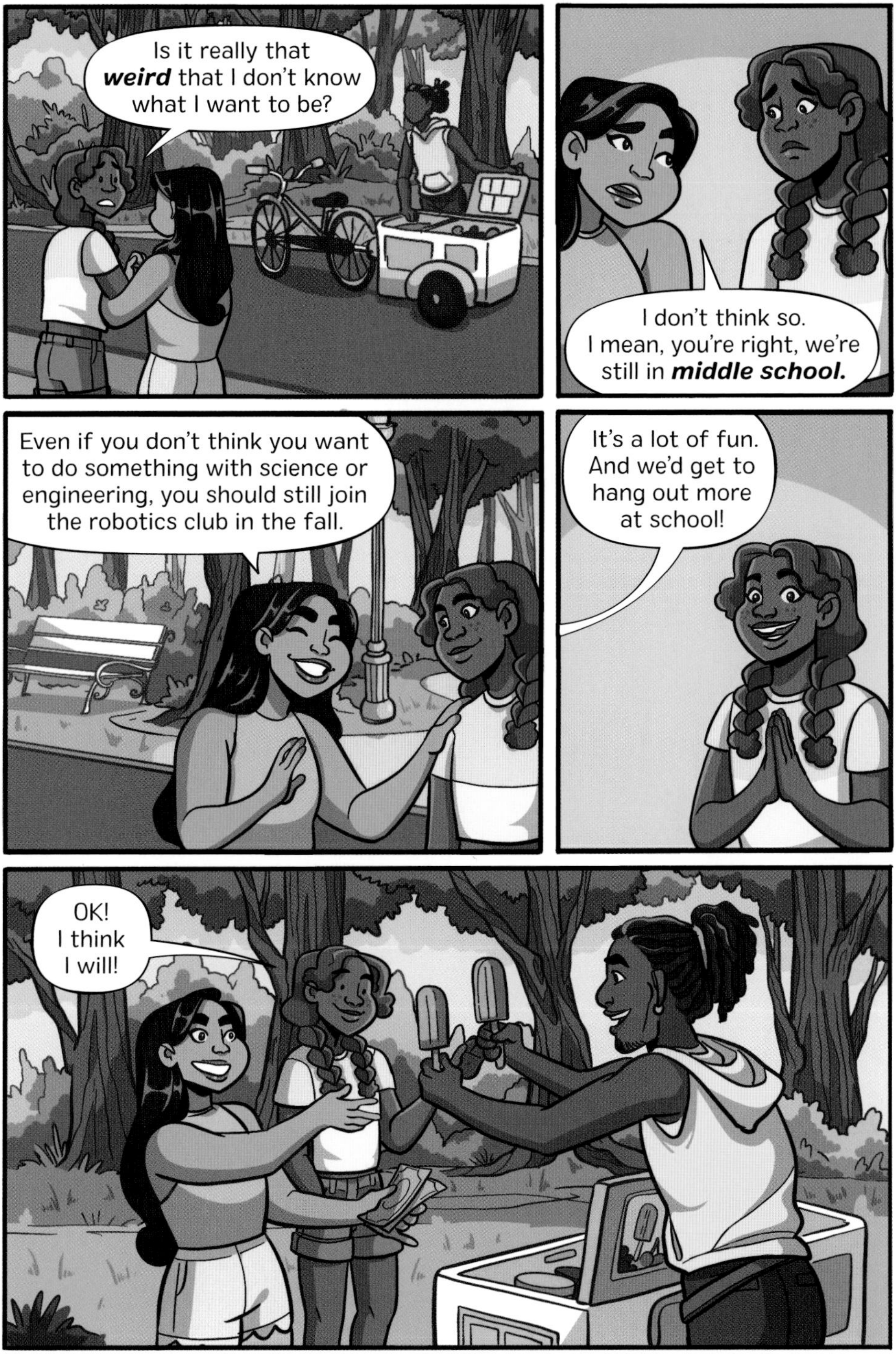
Is it really that **weird** that I don't know what I want to be?
I don't think so. I mean, you're right, we're still in **middle school.**
Even if you don't think you want to do something with science or engineering, you should still join the robotics club in the fall.
It's a lot of fun. And we'd get to hang out more at school!
OK! I think I will!

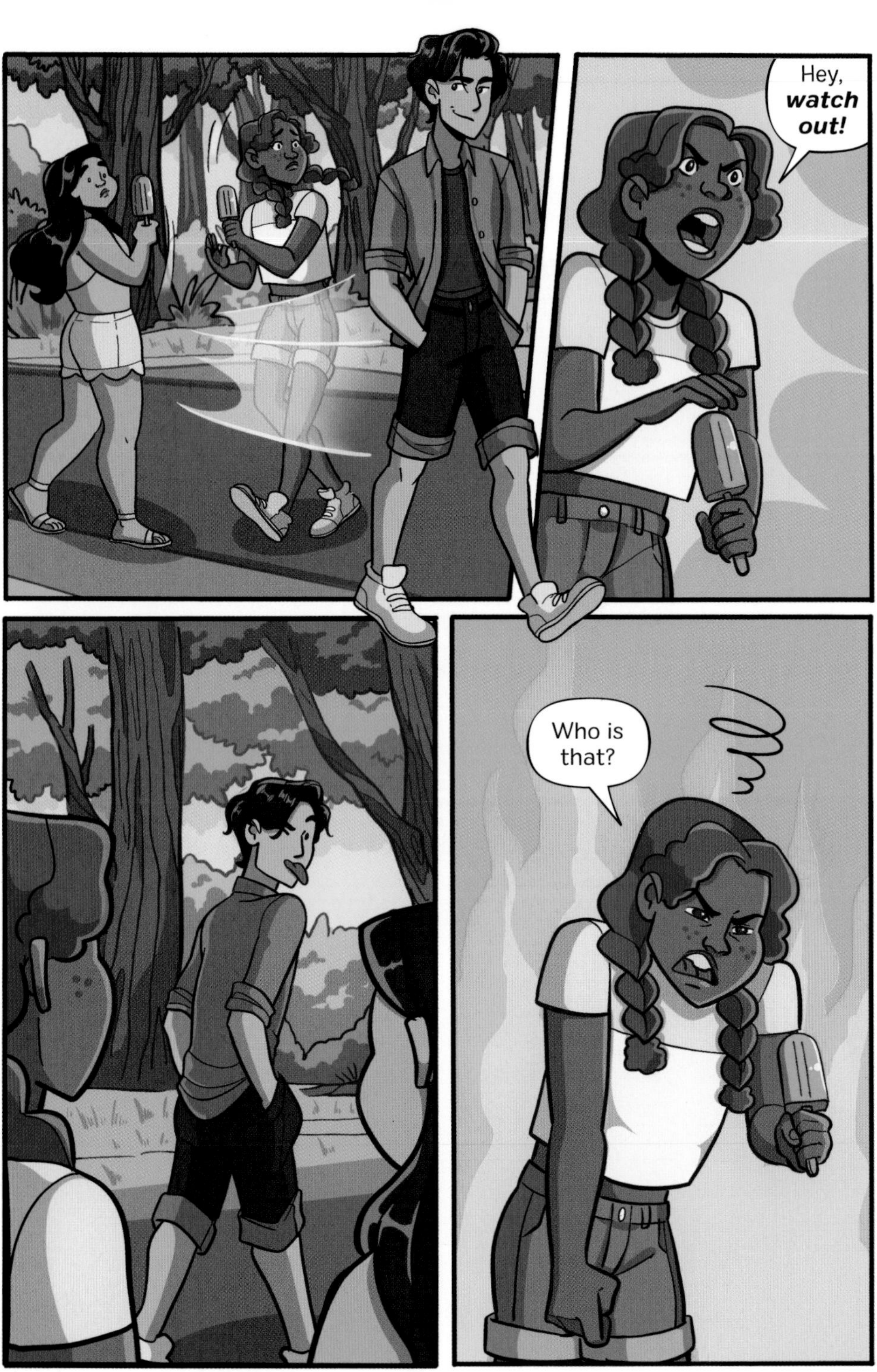
Hey, ***watch out!***
Who is that?

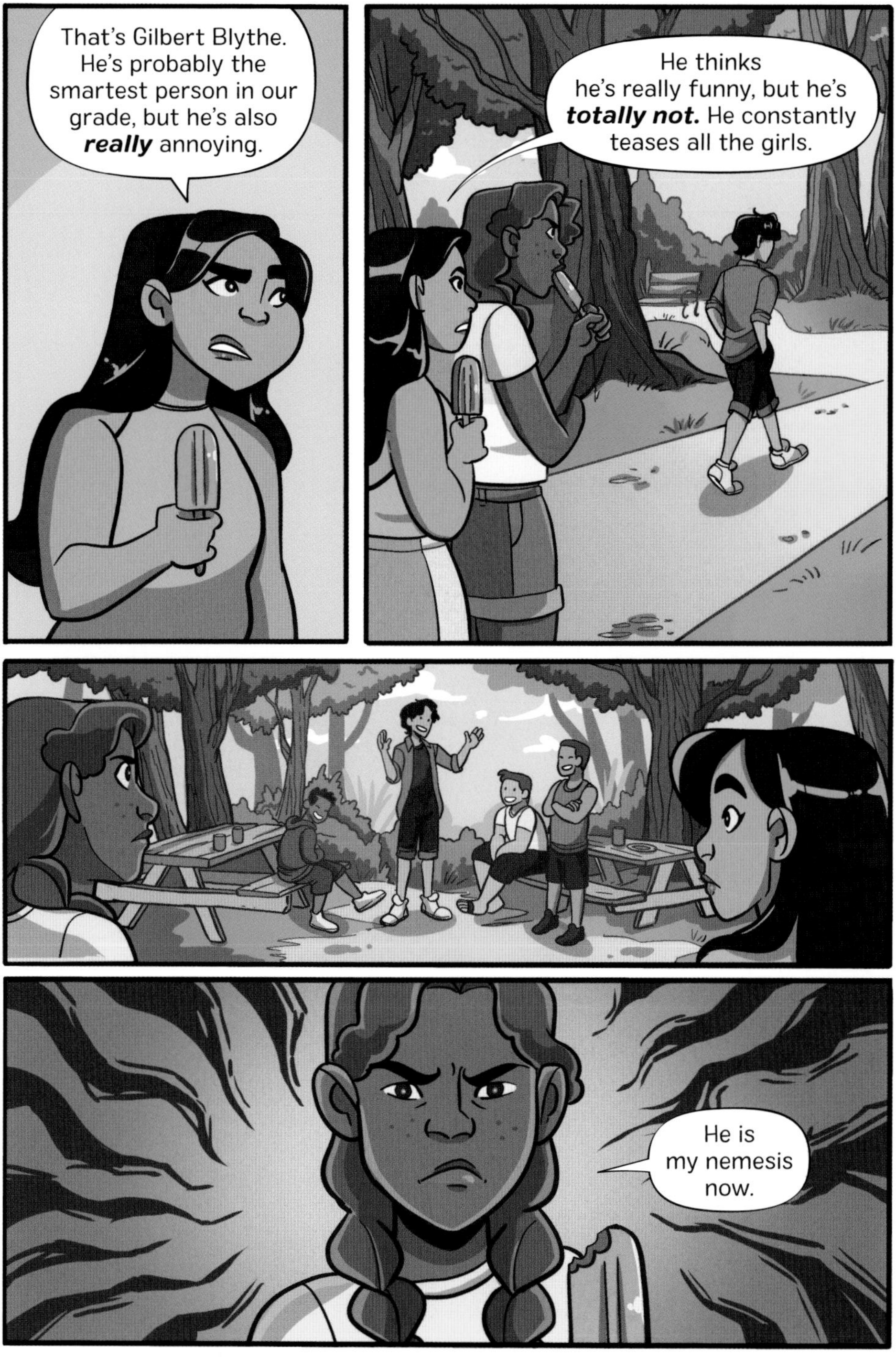
That's Gilbert Blythe. He's probably the smartest person in our grade, but he's also **really** annoying.
He thinks he's really funny, but he's **totally not.** He constantly teases all the girls.
He is my nemesis now.

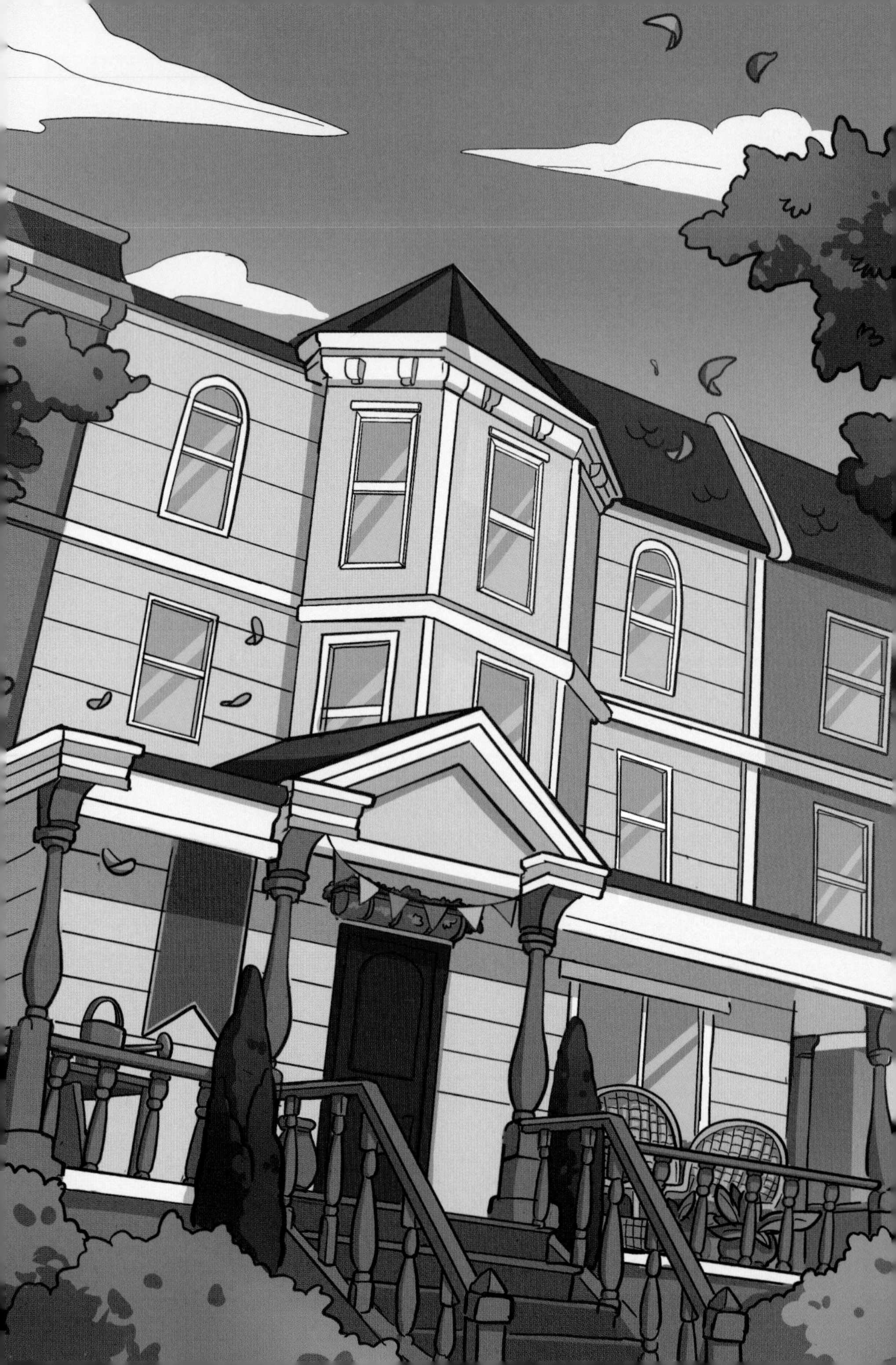

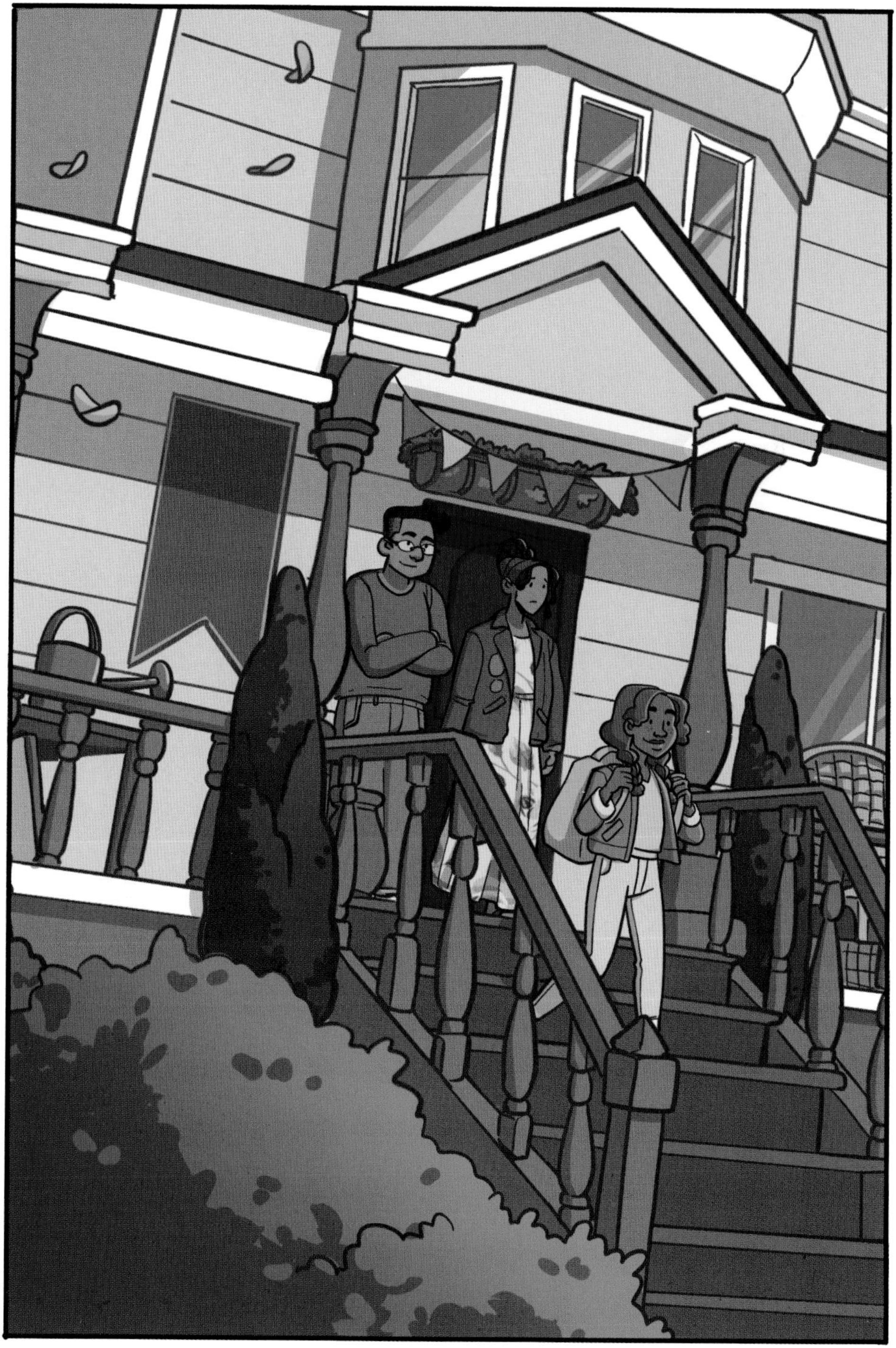

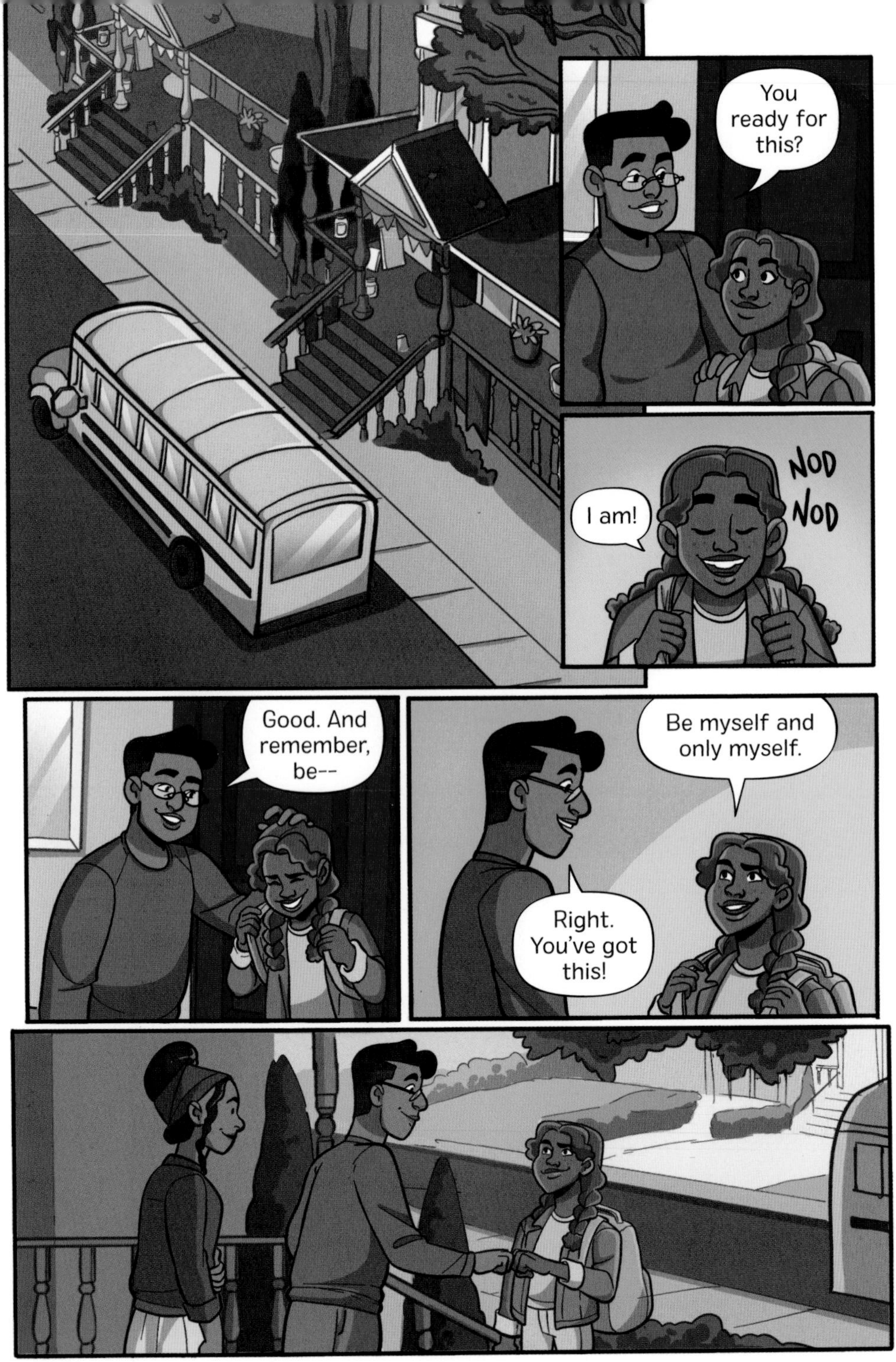
You ready for this?
I am!
NOD NOD
Good. And remember, be--
Be myself and only myself.
Right. You've got this!

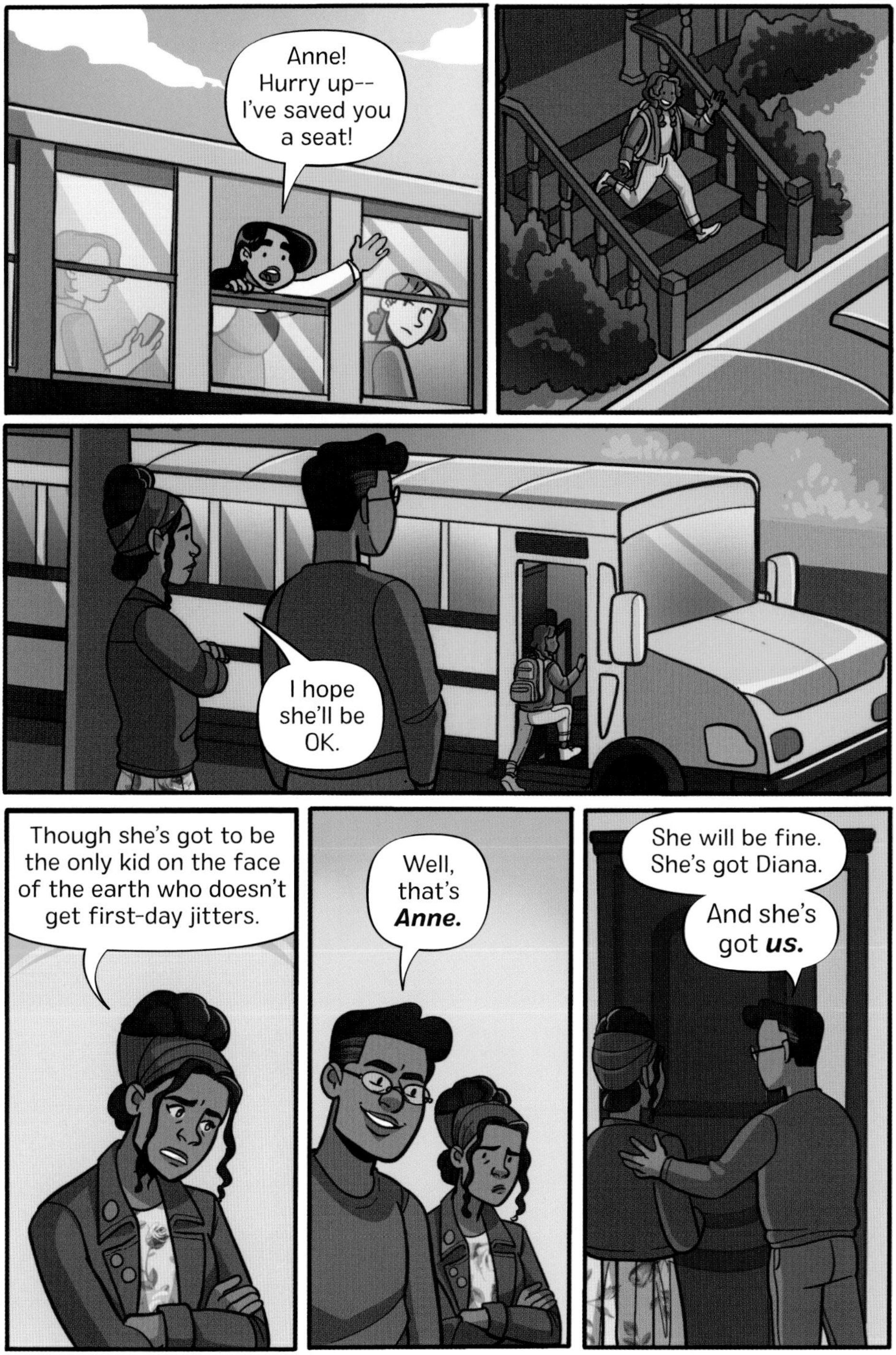
Anne! Hurry up-- I've saved you a seat!
I hope she'll be OK.
Though she's got to be the only kid on the face of the earth who doesn't get first-day jitters.
Well, that's ***Anne.***
She will be fine. She's got Diana.
And she's got ***us.***

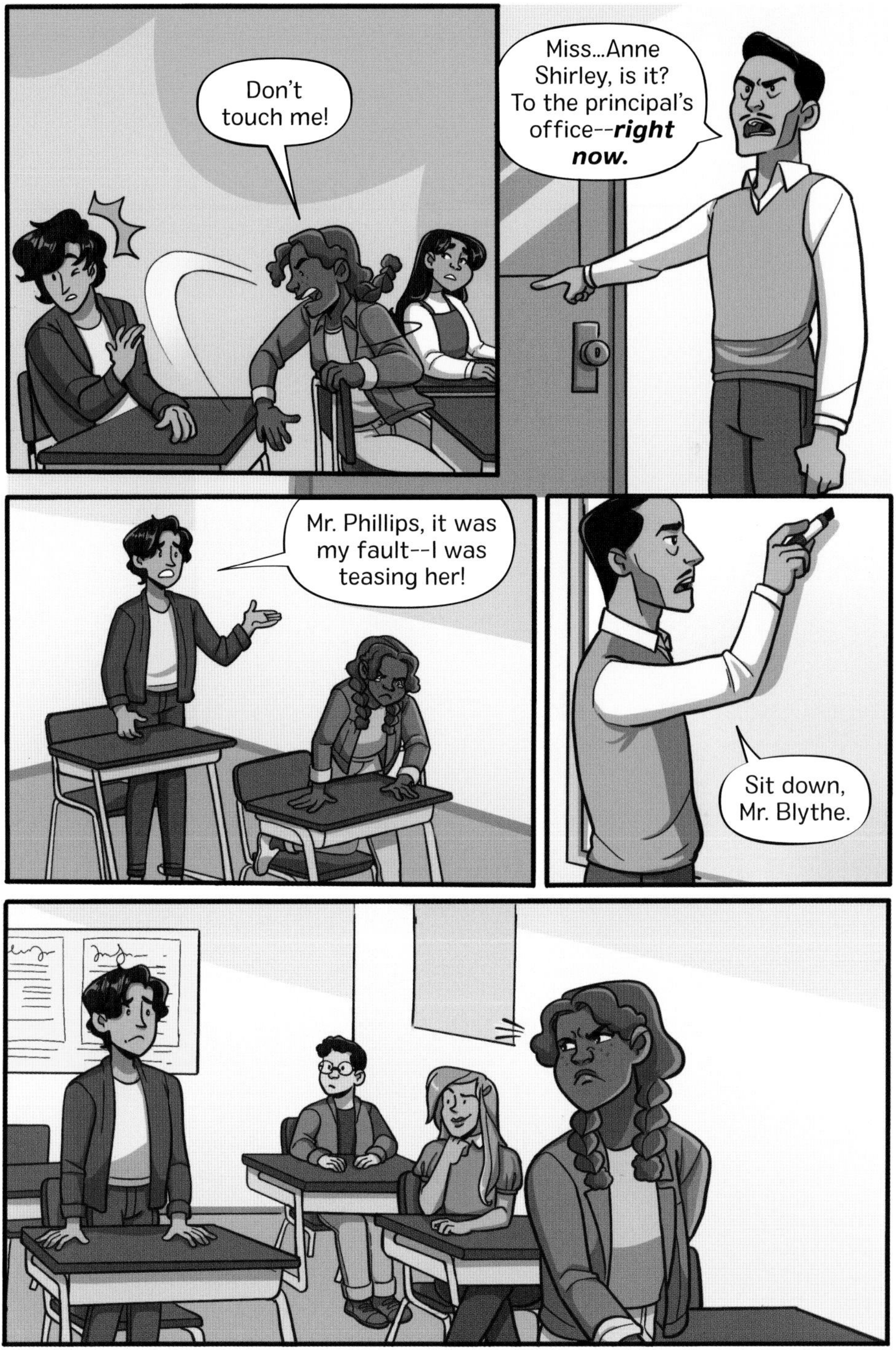
Don't touch me!
Miss...Anne Shirley, is it? To the principal's office--***right now.***
Mr. Phillips, it was my fault--I was teasing her!
Sit down, Mr. Blythe.

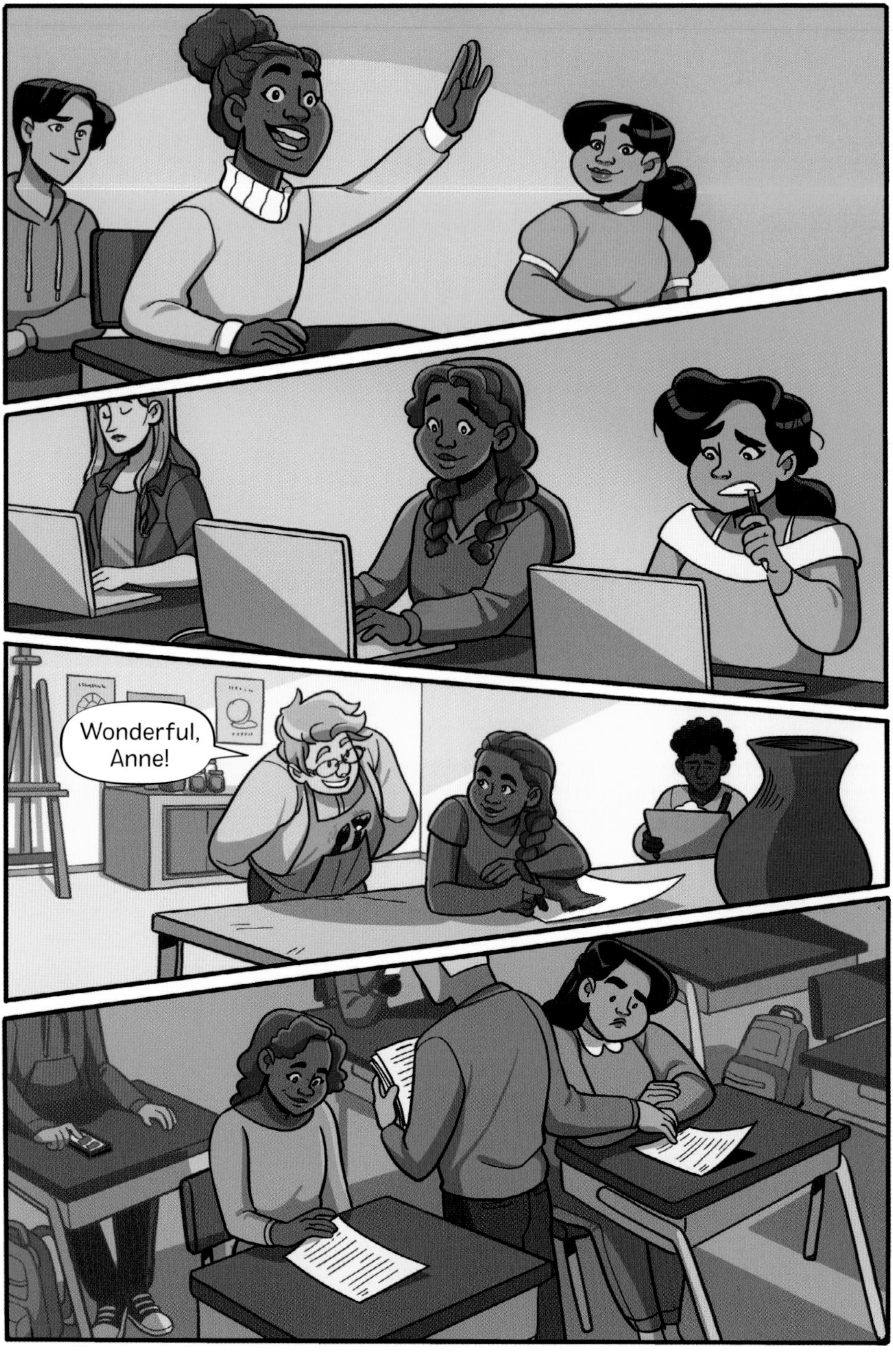
Wonderful, Anne!

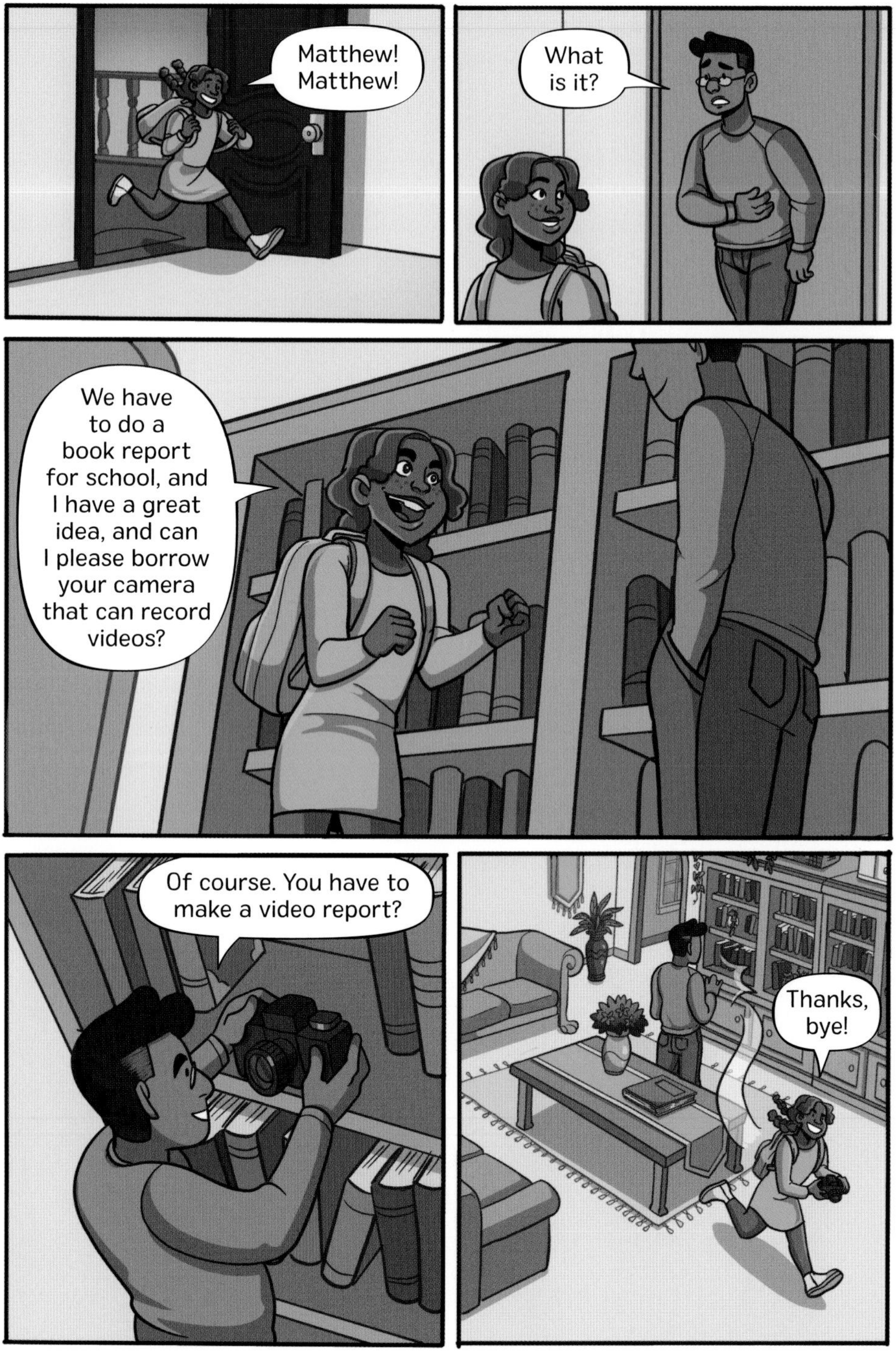
Matthew!
Matthew!
What is it?
We have to do a book report for school, and I have a great idea, and can I please borrow your camera that can record videos?
Of course. You have to make a video report?
Thanks, bye!

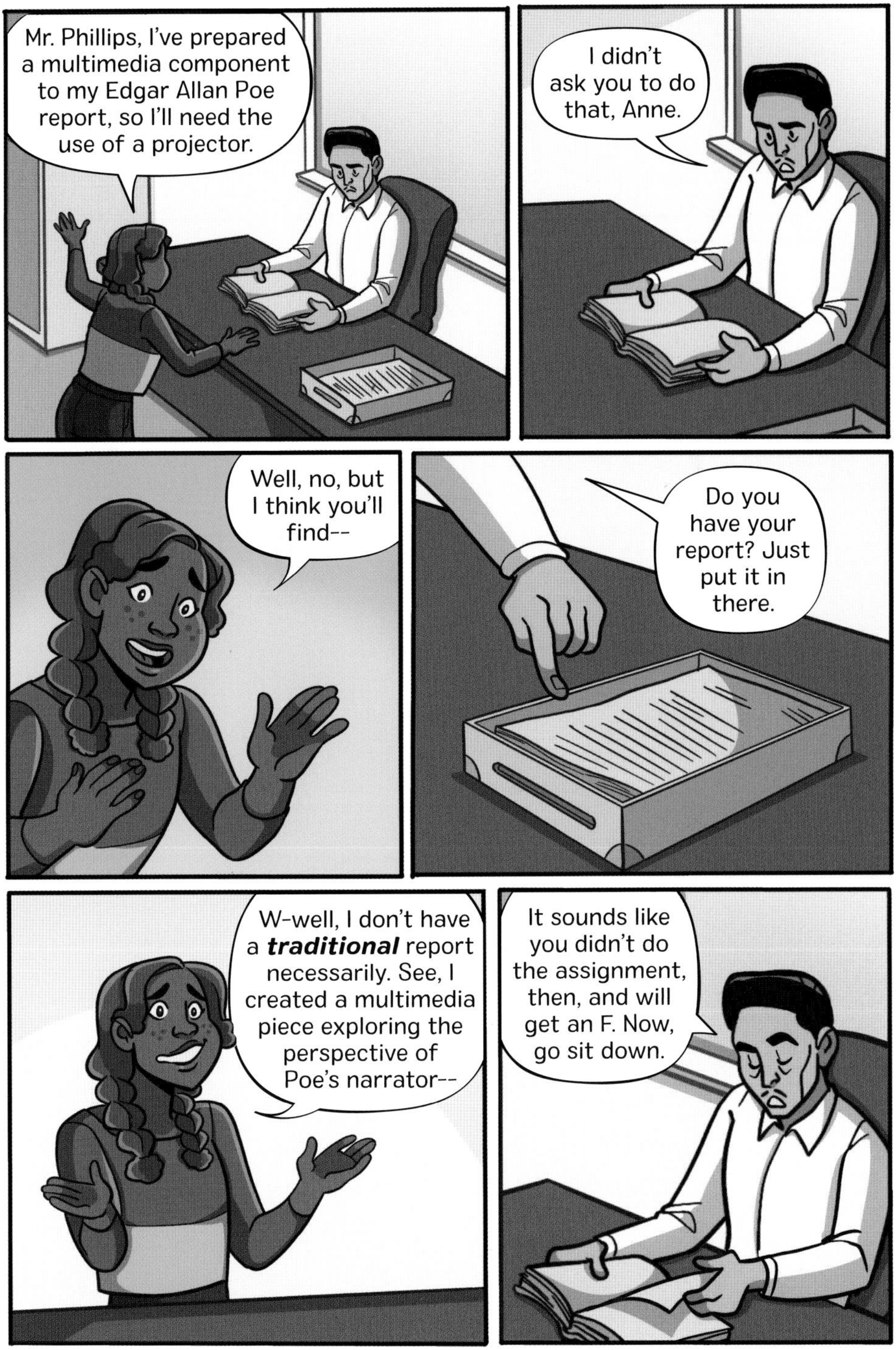
Mr. Phillips, I've prepared a multimedia component to my Edgar Allan Poe report, so I'll need the use of a projector.
I didn't ask you to do that, Anne.
Well, no, but I think you'll find--
Do you have your report? Just put it in there.
W-well, I don't have a ***traditional*** report necessarily. See, I created a multimedia piece exploring the perspective of Poe's narrator--
It sounds like you didn't do the assignment, then, and will get an F. Now, go sit down.

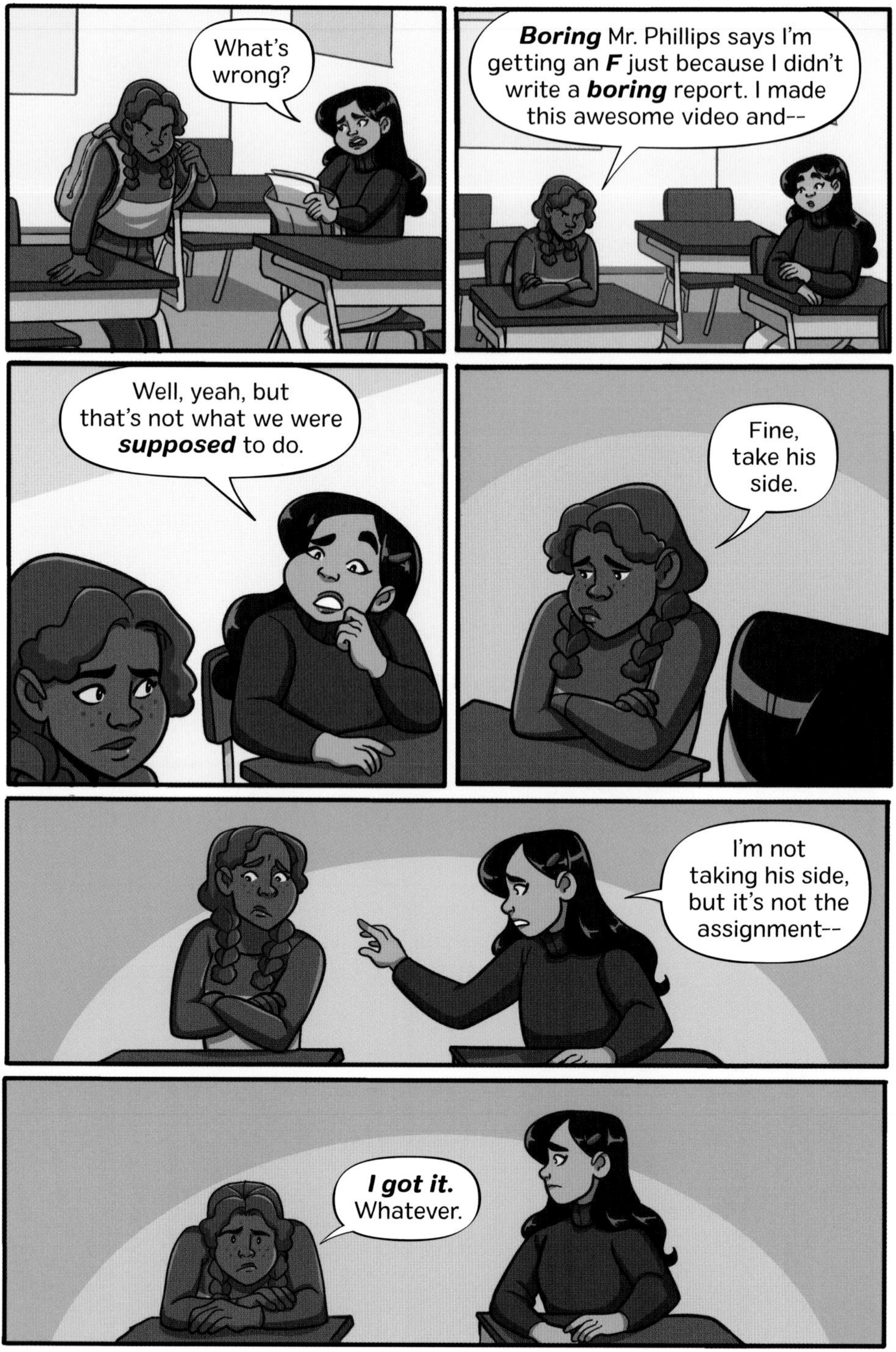
What's wrong?
Boring Mr. Phillips says I'm getting an ***F*** just because I didn't write a ***boring*** report. I made this awesome video and--
Well, yeah, but that's not what we were ***supposed*** to do.
Fine, take his side.
I'm not taking his side, but it's not the assignment--
I got it. Whatever.

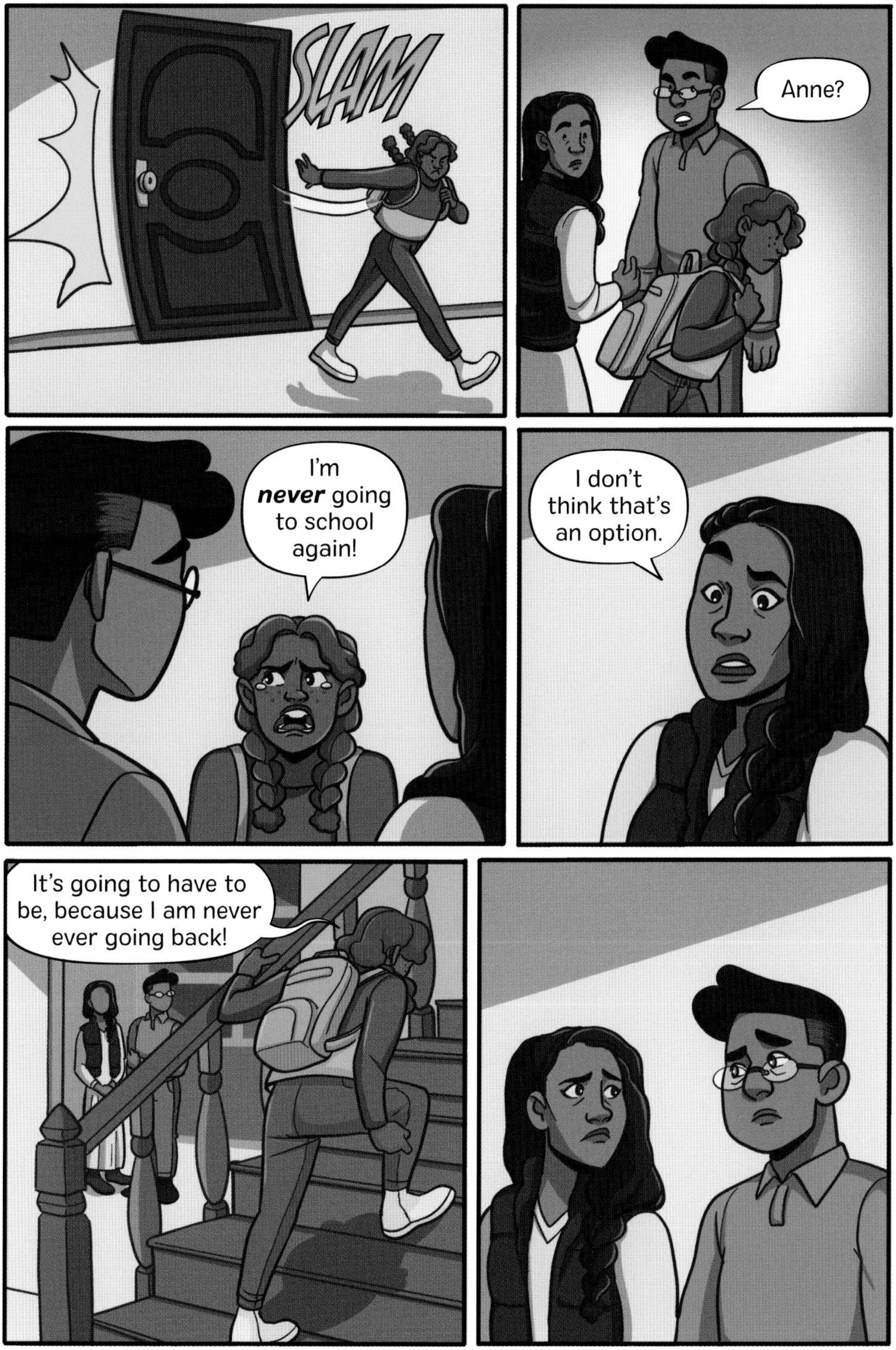
SLAM
Anne?
I'm ***never*** going to school again!
I don't think that's an option.
It's going to have to be, because I am never ever going back!

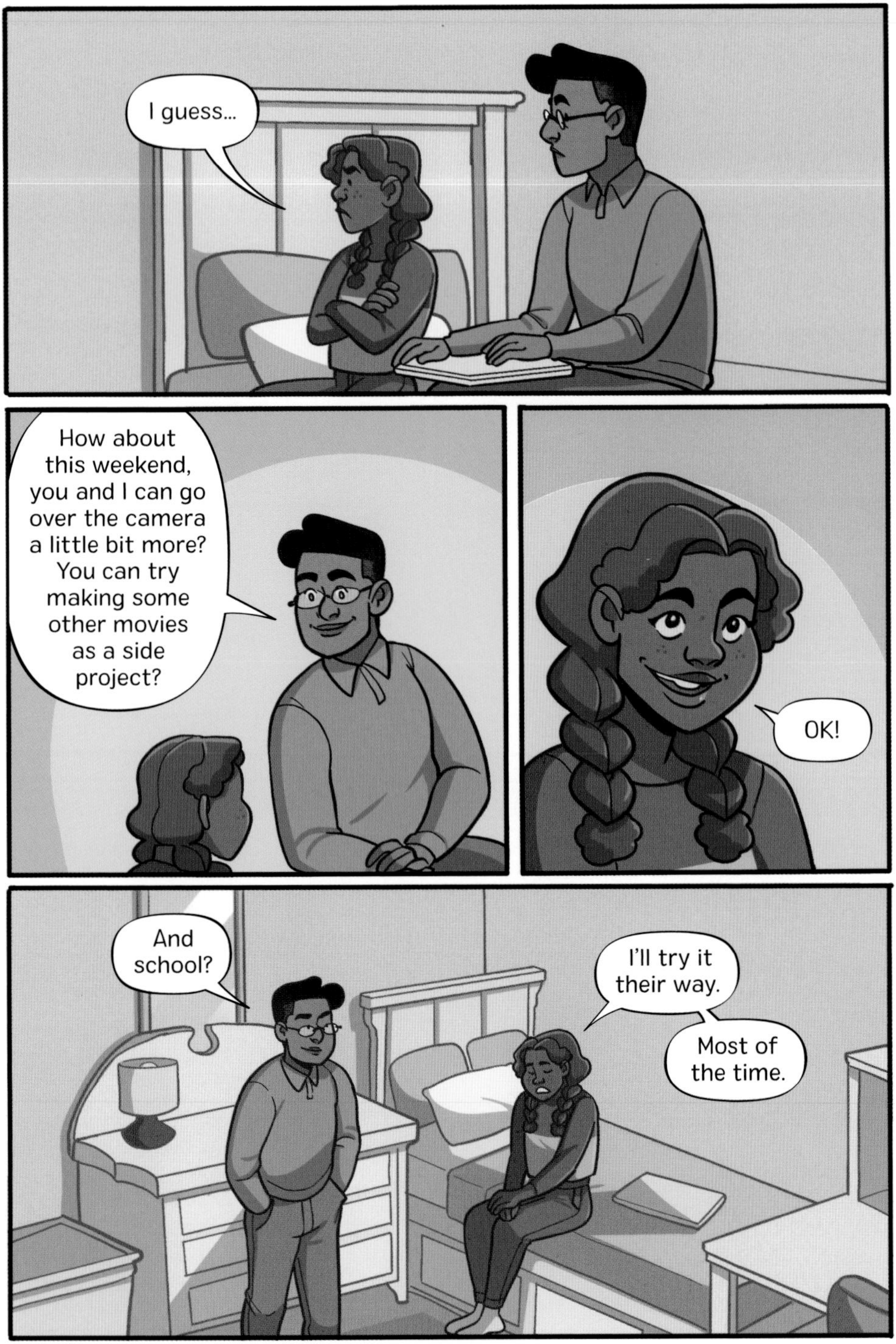
I guess...
How about this weekend, you and I can go over the camera a little bit more? You can try making some other movies as a side project?
OK!
And school?
I'll try it their way.
Most of the time.

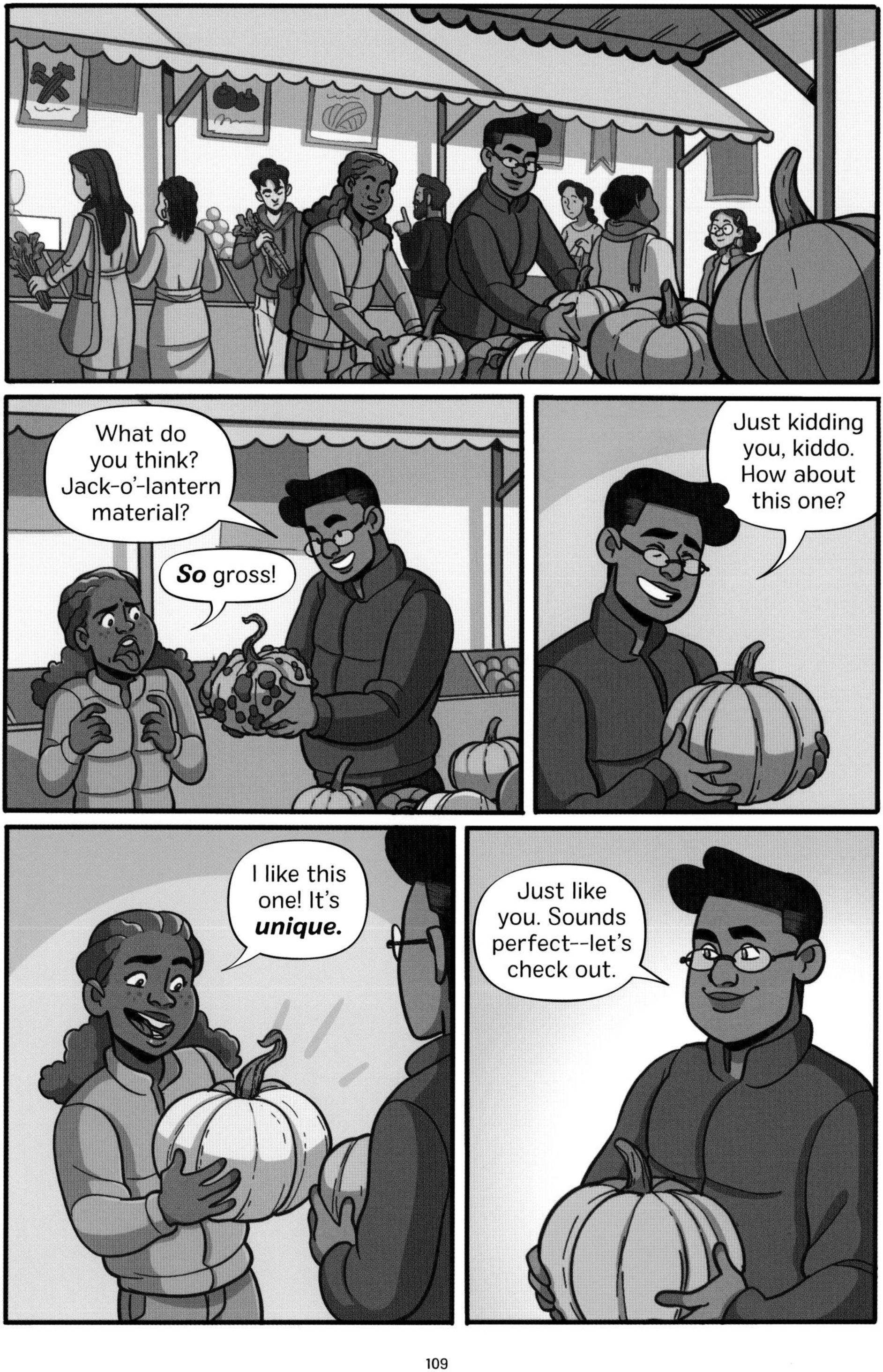
What do you think? Jack-o'-lantern material?
So gross!
Just kidding you, kiddo. How about this one?
I like this one! It's ***unique.***
Just like you. Sounds perfect--let's check out.

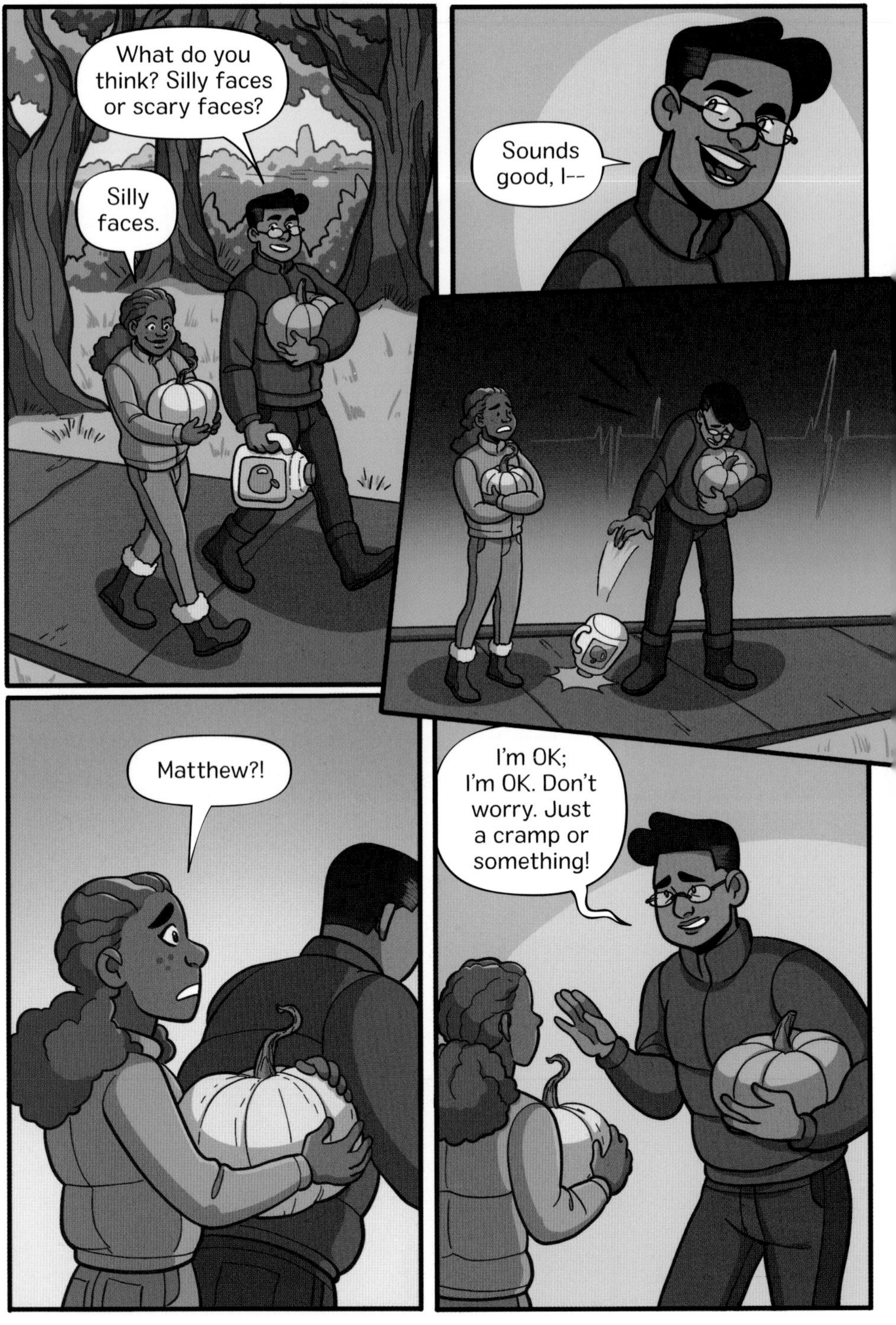

What do you think? Silly faces or scary faces?
Silly faces.
Sounds good, I--
Matthew?!
I'm OK; I'm OK. Don't worry. Just a cramp or something!

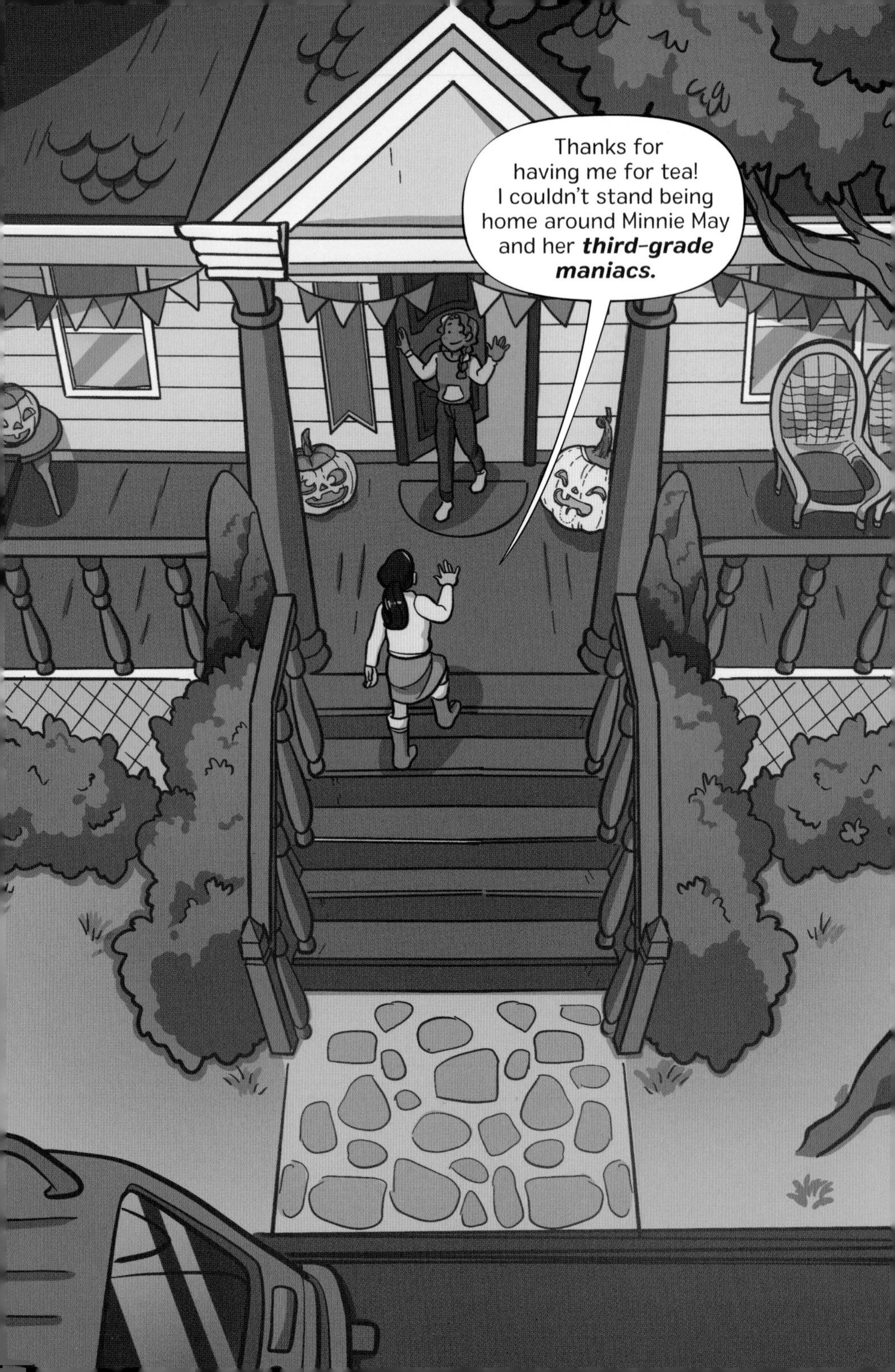
Thanks for having me for tea! I couldn't stand being home around Minnie May and her ***third-grade maniacs.***

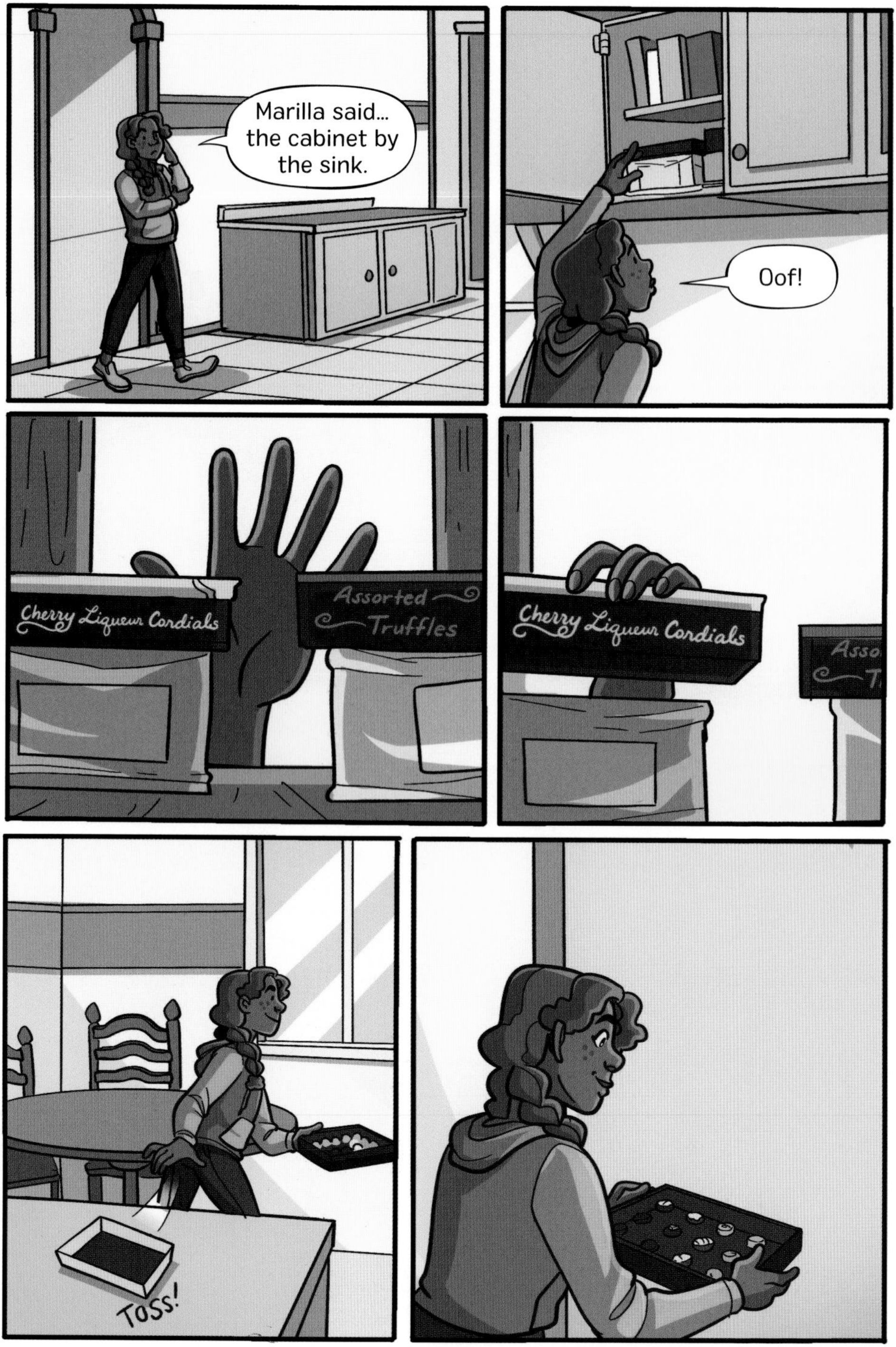
Marilla said... the cabinet by the sink.
Oof!
Cherry Liqueur Cordials
Assorted Truffles
Cherry Liqueur Cordials
TOSS!

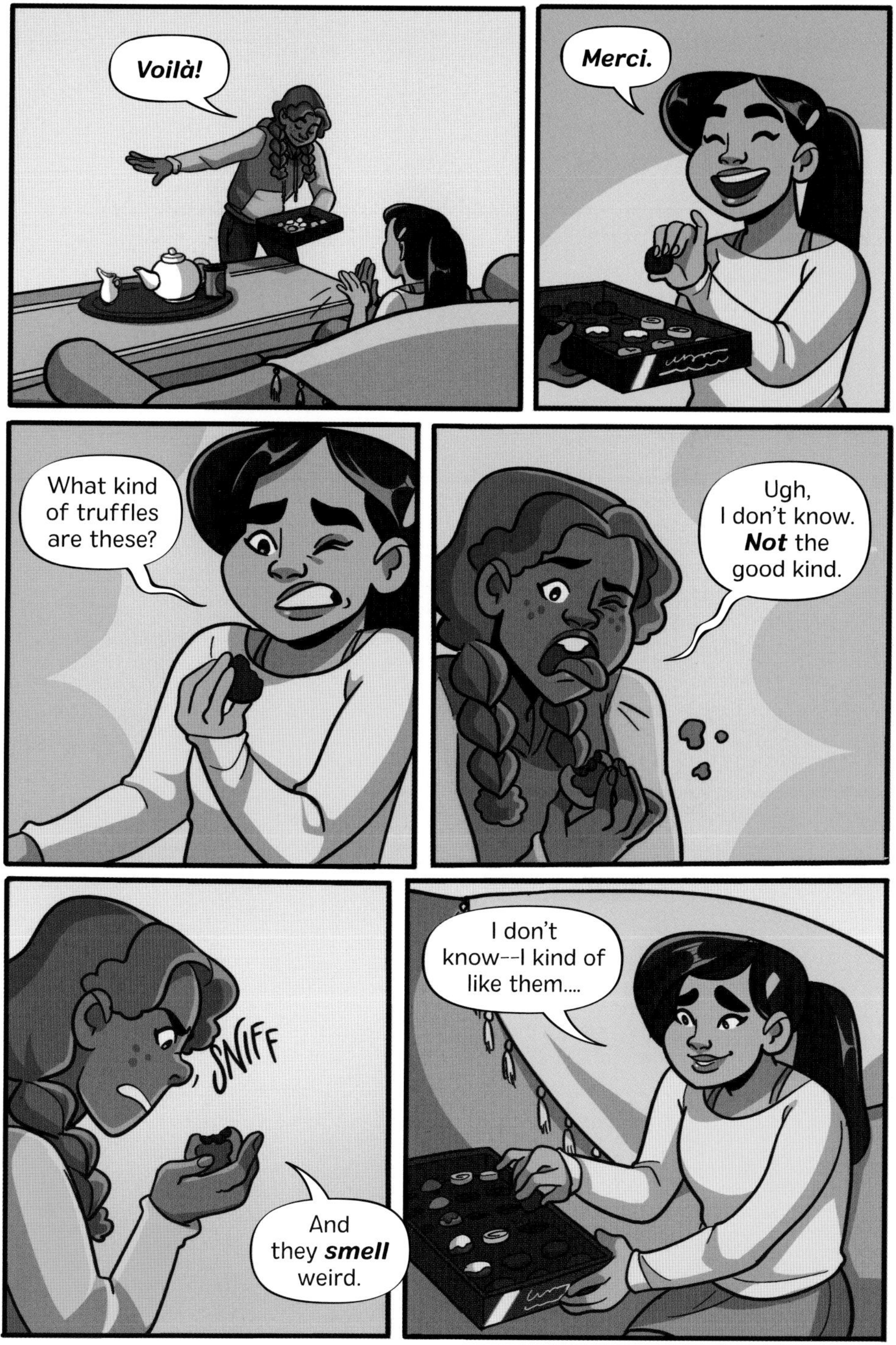

Voilà!
Merci.
What kind of truffles are these?
Ugh, I don't know. Not the good kind.
SNIFF
And they smell weird.
I don't know--I kind of like them....

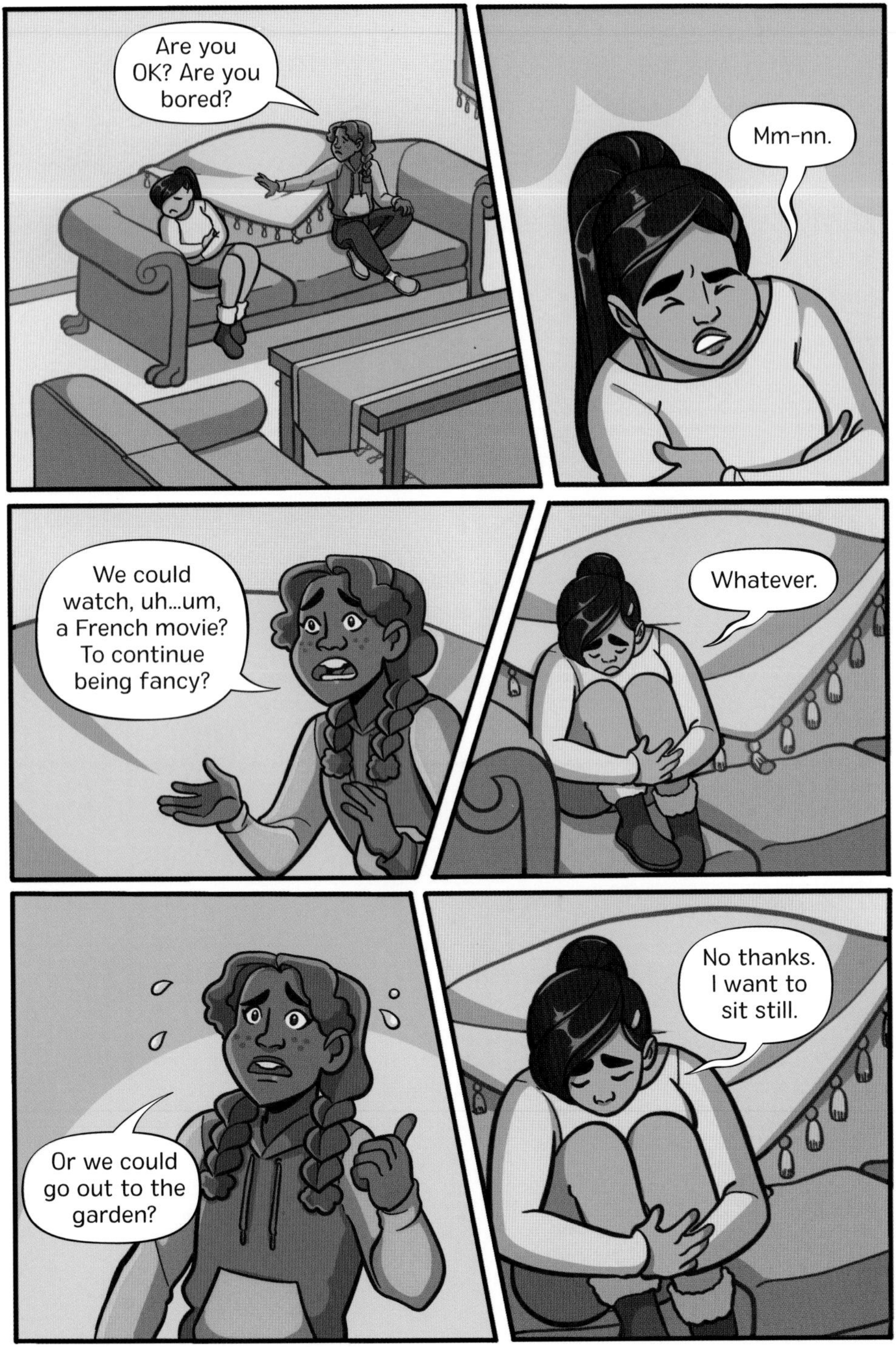
Are you OK? Are you bored?
Mm-nn.
We could watch, uh...um, a French movie? To continue being fancy?
Whatever.
Or we could go out to the garden?
No thanks. I want to sit still.

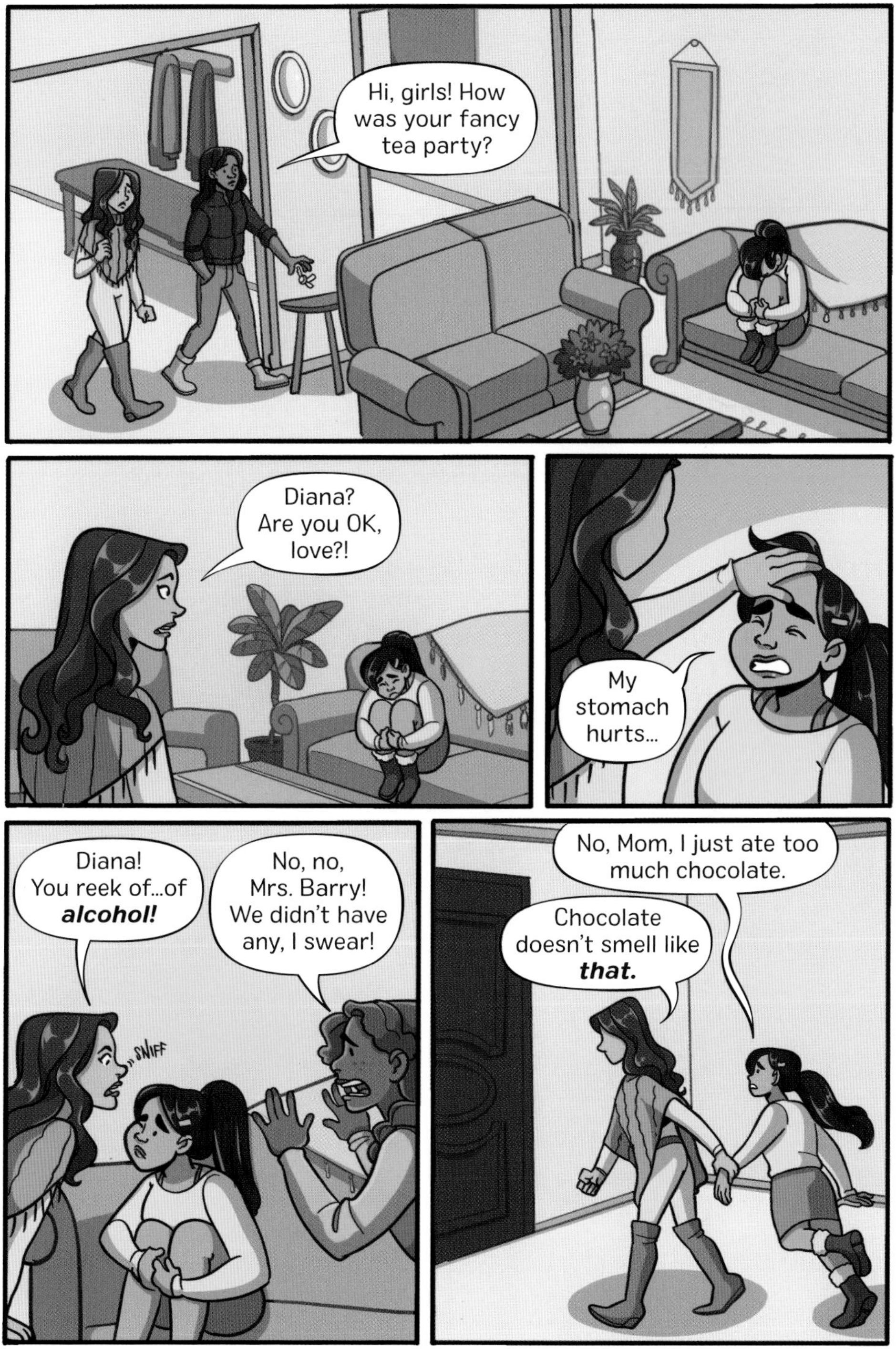

Hi, girls! How was your fancy tea party?
Diana? Are you OK, love?!
My stomach hurts...
Diana! You reek of...of ***alcohol!***
SNIFF
No, no, Mrs. Barry! We didn't have any, I swear!
No, Mom, I just ate too much chocolate.
Chocolate doesn't smell like ***that.***

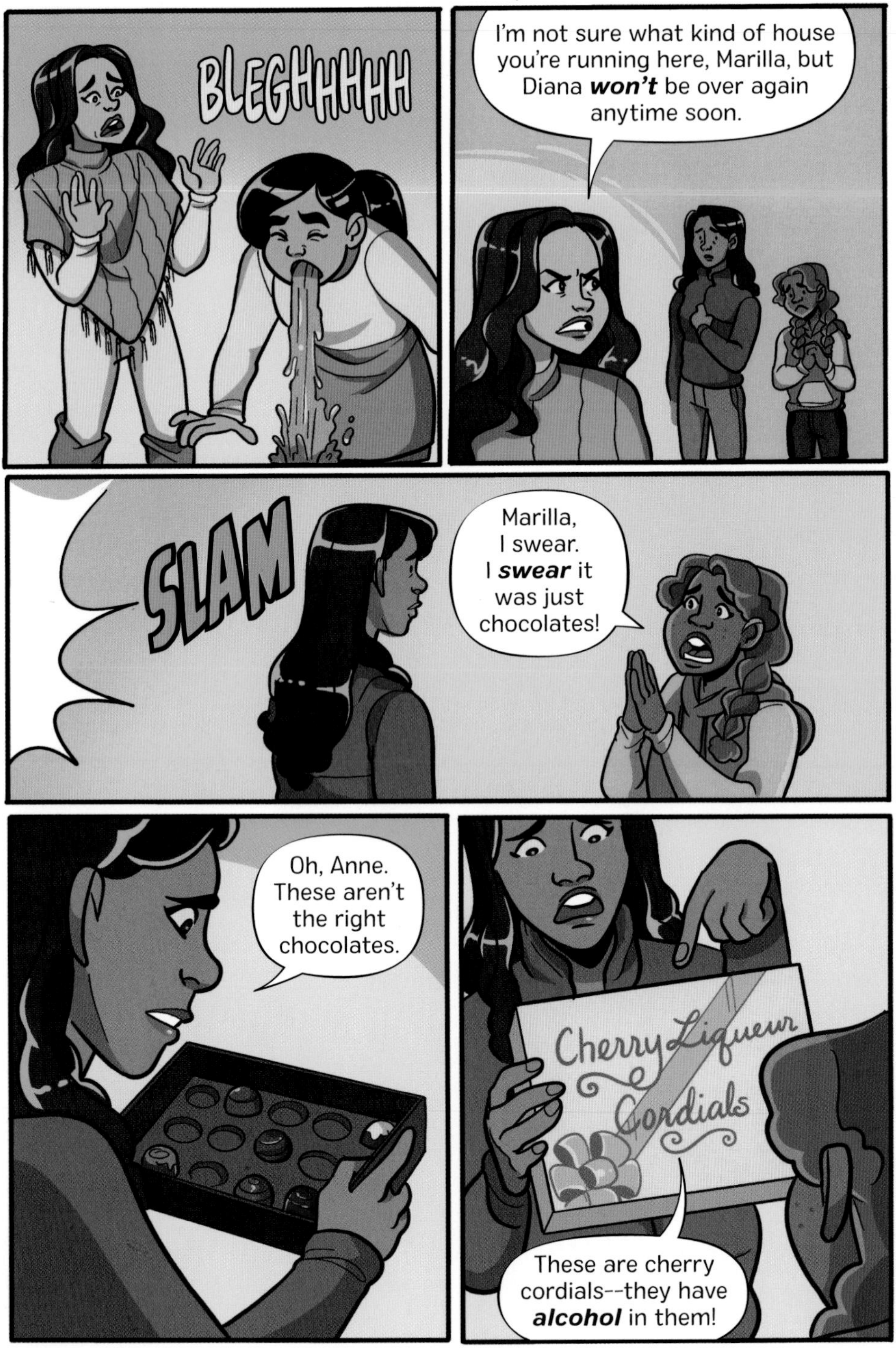
BLEGHHHHH
I'm not sure what kind of house you're running here, Marilla, but Diana **won't** be over again anytime soon.
SLAM
Marilla, I swear. I **swear** it was just chocolates!
Oh, Anne. These aren't the right chocolates.
Cherry Liqueur Cordials
These are cherry cordials--they have **alcohol** in them!

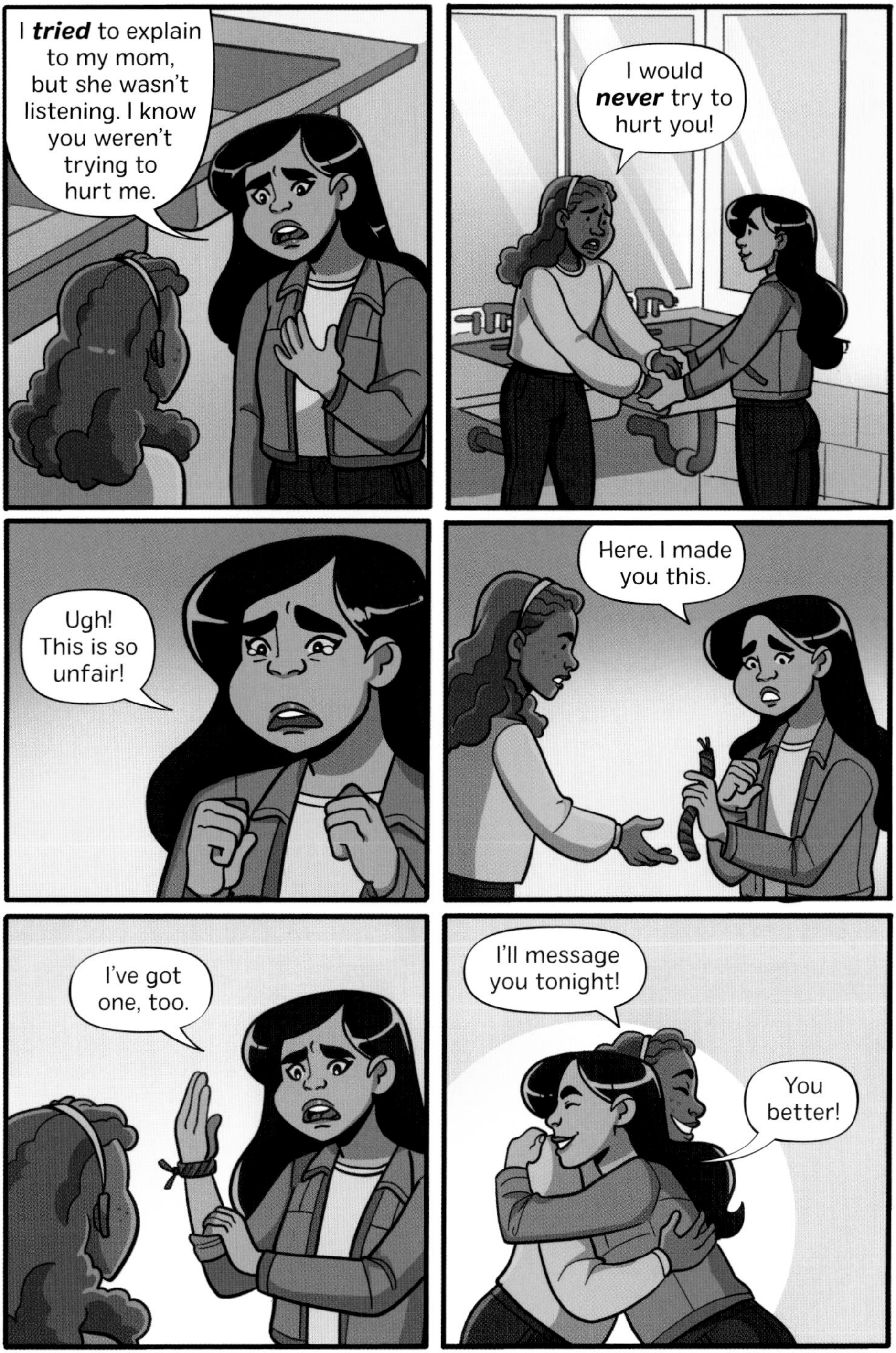
I **tried** to explain to my mom, but she wasn't listening. I know you weren't trying to hurt me.
I would **never** try to hurt you!
Ugh! This is so unfair!
Here. I made you this.
I've got one, too.
I'll message you tonight!
You better!

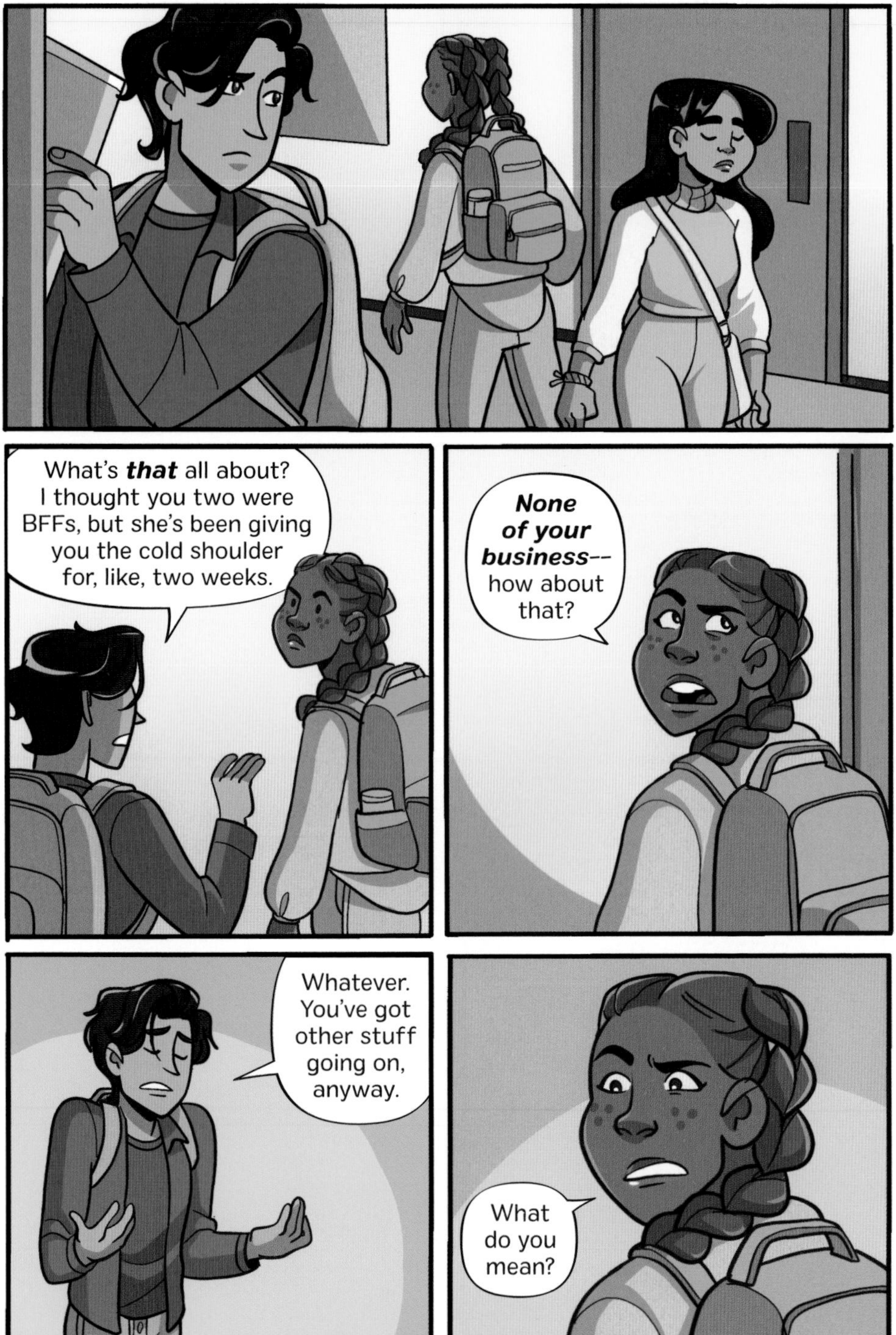
What's ***that*** all about? I thought you two were BFFs, but she's been giving you the cold shoulder for, like, two weeks.
None of your business-- how about that?
Whatever. You've got other stuff going on, anyway.
What do you mean?

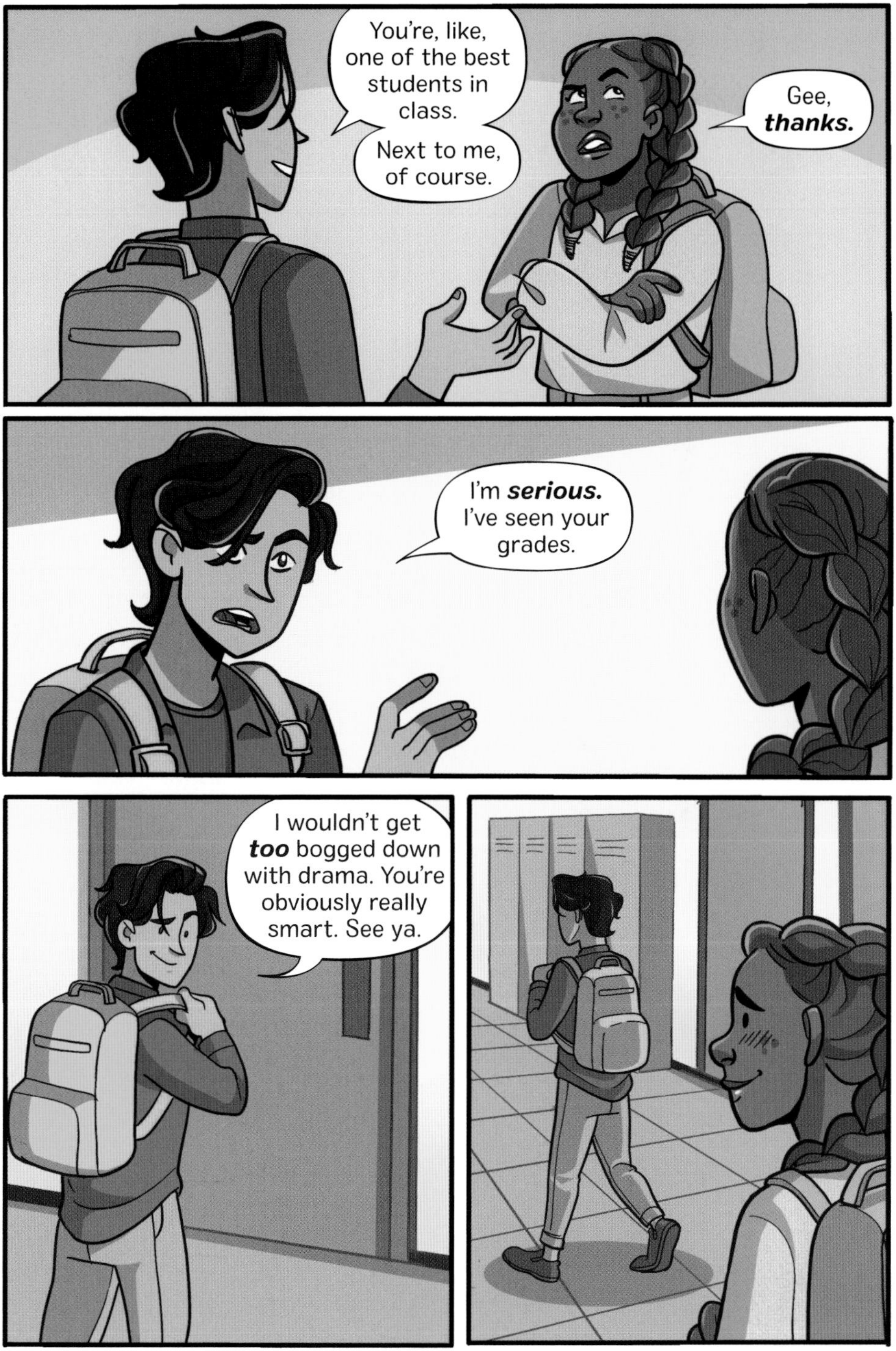
You're, like, one of the best students in class.
Next to me, of course.
Gee, ***thanks.***
I'm ***serious.*** I've seen your grades.
I wouldn't get ***too*** bogged down with drama. You're obviously really smart. See ya.

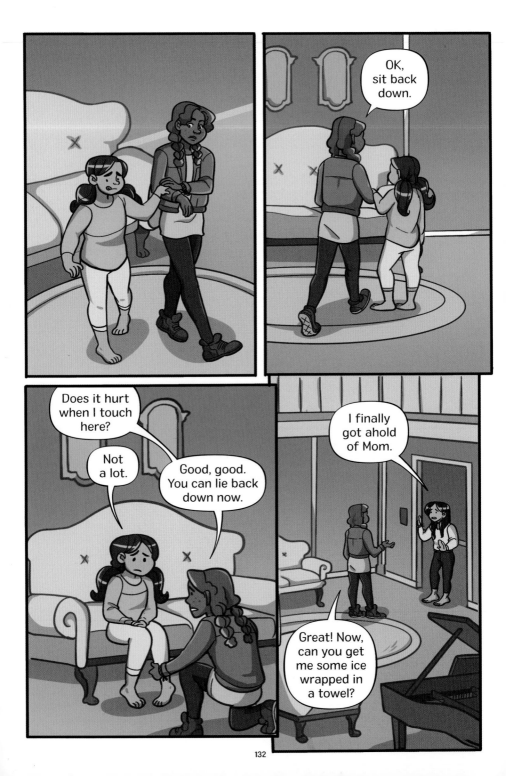

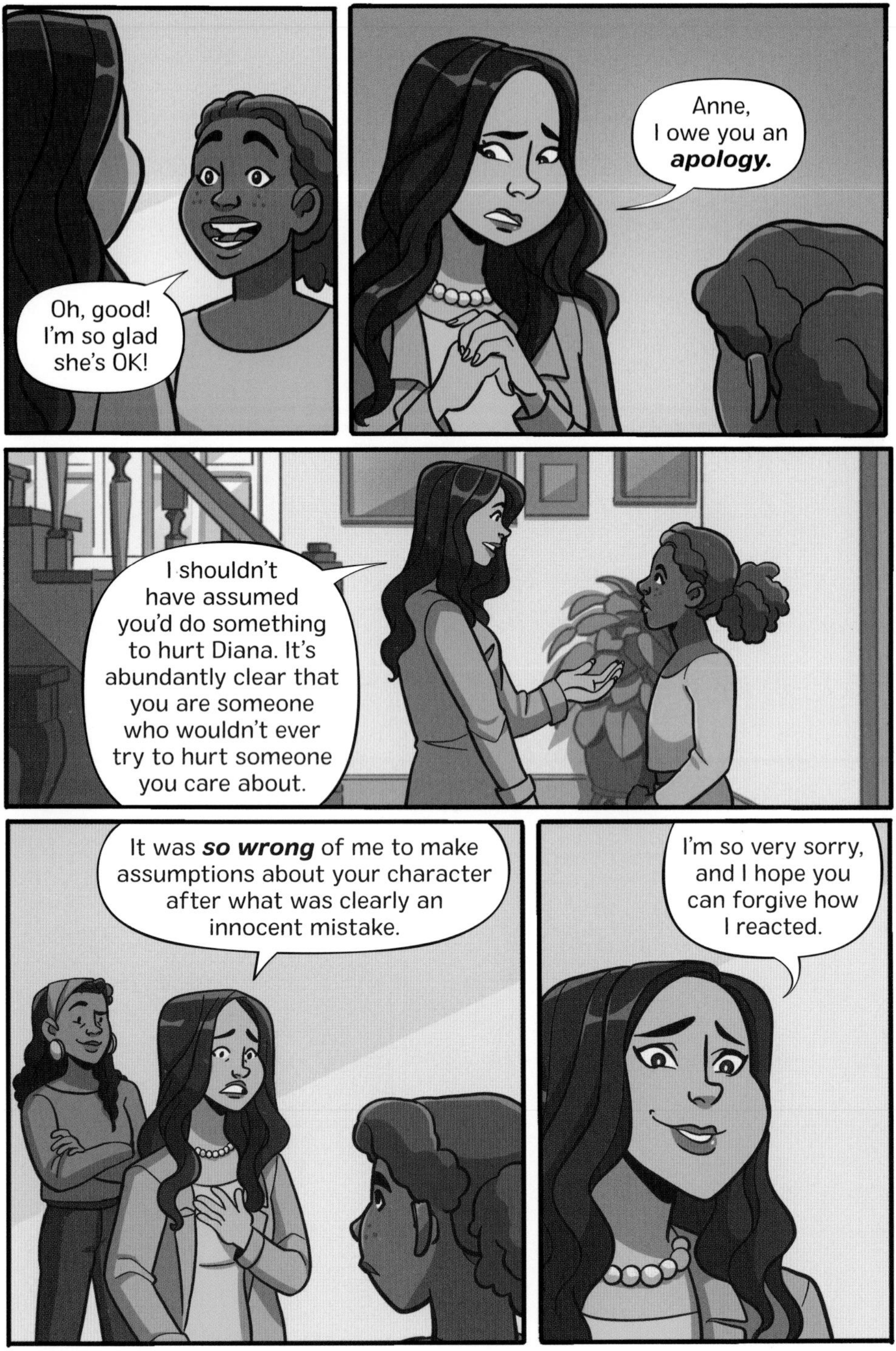
Oh, good!
I'm so glad
she's OK!
Anne,
I owe you an
apology.
I shouldn't
have assumed
you'd do something
to hurt Diana. It's
abundantly clear that
you are someone
who wouldn't ever
try to hurt someone
you care about.
It was ***so wrong*** of me to make
assumptions about your character
after what was clearly an
innocent mistake.
I'm so very sorry,
and I hope you
can forgive how
I reacted.

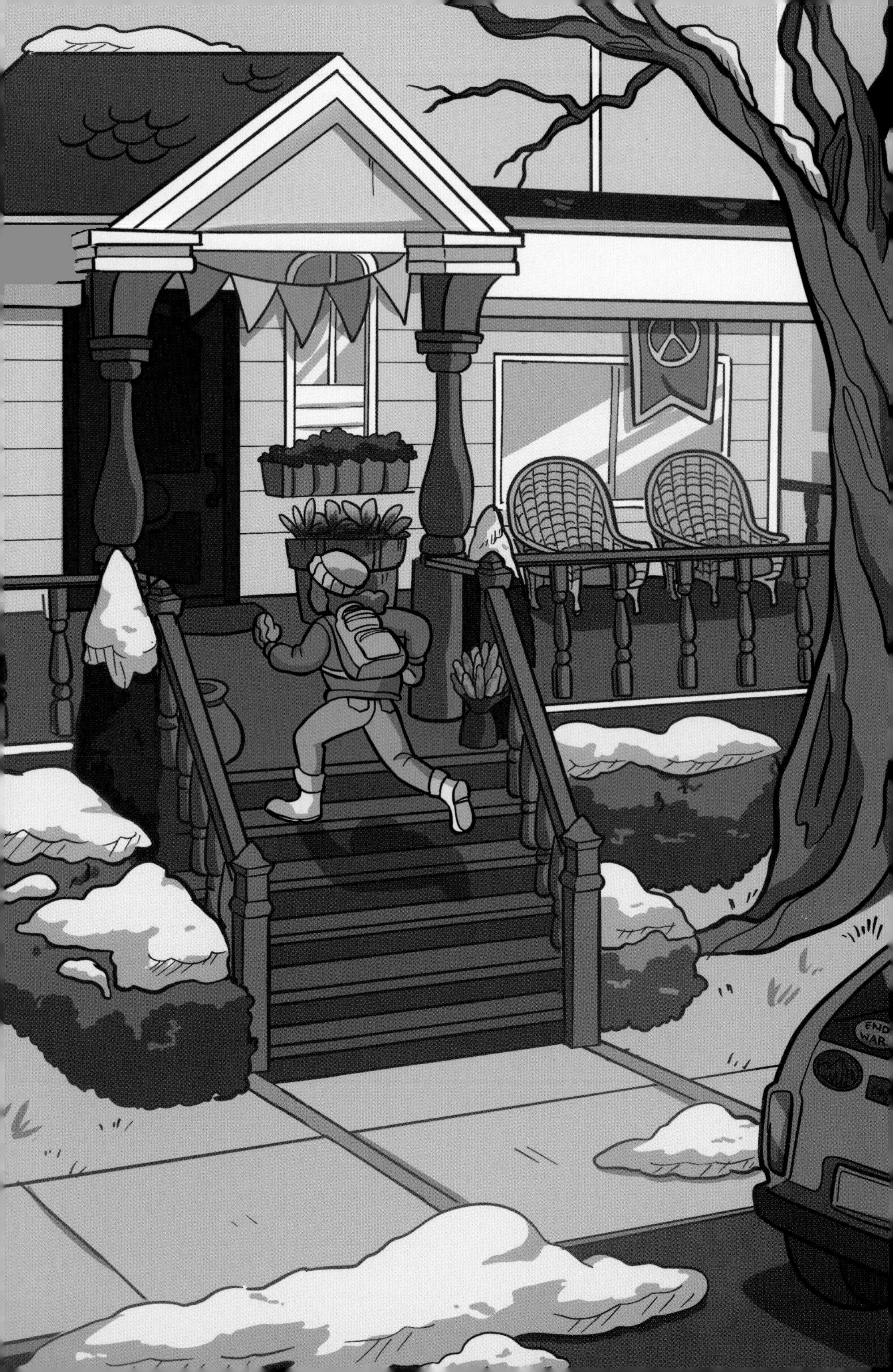
END WAR

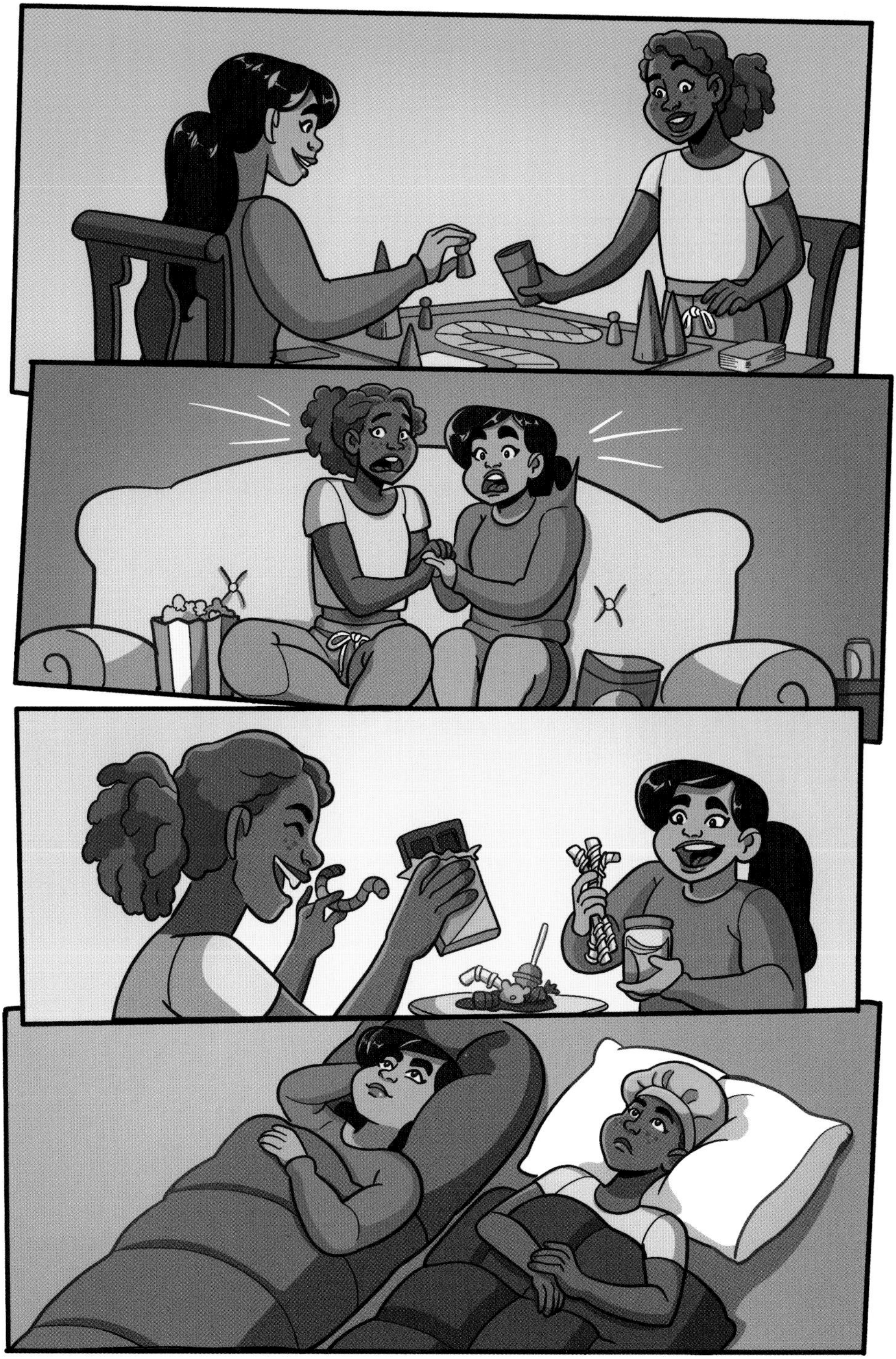

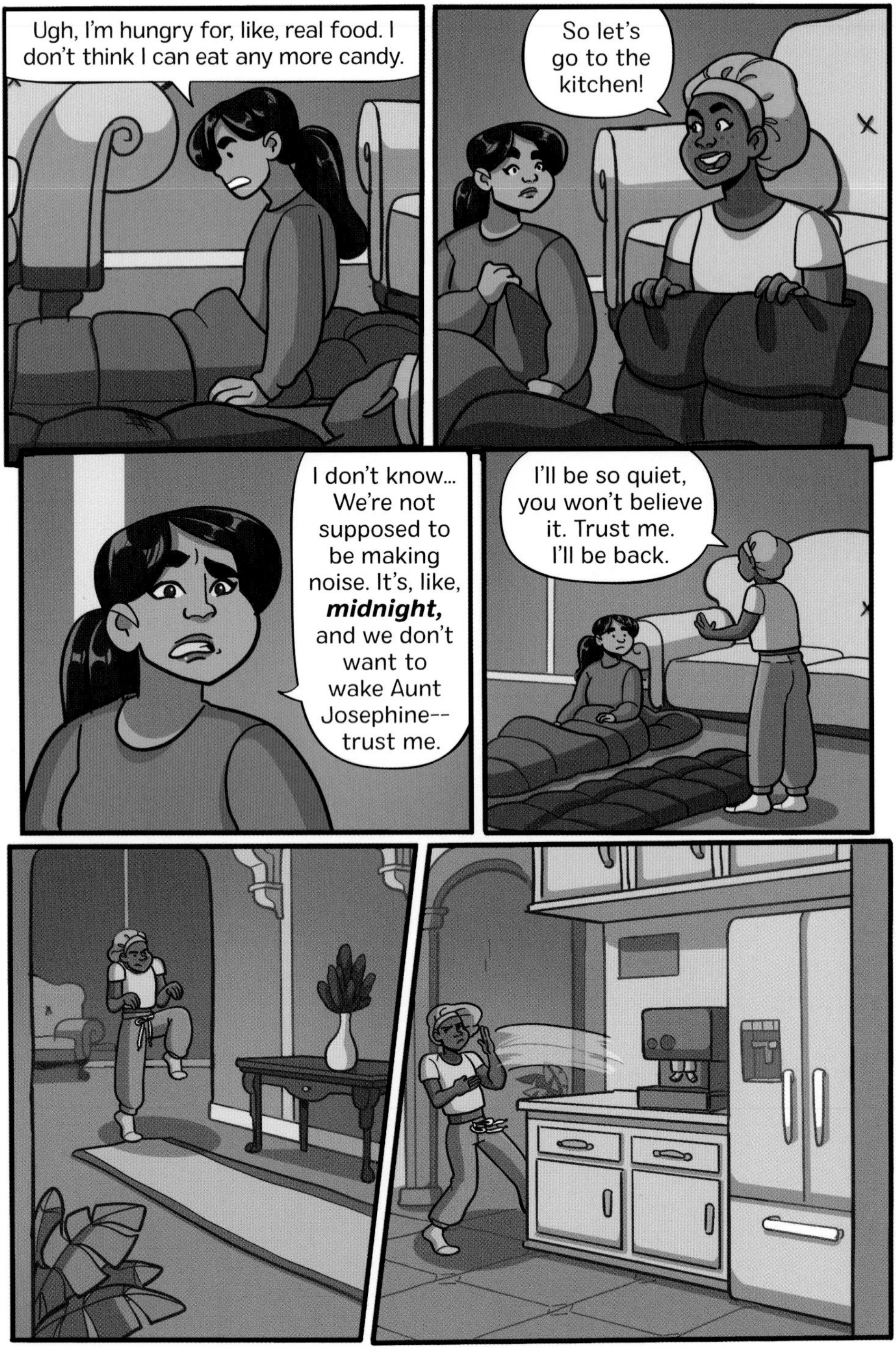
Ugh, I'm hungry for, like, real food. I don't think I can eat any more candy.
So let's go to the kitchen!
I don't know... We're not supposed to be making noise. It's, like, *midnight,* and we don't want to wake Aunt Josephine-- trust me.
I'll be so quiet, you won't believe it. Trust me. I'll be back.

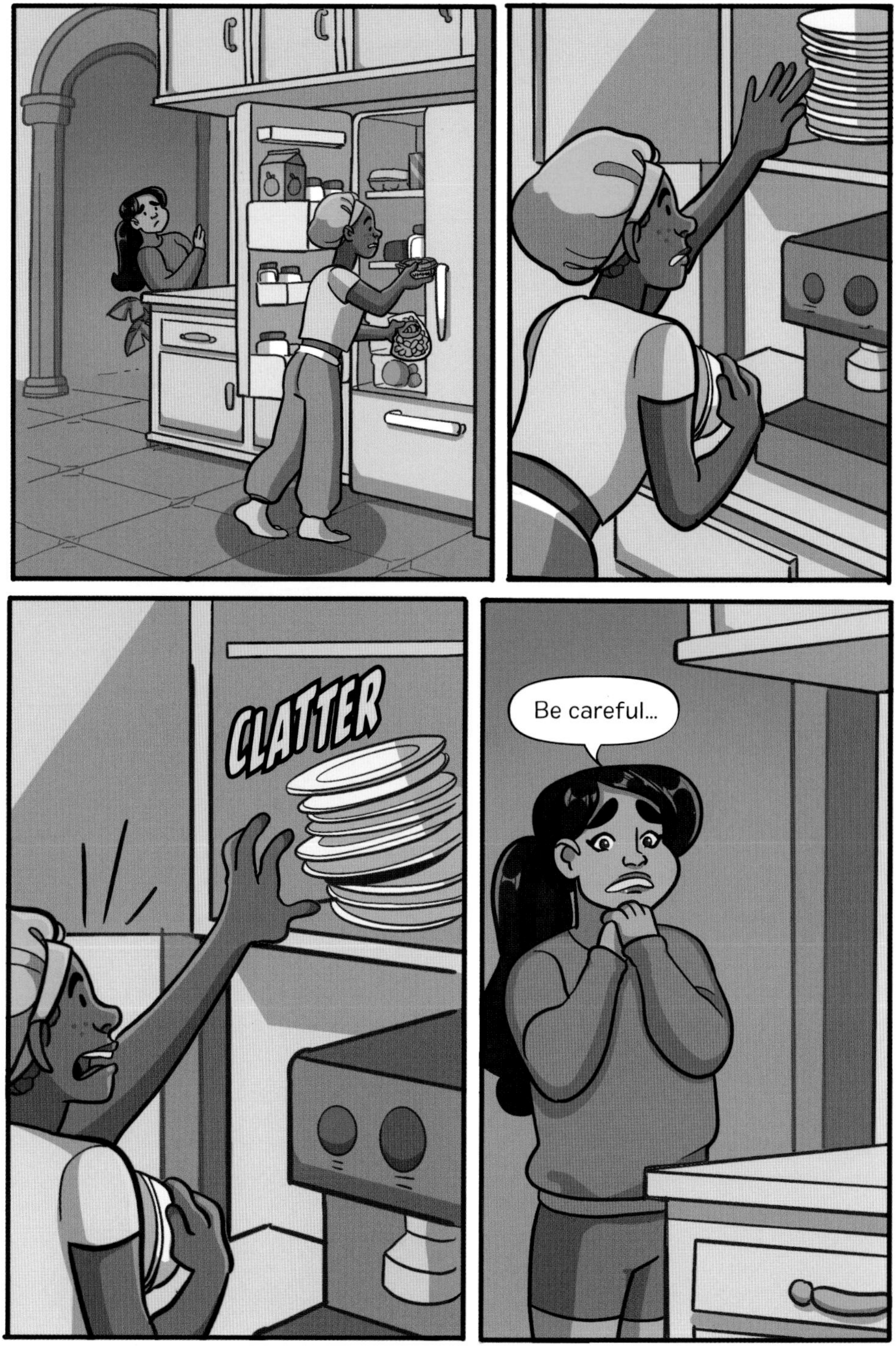
CLATTER
Be careful...

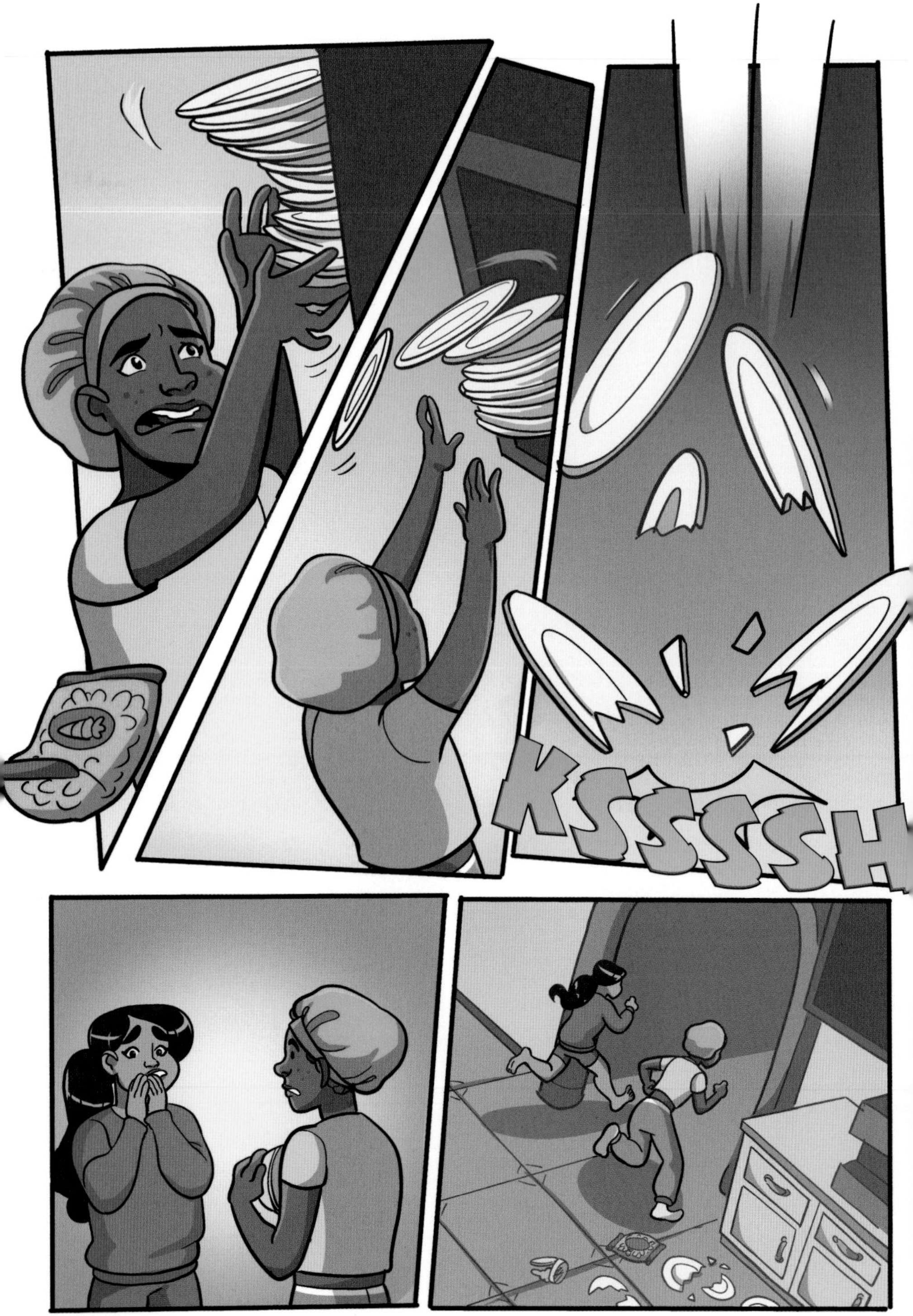
KSSSSH

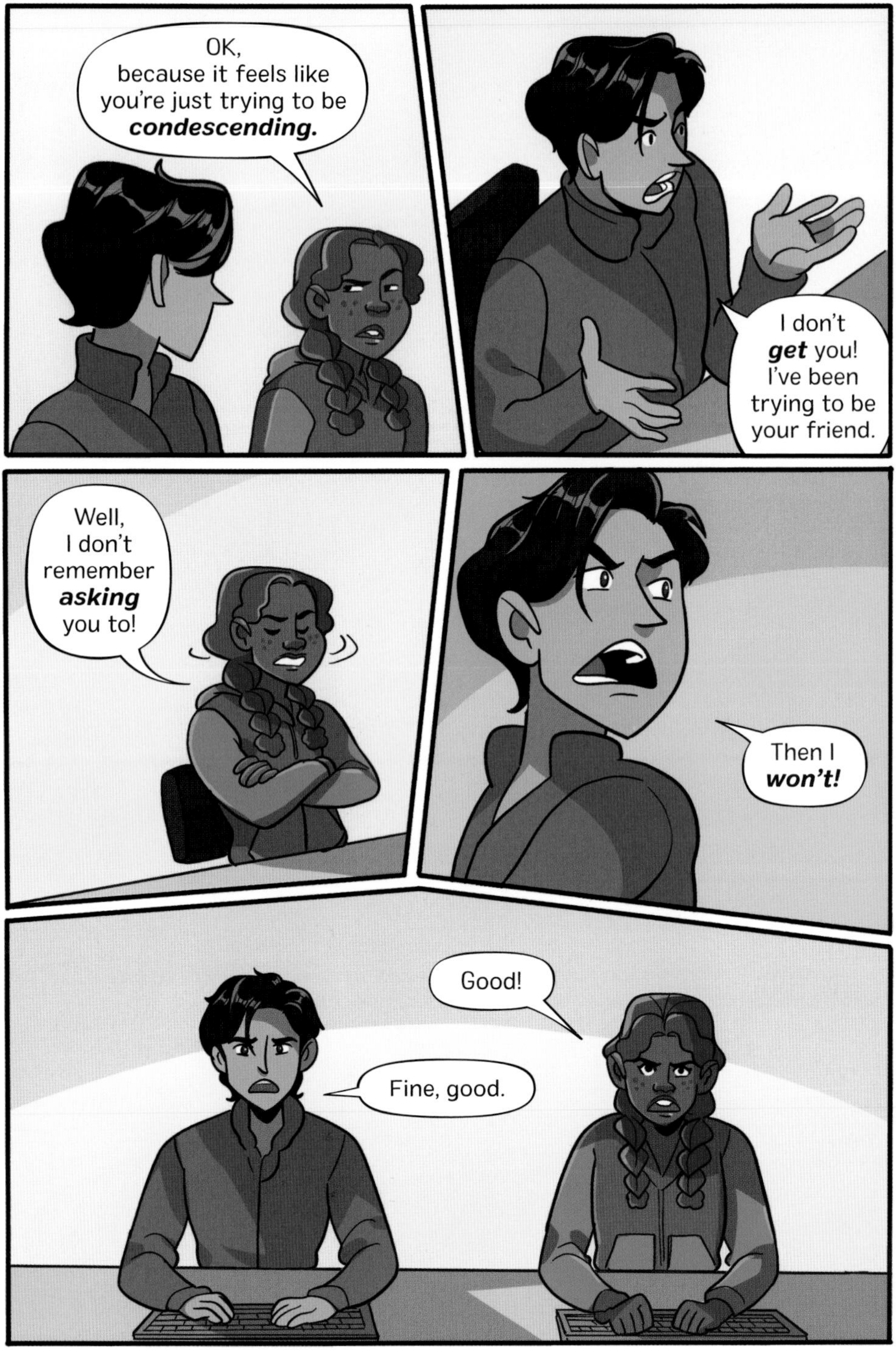
OK, because it feels like you're just trying to be ***condescending.***
I don't ***get*** you! I've been trying to be your friend.
Well, I don't remember ***asking*** you to!
Then I ***won't!***
Good!
Fine, good.

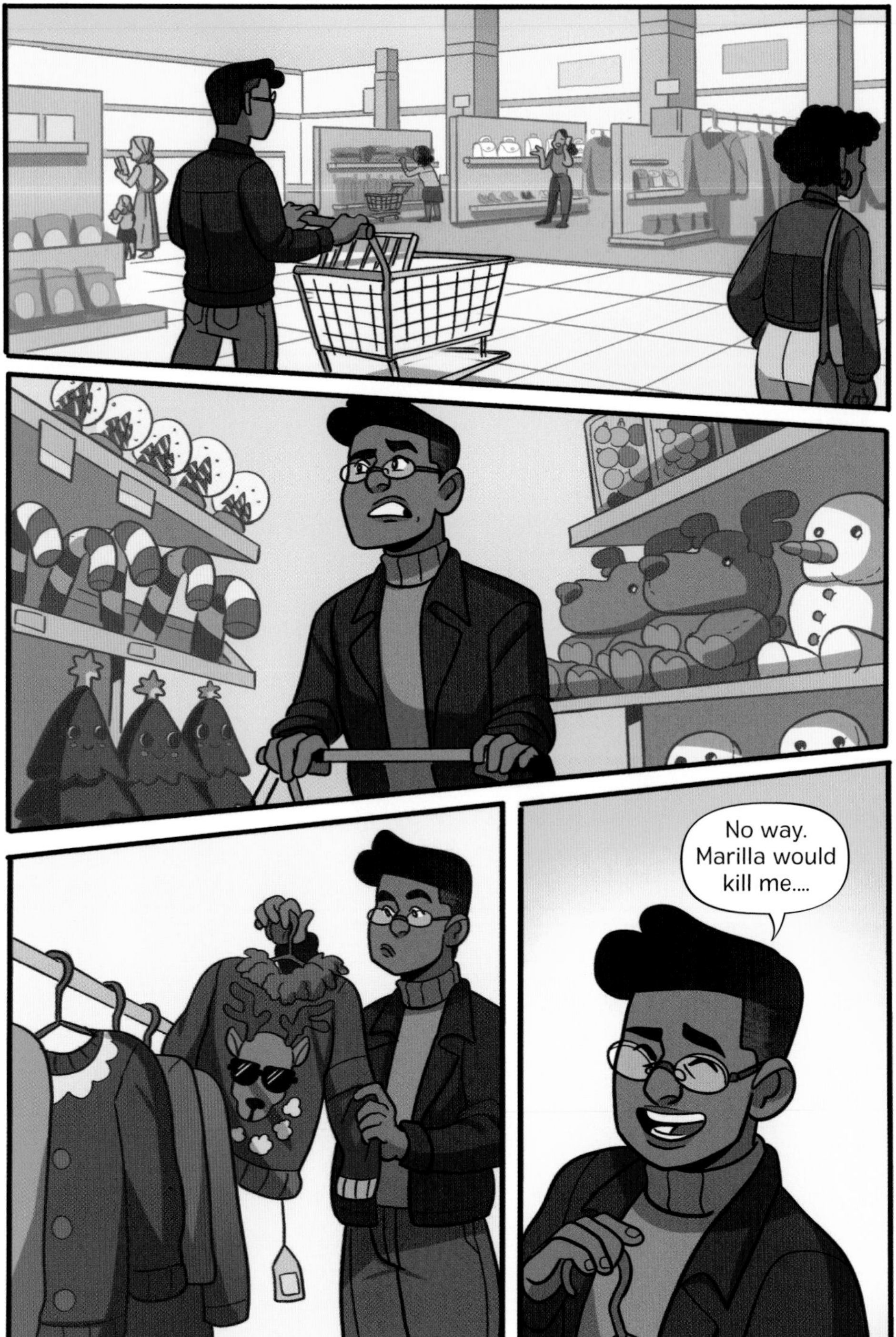
No way.
Marilla would
kill me....

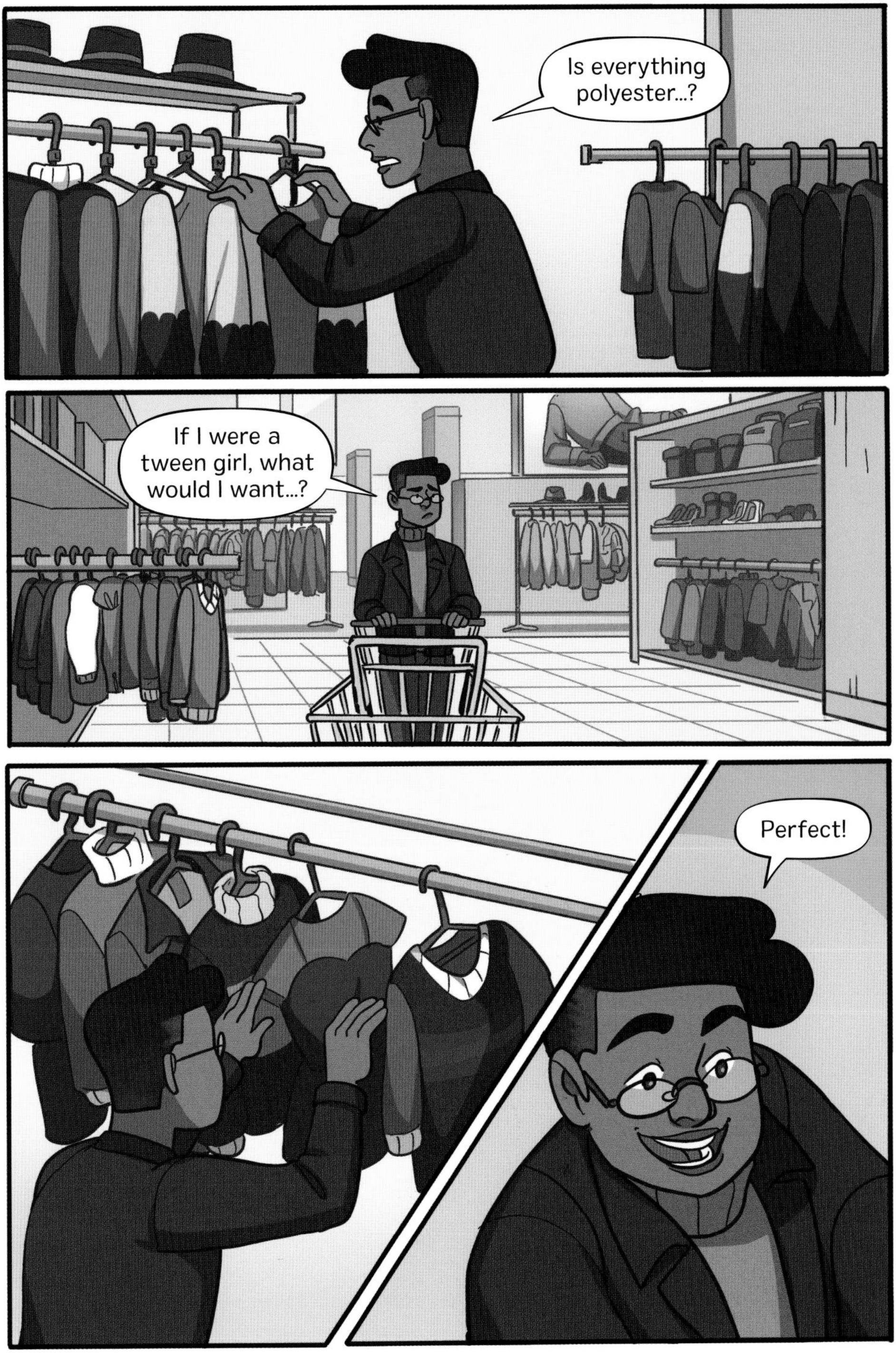
Is everything polyester...?
If I were a tween girl, what would I want...?
Perfect!

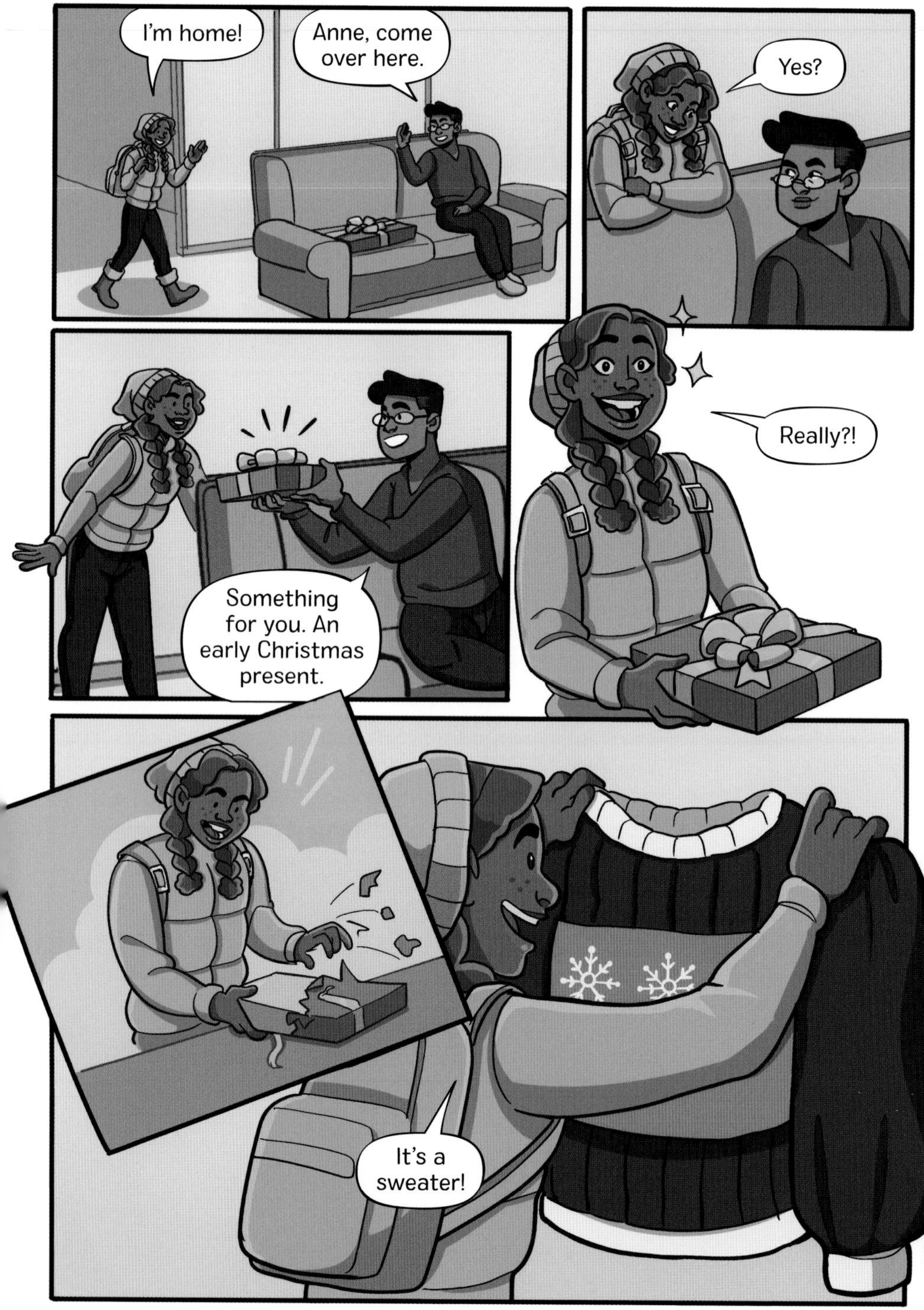
I'm home!
Anne, come over here.
Yes?
Something for you. An early Christmas present.
Really?!
It's a sweater!

163

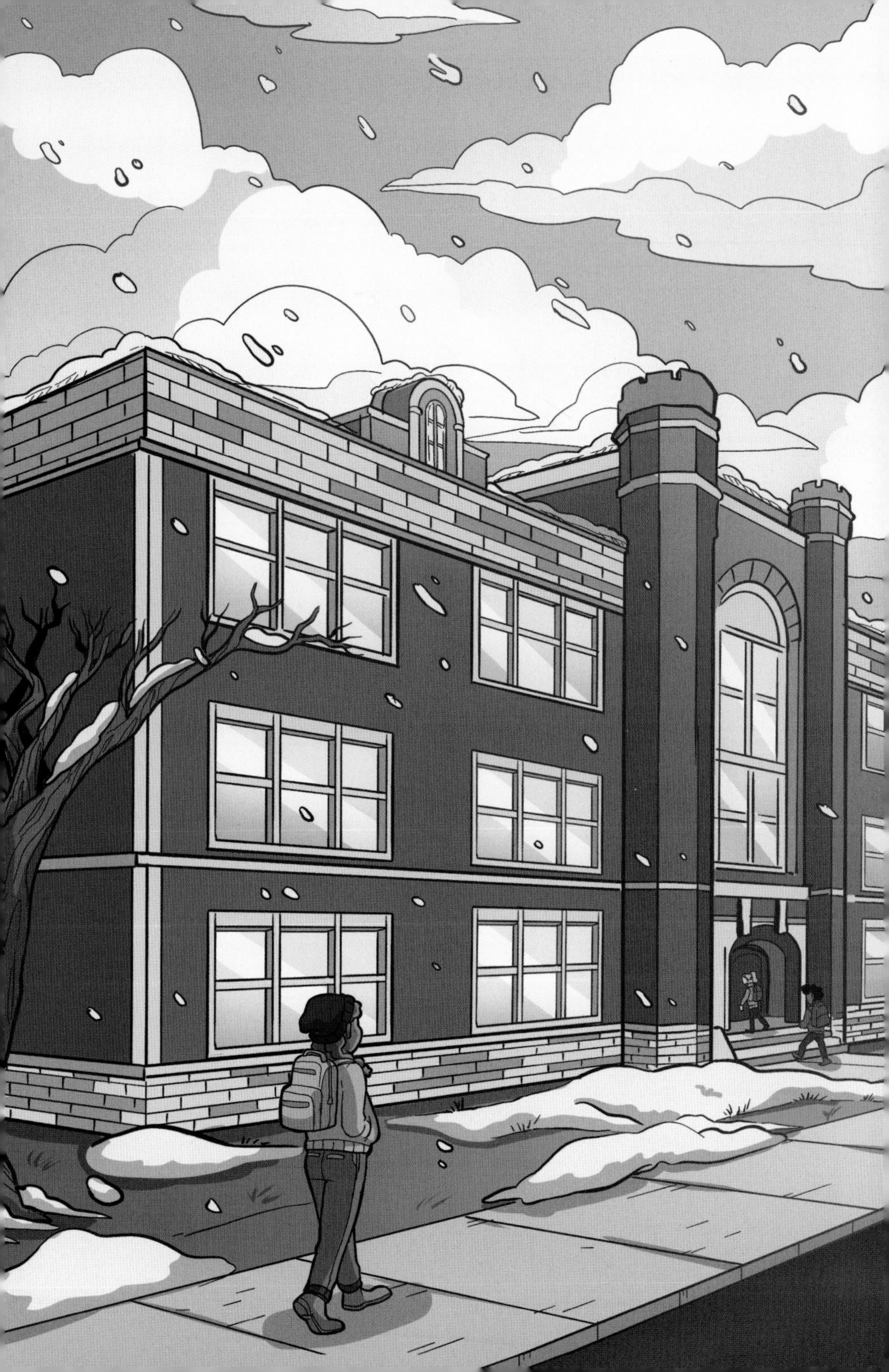

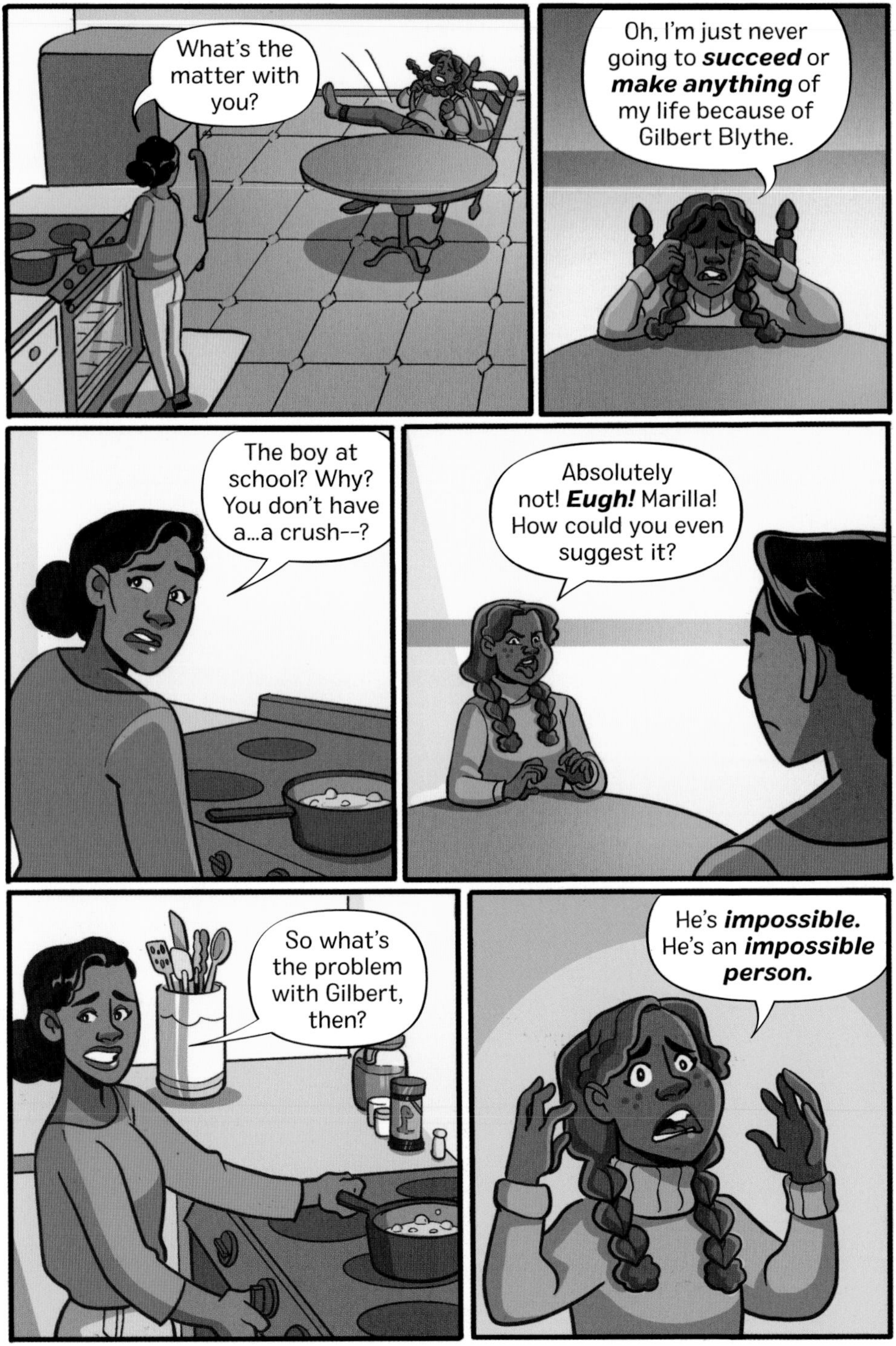
What's the matter with you?
Oh, I'm just never going to ***succeed*** or ***make anything*** of my life because of Gilbert Blythe.
The boy at school? Why? You don't have a...a crush--?
Absolutely not! ***Eugh!*** Marilla! How could you even suggest it?
So what's the problem with Gilbert, then?
He's ***impossible.*** He's an ***impossible person.***

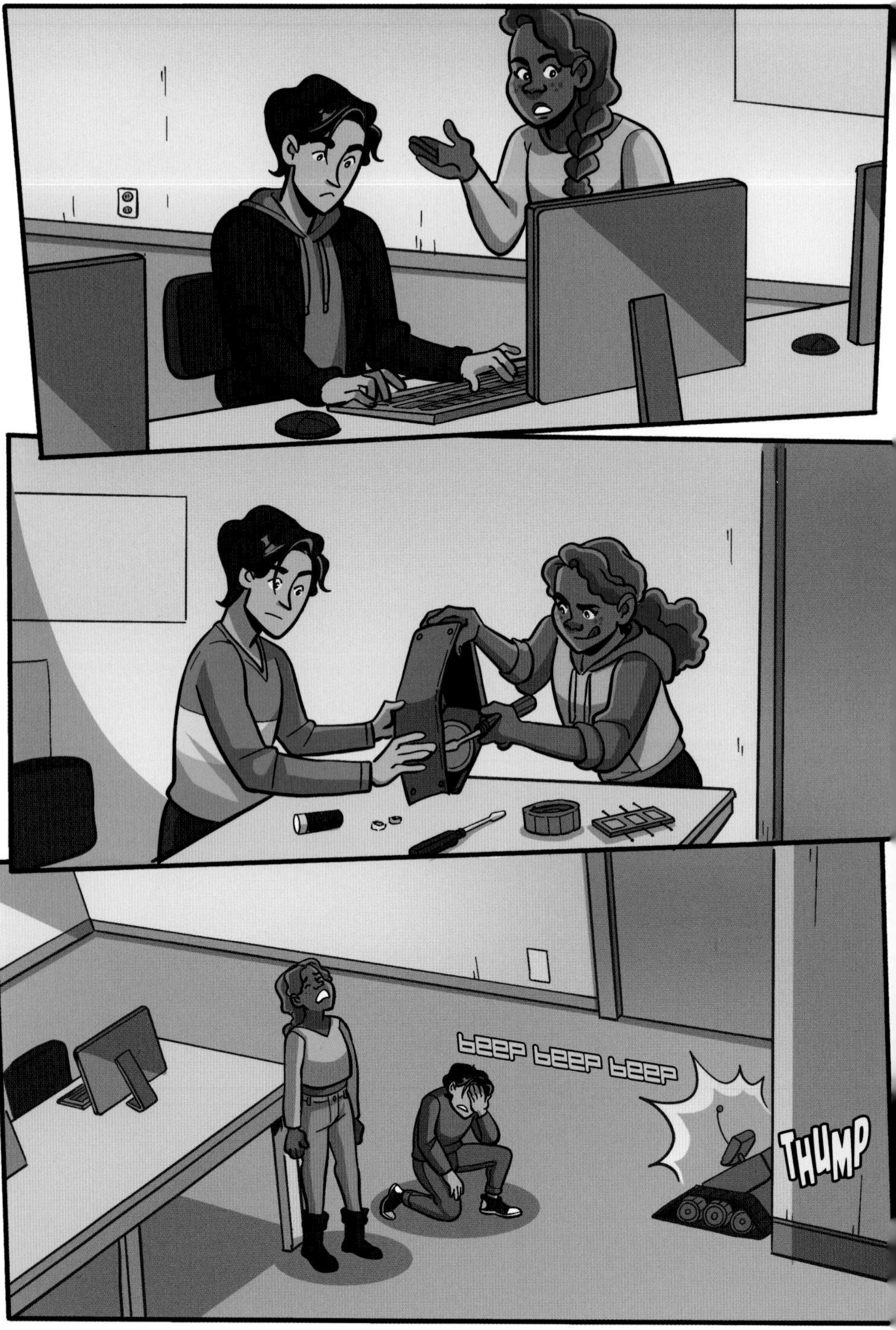
BEEP BEEP BEEP
THUMP

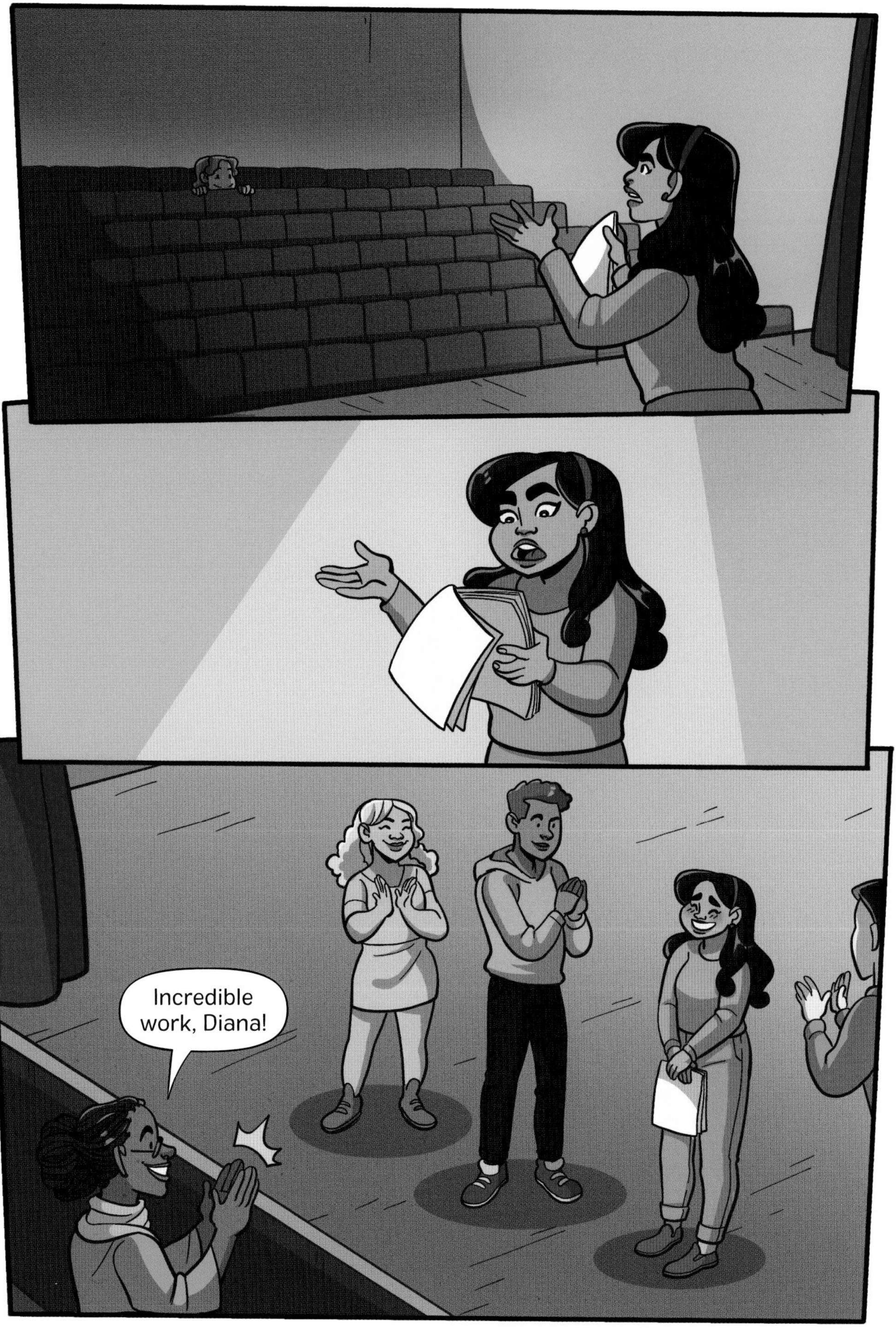
Incredible
work, Diana!

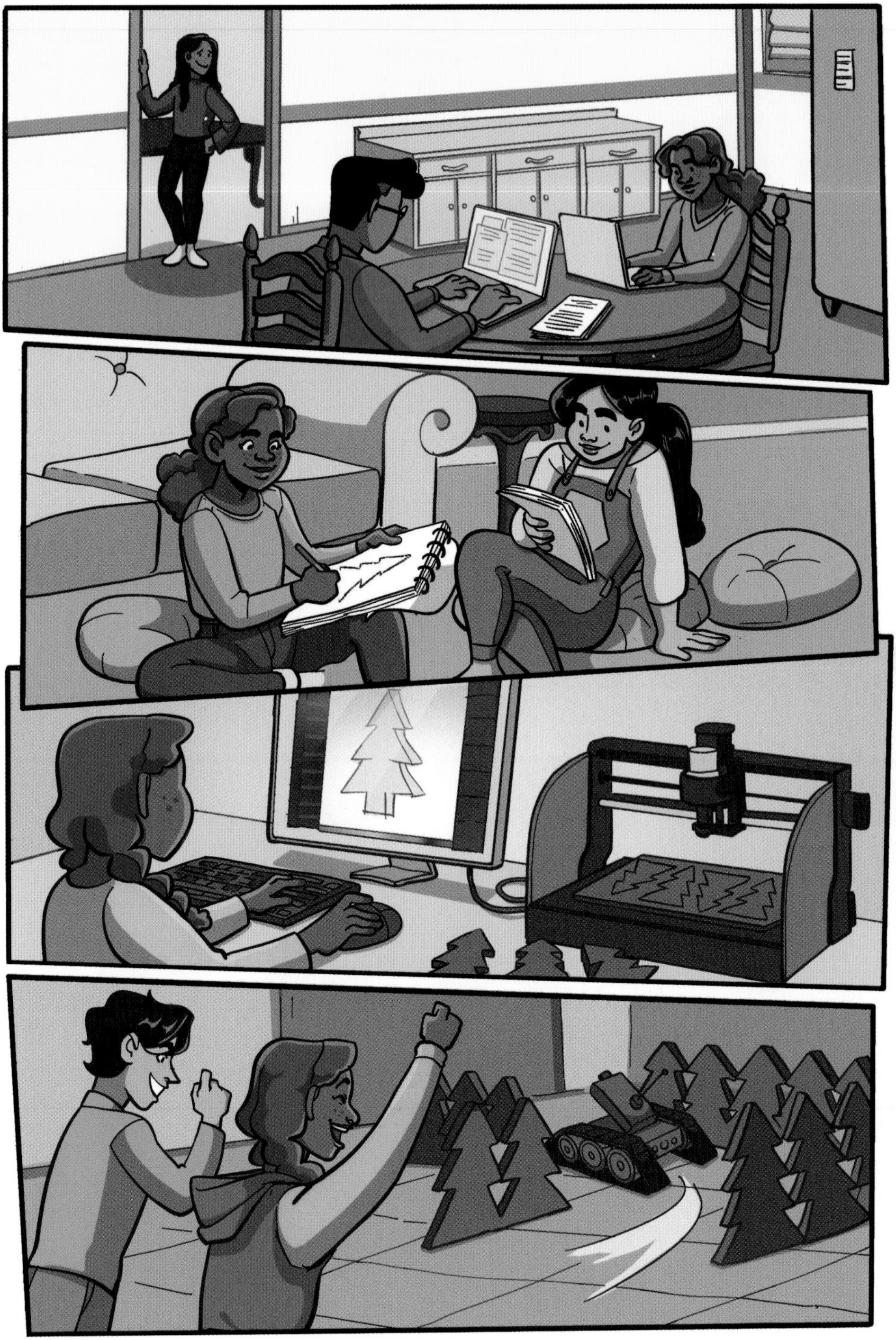

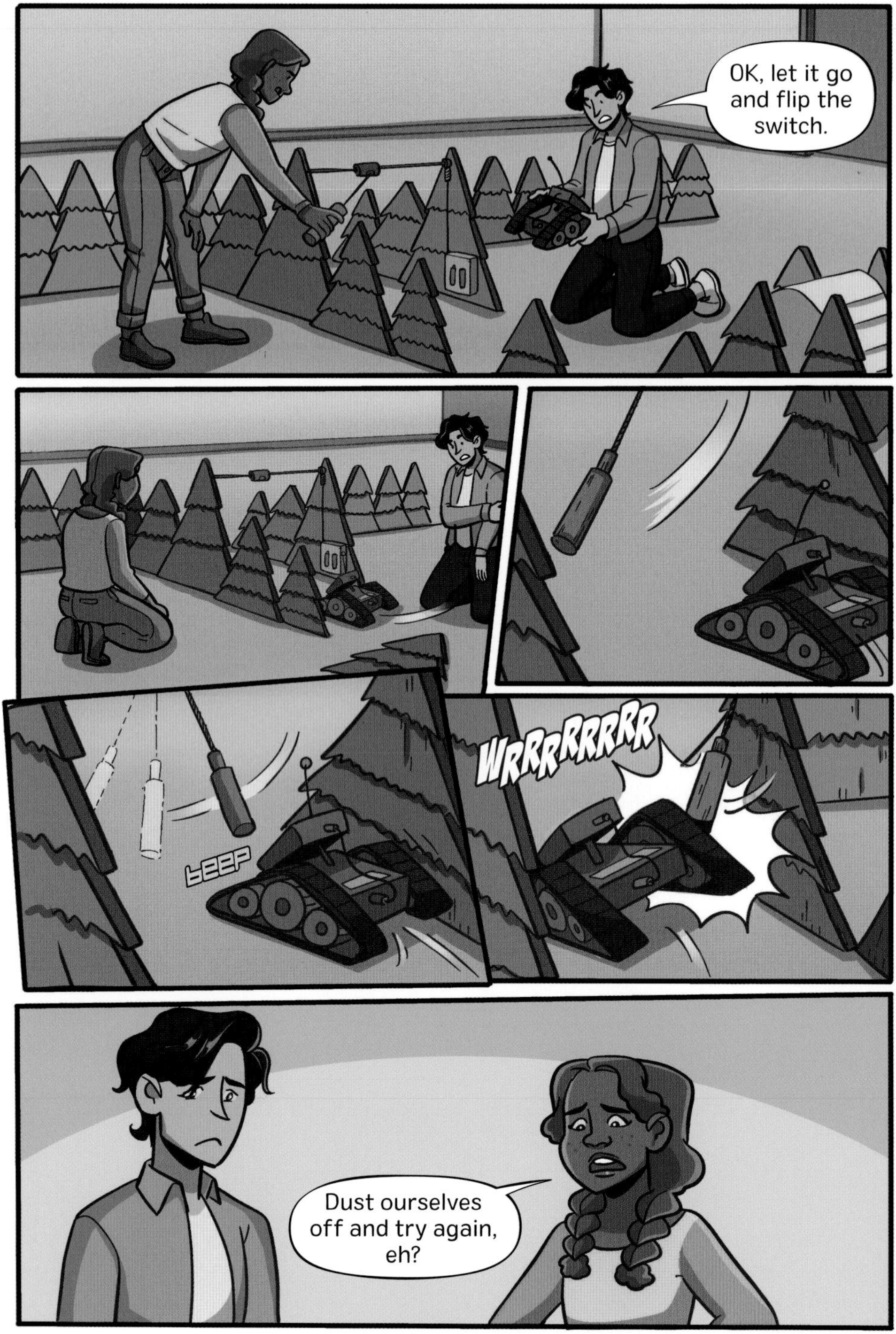
OK, let it go and flip the switch.
BEEP
WRRRRRRR
Dust ourselves off and try again, eh?

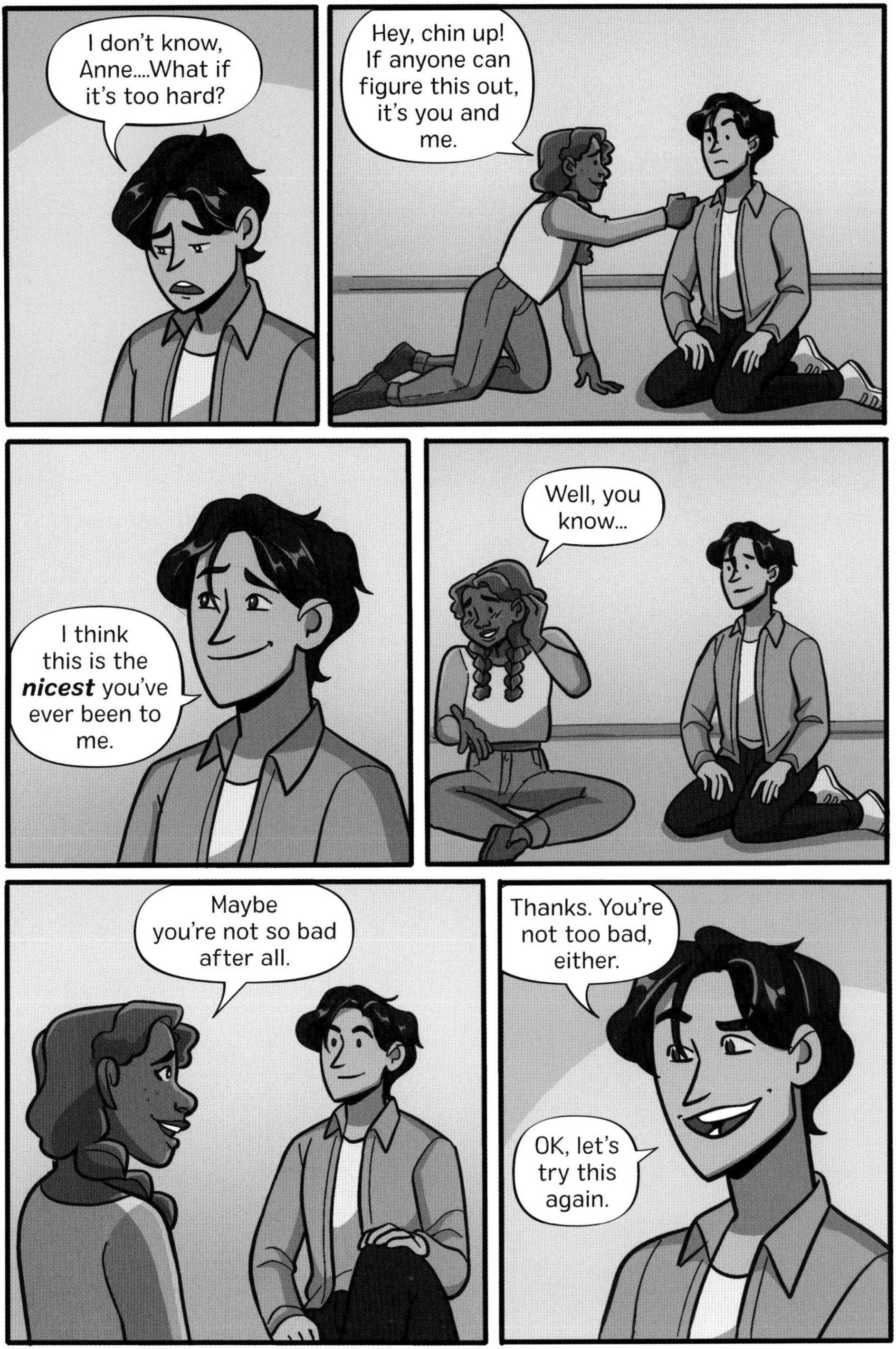
I don't know, Anne....What if it's too hard?
Hey, chin up! If anyone can figure this out, it's you and me.
I think this is the *nicest* you've ever been to me.
Well, you know...
Maybe you're not so bad after all.
Thanks. You're not too bad, either.
OK, let's try this again.

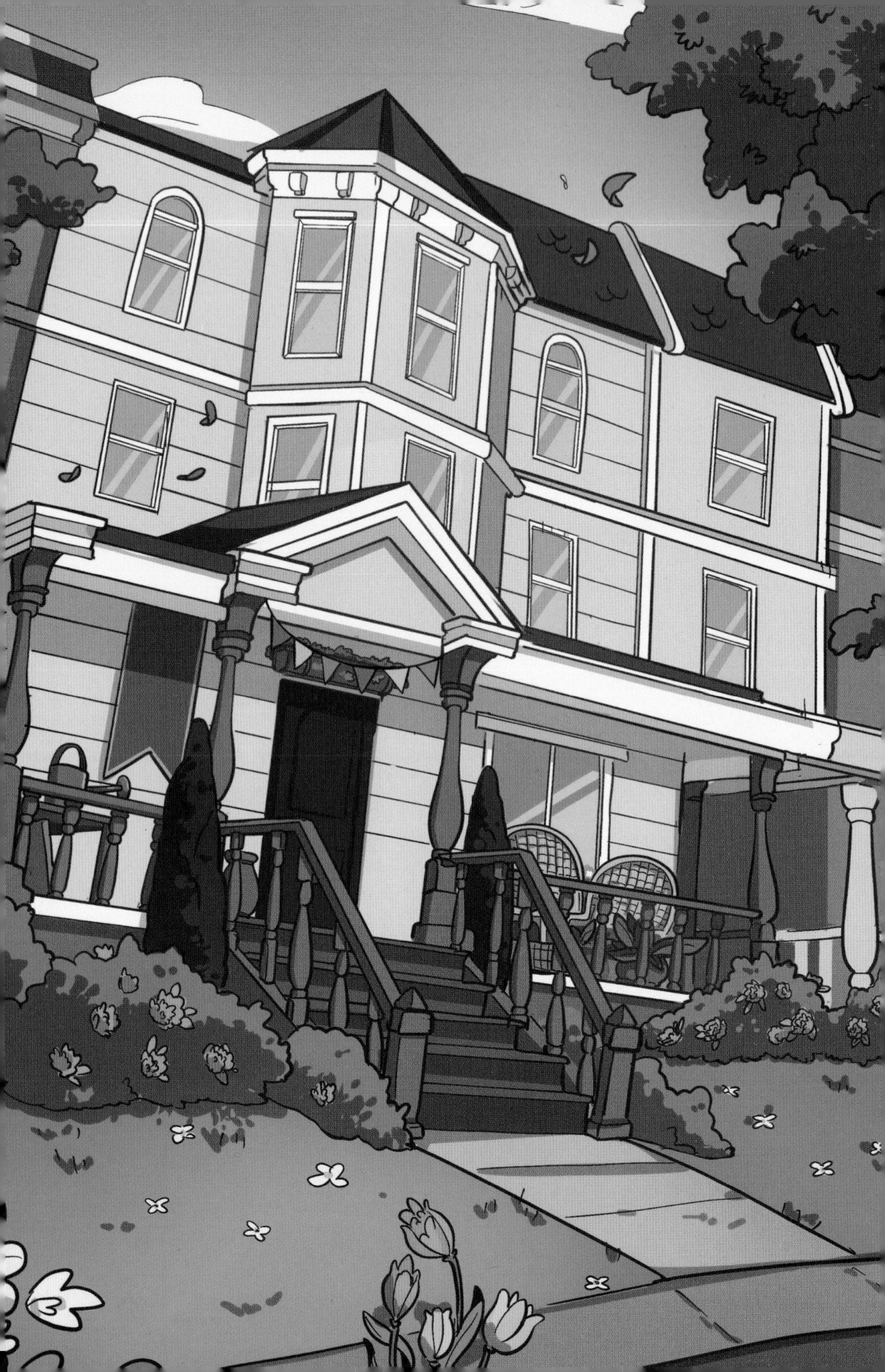

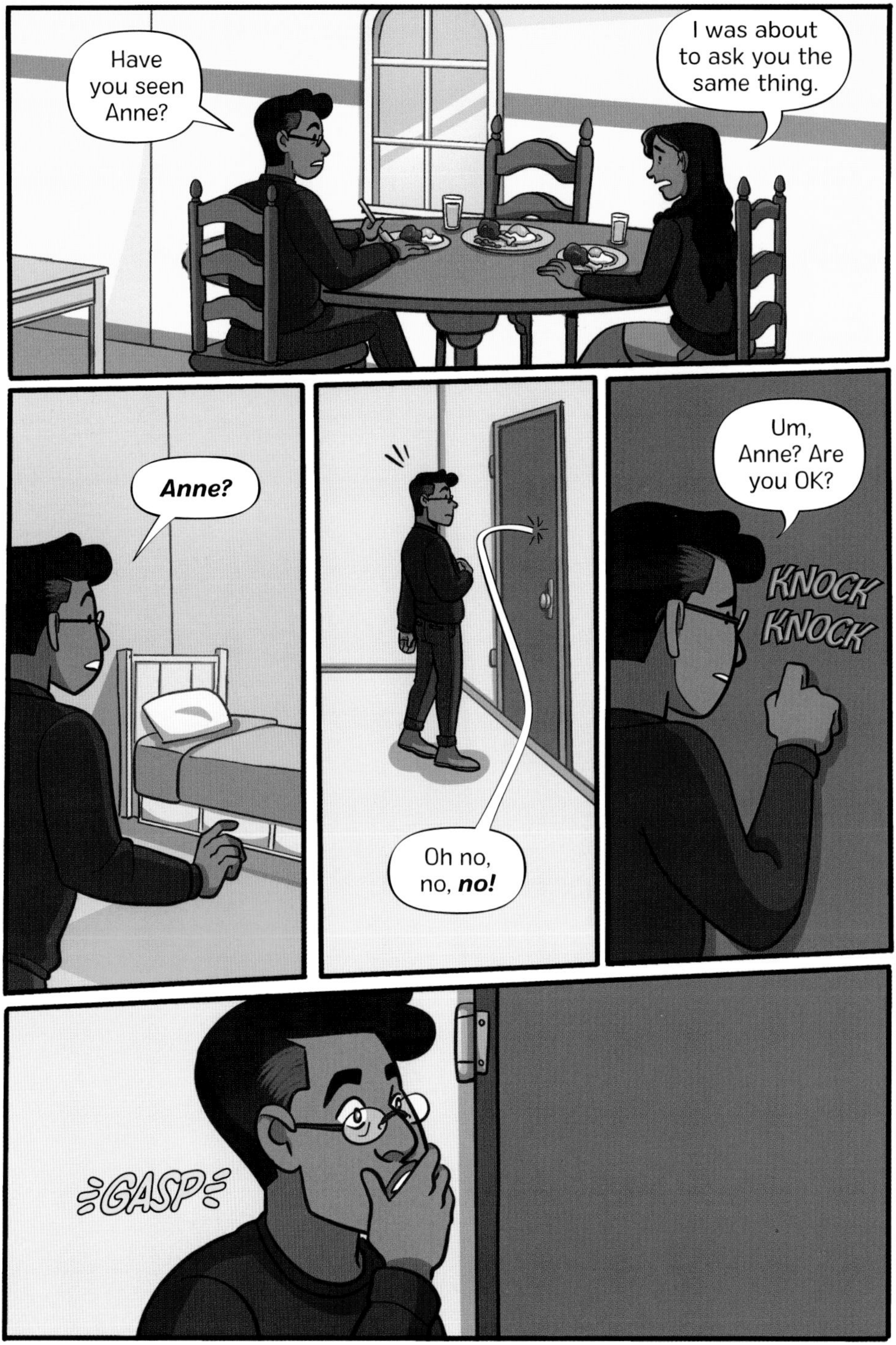
Have you seen Anne?
I was about to ask you the same thing.
Anne?
Oh no, no, no!
Um, Anne? Are you OK?
KNOCK KNOCK
GASP

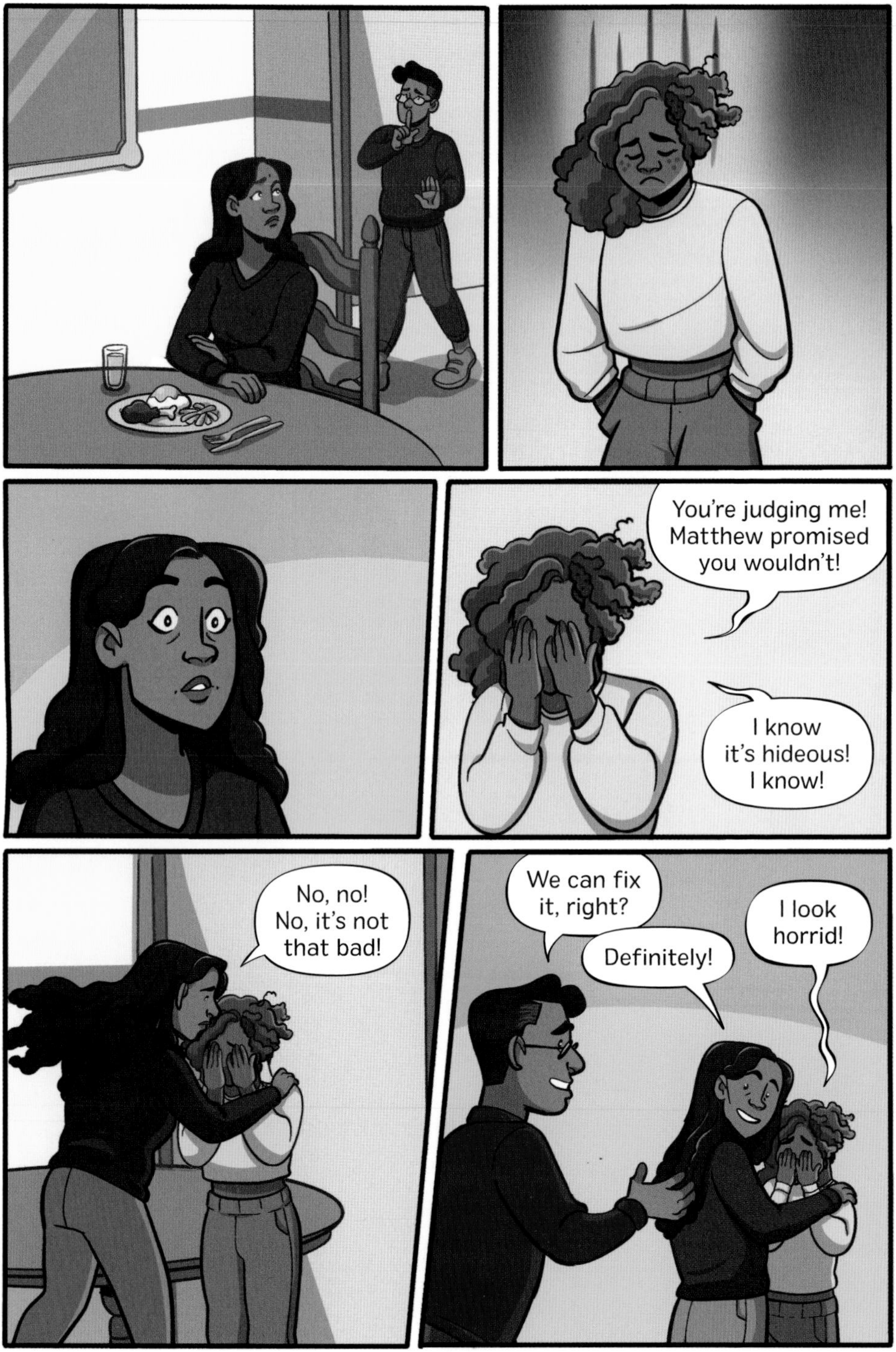
You're judging me! Matthew promised you wouldn't!
I know it's hideous! I know!
No, no! No, it's not that bad!
We can fix it, right?
Definitely!
I look horrid!

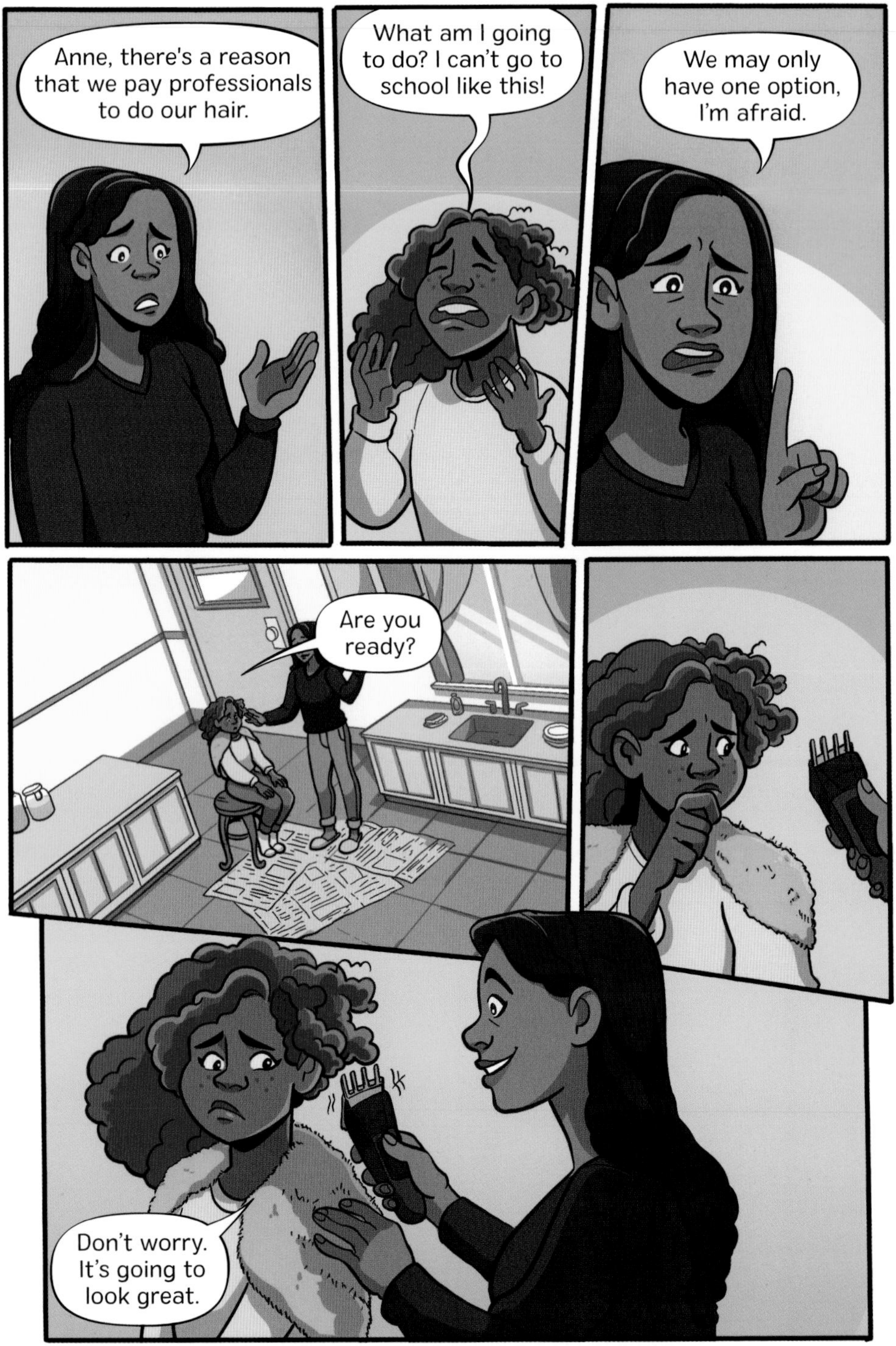
Anne, there's a reason that we pay professionals to do our hair.
What am I going to do? I can't go to school like this!
We may only have one option, I'm afraid.
Are you ready?
Don't worry. It's going to look great.

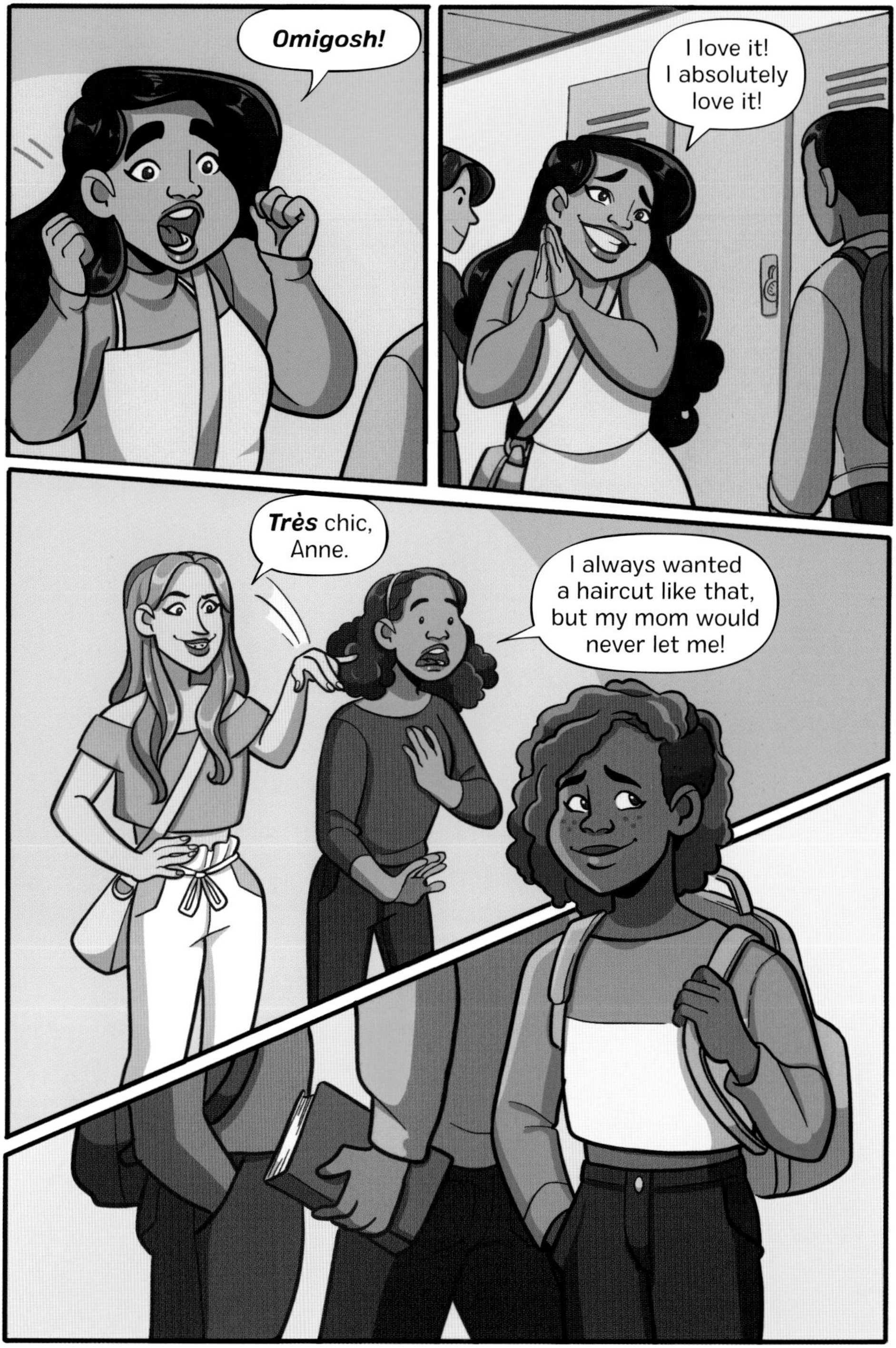
Omigosh!
I love it! I absolutely love it!
Très chic, Anne.
I always wanted a haircut like that, but my mom would never let me!

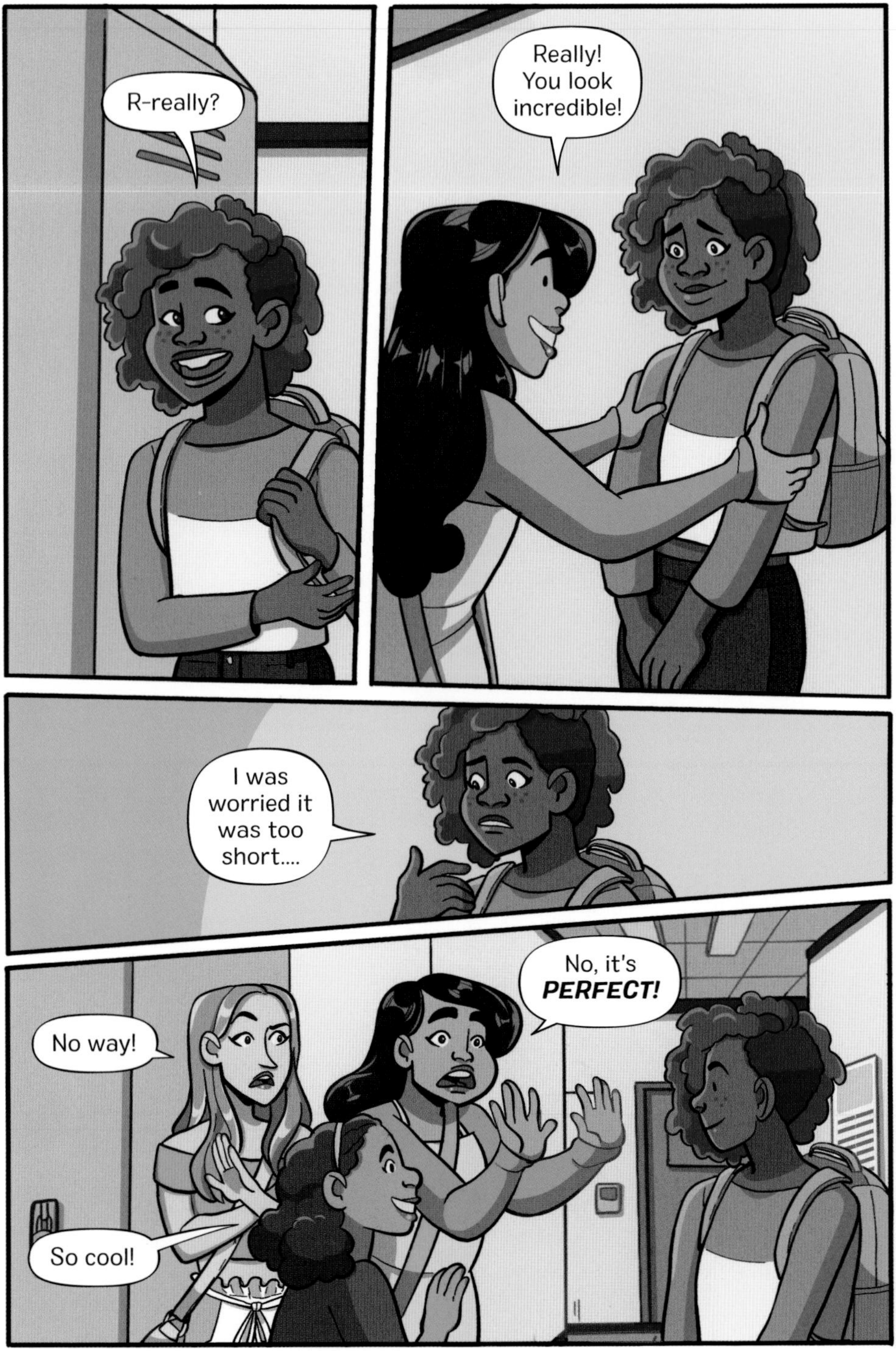
R-really?
Really! You look incredible!
I was worried it was too short....
No way!
No, it's ***PERFECT!***
So cool!

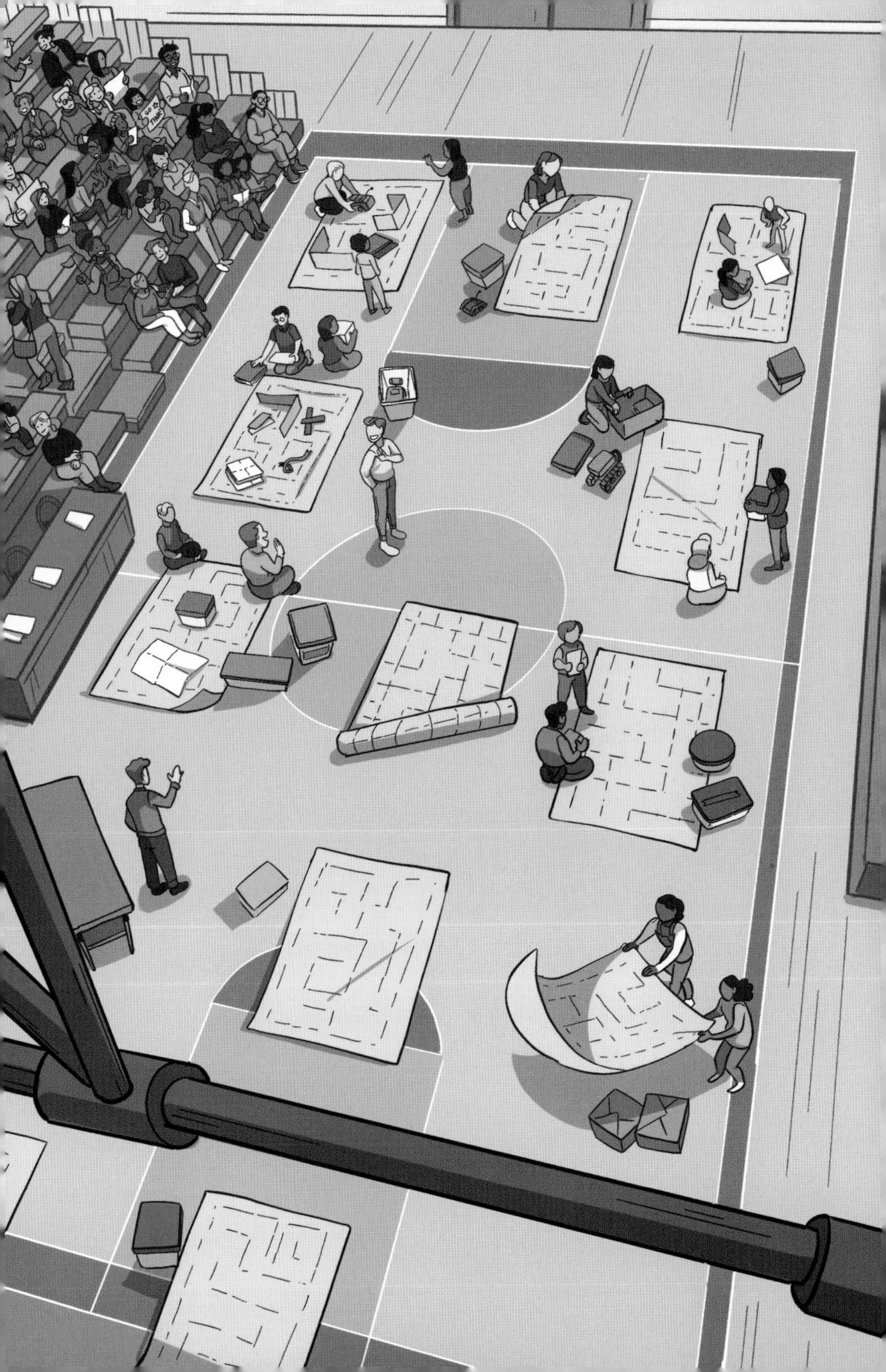
GO ☆ TIAN!

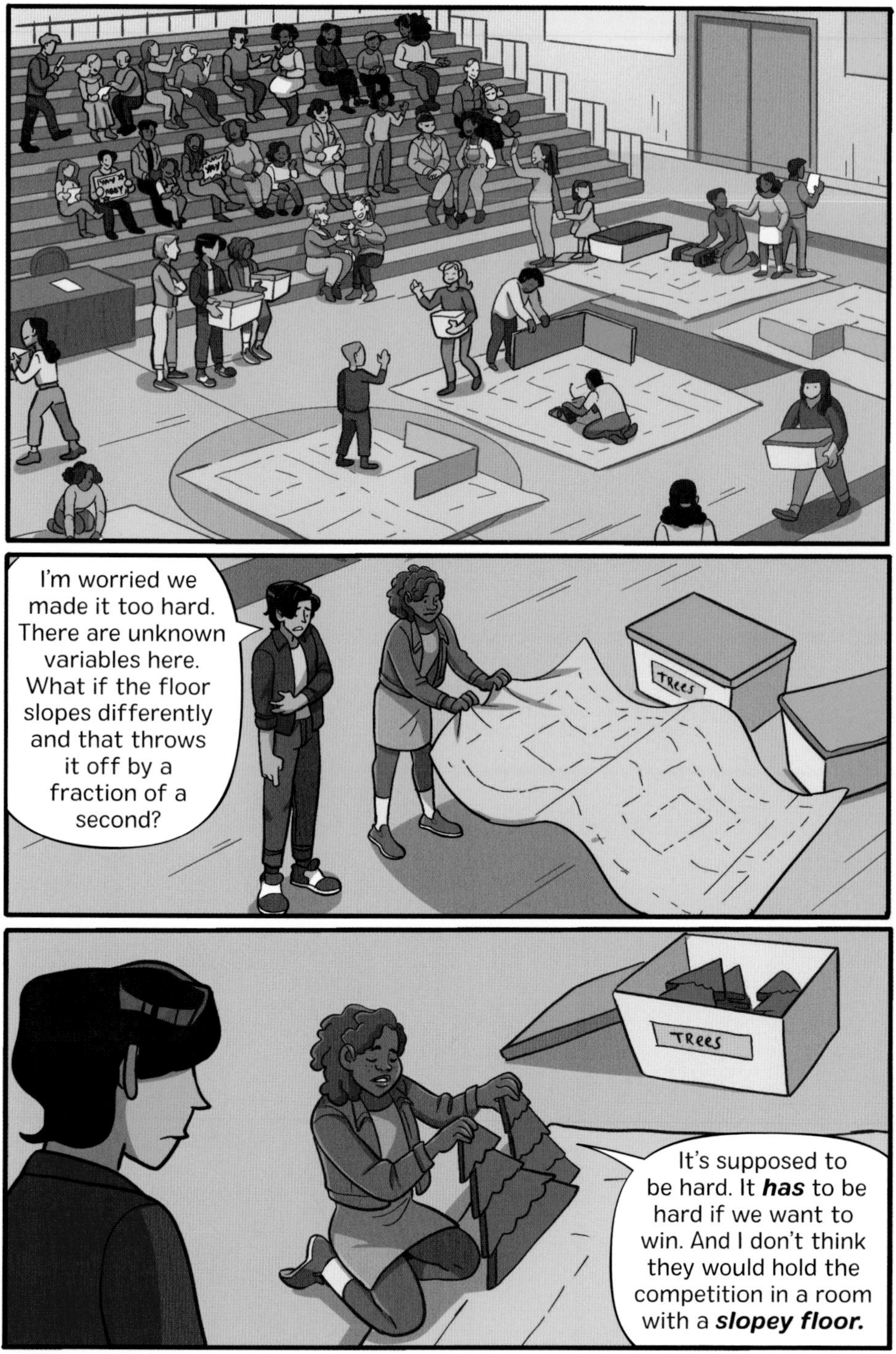
I'm worried we made it too hard. There are unknown variables here. What if the floor slopes differently and that throws it off by a fraction of a second?
TREES
TREES
It's supposed to be hard. It ***has*** to be hard if we want to win. And I don't think they would hold the competition in a room with a ***slopey floor.***

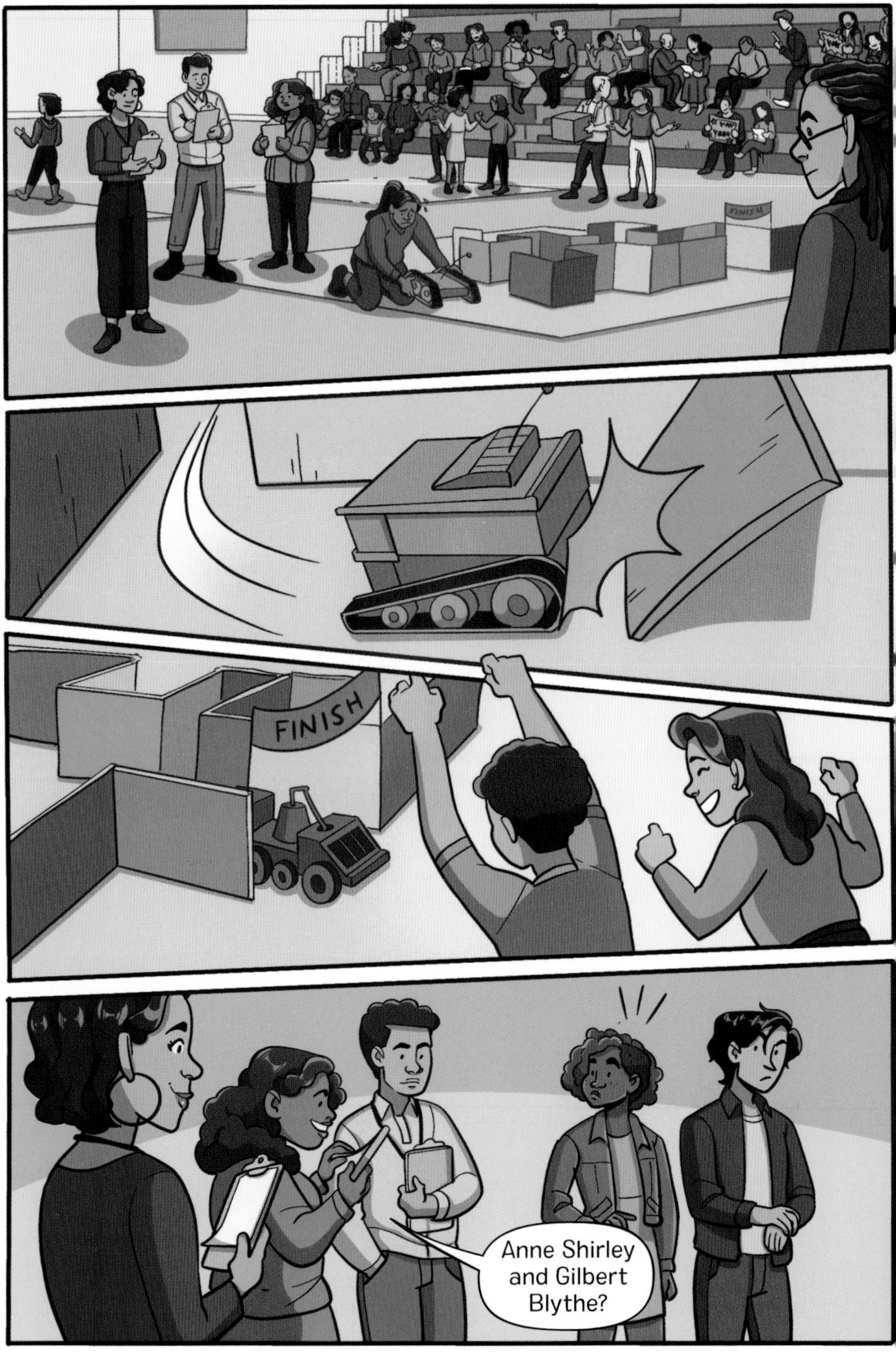
FINISH
Anne Shirley and Gilbert Blythe?

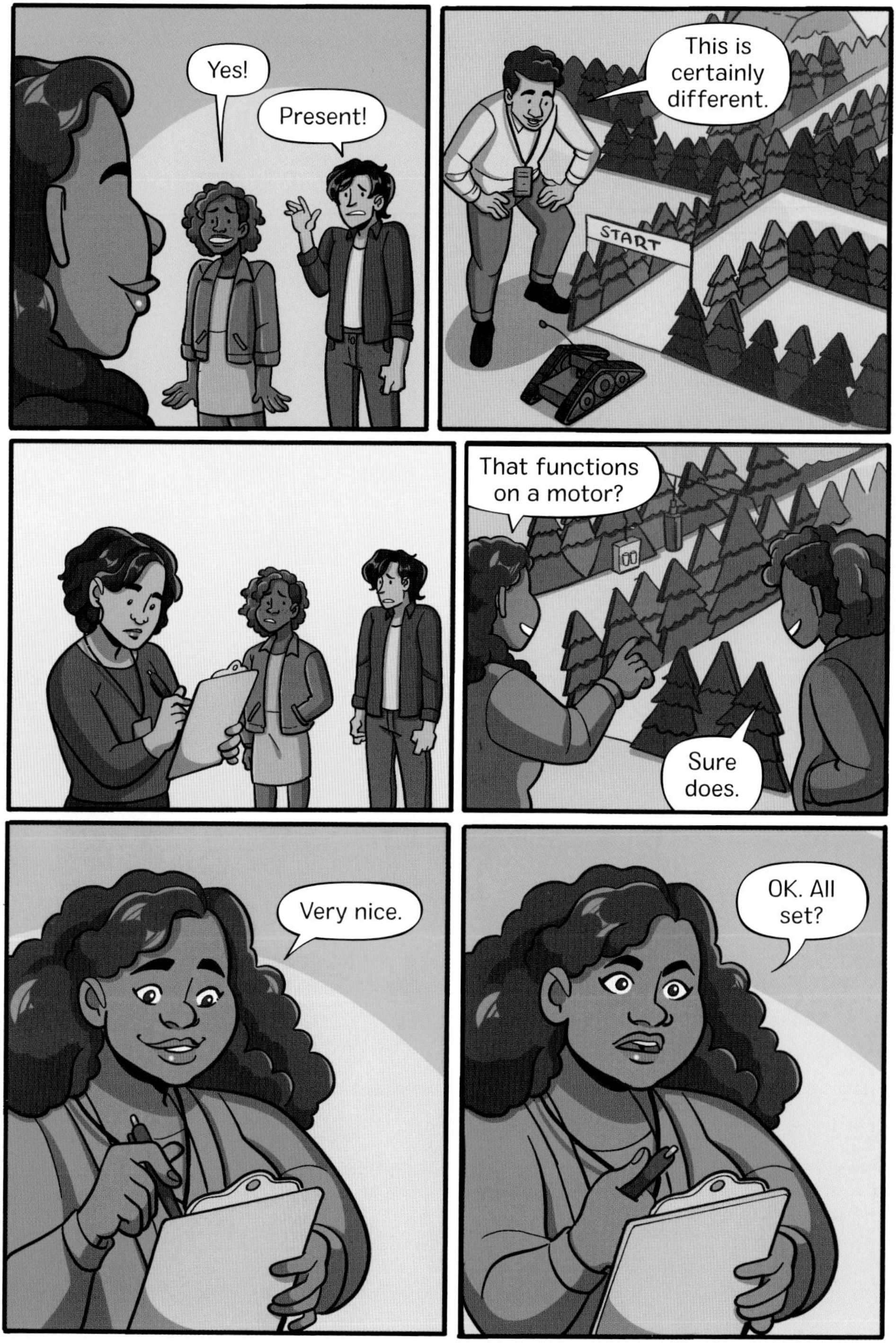
Yes!
Present!
This is certainly different.
START
That functions on a motor?
Sure does.
Very nice.
OK. All set?

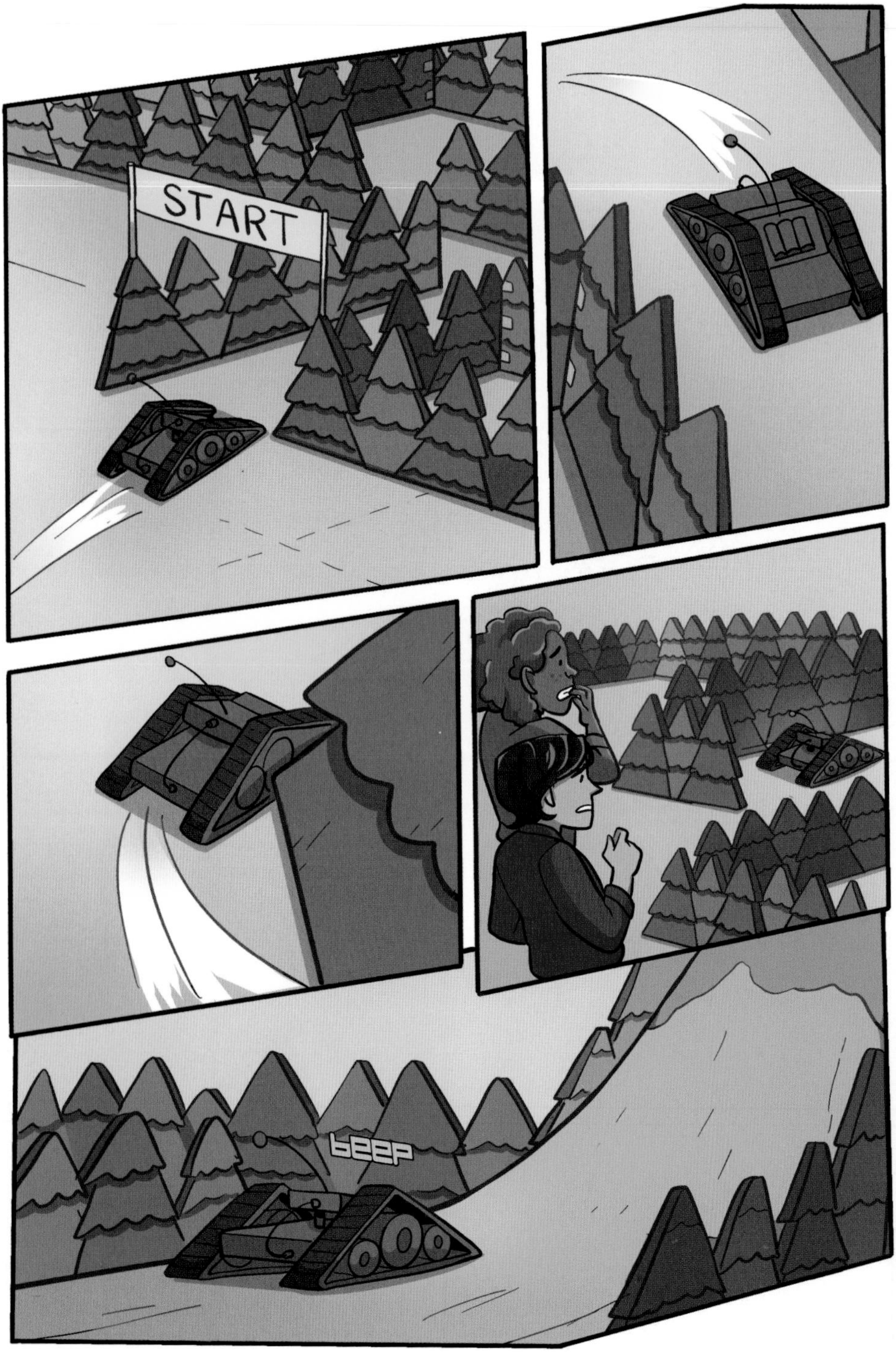
START
BEEP

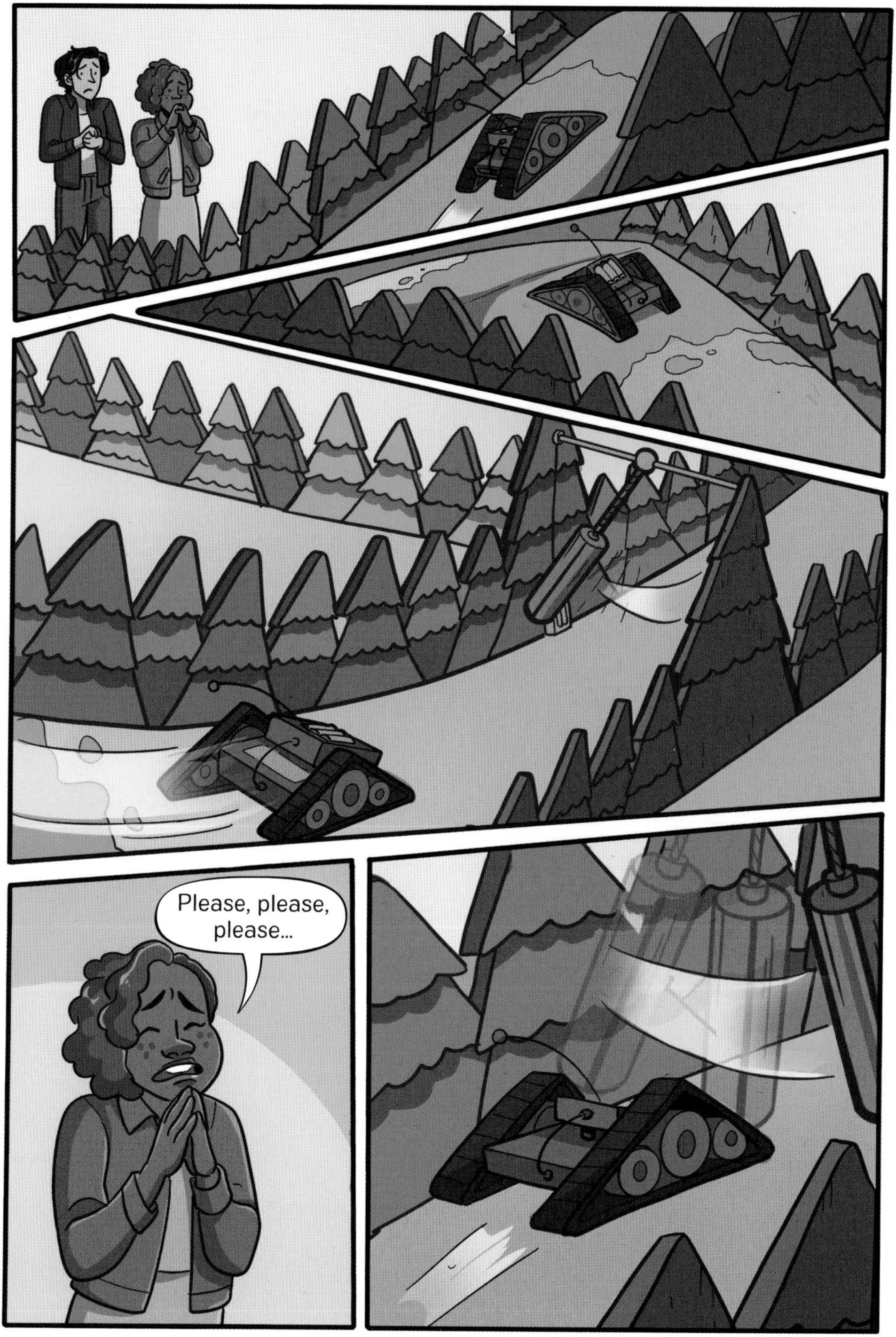
Please, please, please...

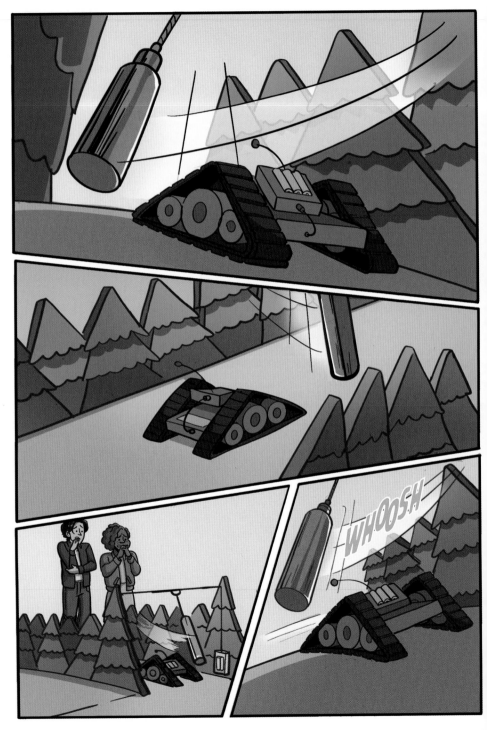

WHOOSH

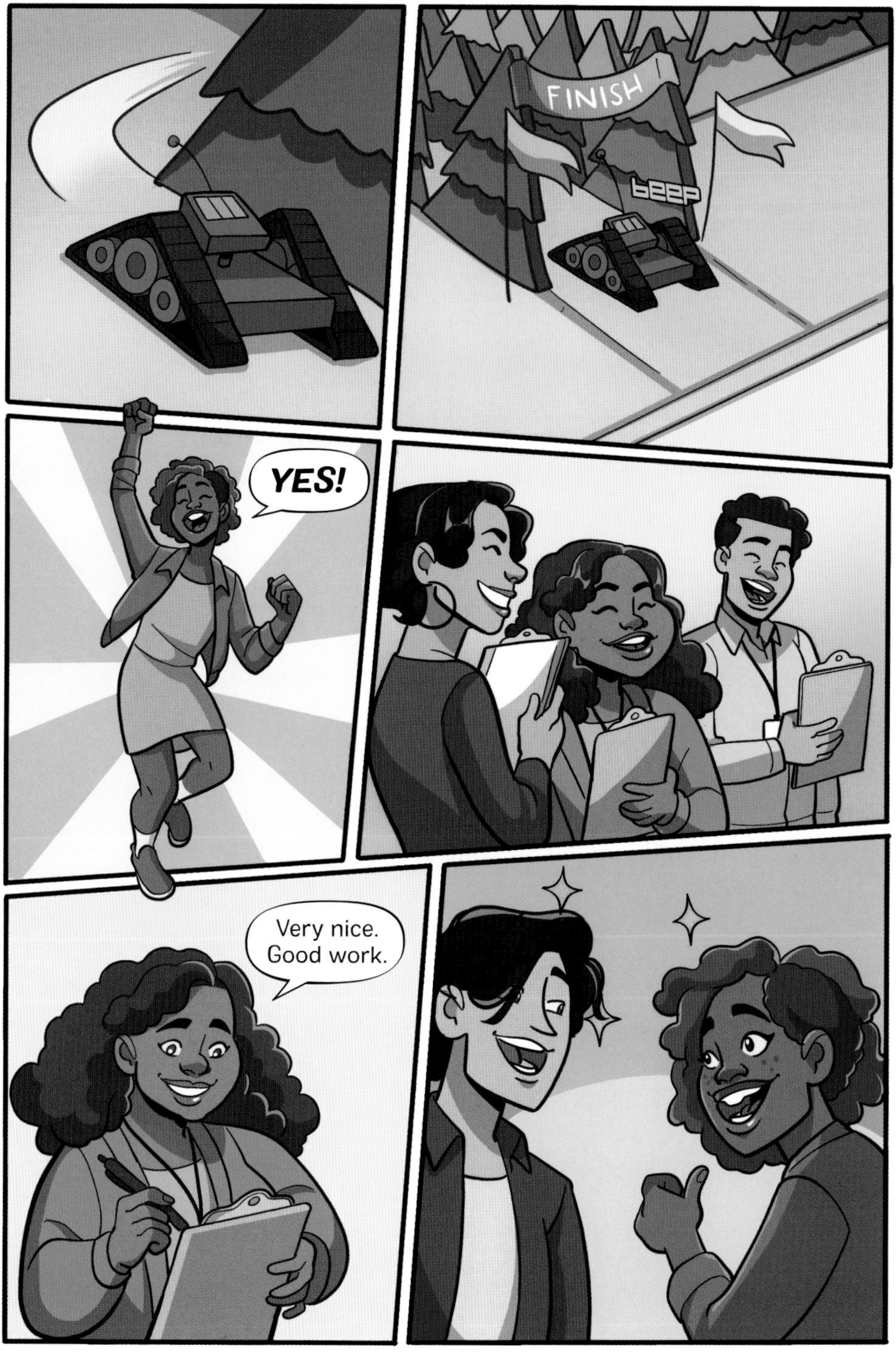
FINISH
beep
YES!
Very nice.
Good work.

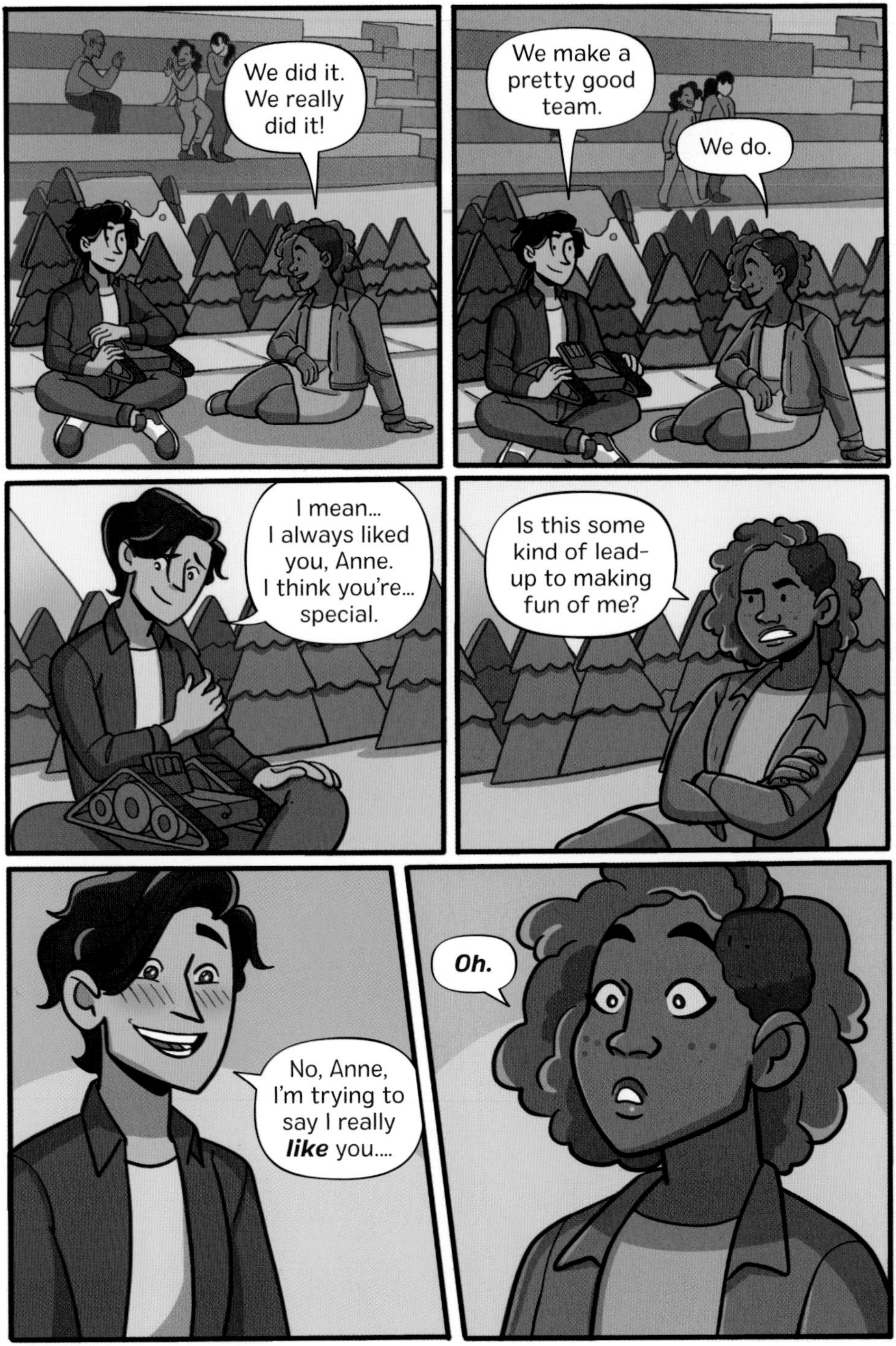
We did it. We really did it!
We make a pretty good team.
We do.
I mean... I always liked you, Anne. I think you're... special.
Is this some kind of lead-up to making fun of me?
No, Anne, I'm trying to say I really ***like*** you....
Oh.

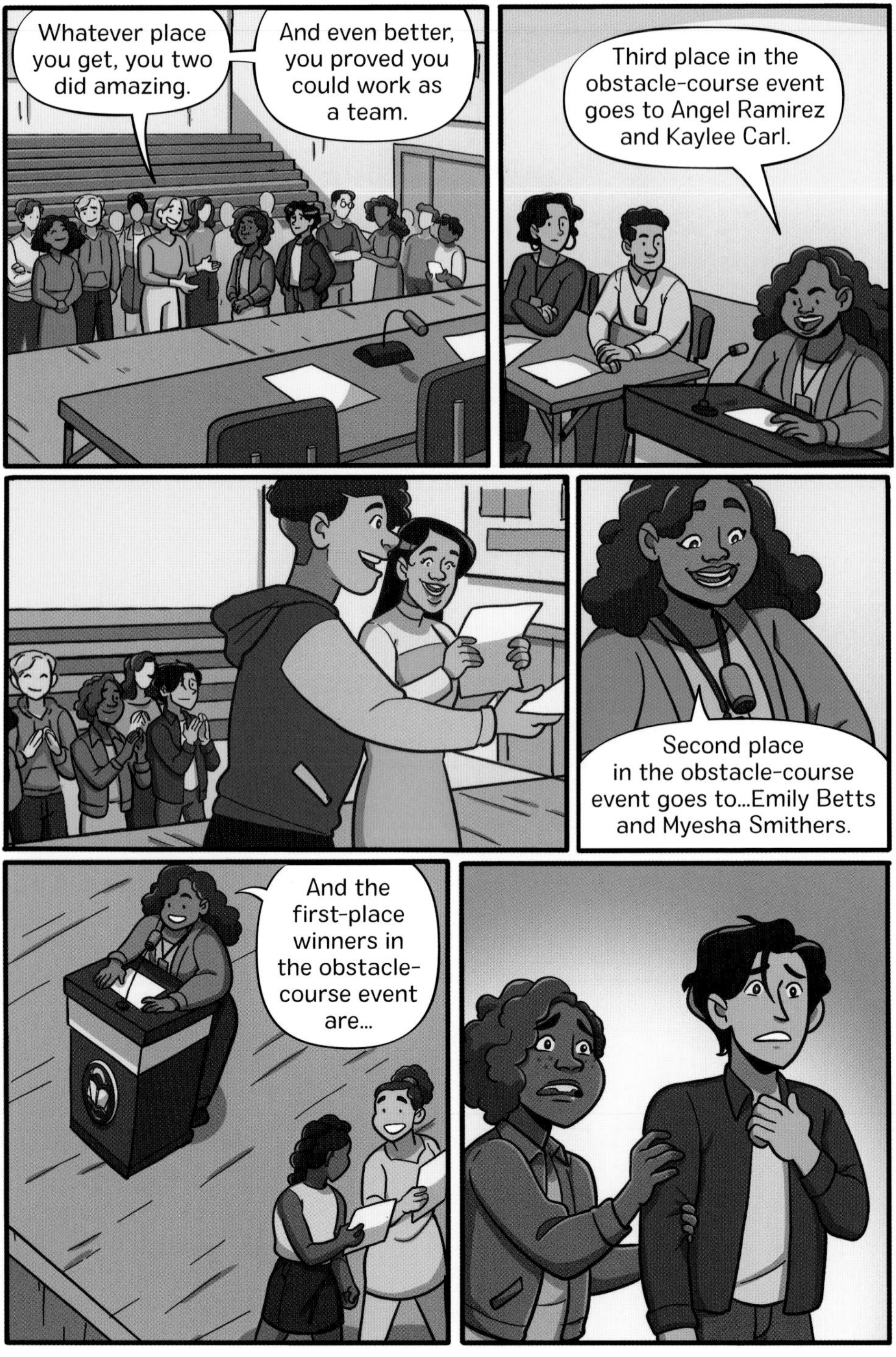
Whatever place you get, you two did amazing.
And even better, you proved you could work as a team.
Third place in the obstacle-course event goes to Angel Ramirez and Kaylee Carl.
Second place in the obstacle-course event goes to...Emily Betts and Myesha Smithers.
And the first-place winners in the obstacle-course event are...

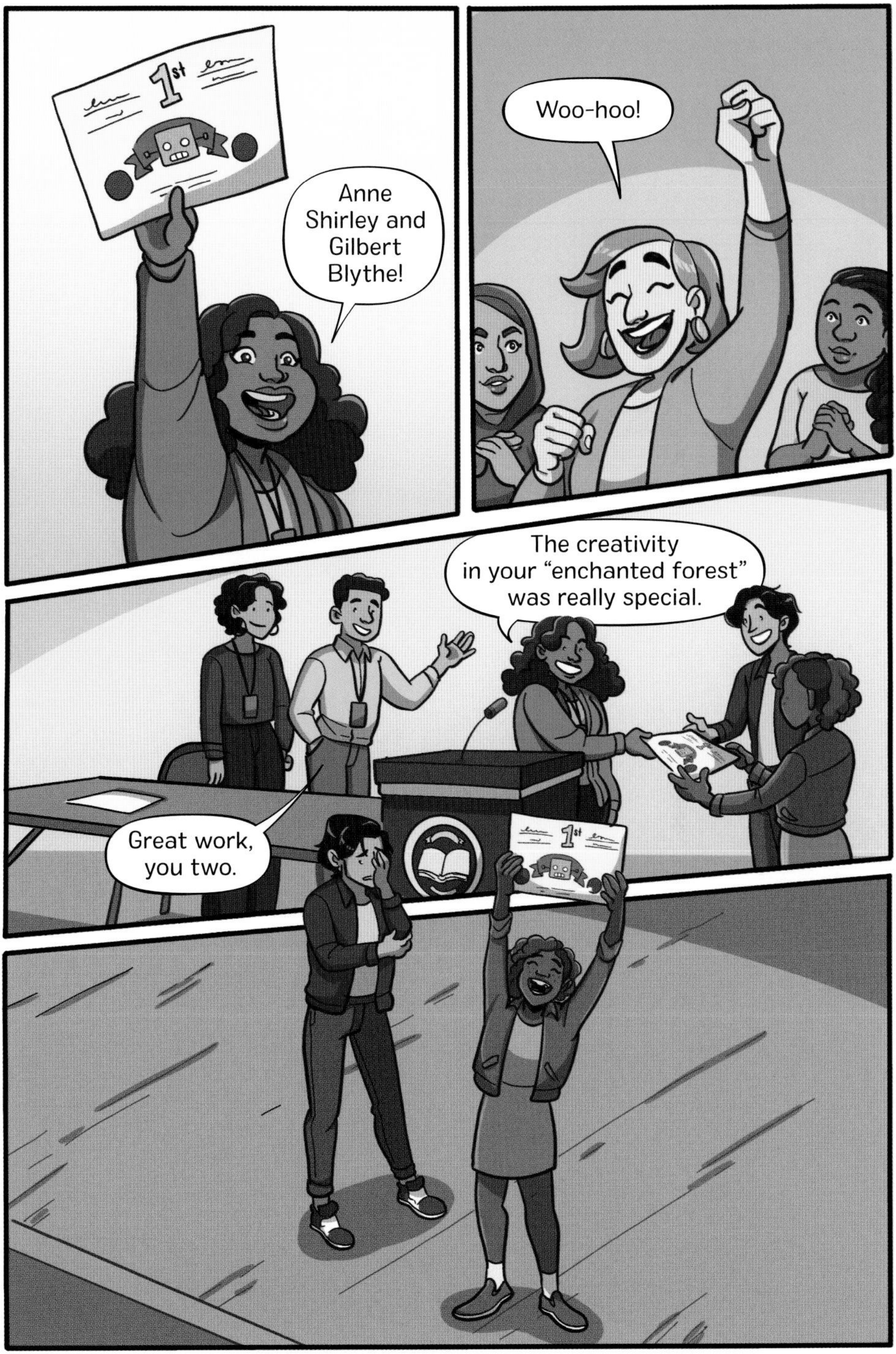
Anne Shirley and Gilbert Blythe!
Woo-hoo!
The creativity in your "enchanted forest" was really special.
Great work, you two.

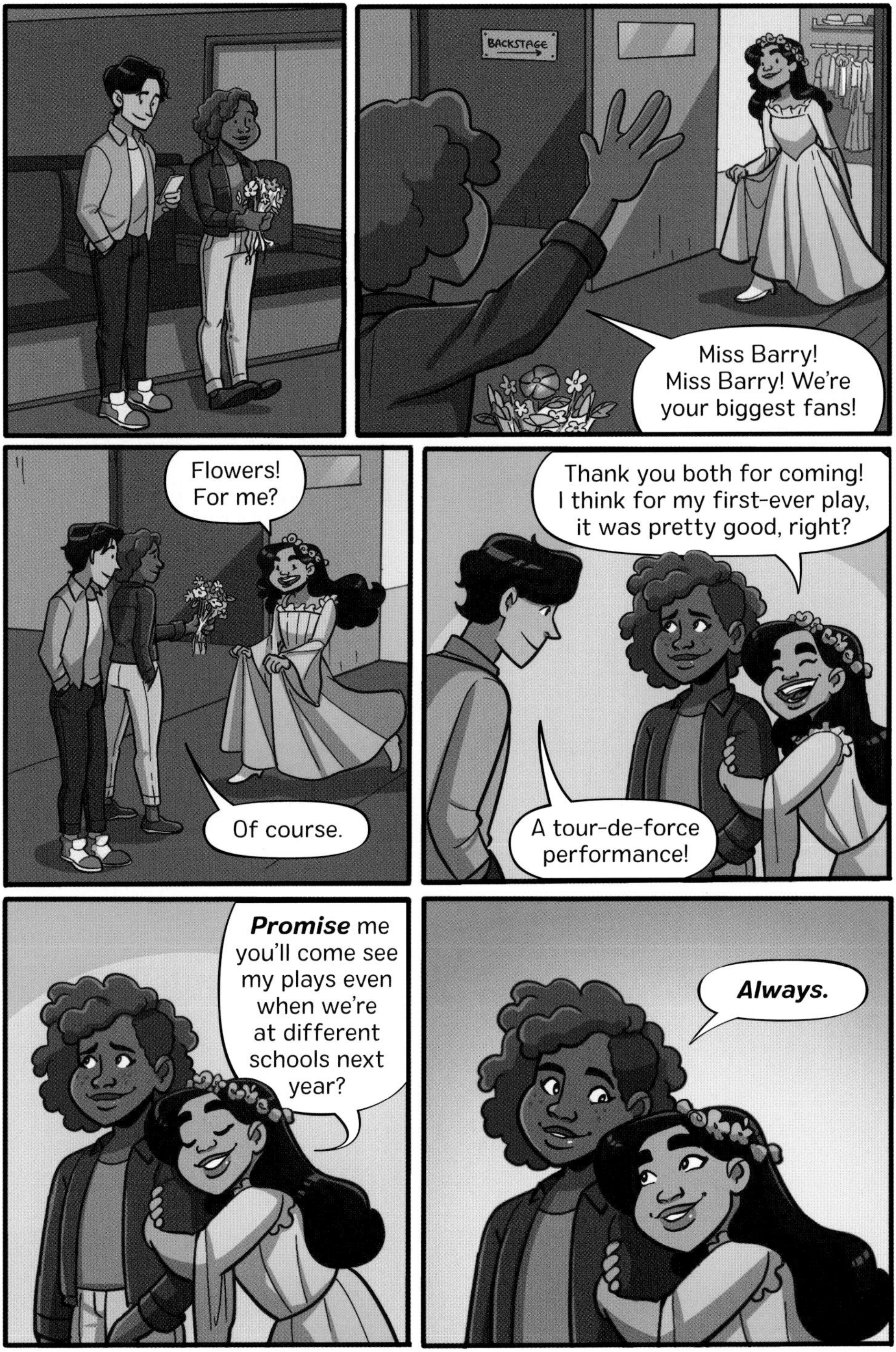
BACKSTAGE
Miss Barry! Miss Barry! We're your biggest fans!
Flowers! For me?
Of course.
Thank you both for coming! I think for my first-ever play, it was pretty good, right?
A tour-de-force performance!
Promise me you'll come see my plays even when we're at different schools next year?
Always.

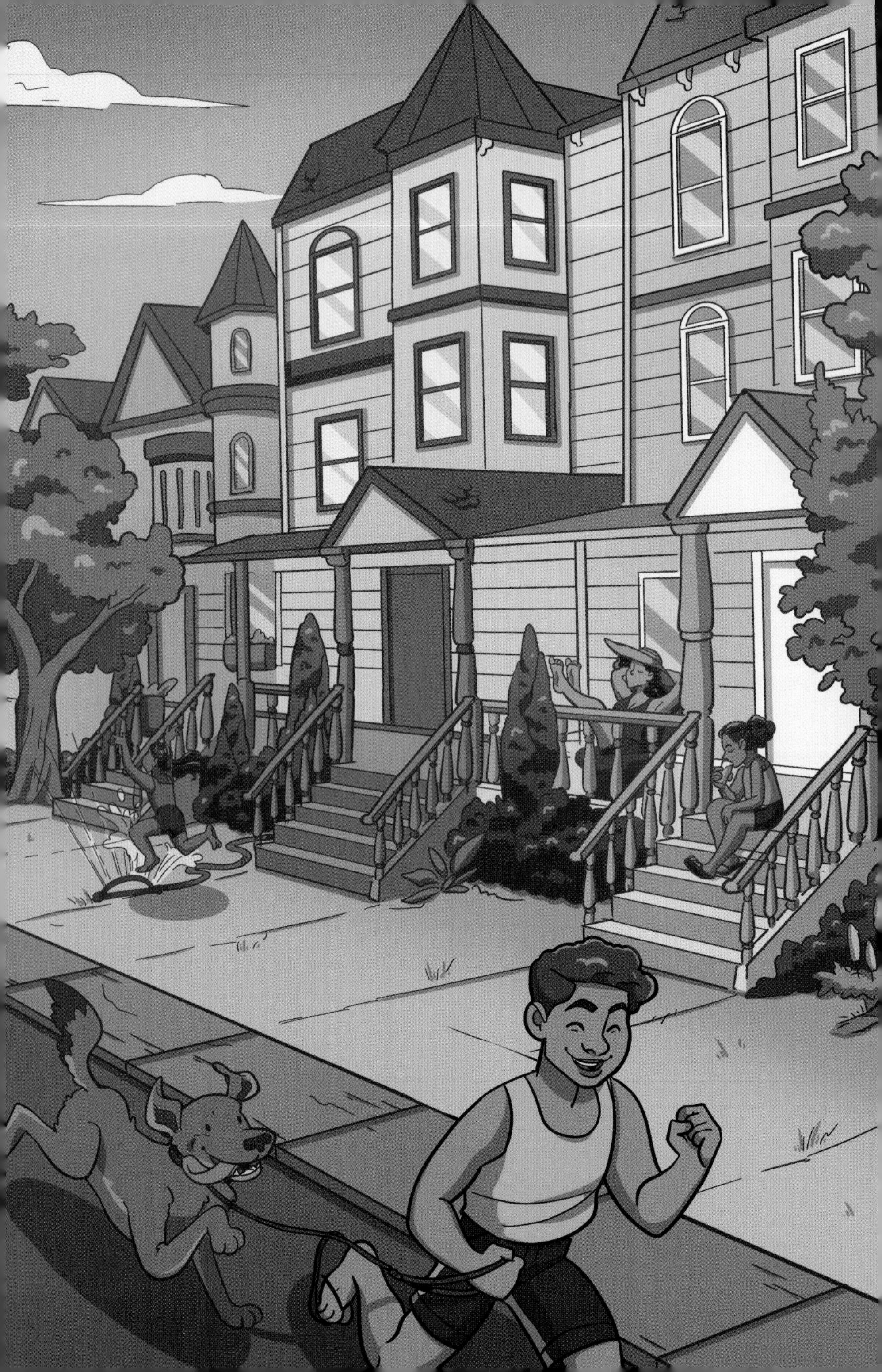

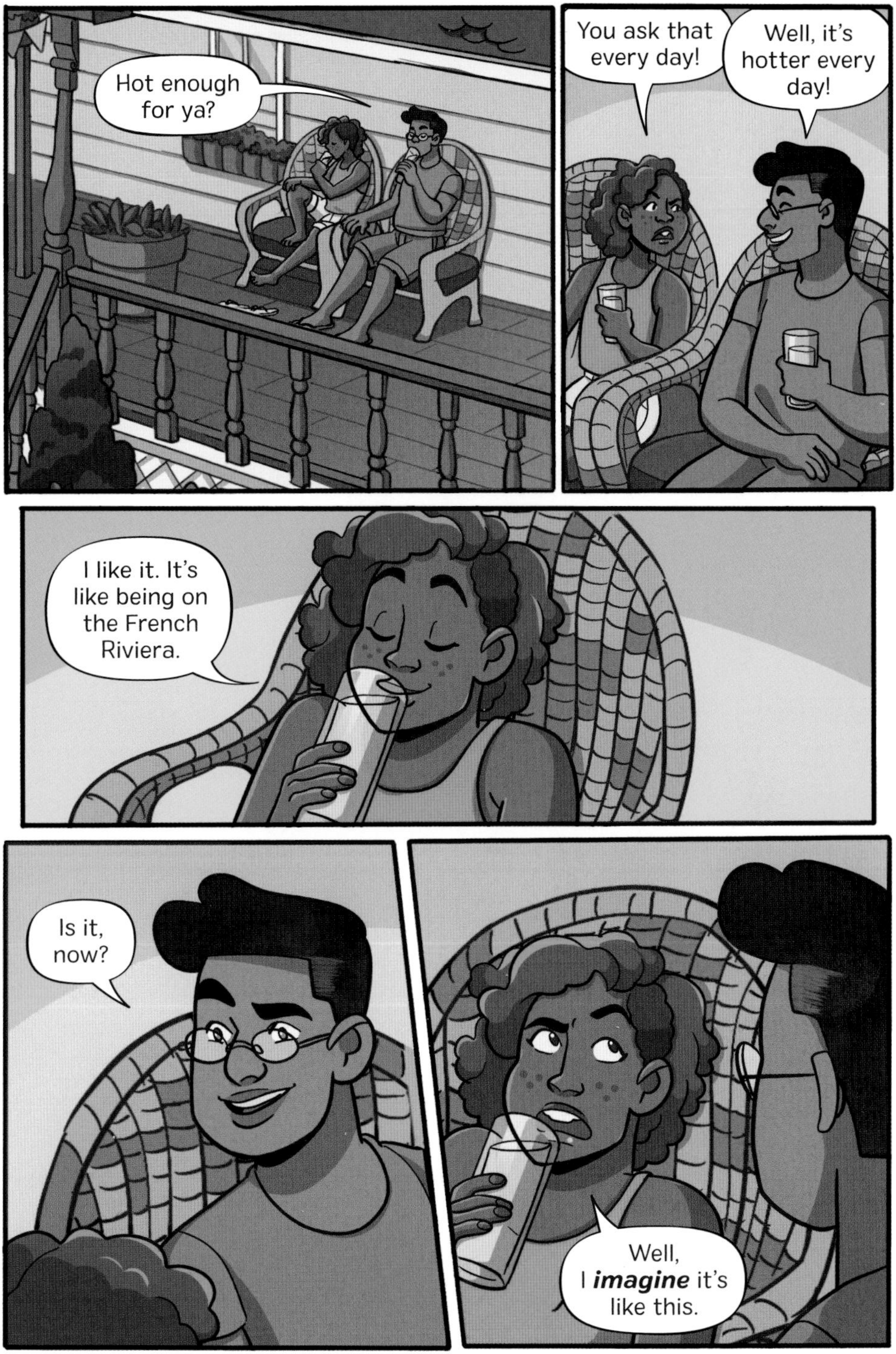
Hot enough for ya?
You ask that every day!
Well, it's hotter every day!
I like it. It's like being on the French Riviera.
Is it, now?
Well, I ***imagine*** it's like this.

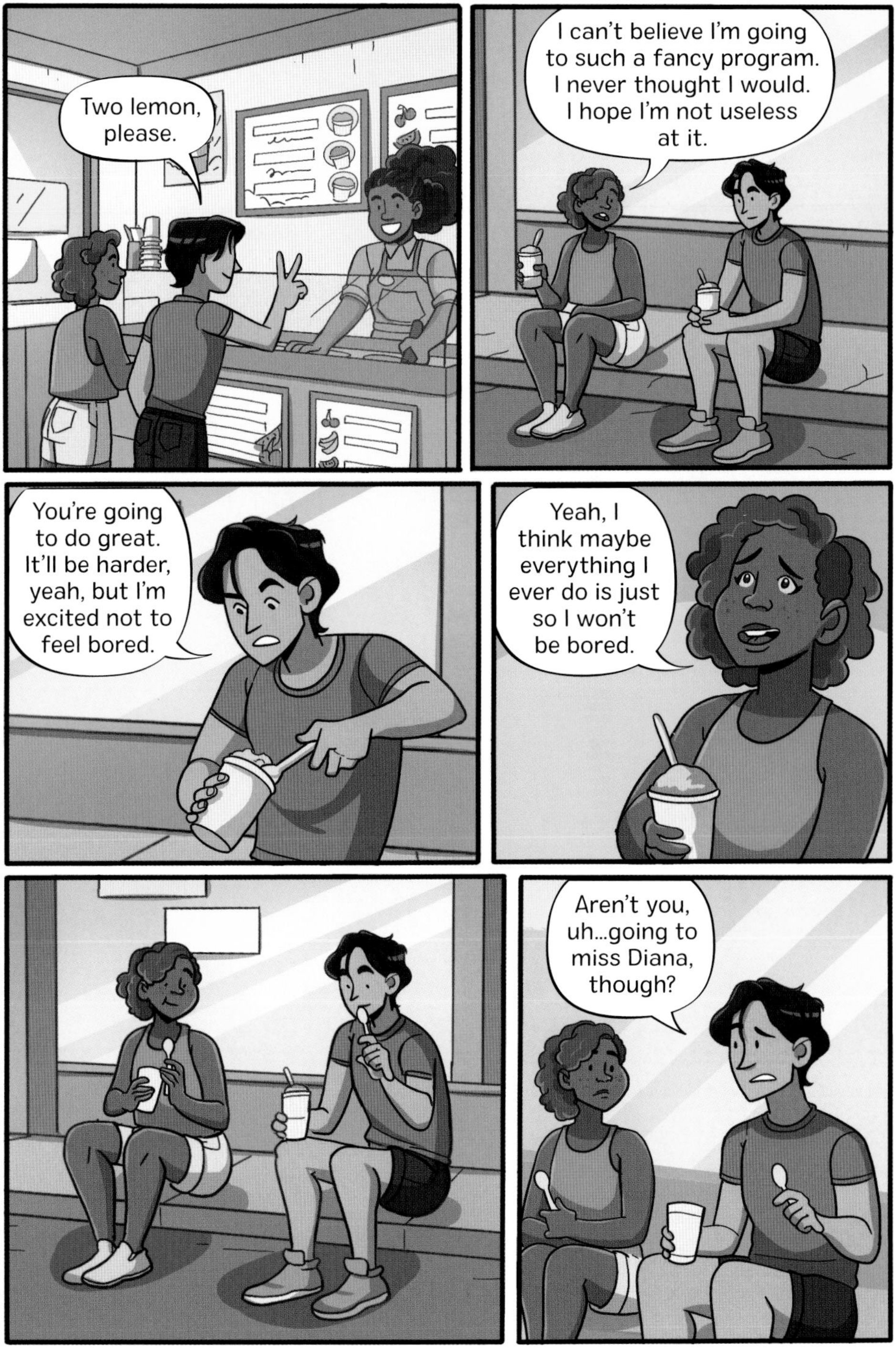
Two lemon, please.
I can't believe I'm going to such a fancy program. I never thought I would. I hope I'm not useless at it.
You're going to do great. It'll be harder, yeah, but I'm excited not to feel bored.
Yeah, I think maybe everything I ever do is just so I won't be bored.
Aren't you, uh...going to miss Diana, though?

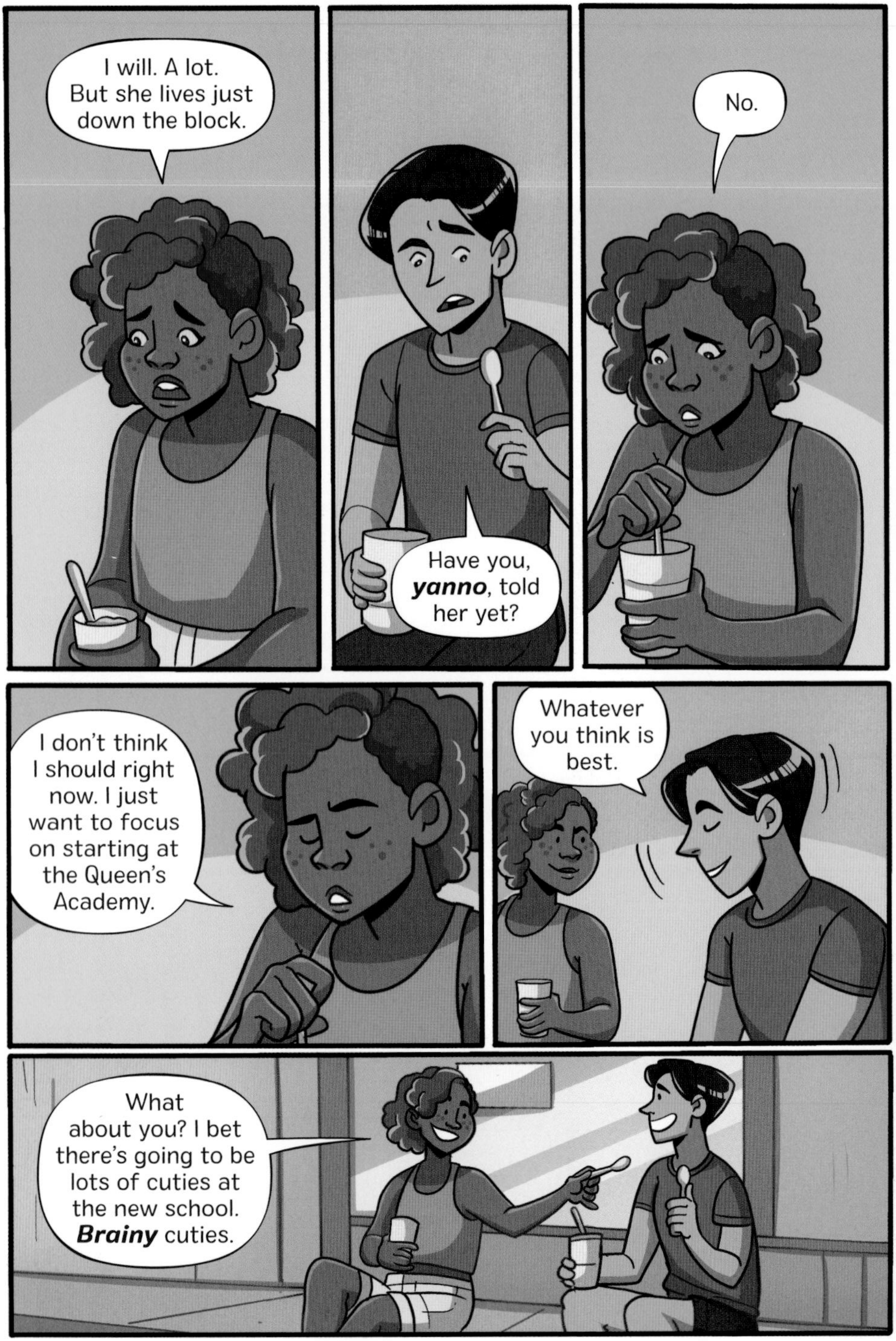
I will. A lot. But she lives just down the block.
Have you, ***yanno***, told her yet?
No.
I don't think I should right now. I just want to focus on starting at the Queen's Academy.
Whatever you think is best.
What about you? I bet there's going to be lots of cuties at the new school. ***Brainy*** cuties.

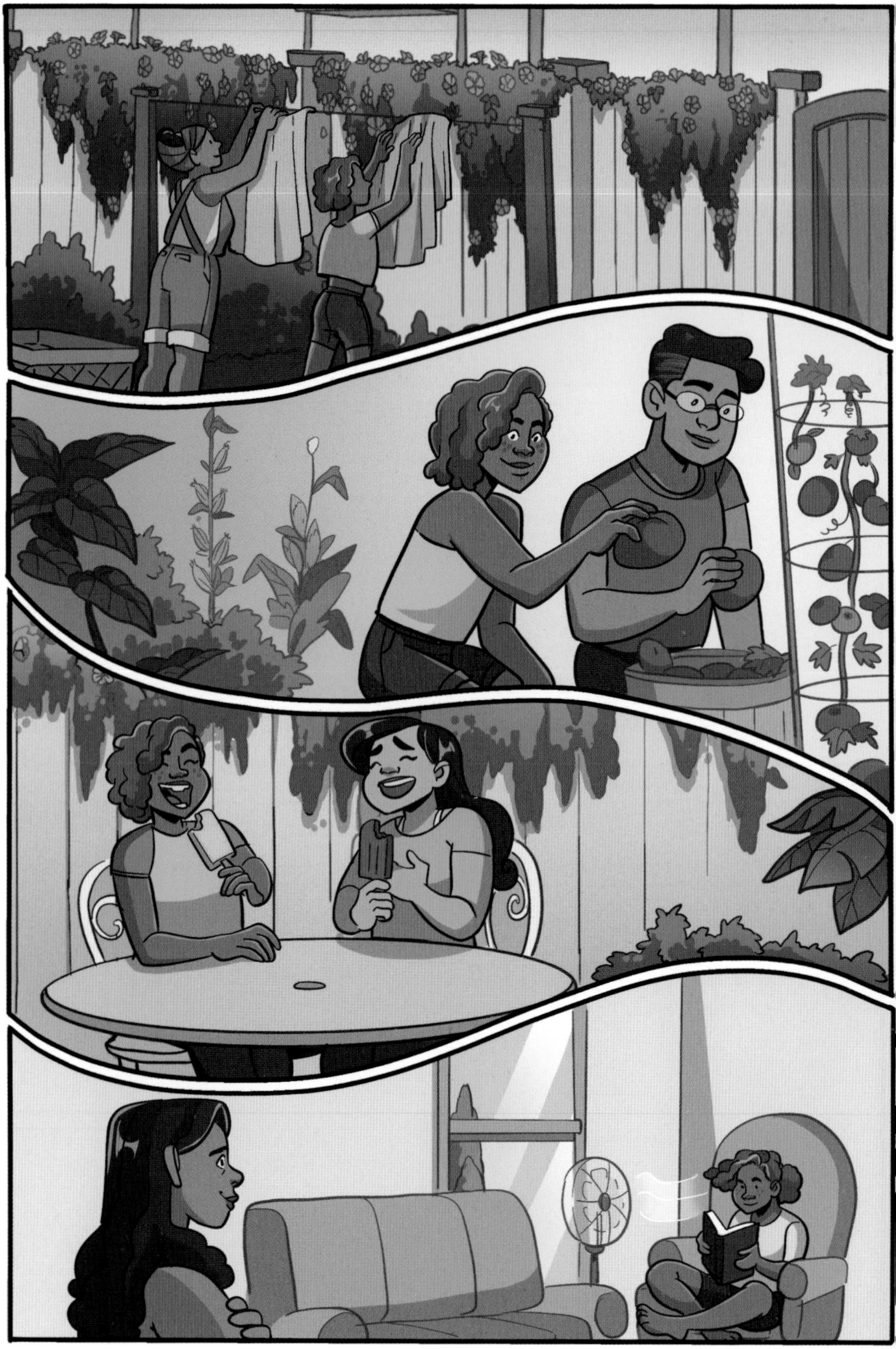

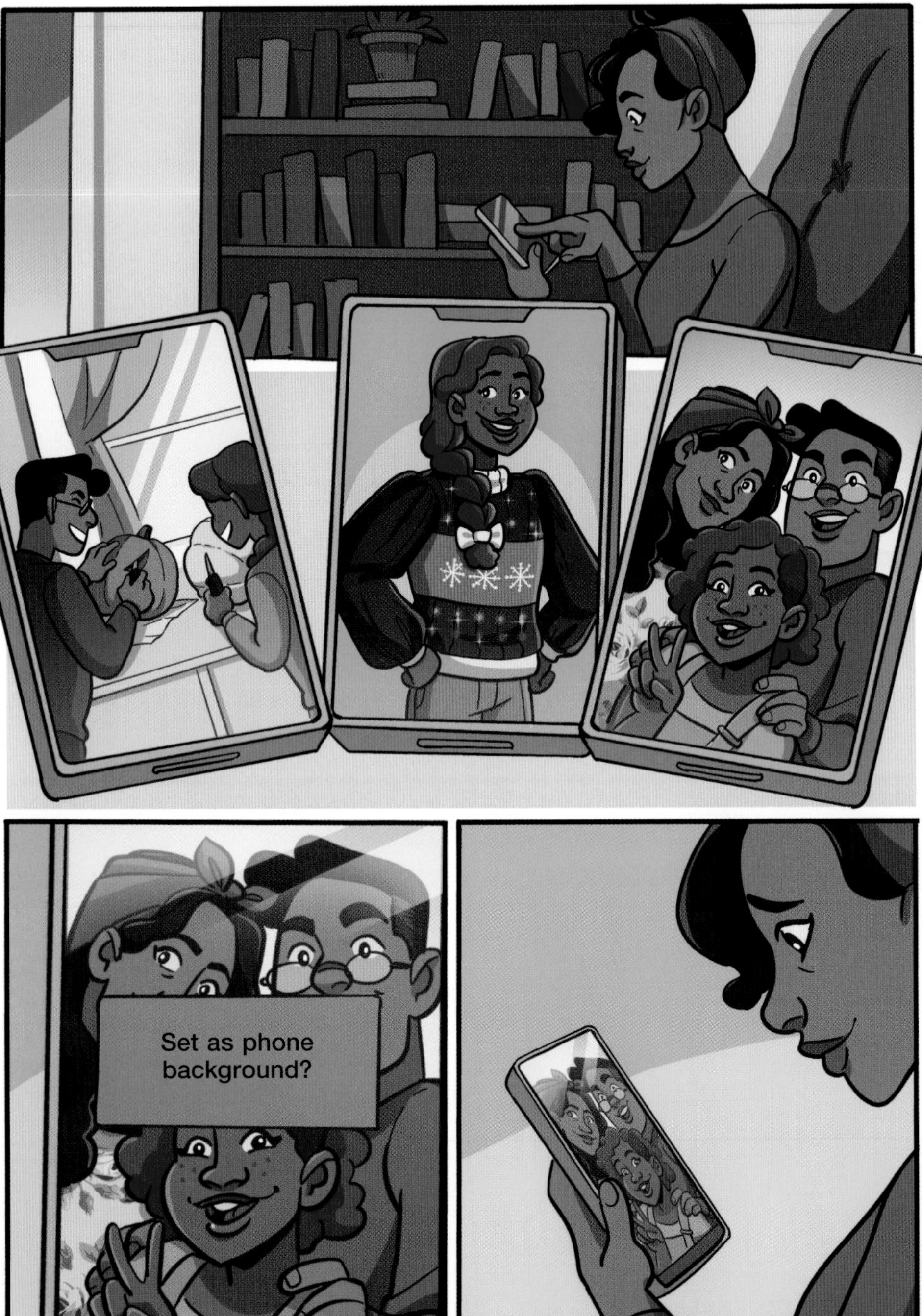
Set as phone background?

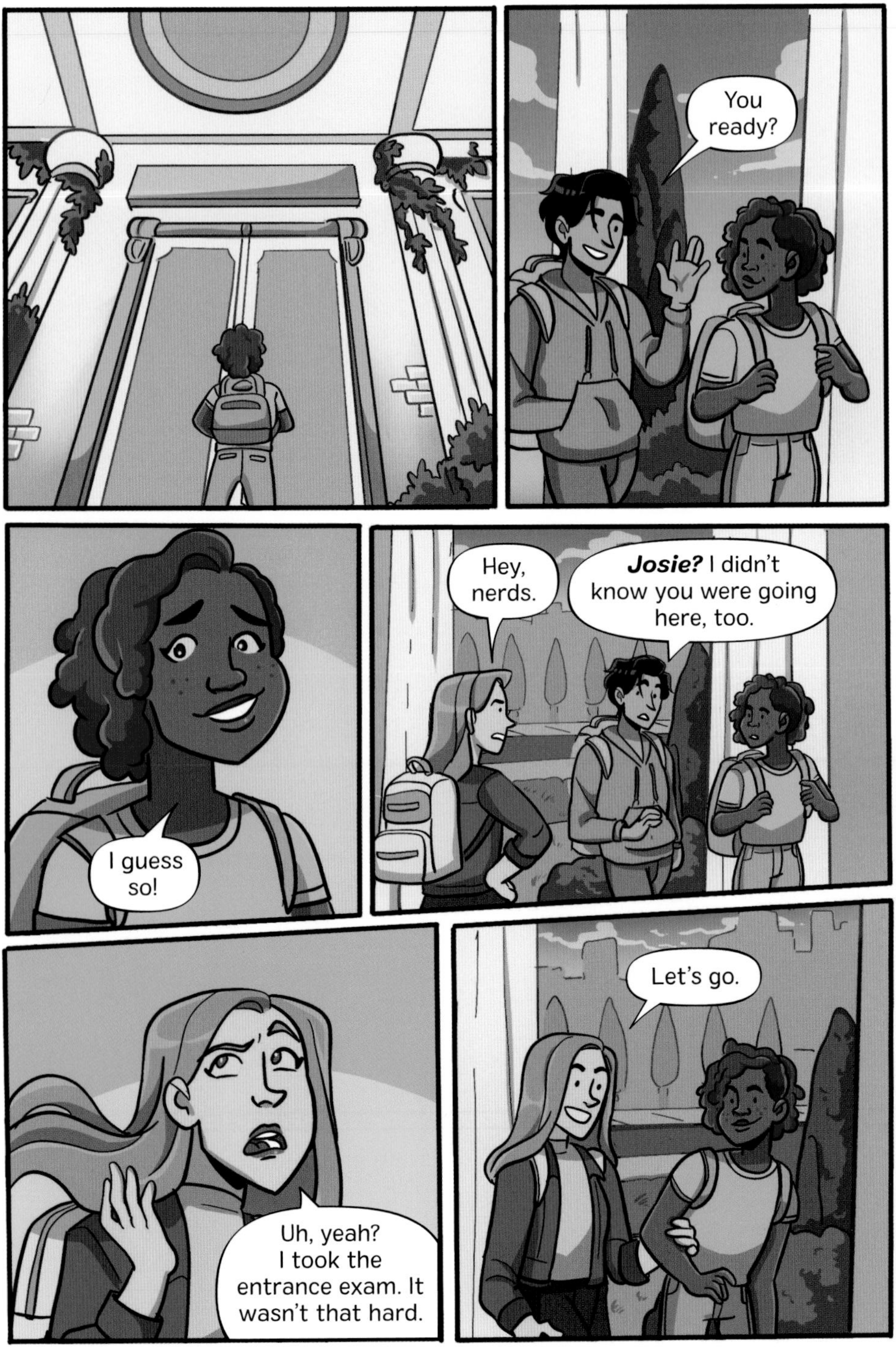
You ready?
I guess so!
Hey, nerds.
Josie? I didn't know you were going here, too.
Uh, yeah? I took the entrance exam. It wasn't that hard.
Let's go.

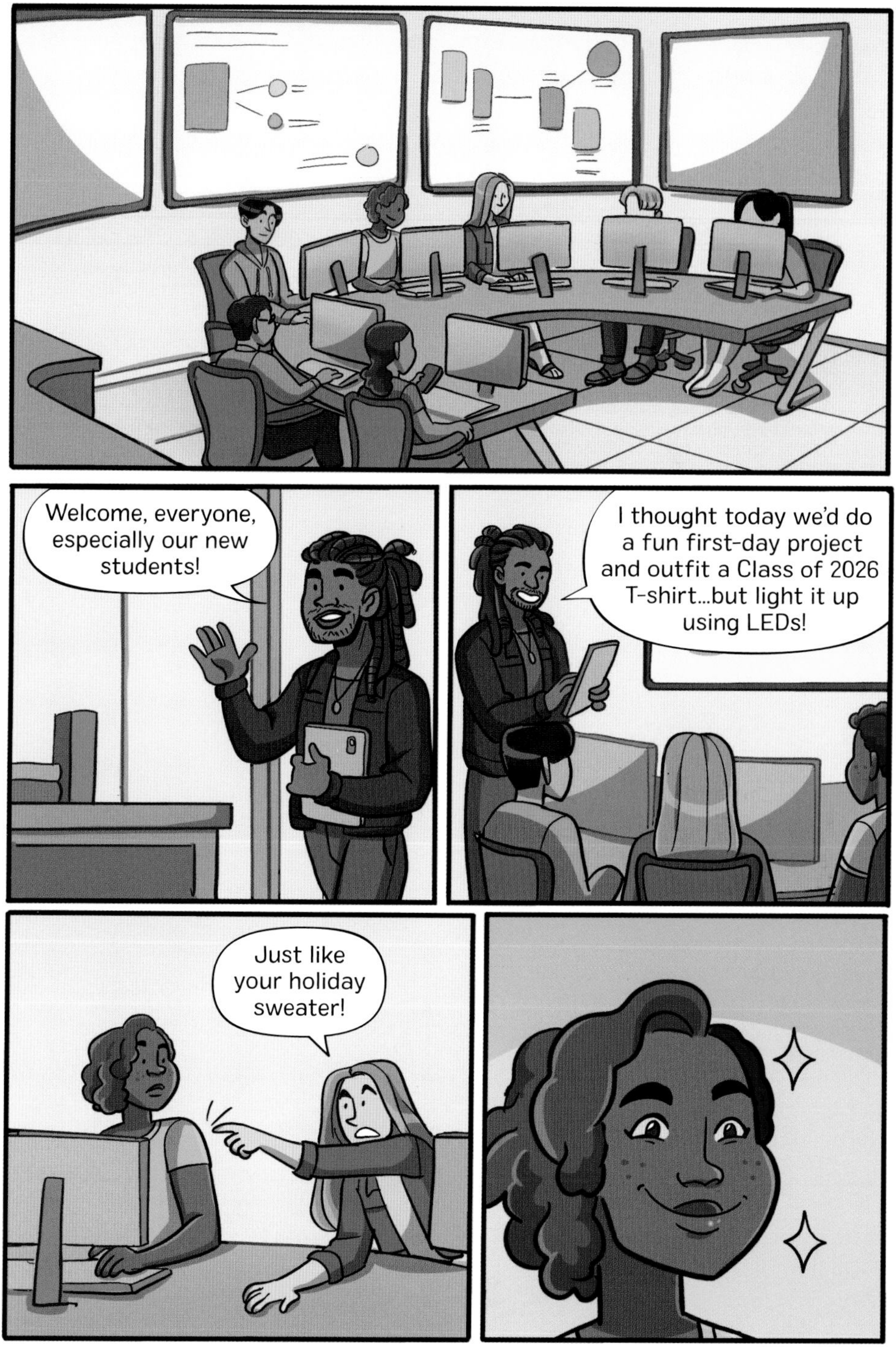
Welcome, everyone, especially our new students!
I thought today we'd do a fun first-day project and outfit a Class of 2026 T-shirt...but light it up using LEDs!
Just like your holiday sweater!

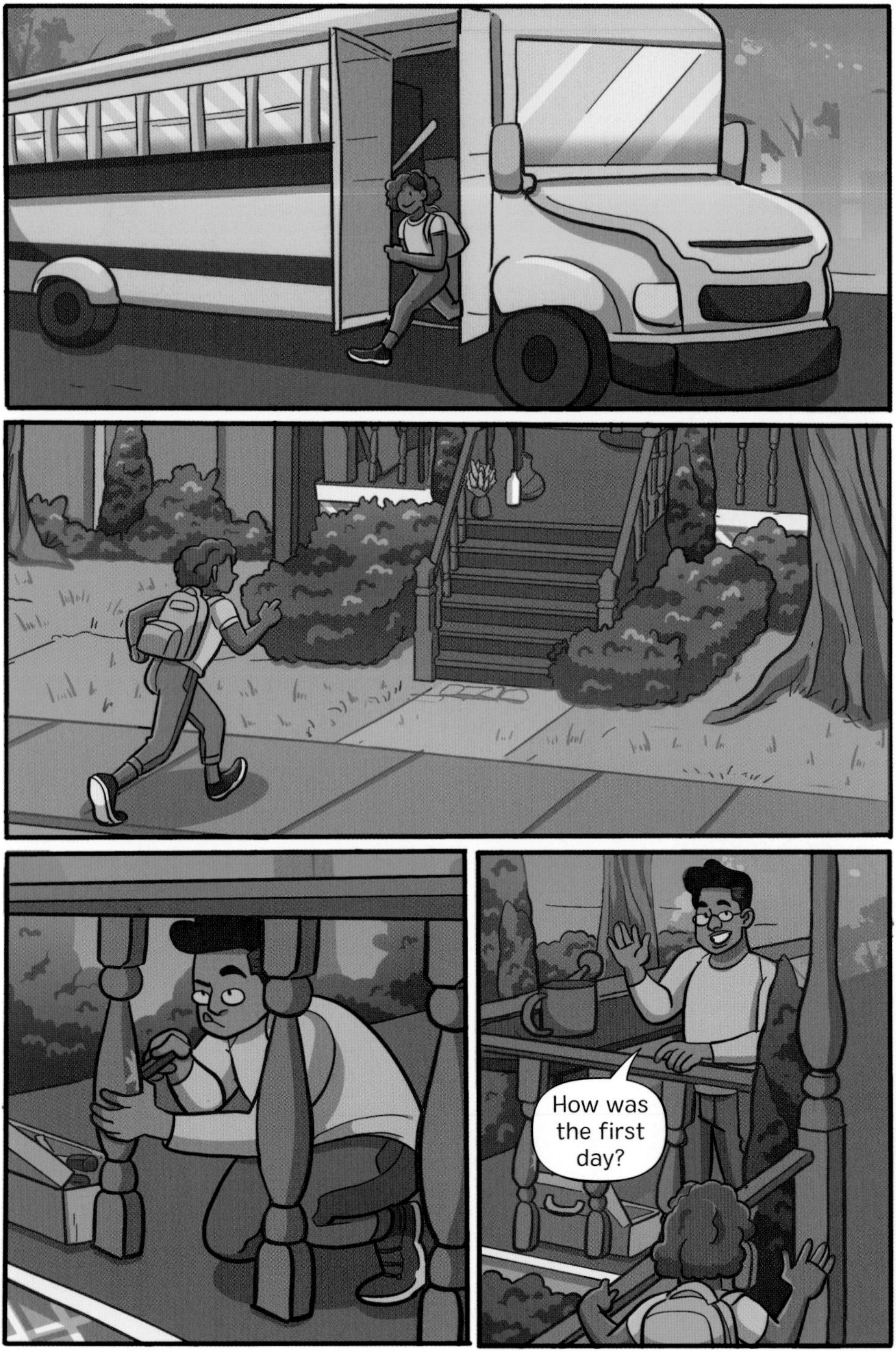
How was the first day?

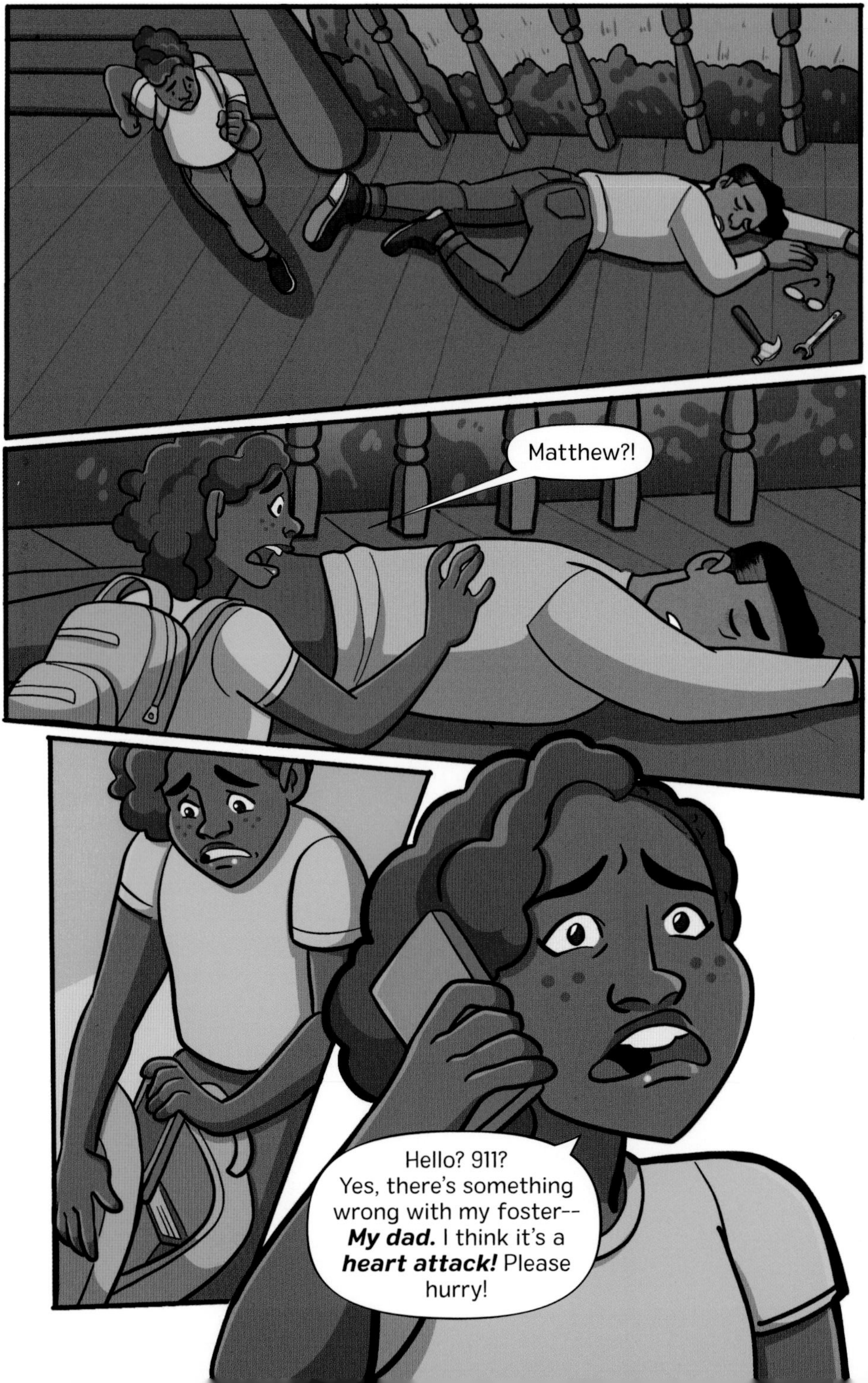
Matthew?!
Hello? 911? Yes, there's something wrong with my foster-- ***My dad.*** I think it's a ***heart attack!*** Please hurry!

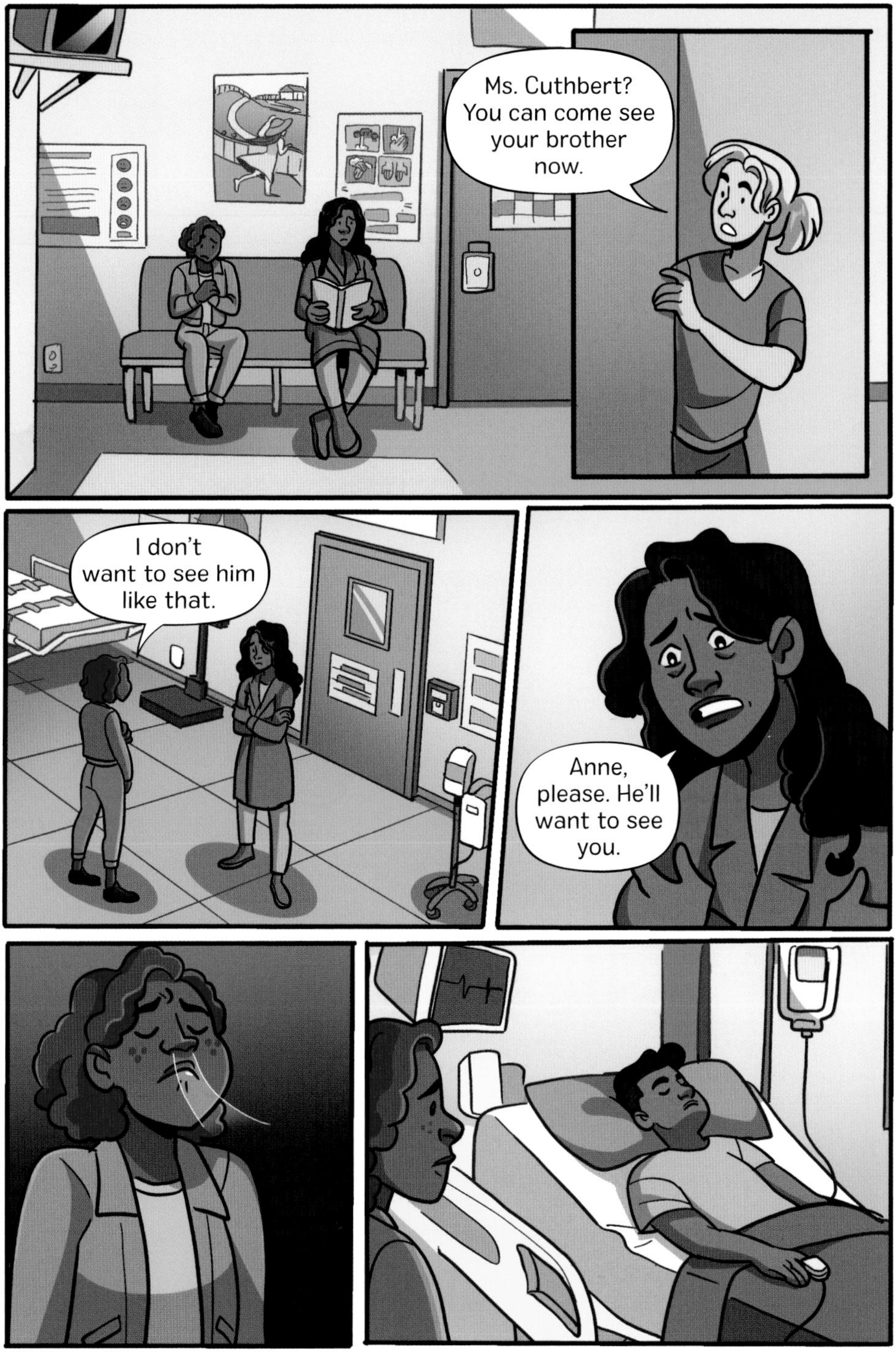
Ms. Cuthbert? You can come see your brother now.
I don't want to see him like that.
Anne, please. He'll want to see you.

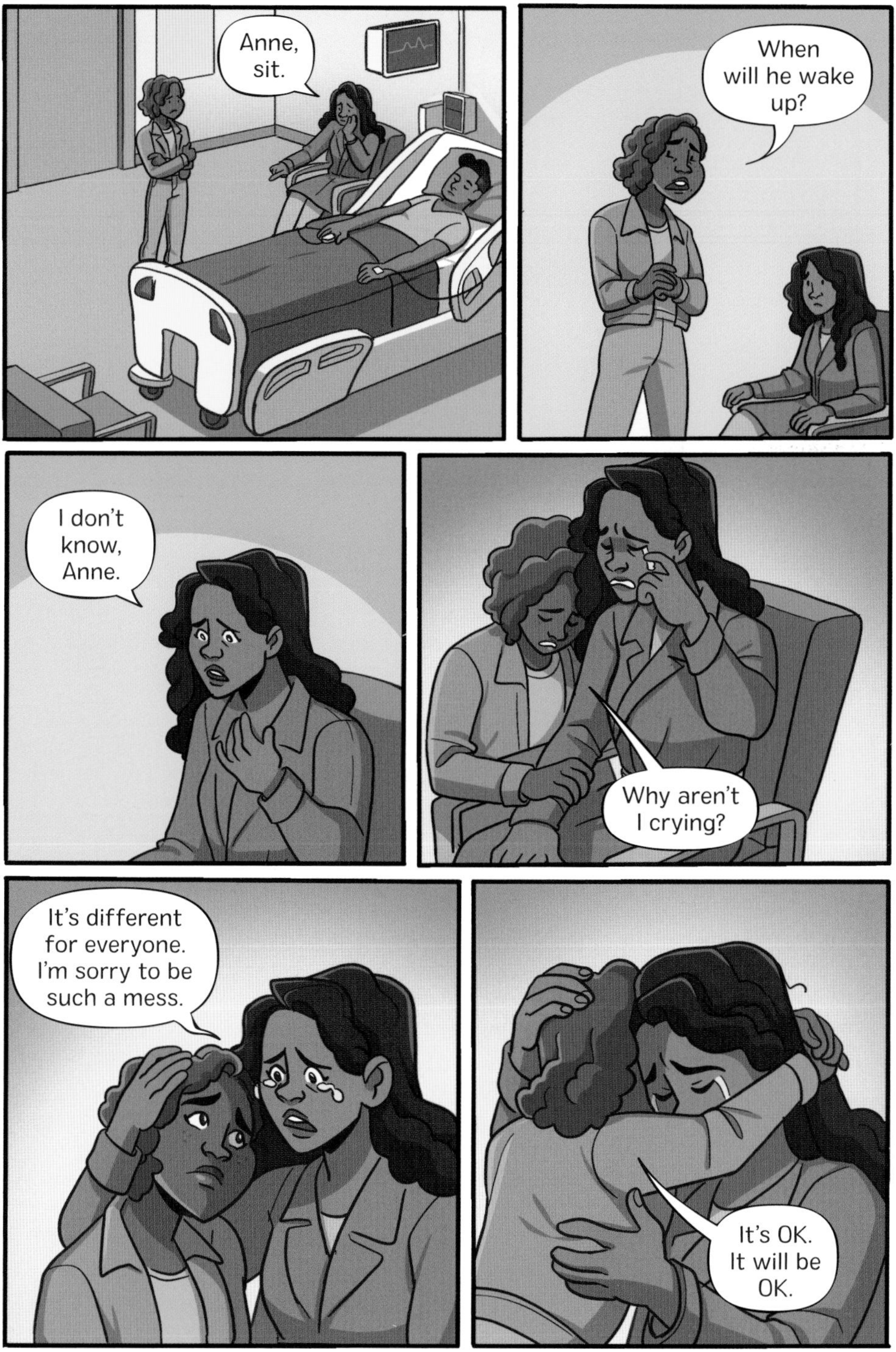
Anne, sit.
When will he wake up?
I don't know, Anne.
Why aren't I crying?
It's different for everyone. I'm sorry to be such a mess.
It's OK. It will be OK.

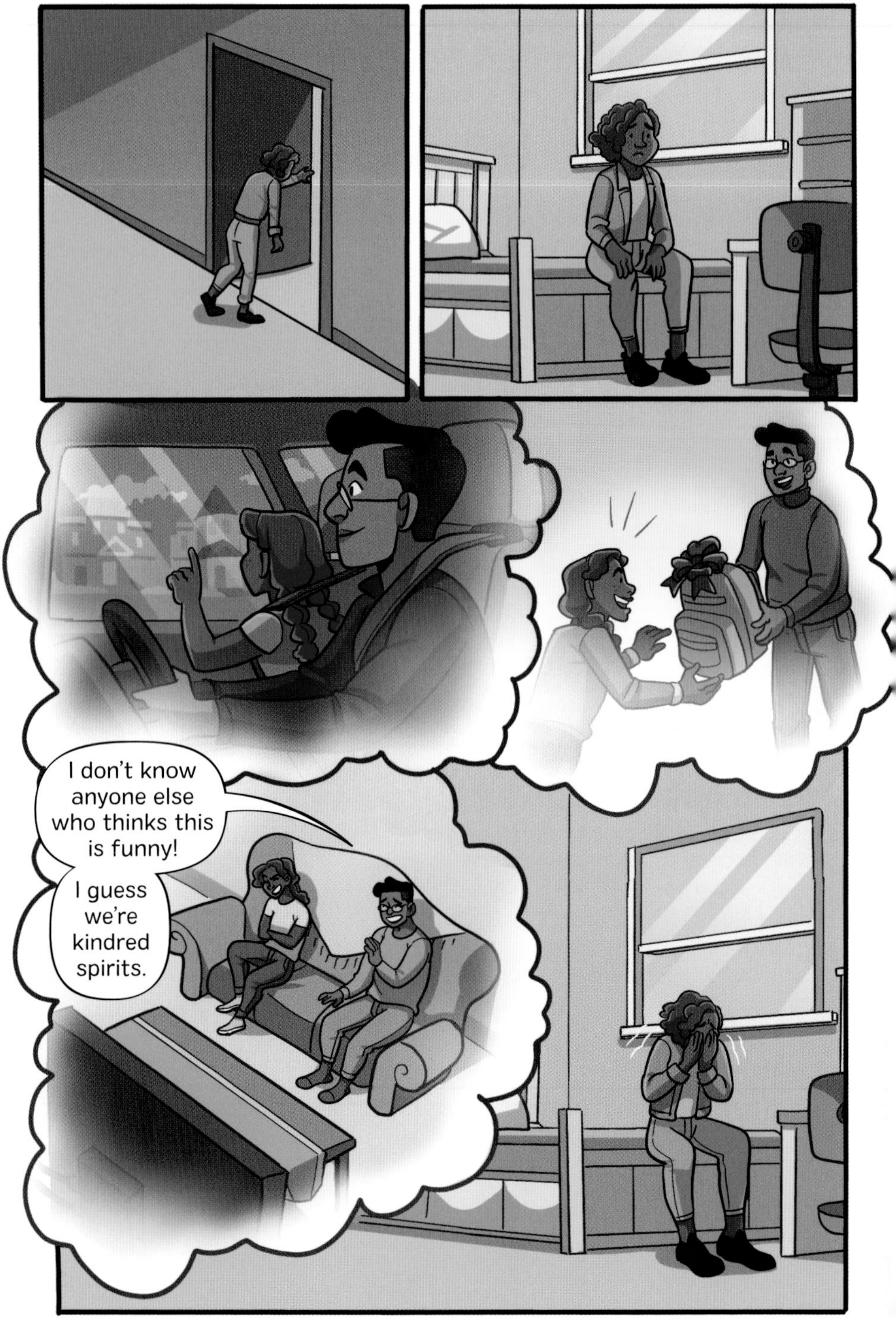
I don't know anyone else who thinks this is funny!
I guess we're kindred spirits.

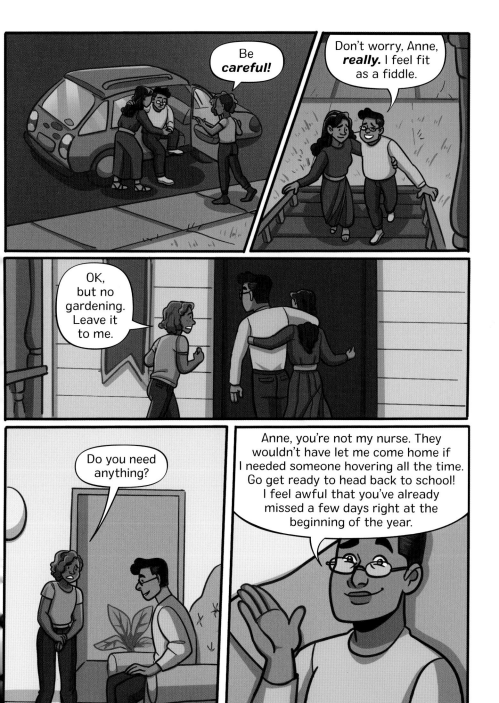

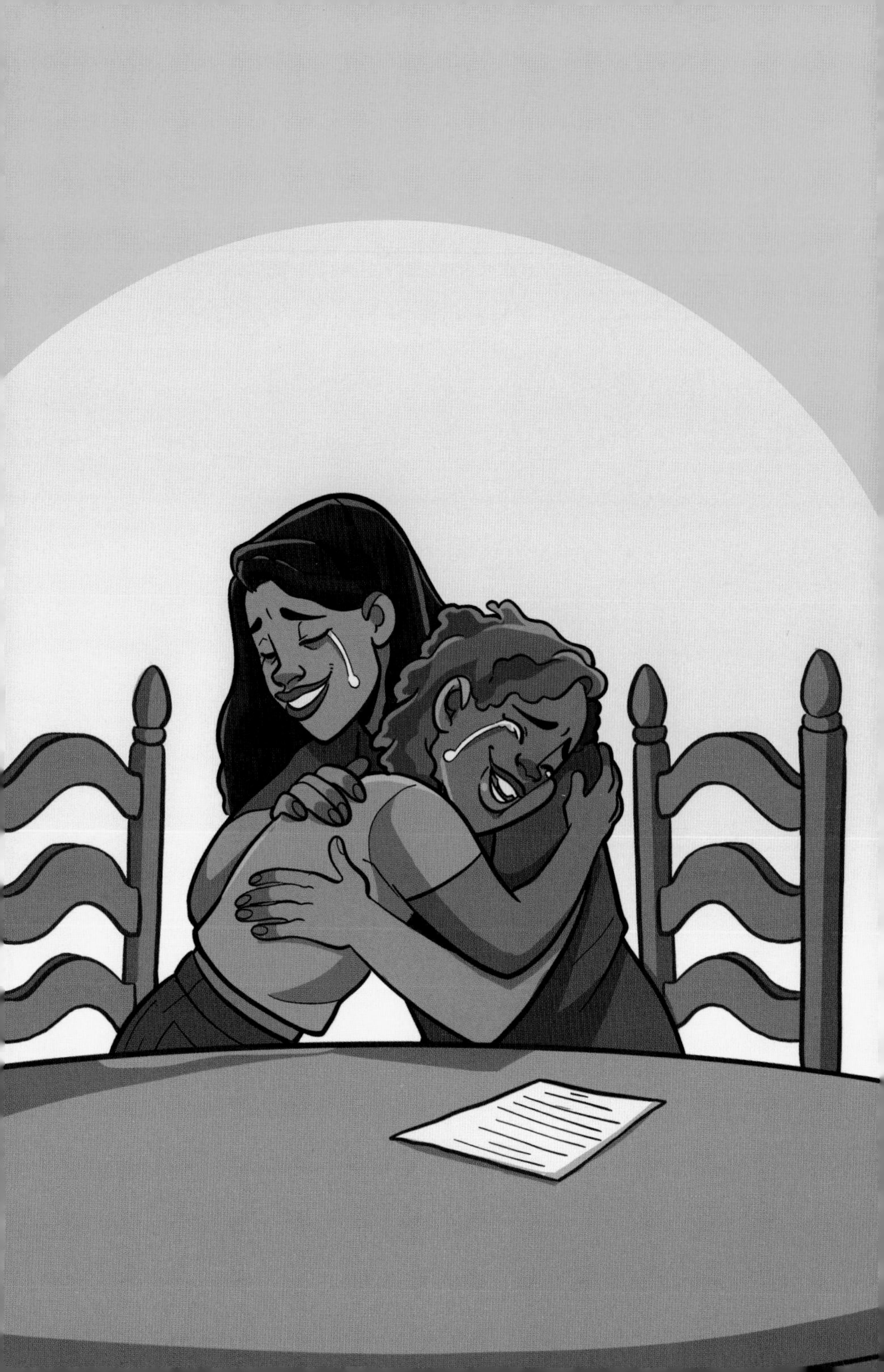

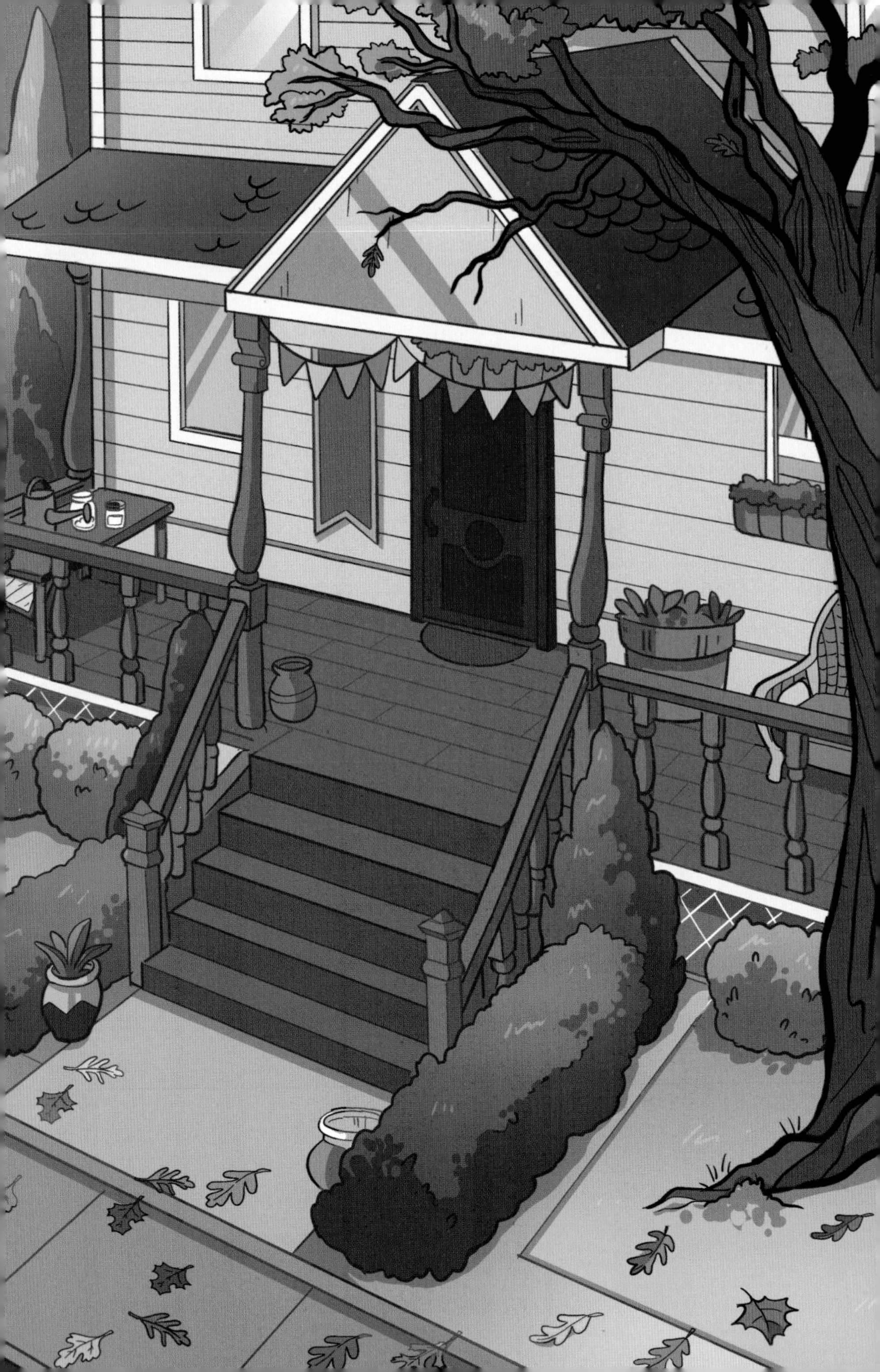

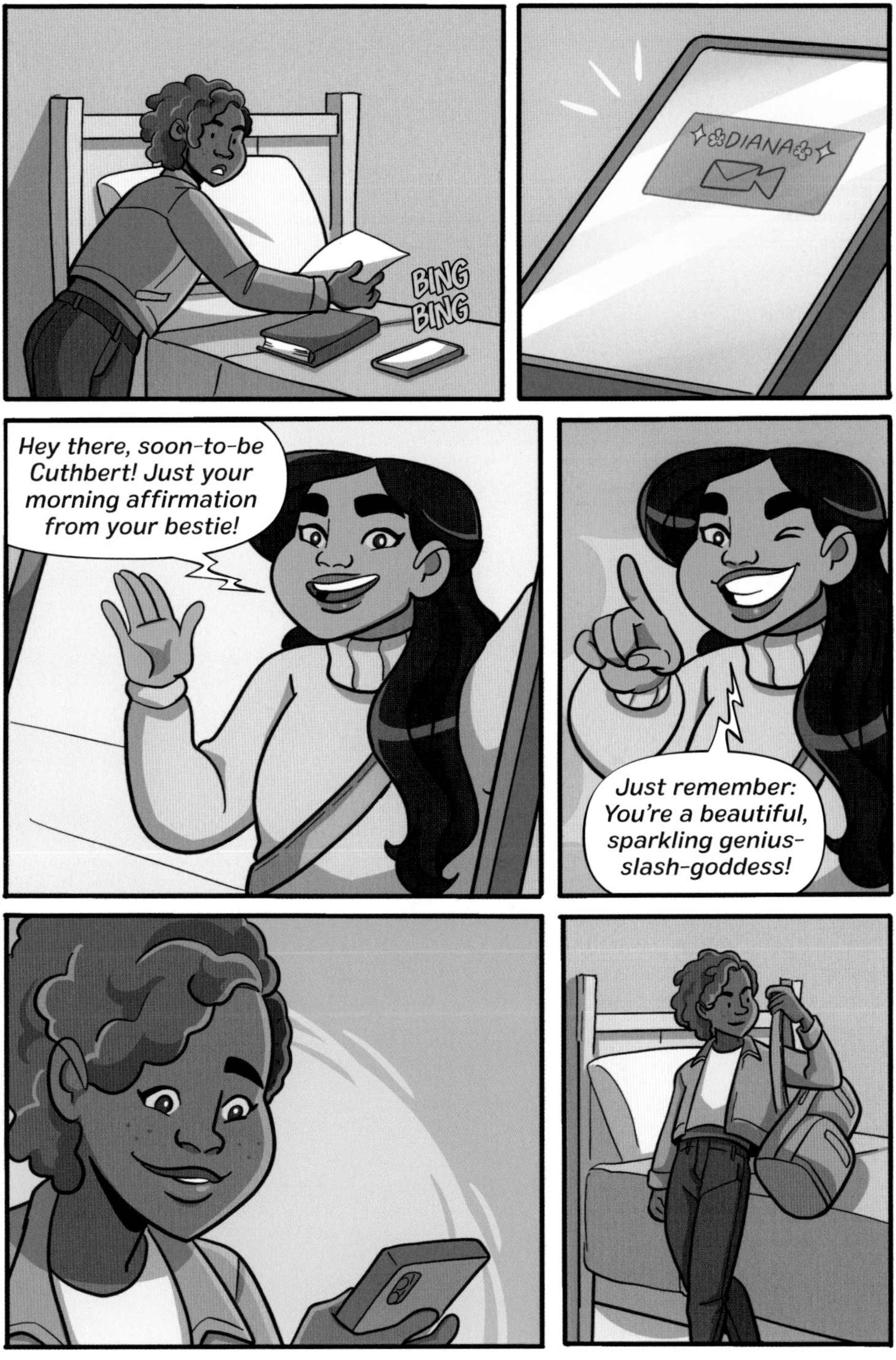
BING
BING
DIANA
Hey there, soon-to-be Cuthbert! Just your morning affirmation from your bestie!
Just remember: You're a beautiful, sparkling genius-slash-goddess!

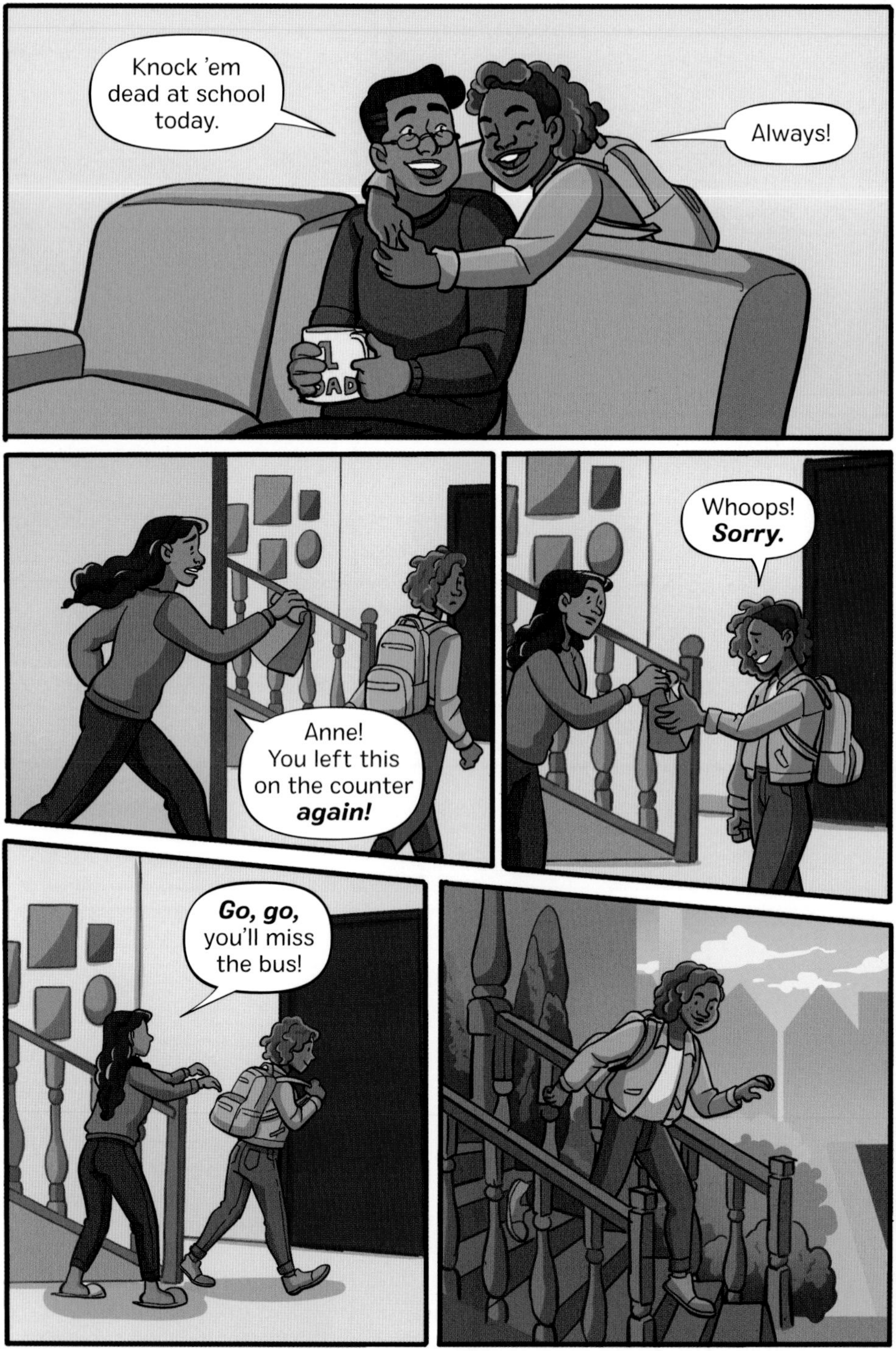
Knock 'em dead at school today.
Always!
Anne! You left this on the counter ***again!***
Whoops! ***Sorry.***
Go, go, you'll miss the bus!

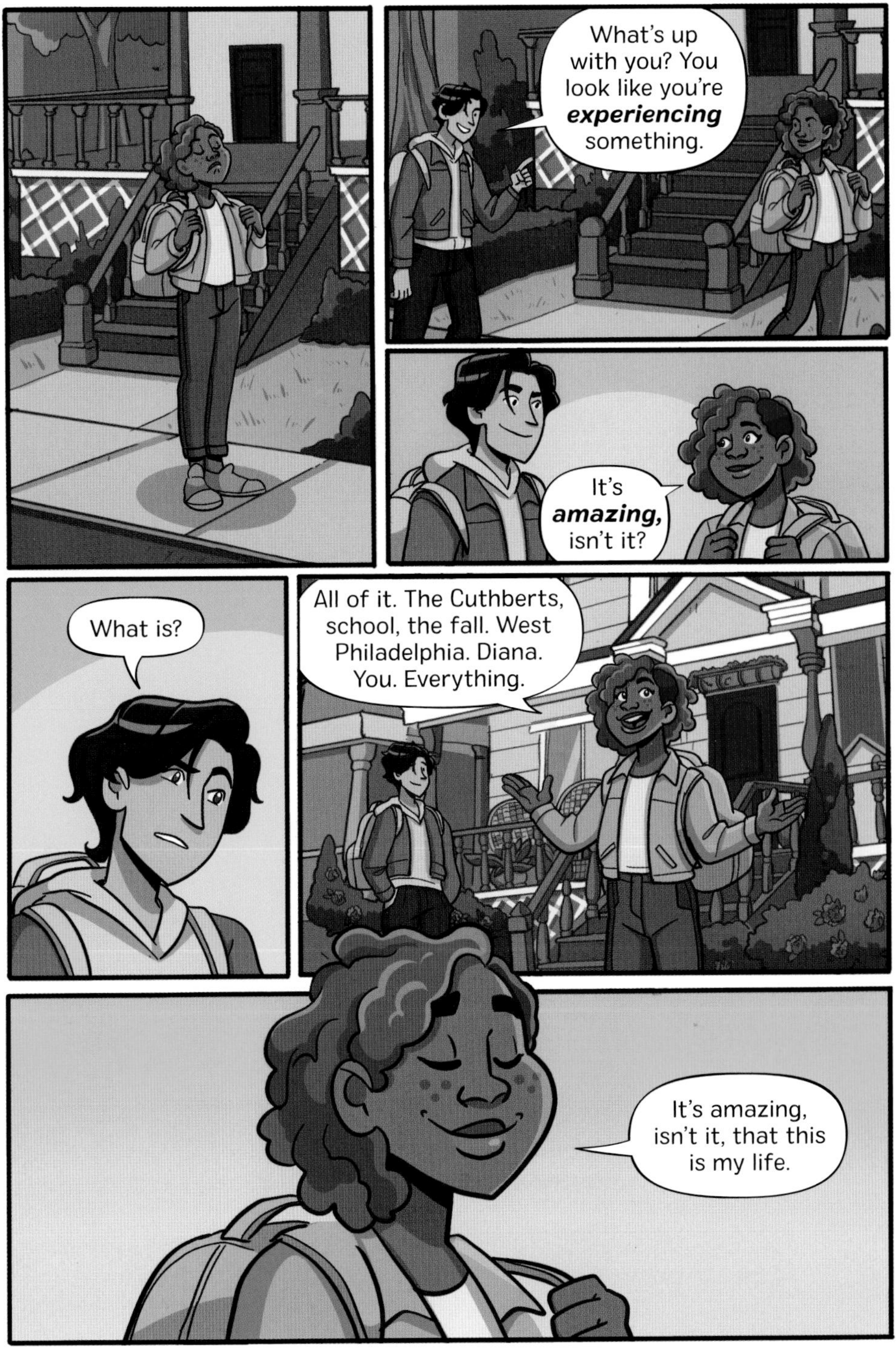
What's up with you? You look like you're ***experiencing*** something.
It's ***amazing,*** isn't it?
What is?
All of it. The Cuthberts, school, the fall. West Philadelphia. Diana. You. Everything.
It's amazing, isn't it, that this is my life.

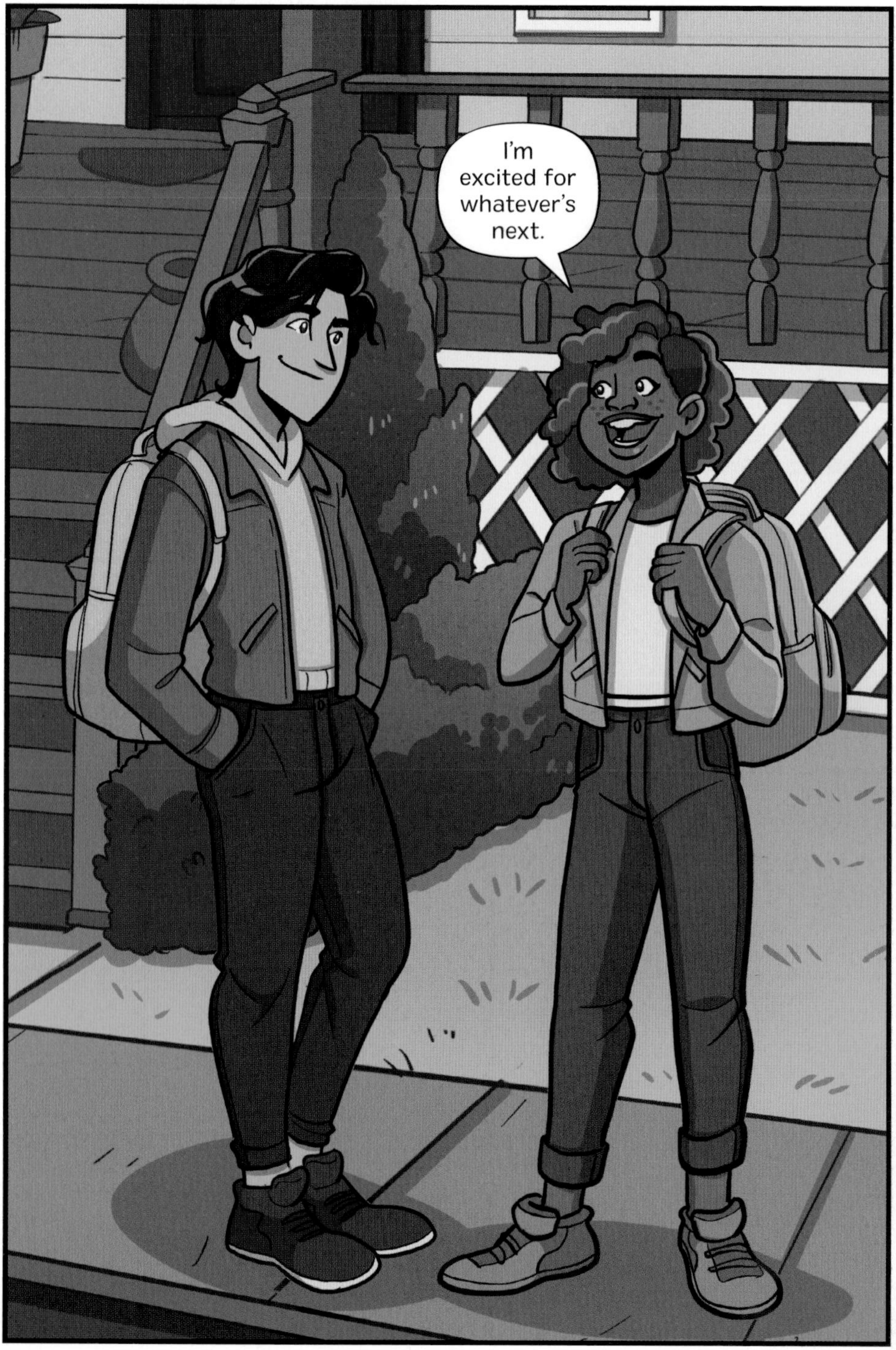
I'm excited for whatever's next.

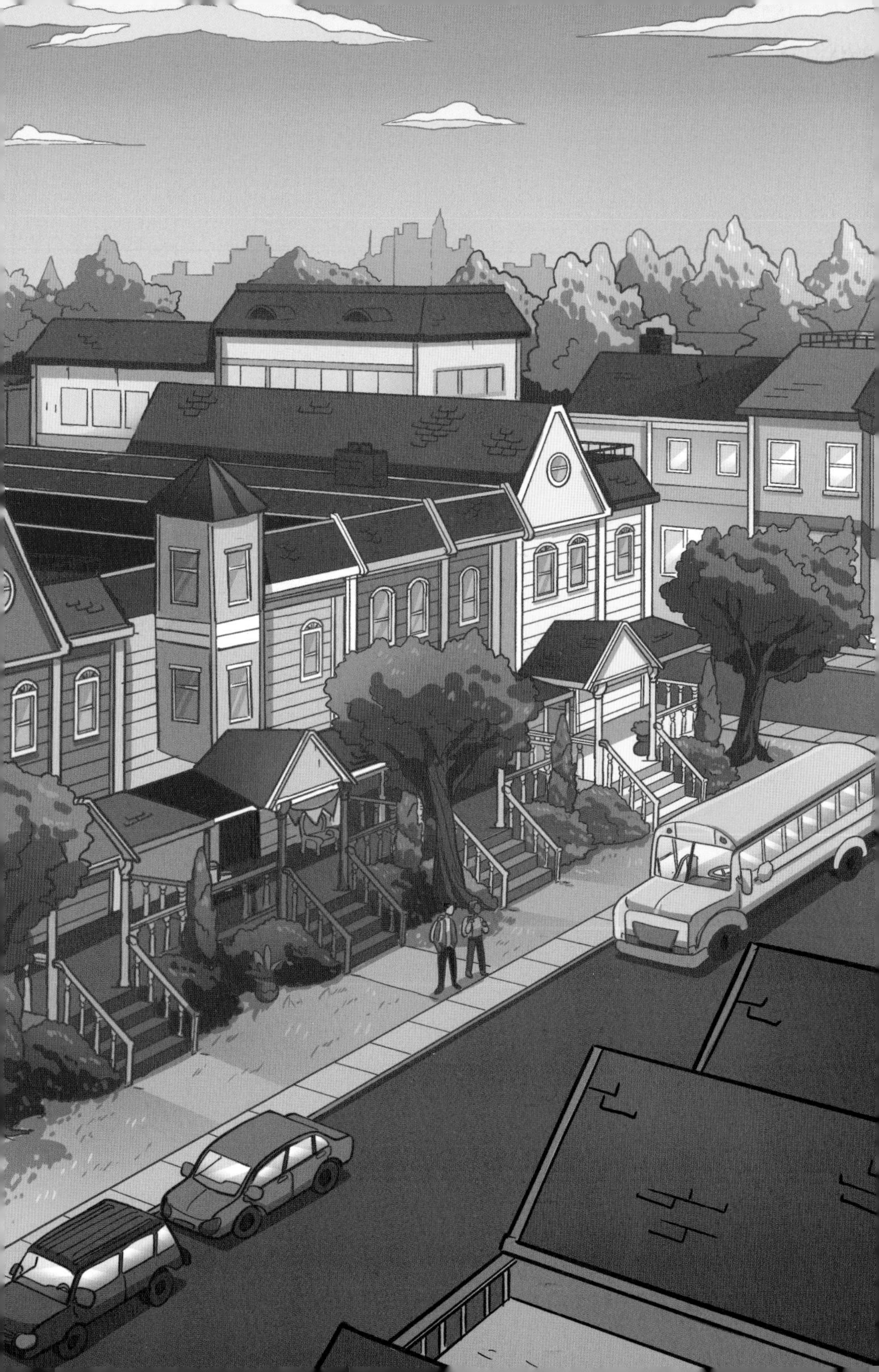

Eugene K. Ahn

Ivy Noelle Weir

is a writer of comics and prose. She is the author of *The Secret Garden on 81st Street* and the cocreator of the Dwayne McDuffie Award–winning graphic novel *Archival Quality*. Her writing has also appeared in anthologies such as *Princeless: Girls Rock* and *Dead Beats*. She lives in the greater Boston area with her husband and their two tiny, weird dogs.

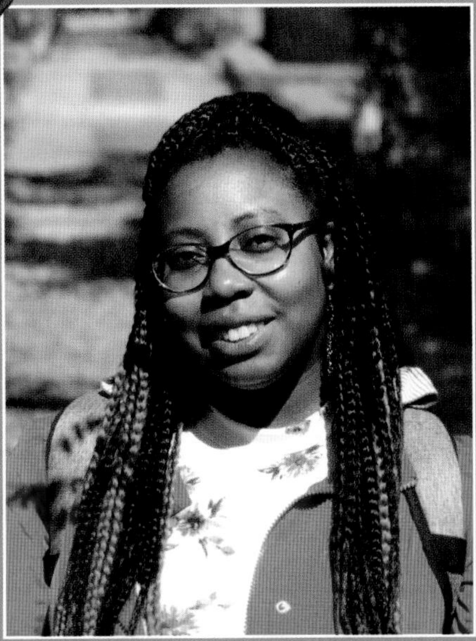

Adeline Kwa

Myisha Haynes

is a Sacramento-based comic creator who loves creating BIPOC-focused stories about friendships, adventure, and self-discovery. Besides her modern fantasy webcomic, *The Substitutes*, her work can also be seen in the award-winning anthology *Elements: Fire*; *Rolled & Tolled*; *Power & Magic: Volume 2*; and Marvel's *The Unbelievable Gwenpool*. *Anne of West Philly* is her first graphic novel.

Author Acknowledgments

Huge thanks to my agent, Anjali Singh, for her wisdom and guidance, and my editor, Rachel Poloski, for her insightful notes and enthusiasm. All the love to my husband, Eugene, for his endless support and encouraging me to take a break when I need it. Love to my mom for always encouraging my writing (and for all the coffee drop-offs). Huge thanks to Steenz for hyping me up and letting me try out my dad jokes on her first, and to Randy Trang for the rides home from work so I could get to writing faster.

Illustrator Acknowledgments

Thanks to my friends, Maria, Rekha, Brenda, Jacquie,
Sam, and Adeline (my resident Anne Shirley Cuthbert
expert), and my comic lunch buddies, Tatyana and
Kaycie, for their continuous encouragement.
Thanks to my agent, Judy Hansen,
for her wisdom and counsel.

Thank you to the team at Little, Brown Books
for Young Readers: Rachel Poloski, Andrea Colvin,
and especially Ching Chan, for their guidance
and patience in bringing this book to life.